Get Caught Reading...

Duets™

Two brand-new stories in every volume...
twice a month!

Duets Vol. #51

Popular Natalie Bishop makes her romantic comedy debut with a charming romp about two couples who start out mismatched, but work it out by story's end. Joining her this month is Darlene Gardner who spins "a delightful tale with an engaging set-up and lovable characters," according to *Romantic Times Magazine*.

Duets Vol. #52

Jennifer LaBrecque returns with a wonderful tale in the Diapers & Detectives miniseries. *Romantic Times* notes that this author always writes "humorous dialogue and lively sc~~ ~~ed Sandra Paul is back w~~ ~~ng." Ms. Paul ne~~ ~~mor and ~~ ~~azine.

Get Ca ~~ ~~ ***mes today!***

Get caught
reading
Harlequin.

D0835139

Two Across, Two Down

It spelled C-O-I-N-C-I-D-E-N-C-E

Chloe gazed at Hank in surprise as they stood in the cab lineup outside the airport.

"What are you doing here?"

"What are you doing here?"

They laughed at their simultaneous queries, then Hank asked, "Were you on this flight? I was on this flight."

"I was in coach," she said.

"I was in first. So, are you going to find Dixie?"

"I guess. Are you going to find Julian?"

"I guess. How about we share a cab?"

They stared at each other for a long moment. "Does Dixie know you decided to join her a day later?"

"Uh, not exactly," Chloe admitted. "And Julian?"

"Nope."

They climbed into the cab with huge smiles on their faces. Absurdly Hank felt like shaking her hand, as if they were allies in crime. And Chloe, feeling the same way, reached out and did just that, giving his hand one hard shake in unspoken, unexpected partnership.

For more, turn to page 9

Up...and down. Up...and down

Sam was just about to swish the credit card up and down through the narrow opening between the door and the wall for the umpteenth time, when a beautiful, long-fingered hand took the card from him. The barrel of a gun was pressed against his backbone. Hell. A lady cop. It had to be a lady cop.

"You have about ten seconds," a throaty voice whispered near his ear, "to explain what you're doing breaking into this P.I.'s office."

"*Trying* to break in," Sam corrected dryly.

"Don't get smart with me, buster. Start talking." Mallory punctuated the command by jabbing the gun deeper into his spine. But something about the gun didn't feel right. Either it had an ultrathin barrel or...

Sam whirled around.

Or it was a tube of lipstick!

"Hey, that's not a gun, and you're no cop," Sam exclaimed.

"Brilliant deduction, Sherlock."

For more, turn to page 197

HARLEQUIN DUETS

ISBN 0-373-44117-7

TWO ACROSS, TWO DOWN
Copyright © 2001 by Nancy Bush

THE CUPID CAPER
Copyright © 2001 by Darlene Hrobak Gardner

This edition published by arrangement with Harlequin Books S.A.

® and TM are trademarks of the publisher. Trademarks indicated with ® are registered in the United States Patent and Trademark Office, the Canadian Trade Marks Office and in other countries.

Visit us at www.eHarlequin.com

Printed in U.S.A.

Two Across, Two Down

Natalie Bishop

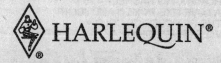

HARLEQUIN®

TORONTO • NEW YORK • LONDON
AMSTERDAM • PARIS • SYDNEY • HAMBURG
STOCKHOLM • ATHENS • TOKYO • MILAN • MADRID
PRAGUE • WARSAW • BUDAPEST • AUCKLAND

ABOUT THE AUTHOR

Natalie Bishop sold her first book to Silhouette when her daughter Kelly was one year old. Since then she's written a variety of stories, from young-adult mystery to preteen horror to adult historical romance. She's even tried her hand at screenwriting and recently sold a script to one of the well-known soap operas on television. This year Kelly turned twenty and by coincidence, *Two Across, Two Down* is Natalie's twentieth book for Harlequin/Silhouette. This story is Natalie's first romantic comedy and she has her daughter Kelly to thank for the plotline. Look for more great stories from this talented writer!

Books by Natalie Bishop

Don't miss any of our special offers. Write to us at the following address for information on our newest releases.

Harlequin Reader Service
U.S.: 3010 Walden Ave., P.O. Box 1325, Buffalo, NY 14269
Canadian: P.O. Box 609, Fort Erie, Ont. L2A 5X3

To Kelly, whose L.A. experiences inspired this book.

1

"I'M SORRY, we're closing," Dixie Kingston said from behind the hostess stand at Diamond's Restaurant on Sunset Boulevard. She had leaned down to stuff several menus into slots into the reception kiosk when she'd heard approaching footsteps. Nobody, but nobody, was getting inside at this late hour.

"I know," a male voice with a decidedly British accent answered. "But I wondered if I could find a quiet corner to sit for a few minutes."

Dixie straightened quickly, certain she'd heard that voice before. Her amber eyes widened in amazement as she regarded the newcomer. Standing in front of her was Julian—*the Julian*—male model extraordinaire! *The* Julian, whose long dark mane and lantern jaw and exceedingly broad chest had landed him on the covers of more magazines, books and television commercials than she could even name. And *the* Julian was *the* spokesman for Primitive Cologne. Just this evening she'd spied his commercial on one of the television screens in Diamond's third-floor bar. A Tarzan-type commercial that was as familiar to the public as was his famous long mane and *mucho*-photographed chest. He was tall, too, she discovered, sizing him up, and he possessed a pair of incredible blue eyes that were Dixie's own particular Waterloo. The man was an icon. A marketing image. As famous as anyone who'd crossed the threshold of Diamond's, one of L.A.'s current hot spots.

All she could do was stare.

"May I come in?" he asked again, a slow smile crossing his lips.

And he knew exactly how charming he was.

Dixie's momentary bemusement ended right there. Diamond's was closing. Her feet hurt. And nobody, not even *the* Julian, was going to stand in the way of her leaving on time.

"They've already herded everyone out of here," Dixie told him. "It's almost two."

A puzzled smile crossed his lips. Apparently *the* Julian wasn't used to being thwarted. "Fifteen minutes?" he asked. "It's been one hell of a night."

She didn't need some one-named, muscled Adonis running the show. She opened her mouth to say as much, then thought better of it. Those eyes really were a fantastic shade of blue. She'd never noticed their color in any of his pictures or commercials. And he was over six feet, which also surprised her, used to actors who were more her own height of five foot seven. But then, he wasn't an actor, really. Well, he wasn't an actor *at all.* Inwardly, Dixie sniffed. She might be one of the ten thousand hopefuls auditioning all over the city, but she'd had training and she knew who possessed talent and who didn't, and although Julian was stunning to look at, he couldn't act himself out of a paper bag.

In her unbiased opinion.

But he was attractive with a capital A and what was another fifteen minutes, anyway? Grudgingly she said, "Okay, fifteen minutes. And if anybody asks why you're still here, tell them Dixie is a sucker for a pretty face.''

He laughed out loud. ''Dixie?''

''Yep. As in, 'deep in the heart of.'''

He gazed at her blankly. Clearly he was not familiar with the song. Well, he was a foreigner, after all. She tried again. ''Dixie cup?''

He nodded. ''Paper cup.''

She gave him a thumbs-up as she glanced into the first floor dining and bar area. Bottles still needed to be cleared and though it wasn't strictly Dixie's job, the sooner the work was completed, the sooner they could all go home.

Julian followed her into the room and seated himself at the end of the bar, watching her work. The bartender lifted his brows at Dixie who said to Julian, ''Ray wants to know if you'd like something to drink.''

''No, thanks. So, you're a hostess here,'' he said, taking the opportunity to open a conversation with her.

''It's not my main ambition, but it pays the rent.''

''What is your main ambition?''

She was almost embarrassed to admit it, it was such a cliché. ''Acting.''

''Had much success?'' he asked.

She gave him a sharp look, but he seemed only mildly curious. ''Well, some.''

''What have you done?''

Recalling the cat litter commercial, her first paying gig, Dixie squinched up her face in remembered horror. Oh, sure. They'd paid her well, but saying, ''Kitties dig Kitty-Diggins,'' a hundred thousand times while holding up a bright pink bag of the loathsome stuff had been a hit to her pride. Still…it was a job, and it had led the way to her recurring role as a cheerleader on "Harrington High," and that had been a huge step up the ladder.

Until she'd blown it.

"I was on a night-time soap. 'Harrington High.'"

"Really?" He nodded appreciatively.

"Have you seen it?"

He shook his head. "No. Sorry."

"That's all right."

"You're not on it any longer?"

Dixie scooped long-necked beer bottles onto her tray and swiped the table with a cloth. "I gave up the job when I made the mistake of chasing after 'true love.' My ex-boyfriend is a tech head, and he got a job in San Jose, sooooo...I followed him to the land of semiconductors and pretty much torpedoed my career in the process. I just got back to L.A. a few months ago."

Julian absorbed this information in silence, staring at her in a way she found slightly unnerving. At length he said, "You're starting over?"

"Trying to. That's the idea, anyway."

Deciding she'd had enough of talking about herself, she asked him, "Why has it been a hell of a night for you?"

"Huh?" He was lost in thought.

"You said it had been a hell of a night."

He expelled a harsh breath and shook his head. "Oh. Yes. Well..."

Dixie set the tray on the bar and turned to meet his gaze. He really was an amazing male specimen. No wonder women threw themselves at him. Although when she examined her own feelings about him, she couldn't dredge up much interest. He was just too—perfect—somehow.

"I was on a date," he suddenly revealed. "She paid to go out with me. Twenty-five thousand dollars."

"What?" Dixie nearly choked.

"It was for charity, and I said I would do it. So, it started out with the two of us and my brother, my agent, which didn't sit well with her, since she wanted to be alone with me. Then Hank left and there I was...." He shuddered. "Then it got messy, and my brother thinks it's the funniest thing that's ever happened to me."

"Twenty-five thousand dollars?" Dixie breathed.

"She spent the evening with her hand on my knee." He arched a brow at Dixie. "I kept worrying she was going to slide it upward."

"Twenty-five thousand dollars!"

He grinned. "Well, I don't come cheap."

From behind the bar Ray snorted, threw down his bar towel and walked out, shaking his head. But Julian had Dixie's attention now. She was riveted.

"So, what happened?" she asked.

"I got out of there as fast as I could. We were in a limo together, and it was getting really tense, and I didn't want her to know where I lived, so I got out at the Standard Hotel, which is where she's staying, and then I made some excuse and called a taxi and here I am." He inhaled and exhaled heavily. "I was going to go home, but Hank's staying with me right now, and I just needed a little bit of time to think things over somewhere else."

Dixie absorbed this information. "The dark side of being a celebrity."

"Earlier today I was accosted at lunch by a group of women," he said reflectively, as if from a long distance away. "One of them kissed me just after I'd taken a bite of salad. I kept thinking I might choke to death before she backed off.''

Dixie shook her head and half laughed. ''I see the problem, but it's kind of hard to feel sorry for you. I mean, look at you....'' She waved to encompass his lean form. He wore a blue shirt, open to the navel, with sleeves rolled to his elbows, and a pair of black jeans and an expensive-looking pair of Italian leather boots. ''When you're a struggling actress, it's just difficult to feel empathy for the successful.''

''You're pretty candid.''

Dixie didn't answer immediately. She'd been told the same thing in a lot less flattering ways. Her sister, Chloe, had pointed out that she had a big mouth on more than one occasion, but with Chloe, that was really like the pot calling the kettle black!

''So, you're auditioning now?'' he asked.

''I'm with L.A. Artists. They've been sending me out.''

''Are you taking any classes?''

''Not at the moment. I'd like to sign on with Palmer Michaels, but his classes are impossible to get into without some kind of recommendation.''

''I know Palmer.''

Dixie, who'd been scanning the rest of the dining area and keeping an eagle eye out for her boss at the same time, knowing she would be accused of slacking in some way if she weren't constantly moving, gave Julian a long look. ''You do?''

''I could put a word in for you.''

''You would do that?'' Dixie asked in astonishment.

He nodded, slowly and thoughtfully. ''I was just wondering if you might do something for me.''

Dixie's spine immediately stiffened. "What?" she asked suspiciously.

"Relax." He lifted a palm to her fears. "Actually, it's an acting job."

"What kind of acting job?"

After a moment of careful thought, he said slowly, "I need someone to play the part of my fiancée...."

JULIAN GAZED HARD at the woman in front of him. She was clutching the bar as if it might suddenly sprout wings and fly away. He knew he was being reckless. But he was a man who trusted his instincts, and his instincts told him to take this chance.

It had been an impossible day from start to finish. He'd joined Hank for lunch at Mel's Diner and things had gone downhill straightaway. The restaurant made famous in *American Graffiti* was too exposed for someone as recognizable as himself, but Hank was either oblivious to, or didn't give a damn about, Julian's dilemma.

"Oh, relax," Hank had told him in that irritatingly breezy way he had. "The least you could do is put a smile on your face. It's just one date."

Hank was his brother, his manager, his agent and his friend. He was the person who'd paved the way for Julian, and if asked, Julian would admit that he owed his career to him. But that didn't mean his younger brother couldn't annoy the hell out of him.

"She paid too much money, and she would have paid even more if she'd had to," Julian told Hank. "I think the woman's a stalker."

"She's just motivated to meet you," Hank disagreed.

"She has met me," he reminded Hank, thinking of

the last time he'd run into this particular woman. He'd been on a tour promoting Primitive Cologne. The tour had finished in Los Angeles, and he'd wanted to just go home and sleep, but there had been one last megapush where he'd been on stage and available for autographs while women lined up for the fragrance and a chance to meet their idol. This woman had refused to stand in line, had damn near demanded she go out to dinner with him, had positioned herself at his side as some kind of uninvited bodyguard and then acted as if she owned him.

But the worst of it was she was just one of many. Julian found himself living a nightmare that many men would have considered a dream. Women wouldn't leave him alone. Night and day, day and night, and again and again... He was hounded by hordes of women, and it was becoming a serious problem.

"I'm not going tonight," he told Hank.

"Yes, you are."

"No, I'm not."

"You have to go," Hank argued, picking up his hamburger and biting deeply. Around a mouthful of food, he mumbled, "It's for charity."

With a groan, Julian closed his eyes and counted slowly to ten. Hank just wouldn't let himself understand. Henry "Hank" Ashby might be a financial wizard, but he refused to recognize Julian's women problems. Not that Hank didn't have his own to contend with, as well. Though Julian's hair was darker, almost black, and Hank's was a more chestnut brown, their faces were similar enough for Hank to get the occasional double take, even though Hank's hair was a more conventional length. And women liked him pretty well, too. Hank, however, kept himself out of the limelight, so his problems were far less serious, at least in Julian's eyes.

Julian had watched his brother take another lip-smacking bite. The way Hank tucked into a greasy hamburger made Julian shudder with real disgust; hamburgers weren't on his own personal diet. Seafood and a certain amount of good pasta were his staples, and today, because Hank had picked the restaurant, Julian was limited in his choices. And it was also damned irritating that Hank's physique was nearly as toned as his own since Julian worked out religiously, and Hank's efforts were kind of hit-and-miss.

Hank, for being a Brit, was about as American as it came. Worse, he'd taken to wearing surfer shirts and khakis and looking as if someone had dragged him in off the beach. As Julian watched, Hank smothered one of his French fries in a mound of ketchup, then popped it into his mouth. Julian actually groaned aloud. Watching others eat all that greasy stuff could nearly do him in, and he'd glanced around the environs of Mel's Diner to keep his eyes off Hank's munching mouth. Several other customers waved at him, and he waved back. How had he ever let Hank talk him into coming here?

And that's when it happened. A group of girls, apparently encouraged by his wave, suddenly swooped down on him just as he'd forked a bite of Caesar salad in his mouth. The next thing he knew he was in a lip lock, and Hank was practically choking with amusement. Hank, in fact, half-toppled out of his chair, fighting back a tide of laughter that nearly sent him to the floor.

Hank was a regular *hardy har har*.

"Oh, get over it," Hank told him when the girls

finally let him come up for air and departed. "You're *the* Julian," he said simply. "It comes with the territory."

Julian had glowered at his brother as Hank swirled another French fry in the mound of ketchup and stuck it in his mouth. "Let's get something straight. I'm Julian because you made me Julian. This is your fault, you know."

Hank grinned like a devil, his steely blue eyes a reflection of Julian's own, sparkling with barely repressed mirth.

"You think this is funny, don't you?" Julian accused dourly.

"Lighten up, bro."

Julian snorted.

"Excuse me? I'm sorry to bother you. But could I get a picture with you?"

Julian, who had just dared to swallow another bite of Romaine lettuce, looked up at the middle-aged woman with the Minolta camera. Another problem with having Hank pick the restaurant. Outside the three or four Julian frequented on a regular basis, where the clientele respected his privacy and left him alone, here he was a sitting duck for every autograph hound and celebrity gawker within a hundred yards.

"He'd be happy to," Hank answered for him.

Throwing his brother a black look, Julian pushed back his chair and got to his feet. At six foot three, he towered over her five-foot frame.

"Oh, thank you, thank you," she declared as Hank took the camera from her shaking hands. "It's for my daughter. Not me."

Hank shot Julian an *oh, sure* look. Julian placed his arm around the woman and smiled.

Click.

"Thank you, thank you!" She gushed again, beaming.

"You're welcome," Julian told her as she hurried away with her treasure.

"You can really throw that accent on," Hank observed.

"Well, you've practically eradicated yours," he observed right back.

"So?" He lifted both palms. "I'm an American now. A Californian."

"You're a pain in the b-u-t-t."

"Oh, stop whining. It won't be that bad tonight," Hank told him. "A couple of hours, and you're done."

A couple of hours...

It had been a night of pure torture, as far as Julian was concerned, and as much as Hank might needle him, he'd been glad his brother was there to help deflect his "date." When she'd managed a discreet trip to the ladies' room, Julian had leaned toward Hank and muttered, "Do you see where her hand is?" hoping to rouse Hank's slumbering anxiety.

"She just wants to sleep with you."

"Oh, God..."

"Of course, that's entirely up to you," Hank added with a nonchalant shrug. He checked his watch. "Time for me to skedaddle and leave you lovebirds alone."

Murder had actually entered Julian's mind. But when Hank was gone and his "date" was back, his mind turned to escape. As soon as humanly possible, he'd wrapped up the meal, guided the limo driver to the Standard Hotel, brushed his lips across the lady's cheek and vamoosed as fast as possible for Diamond's.

Which brought him up to the moment and the growing certainty that he'd walked into the right restaurant at just the right moment and encountered just the right woman.

But she was frozen in place, as if she had forgotten how to move.

"Are you all right?" he asked.

Finally, she relaxed her grip on the bar and gave him a long, searching look.

"You want me to play the part of your fiancée?"

"I'd like someone to run interference, and when we started talking, it just seemed like it should be you." As she mulled it over, he said, "I'd be happy to help you in any way in your career. We could…strike a deal," he suggested.

And with that he stuck out his hand, and Dixie, staring down at his outstretched fingers, decided there was no time like the present to jump-start her flagging career. Ignoring the clamoring doubts that filled her brain, she clasped his warm hand, looked up at him and breathed, "Deal," before she listened to the sane part of her mind.

"There's just one catch." She snatched her hand back, and Julian shook his head to allay her fears. "No, no. Don't worry, this is on the level. I just don't want to tell anyone—and I mean *anyone*—that it's a fake. If the truth got out, it would be ten times worse than what I'm facing now. So I need the world to think it's real. You'll have to keep the secret from everyone."

Dixie thought of her sister, Chloe. "But…"

"No one." He stressed the words. "And I'm going to make myself believe it's a real relationship, so that I can play the part."

Alarmed, Dixie reiterated, "But it is just acting, right?"

"Absolutely. I want a real relationship like I want root canal," he said with finality.

Dixie stared at him, amazed at this odd turn of events. It was her lucky day! Julian was going to get her into Palmer Michaels' Acting Studio, and all she had to do was pretend to be his fiancée.

How hard could it be?

"You're on!" Dixie declared, grabbing his hand again and giving it a hard shake.

And that's how the deception began.

2

"I'M HAVING a high self-esteem day."

Dixie glanced at her sister, Chloe, over the top of her skinny tall decaf vanilla latté. She tentatively slurped in a bit, managed to avoid burning off the top layer of her lips, and asked, "Why?"

For an answer Chloe pushed the *New York Times* crossword puzzle in front of Dixie's nose. "I got number fifty-six. See?" She tapped the end of her pen onto the newspaper several times. "And it's a Saturday," she added mysteriously.

Since Dixie would no more attempt any kind of crossword puzzle, she was almost afraid to ask what this cryptic comment meant. Her sister, ten years her elder, would probably tell her in her own unique way. Chloe's brain was an encyclopedia of facts and ideas, and it explained why she was so well-respected in the law firm where she worked as general dogsbody. She might not be a lawyer herself, but she kept even the most acclaimed attorneys on their toes.

Dixie, however, didn't work that way. All she wanted to do was act, and it would be nice, once in a while, if she actually got paid for her effort. Not that she required tons of funds. Heavens, no! But a pittance now and again would be really appreciated and make her stop feeling like such a cadger at her sister's modest two-bedroom home outside Manhattan Beach.

Now, Chloe held up the paper and smiled at it. "The puzzle gets harder as the week goes on. This is Saturday, the hardest day, and I'm burning through this thing!" Her gray eyes full of contentment, she inhaled a deep breath and asked, "Does it get any better than this? I ask you. Does it?"

Dixie buried her nose in her latté and considered things. Ever since her strange meeting with Julian the night before, she'd been dying to tell her sister what had happened. But she couldn't. She'd promised. And so she'd spent the morning thinking, thinking, thinking—and trying desperately to keep her word.

Chloe tilted her head to look at her sister. "You certainly have been quiet this fine day. What gives?"

They were seated at a postage stamp size table near a window at Java Beach, their favorite coffee shop, about a block off Manhattan Beach itself. Since it was Saturday, Chloe didn't have to be at work. She'd been employed at the law firm for as long as Dixie could remember, practically from the moment their mother died from breast cancer and Chloe took Dixie under her wing. Chloe ran that office. Without her, Dixie was certain the place would simply shut down. Luckily, the powers that be understood her worth and paid her well enough so that she'd managed to save up a down payment to put on the little house in this prime real estate market.

It was Dixie's turn to make some money. She'd been fretting over her half-baked acting career, but now—now!—Julian had opened a door for her.

If she could only tell Chloe about this opportunity, but Julian had been very specific. Frustrated, she leaned her chin on her palm and sighed.

"Is it that restaurant job?" Chloe waved a blithe

palm in the air, dismissing what she believed to be the cause of Dixie's current blue funk. "You're hooked up with L.A. Artists and going out on auditions all the time. Something'll pop. And then you can quit."

"I don't mind working at Diamond's. I'd like to make more money, but it's okay."

"It's Jeff!" Chloe suddenly decided. "Now, listen to me. You're too good for that total tech brain and besides, he's burrowed into that hole of his in San Jose. You're better here in the good old City of Angels with me. Trust me."

"It's not Jeff," Dixie stated firmly. "That relationship is over with a capital O. And don't say it, I know I was an idiot for giving up my role on 'Harrington High' just to chase after him."

"I wasn't going to say anything."

"I'll never do that again," Dixie vowed. "Career first, romance second. Period."

"Or maybe third or fourth." She glanced at her sister's soft golden bob, round amber eyes and pert little nose and said, "Jeff was the idiot."

"Hear, hear." Dixie lifted her latté in a toast.

"Romance is not a positive experience."

Now, that was taking things too far. Especially since Dixie needed to alert Chloe to her new "engagement." She was debating which opening to use when an attractive man walked through the door, spied the two sisters and winked as he cruised up to the counter.

Chloe snorted and rolled her eyes. "Too good-looking," she declared with a sniff. This was Chloe's mantra: The better the man's appearance, the worse his character.

Good grief. What was she going to say about Julian? Dixie thought with growing anxiety. Her sister's six-year relationship with one of the law firm's most charismatic and handsome attorneys had sputtered and died. He'd moved to another firm, met a woman his first day on the job, then married her within the month. Though she didn't talk about it much, the experience had devastated Chloe, and to this day the more attractive the male, the less she trusted them. Dixie had found herself worrying on more than one occasion that her own date of the moment might be too good-looking, and she'd had to shake herself back to reality. Chloe's fears weren't hers.

But, *Julian!*

As if her guardian angel were looking out for her, Dixie's eye caught sight of a celebrity item headline from the paper. Snatching up the page, she said, "Chloe, listen to this. 'Julian re-signs with Primitive Cologne. The ad campaign which made the romantic hunk famous is about to film another series of steamy jungle spots. Female hearts beware! Your faux-Tarzan will be swinging across television sets this fall. The enormous pecs and legendary locks of your single-named hero are primed and ready. Ah, yes, romance is in the air. You'll be able to smell it!'"

"And?" Chloe asked as Dixie folded up the page.

Dixie chewed on her lip, conscious of her sister's mystified frown. "Well, I haven't been sure how to tell you this, but..."

"Yes?"

"I've got a date with him tonight." She couldn't just say she was engaged. Chloe would never believe her.

"Him? Who? *Him?*" Chloe's horrified gaze jumped to the page. She snatched at it, dragging it from beneath Dixie's elbow and gazing at Julian's picture as if she'd never seen his chiseled profile before. *"Julian?"*

"He came into the restaurant last night and asked me out. I wasn't sure how to tell you." Dixie braced herself for the onslaught that was sure to follow.

She wasn't disappointed.

"You have a date with *Julian?"* Chloe fairly shouted.

"Shh!" Dixie admonished, glancing around.

"The Julian? *Tonight?"* She was utterly flummoxed. "Why didn't you tell me?"

"I just did."

"Oh, my God. Oh, no." Chloe shook her head and stared at Dixie as if she were out of her ever-loving mind. "You can't go out with him. He's—he's a cartoon!"

Dixie snatched back the page and glanced at the black-and-white picture of the famous male model. "He's handsome as sin. And masculine. Look at that body and check out that jawline."

Chloe's gaze stayed riveted on her sister's face. "You're kidding, right?"

"Women drape themselves all over him. He practically has to hide from them. Personally, I don't know how he stands it."

"He *loves* it!" Chloe's snort was loud enough for the man and woman seated at the next table to send her a look.

Dixie heaved a sigh, gulped the end of her latté and got up from the table. Chloe, however, stayed rigidly seated.

"Why shouldn't I go out with him?" Dixie demanded. "Give me one good reason."

Chloe's eyes narrowed, a sure sign that she was

thinking hard. She leaned back in her chair and brushed at the brownish-gold curls, which ran riot no matter how she tried to tame them. She and Dixie looked a great deal alike, but Chloe's eyes were gray, not amber like Dixie's, and her hair, though near the same length, possessed more curl and body than any human being should have to deal with.

Clearing her throat as if she were about to pronounce judgment, she said, "I'll give you three reasons—the three rules I have where men are concerned." She ticked off one finger. "You can't date anyone whose hair is longer than yours." A second finger pointed skyward. "You can't date someone who does not possess a last name." A final finger joined the group. "And you can't date someone whose chest is bigger than yours. Sorry. Julian's out."

Dixie glanced down at her own chest. She was no Dolly Parton, but that was really hitting below the belt. "Well, you're just going to have to get used to the idea!" she told Chloe. Slinging her purse over her shoulder, she then snapped her fingers. "He said he's got a brother. Why don't I call him, and we can make a double date!"

Chloe choked on her straight black coffee and spilled half her cup across the crossword puzzle. "Now, look what you made me do," she said in a forlorn voice.

"Oh, it's my fault, is it?" Dixie grinned.

"And you're not going out with *the* Julian, no matter what you think."

"Like you have anything to say about it!" Dixie waved her away and headed out the door to the car. As soon as she was outside, she exhaled, blowing her blond bangs away from her face. If this was how she was going to react after the mention of just one date…!

What would it be like when she revealed her "engagement"?

She shuddered. The future did not bear thinking about.

"SHE'S GETTING OFF early tonight, and I'm picking her up at the restaurant," Julian told Hank, keeping his expression neutral as he rolled up the sleeves on his shirt and examined his reflection in his dresser mirror. Behind him, caught in the mirror, his brother's face was a mask of consternation.

"You met her last night," Hank said in disbelief. "She's a hostess at Diamond's. You're taking her to your favorite restaurant, the one you never take anyone to because you don't want people to know where you eat?"

"That's right."

"But you're going to walk into that restaurant and put her on your arm, plain as day, so that everyone sees?"

Julian shrugged. Picking Dixie up at Diamond's was part of the plan, all right. If he wanted the media to learn of his new romance—and he did—then he couldn't pay for better advertising than the kind of stir his dating Diamond's hostess would bring.

Hank was utterly flummoxed. This wasn't the usual Julian kind of move. "Want me to come with you? I'd like to meet her."

"Sure." Julian smiled affably. "You can go in first and make sure she's there, but you're not coming out to dinner with us."

"Wouldn't dream of it," Hank said dryly. "If you

want, I can just fetch her and bring her to the car, that way you won't have to show yourself at all.''

"But that would be rude."

"Damn straight," Hank agreed, gazing thoughtfully at Julian. "But since you're so concerned about all your adoring fans, I just thought—"

"Dixie's special. I don't want to ruin this before it even gets started." He cut him off.

Hank's jaw actually dropped. It was all Julian could do to keep from laughing. Ducking his head to hide his expression, he headed for the front door. "Coming?" he asked.

Hank slowly followed after him, confusion written clearly across his expressive face. At Julian's Mercedes, he asked, "She's really all that?"

"All that and more," Julian assured him.

DIXIE'S FACE was flushed, her heartbeat erratic, her composure completely out of whack. It was all fine and good to agree to this deception with Julian, but she could scarcely keep her mind on her work with their date imminently approaching. And it wasn't because she was wildly attracted to him. To her, he was little more than a stranger she was mildly interested in. It was knowing the reactions of her co-workers and patrons of the restaurant when Julian strode in, big as life, to pick her up.

She seated a couple on the first floor patio overlooking Sunset Boulevard. The patio was already choked with crowded tables of people. Glancing at her watch, she inhaled a nervous breath. Half an hour longer.

Back at the hostess stand, a newcomer was waiting impatiently for her return. He gave her the once-over as she greeted him with her standard, "Hi, I'm Dixie. Welcome to Diamond's."

"I'm Hank," he said, extending a hand.

That voice…those blue eyes… She blinked at how familiar he seemed. "You sound British," she said.

He lifted one brow. "And I try so hard to talk like a Californian…dude."

She gathered up a menu and nodded to the anxious-looking group waiting in line. "Just a little bit longer," she told them, then turned back to the newcomer. His face was so incredibly familiar. "Have you been here before?"

"Uh-huh." He seemed about to add something further, but then his gaze skated down her shapely legs, and Dixie suddenly worried if her skirt was too short.

He was dressed in khaki pants and a rayon shirt covered with surfboards. For Diamond's, it was pretty casual, but it worked for him. She was about to ask him which floor he would like when he inclined his head, smiled and confessed, "I'm Julian's brother."

The penny dropped. "Oh! *Hank!*" she declared. Of course! "He mentioned you!"

"He mentioned you, too," he said reflectively.

"Where is he?" she asked. She couldn't seem to take her eyes off him. If his hair were darker and longer, and he wore a shirt open to his navel, he could almost pass as his brother. Except he seemed so much more—sexy.

No. Untrue. Julian radiated sexiness, and this guy was way too casual. Still, his whole way of being struck a deep chord inside Dixie that resonated wildly even while she desperately tried to silence it.

"Julian walked in ahead of me," Hank revealed.

"You weren't at the desk, so he went upstairs to find you."

"He did?"

"I guess he was—anxious—to see you."

They stared at each other. Dixie wondered, then, what Julian had told Hank about her. For inexplicable reasons a blush worked its way up her neck and burned her cheeks. "I'd better find him."

A squeal of feminine voices floated down to them. "Too late," Hank said, his lips quirking. "I'll come with you," he added as Dixie turned toward the steps.

They'd just crested the top stair when a cry sounded. Glancing inside the second floor bar, Dixie saw Julian standing in the center of a gaggle of women. Bright smiles and tight dresses and bare limbs and loud giggles seemed to engulf him.

Spying her, Julian's face cleared. "Dixie!" he called, extending one muscled arm in her direction. The women's heads swiveled as one. Reluctantly, they stepped aside so that Julian could reach her side. A collective groan sounded when he suddenly scooped Dixie into his arms and smacked her hard on the lips, stunning her to immobility. "Sorry," he whispered in her ear as soon as the kiss ended. "Hope you don't mind."

"No, I…no," she stuttered.

The women stared in unbridled shock. Julian brushed back his hair, gazed at the throng for a moment and said, "Ladies, I'd like you to meet my fiancée, Dixie, um…"

"Kingston," she whispered through stiff lips.

"Kingston," he repeated, his arm draped familiarly over her shoulders, hugging her close.

As the women gasped and cried and glared daggers

at her, Dixie glanced over at Hank. The stunned look
on his face was indescribable. He returned Dixie's
gaze and held it, and she swallowed hard and hoped
she looked a lot happier than she felt.

3

CHLOE BRUSHED BACK a strand of curling brown hair and eyed Dixie carefully. Her sister was buttering her toast with all the concentration of an athlete preparing for the big game. It was all Chloe could do to keep from ripping the knife from Dixie's hand and demanding her attention. But she'd been told by an ex-therapist, a man she'd gone to once when she was trying to get over the breakup of her last relationship, that she had a tendency to take control. An older sister's bad habit that also seemed to affect her few and miserable relationships with the opposite sex. So, with newly acquired self-restraint, she mentally grabbed the knife, mentally tossed the tub of butter across the room and mentally screamed at the top of her lungs, "What happened with Julian, for God's sake? Spit it out! I haven't got all day!"

But all she said was, "Well?"

"What?" Dixie asked, looking up innocently.

Chloe stabbed her grapefruit, counted to ten, then smiled as if she didn't have a care in the world. Dixie wasn't the only one who could act when called upon. "How was your date?"

"Fine."

Give me strength, Chloe thought. Beneath the table her fingers dug into her own knee. "Dixie..."

Dixie glanced at her, her brow furrowing as if she

found her sister entirely incomprehensible. "I met his brother, Hank. Did I tell you that?"

"You haven't told me anything," Chloe reminded her through a tight smile.

"Well, I actually saw him first. Julian was already inside, but I didn't know it. So, I started to talk to Hank...." Her voice drifted off. She didn't understand it, but her reaction to Hank had been, well, surprising. She'd hated putting the deception over on him. Just as she hated putting this deception over on Chloe.

But she had to be strong. Stalwart. Discreet.

So thinking, Dixie clamped her mouth shut and set about buttering another slice of toast. She hadn't taken even one bite out of the first.

"Are you going to eat either of those?" Chloe asked, indicating Dixie's two slices of toast. "Or are you stockpiling for the next millennium?"

"Do you think my white skirt is too short?" Dixie asked, gazing at her sister as if it were the most important question on earth. "I mean, it *is* short. But is it too short?"

"Dixie!" Chloe sighed in exasperation.

"I'm never wearing it to work again," she suddenly declared. "All the waiters dress in black, and black seems to be the only color the patrons wear, as well. Of course, the hosts and hostesses can wear any color. We're just supposed to look nice. You know, be an attractive picture to the guests. But the white skirt has got to go." Dixie bit hard into one of her pieces of toast. Her bathrobe fell off one shoulder, and she tugged it back.

Chloe, who also sat in her bathrobe on this lazy late Sunday morning, regarded Dixie with suspicion. She was deliberately holding out on her. "Something happened, didn't it?"

"No."

"Did he make some kind of—*pass* at you?"

"No!" Dixie started to laugh. "He was a perfect gentleman."

"Then what?" Chloe demanded.

Dixie tilted up her chin, offering Chloe her little minx smile that was her trademark. Her bobbed, blondish hair curved in at her chin, the golden strands varying in shades, some nearly the exact shade as her eyes. Head shots never did her justice. She was much prettier in person, or maybe on camera. Chloe, on the other hand, couldn't tame her brown curls if a steamroller ran over them, and her own eyes were that silvery shade of gray the Pacific Ocean sported on a cold day.

"Actually, we, um, really hit it off," Dixie told her. "So, we're going out today, too."

"*What?*"

"I knew you'd be upset, so I didn't want to tell you. Here…" She grabbed the paper and searched through the pages until she found the Sunday crossword puzzle. "It looks twice as large as yesterday's."

"It is." Chloe snatched the paper from Dixie's hands and folded it on the table. "Okay, no more fooling around. Details. I need details."

Tucking a strand of hair behind one ear, Dixie bit into her toast once again. She was having difficulty meeting her sister's penetrating gaze. Acting was an art, one she continually tried to perfect, but Chloe knew her so well that Dixie wasn't completely certain she could keep up this charade.

And it didn't help that Julian had actually *told* Hank

that they were engaged! The memory of the look on his face was enough to make her wince. Good grief, how was she going to pull this off? She'd been too stunned last night to do more than offer a sickly smile to all and sundry, and Hank had grown instantly silent.

She'd spent the rest of the evening in a numb haze. That last dark look Hank sent her was enough to send her into a vortex of depression. He'd disappeared almost immediately afterward, and then Julian had taken her to a quiet Italian restaurant where the food was apparently to die for. Not that Dixie would know, because everything she tasted was like ashes on her tongue. Julian's attempts to engage her in conversation had met with limited success, and he'd finally had to snap his fingers in front of her face to gain her attention.

"Are you all right?" he'd asked.

She'd nodded jerkily. Yes, she was all right. Of course she was all right! This was an opportunity to kill for. It was a windfall for her career of a magnitude she could only dream about! And hadn't she just sworn to put her career first, above everything else? So, why should she care what Julian's brother thought of her?

Eye on the prize...

"I'm perfect," she told him, to which Julian smiled.

"We've made a great first start. Tomorrow, let's take it a step further. We'll go shopping on Rodeo Drive. Then, Monday I have a meeting with Primitive Cologne. I want you to go with me."

"You do?" Dixie had blinked in astonishment. Things were moving so fast!

"I'm doing a new series of those Tarzan-type commercials. You could be—Jane,'' he said, spreading his hands in an unasked question.

She'd nearly jumped across the table and returned that huge smackeroo he'd laid on her earlier!

''And then Palmer Michaels wants to see you tomorrow at two. He says there's room for one more in his acting class.''

Dixie had been struck dumb. She'd squeaked out a thank you, which Julian had brushed aside.

''You're my fiancée,'' he told her with a smile, as if that answered everything. Which, actually, it did.

But she couldn't tell Chloe any of this yet. Chloe's aversion to Julian was plain as day, and Dixie wasn't quite sure how her sister would take the news.

''I don't believe you're going on another date with him!'' Chloe was saying now. ''I don't believe it!''

''He's a nice guy.''

''Nice—guy?'' She shook her head and actually pressed one palm to her forehead as if she were having trouble holding the thought inside, it was so repugnant. ''Dixie! We're talking about *the* Julian!''

''It's just another date,'' Dixie mumbled, having difficulty swallowing. What was the deal with this bread anyway? It was likely to choke her to death all of a sudden!

''It's not just a date. It's never just a date when it's with a celebrity,'' Chloe argued heatedly. ''I mean, there's paparazzi and other people. Everyone will recognize him, and there you'll be. Sitting at lunch, or dinner, or a movie, or something, and everyone will be staring at you. Well, at him, anyway. It'll be *weird!*''

''Have you forgotten that I want to be an actor? It's the price of fame. I can handle it.'' Chloe blinked, currently out of complaints. As her fertile mind began working overtime, Dixie added for good measure, "And besides, didn't I just say I wanted to get my career on track? A date with Julian certainly can't hurt."

"*Another* date."

"For Pete's sake," Dixie declared, thinking Chloe was getting entirely too close to the truth without even half trying! If only there were a way she could clue Chloe in without revealing Julian's whole plan. "Look, Julian is internationally known. I'm trying to establish myself in a tough business, and if I'm seen with him at some fancy restaurant, well, so what? I've been knocking on doors for months and no one's opening them. If this helps…" In lieu of finishing, she let Chloe come to her own conclusions.

But Chloe was in no mood to herald the benefits of Julian's celebrity. Instead, she bit rather viciously into her own piece of unbuttered toast and said, "Oh, I see. Hang around with Julian and somebody might actually notice. Somebody important. And then all of a sudden the buzz is on Dixie Kingston. Wow! Who's that beautiful starlet with Julian? Maybe you could even set up a picture of you and Julian coming out of some No-Tell Motel and pretending to hide from the cameras!"

Dixie narrowed her eyes. "Why do I suddenly feel like I need to take a bath?"

Chloe waved her away, realizing she may have gone too far. "Because you just got up and you're all sleepy and mungy and you probably smell, too."

Shoving her chair back, Dixie said, "Then I'd better go take care of the problem."

"You've got to get ready for your date," Chloe agreed a bit tightly.

"He's coming to pick me up at noon. Just be nice, okay?"

Chloe dropped her toast. "Julian's coming here!" she practically shrieked as Dixie headed to the shower. "*Here?* Why didn't you say so? Dixie, this place is a disaster. Dixie! *Dixie!*"

But all she heard was a soft roar as Dixie turned on the taps, followed by the muted sound of hearty laughter.

SLAM! Hank practically threw the phone onto its base, damn near sending the whole thing rocketing to the floor. He was going to wring Julian's neck! He paced around the room, entertaining himself with ways to foil his brother.

He grimaced. Wouldn't that be dishy for the newshounds? He could read the headlines now: Julian's Brother out of Control, Nearly Murders the Romance King…Julian's Brother Doing Twenty-Five To Life After Killing Most Beloved Man on Earth—Women Across the World Mourn…or, better yet, Jealous Brother Strangles Romance Idol Over Woman in Short White Skirt.

Gnashing his teeth, Hank stalked across the cream marble floor of Julian's home and threw himself onto the black leather sofa. A bachelor pad. That's what it was. A place to bring chicks.

For a few moments Hank nursed his anger, then he drew a long breath and sought to calm himself. Julian was not the kind of guy who brought home chicks. He didn't spend a lot of time with women in general because they invariably wanted something from him. It was rare for him to even look twice at a woman.

So, why does it have to be Dixie?

Hank shook his head at his own stupidity. What was it about Dixie that had turned *him* inside out last night? She was, after all, just a girl.

A very attractive, shapely, ingenuous girl with a bright smile and shining blond hair and a pair of calves that curved lusciously and...

He clamped his hands over his ears and squeezed his eyes shut in an effort to shut his brain down. Engaged? They *couldn't* be! She was just another groupie who'd fallen under Julian's spell. But he seemed to have fallen under hers, as well!

There has to be a catch, he told himself. Despairingly he remembered the tender way Julian had looked at Dixie and her bright, beautiful, stunned face when he'd introduced her as his fiancée. And then the way she'd blushed.

When was the last time he'd actually seen a woman blush?

He'd felt his own heart begin a hard, heavy beating, much like the tempo and sound of a funeral dirge.

He'd been bowled over by her as soon as he laid eyes on her. Of course it was because she was Julian's date, or at least that's what he told himself. But Hank had fully expected to feel nothing for her; for some reason he and Julian did not click over the same kind of women. But then—*whammo!* It was as if he'd been hit by Cupid's arrow right between the eyes.

No!

He paced around the room. He absolutely refused to believe it had been love at first sight, especially since she was Julian's girl. And besides, what did he know about her really? A hostess at Diamond's. Probably a gold digger. Most women were, in Hank's opinion.

The person to really talk to about this situation was Julian himself, but big bro had been sleeping late today while Hank had tossed and turned all night, wishing his condo were ready and he could move out of his brother's house. Hank had been awake the night before, waiting up and channel surfing when Julian came in, but though he'd had the opportunity to ask all sorts of questions then, and his mind was buzzing with anxiety, he'd found himself unable to even speak Dixie's name.

Julian had broached the subject first. "So, what do you think of her?" he'd asked casually.

Hank just stopped himself from asking, "Who?" because he knew his brother would see right through that. "Dixie? She seems—fine."

"Just fine? That's all?"

Hank flicked through several channels. "You were kidding about the engagement part, right? Some kind of inside joke between the two of you?"

Julian had hesitated. And when his answer came, it was rather cagily put. "I like being off the market."

"You really are engaged?" Hank had asked.

His brother nodded, watching him closely.

"Why?" The question had been wrung from him.

"Because Dixie's the best thing that's happened to me in years," Julian answered without a shred of hesitation.

The ring of truth in those words had been monumentally depressing. Hank hadn't been able to muster the gumption to inquire about the whole thing any further after that, although today he planned to list all the reasons to Julian about why he couldn't be either engaged or married.

As if hearing Hank's unspoken thoughts, Julian came through the door to his bedroom and sauntered into the living room, wearing a bathrobe and a cat-and-canary smile that really set Hank's teeth on edge.

"So, Lazarus has risen," Hank muttered.

"No reason to get up early," Julian said with perfect logic. He glanced at his watch. "I've got over an hour before I'm supposed to be at Dixie's."

"You're going to her place?"

"We're having lunch and then who knows? Might do some shopping together."

"Shopping?" Hank had to fight to keep his jaw from sagging.

"We haven't looked at rings yet. Thought we might go to Tiffany's. Check things out."

"Tiffany's?"

Julian nodded. "What do you think about a September wedding? That gives us all summer to put this thing together."

Hank just managed to keep from repeating "wedding" like he'd parroted every other question. "You're serious?"

Julian cleared his throat and regarded Hank with a frown, as if he didn't know quite how to deal with his younger brother. And that's when Hank's brain finally clicked into gear. "You can't do this, Julian. Your image will suffer. You're the Adonis of this planet, and if you mess with that, poof! Bye, bye, career. A career that I launched for you, damn near single-handedly."

"Oh, really?" He arched a brow.

"All I'm saying is now is not a good time to be in

a steady relationship. We've got this whole eligible bachelor thing going, and I don't want to mess with it.'' Hank paced some more, then stopped and wagged a finger in front of his brother's handsome face. ''In fact—in fact—I've been thinking about arranging a contest where the woman who can name the most facts about you wins a date. What do you think?''

''No more contests! I don't want them to know anything more about me than they already do! I'm done with all that, Hank! I need some quiet time—with Dixie.''

''Nope. No good.'' He shook his head.

Julian eyed him in that calculating way he sometimes had, as if he found something lacking in his younger brother. It really got to Hank. ''I knew this would be your reaction.''

''Of course it's my reaction! How else could I feel?''

''You could be happy for me.''

Knowing he was acting like a two-year-old, Hank simply shook his head and flopped down on the couch again, set to channel surf until hell froze over.

Or Julian gave up the idea of seeing Dixie again.

A moment later he jumped to his feet and headed outside for the paper in the driveway. His own fears were getting the better of him. Snatching it up, Hank looked for the section devoted to celebrities and news makers. Scanning downward, he stopped in his tracks just inside the door.

''What?'' Julian asked, heading for the kitchen and a glass of orange juice. Hank followed, newspaper in hand.

''It looks like your engagement already made news.

There's a quote here from one of your one-night stands," Hank observed.

"One-night stands!" He stopped short. "I don't have one-night stands and you know it!"

"Well, tell that to Mimi."

"Who's Mimi? Let me see that!" Julian snatched at the paper, but Hank kept it just out of reach.

"She says you slept with her. She goes into some detail about your various assets, and I've got to tell you, she's rather explicit when she comments on the size of your—"

Julian grabbed Hank in a headlock and ripped the paper from his unresisting fingers.

"—chest," Hank finished, and then broke into paroxysms of laughter.

Forced to suffer through Hank's ensuing coughing attack brought on by his overwhelming fit of humor, Julian glanced over the page Hank had been reading from. Slowly, he folded up the paper and faced his brother. "There's nothing here."

Hank stopped laughing. "You almost sound disappointed."

Julian rolled up the newspaper and tossed it back at him. "I'll be happy when the world knows about Dixie and me," he said, heading for the refrigerator.

"You could always put out a press release," Hank said tightly.

He shrugged. "Maybe."

Frustrated, Hank grabbed his laptop computer from where he'd folded it up the night before. He flipped it open and switched on the On button. "I'll make a note," he said gaily, still hoping Julian would break down and admit that he'd pulled a hoax on his brother, just for the hell of it.

But that wasn't going to happen. Julian finished his orange juice and returned to his bedroom, whistling. He stopped at the door. ''She's got a sister. Want to make it a double date?''

A vision flashed across the screen of Hank's mind: killer smile, eyes the shade of hammered gold that crinkled at the corners with suppressed humor, red blouse with crisscrossing strings across a delectable bare back, long, long legs and painted toenails and a short white skirt...

But that image was of Dixie.

''What's the sister like?'' Hank asked without much enthusiasm.

''I think it's time we found out.'' Julian's disembodied voice floated from around the corner.

Sure. Why not? What did he have to lose, anyway?

Only my sanity, he thought despairingly and wished Dixie's image wasn't floating in front of the computer icons on his screen.

4

"I'M NOT IN THE MOOD for a date," Chloe told her sister stubbornly for the fifth time. No way was she going to subject herself to a day in the company of Dixie and Julian. "Sorry. No can do."

"Come on. It'll be fun," Dixie begged. When Julian had phoned and suggested he bring Hank along, Dixie had jumped at the idea. This was not a good sign, she supposed, but she couldn't help herself. Now she just needed Chloe to play along.

But now Chloe clapped her hands over her ears. "La, la, la, la, la," she sang at the top of her lungs as she headed down the hall toward her bedroom and away from Dixie. Chloe didn't like the idea of her sister dating a celebrity. Something was wrong about it that she simply couldn't name, but it existed. Oh, yes, it did.

Lifting one hand, she heard some rather pungent muttering from the direction of the living room. "What?" she called loudly.

"You're making a big mistake."

"What?" she repeated.

More muttering. "Never mind," Dixie yelled repressively. "But when Julian gets here, be nice."

"Nice is my middle name."

"Sure it is," was her sister's dry response.

JULIAN PULLED UP across the street from the address Dixie had given him. Stepping from the car, he examined the one-story house with the wide front porch. It was little more than a bungalow, but its fresh coat of paint and clean, well-tended grounds revealed how much care had been taken on its upkeep. Add the skyrocketing prices around this area to its general appearance and that meant the place must be worth more than even he suspected.

But calculating monetary worth was Hank's area of expertise, not Julian's. From his point of view he simply liked what he saw. The house wasn't nearly as huge and rambling as his own Beverly Hills mansion, but it had charm.

Which was how he introduced himself to the woman who threw open the door to his knock. "Hello," he said, sticking out his hand. "I'm Julian. This is a really charming home."

The woman gazed at his hand as if it were covered with warts. Slowly, reluctantly, she shook it. The sister, he realized, remembering Dixie's words. The one who'd refused a blind date with Hank. For the life of him he couldn't recall her name.

"Charming?" she said.

Her handshake was firm. Actually, it was a viselike squeeze. Julian lifted one brow. "You must be Dixie's sister."

"Chloe Kingston." She swept her hand back as if touching him might poison her. Julian had the absurd notion she could only just keep herself from wiping it off. Stepping back from the door, she invited him in with a sweep of her hand. "At your service."

Julian's smile was mystified. He'd experienced a lot of reactions from women over the years, but he couldn't recall ever being so actively disliked at first glance. For that's what it was. This woman disliked him. *Hated* him, it appeared. "Is this your house?"

"Yes." She didn't seem to know what to do with him. "I'm sure Dixie will be right out. Would you like a seat?" She indicated a tan chenille-covered armchair. Julian sank into the cushions and found that the springs were less that youthful. His hips darn near touched the floor and his knees nearly knocked his chin.

This caused her to place a hand over her mouth, as if she were fighting a serious attack of the giggles. "The couch is in better repair," she said apologetically.

With a certain degree of effort, Julian levered himself out of the chair and onto the couch. It nettled him a bit that she was so amused at his expense. Glancing out the window, he realized he could see a sliver of beach through several buildings across the street. "I haven't been to Manhattan Beach much."

"I'm sure," she said on a laugh, then caught herself up short. "I mean...oh?" she asked, as if she were reading a line.

Julian stared at her curiously. Her hair was medium-length, medium brown-blond, with a natural curl that made her seem quite young. He'd pin her age at somewhere in her late twenties to early thirties. Her eyes were wide and gray and her mouth...

Here Julian's brain tripped on its own wave of thought. Her mouth was luscious. That's what it was: *luscious*. Wide and pink and soft. And the way she worried her bottom lip with her teeth was downright cute. But she seemed as prickly as a porcupine, and he was struggling for something else to say when she perched on the overstuffed arm of the chair he'd just vacated and gave him a hard stare.

"So, what's the deal?" she asked him, that beautiful mouth forming the words rather tightly.

"The deal?"

"With Dixie. She told me how women drape themselves all over you. I can see that. You're…well…"

"I'm…?" he prompted.

She lifted a brow in a thoroughly enticing way and spread her hands apart as if measuring his shoulders. "Well-equipped," was her rather startling answer. Before he could respond, she came at him from another direction. "Do you possess a last name?"

This was territory he'd been over a thousand times. For an answer he pulled out an American Express card, held it out to her and fought a smile. "Julian" was printed across the bottom and nothing else.

Chloe sniffed at this as if it were the most childish thing she'd ever run across. "I see," she said.

"If you're worried about Dixie, don't be. I promise to behave."

His slow smile started a strange reaction in Chloe's chest. Her heart seemed to lug down, pound painfully for about four beats, then speed into overdrive. Clearing her throat, she glanced over her shoulder, certain she was about to do something utterly embarrassing like throw up or pass out or worse. "I'll get Dixie," she told him, rising to her feet in a spurt of energy and struggling hard to saunter nonchalantly down the hall when all she wanted to do was run, run, run!

"What?" Dixie asked on a gasp as Chloe burst into the bathroom and gently, almost secretively, closed the door behind her.

"Shh!" Chloe admonished, a finger to her lips. "He's out there."

"Julian?"

"*Yes! The* Julian. Who else would it be?"

"I was just wondering.... I guess I thought he might bring Hank anyway," Dixie answered lamely.

"Oh, that would be just great. After I explicitly said no." She heaved a sigh. "No, it's just Julian. Good God. He's taller than I thought he was."

"And better looking?"

Chloe gave her a sharp look. "Yes. Why?"

"I just noticed he's better-looking in person. So's Hank. Good-looking, I mean."

Chloe pressed her hands to her cheeks, her face flushed. "I don't like this one bit. You know how I feel about good-looking men."

"Then Julian and his brother are both lost causes, so you might as well give up now," she advised, applying a touch of peach lip gloss. "There. What do you think?"

Chloe regarded Dixie from head to toe. The lightest dusting of eyeshadow and mascara complimented her eyes, making them seem even rounder than usual. Their gold color sparkled, and the corners of her mouth curved up mischievously. She wore a watermelon-colored sundress, a shift with a slit up one side that hinted at more thigh than it actually delivered. A pair of rope sandals that laced around her ankles completed the outfit.

She looked like a million bucks.

"I think he's gay," Chloe said.

"*What?*" Dixie started laughing and could scarcely stop. She doubled over in an effort to contain her mirth but laughter spilled out in choked ripples.

"I'm serious. Have you ever heard of him with a woman? I mean, think about it. No photographs apart from the ones that are staged. Lots of male models are gay. Most of them, I think."

"Julian's dated lots of women. That actress, for one. I can't think of her name right now...." Dixie rolled her eyes at her sister.

"How do we know she's for real?"

"And that model! Britta!" She snapped her fingers.

"Could have been a setup."

"Chloe, he's not gay," Dixie whispered.

"You don't know that."

Dixie gazed at her sister in exasperation. "Does he strike you as gay? I mean, you have gay friends. So do I. Does he strike you that way?"

Chloe would have dearly loved to tell her sister that yes, Julian hit every gay stereotype there was and added a few new ones to boot. But truthfully, Dixie was right. Chloe had a number of gay friends, and she'd never had the reaction to them that she had to Julian. But she wasn't about to cop to that. "He said my house was charming."

"Well, then, by all means, let's call the Gay Police right now and have him taken away," Dixie said, opening the door to the hallway.

"You laugh now," Chloe warned.

"And I'll be laughing later. So will you." She hesitated then. "Come with us, Chloe. I'm sure Hank's around. We can make it a foursome. You'll have a good time."

"No..." She vehemently shook her head, then made a face, torn.

"Come on, come on!"

"Call me later," she suddenly acquiesced. "Maybe I can meet you somewhere."

"Perfect!" Dixie delightedly gave her sister a hug and whispered, "Goodbye," then headed into the living room to meet Julian who immediately stood up and kissed her lightly on the cheek before escorting her to the door.

Watching them leave from the window, Chloe felt oddly exhausted. She continued to keep an eye on their departure as Julian turned his Mercedes around in the street and the machine purred away. Dropping the curtain, Chloe sank onto the couch Julian had just vacated and reached for the Sunday crossword puzzle, but no matter how long she stared at the little white-and-black boxes she couldn't get her mind in gear. Julian's face seemed to be superimposed over everything she looked at and it was a damned fine face at that.

With all the energy she could muster, Chloe concentrated on a six-letter word for "Handsome one," and for the life of her all she could come up with was "Julian."

THE RESTAURANT Julian chose was a small bistro with black-and-white striped awnings and paned glass partitions, which cut the dining room into cozy nooks. One of the servers rushed to help him, and Dixie realized he was almost a friend.

"Come here often?" Dixie asked him.

He smiled. "The food's great. This is a place that people know I come to, so we might get some paparazzi, which is all part of the plan."

"What is the plan, exactly?" Dixie asked, opening her menu. "Let's go over it again. And thanks for not blurting out that engagement thing to my sister. I think she needs a little more time to adjust.''

"It could hit the papers by tomorrow," Julian told her. "She'd better start adjusting."

Dixie made a face and buried her nose in her menu. She was having a heck of a time getting used to this idea herself.

"If I'm engaged, I'm off the market," Julian said. "People will finally realize that I'm not looking for a missus because I've already got one ready to take the plunge."

"Ready?" The waiter materialized beside their table, pen in hand.

"Umm…"

She wasn't really hungry. She'd had toast with Chloe, and Julian's words had stolen her appetite in a hurry. But as he was ordering a fish dish that sounded wonderful, she scanned the menu, the words seeming to run together in front of her eyes. She felt as if she were on a roller coaster and was unable to get off.

"Chicken Caesar salad," she told the waiter.

"See there?" Julian lifted his water glass in a salute. "We even eat alike. Hank's diet could give me nightmares."

Here was a subject that caught her attention. "Why? What does he eat?"

"Hamburgers, steaks, French fries, terrible stuff…" He shuddered.

Dixie had a mental image of Hank chowing down on a huge American meal, his eyes twinkling at the disgust on Julian's face. "I like hamburgers sometimes," she admitted.

"What about your sister?" he asked casually.

"Chloe?"

"I'd have to agree with you that she won't adjust to this idea very well. She seemed less than happy to meet me."

"Oh, that's just the way she is." Dixie waved Chloe's attitude away. "She feels like you do about food. She really can't handle red meat. And greasy foods give her nightmares."

"She's older than you are?"

"Ten years, but don't tell her I told you." Dixie smiled.

"Has she ever been married?"

"No."

"Steady boyfriend?"

"Past tense. There was one, but when she kissed him he turned into a frog."

Julian grinned. "Hank got involved in a relationship that was sort of like that."

Dixie stopped with her water glass halfway to her lips. "Oh, yeah?"

"A model."

Depression hit like a hammer. Dixie could find no response to that remark, and she was glad when her salad was delivered so she wouldn't have to talk. Of course Hank would have been with a model! she thought with a pang. Julian had been involved with that Britta something-or-other. Tall, thin, pouty and beautiful... Yep. A living nightmare. If Hank's model was anything like Britta, the rest of the female population might just as well give up the ghost.

"Chloe wants me to call her later. Do you think Hank would meet us, and make that double date after all?"

Julian's interest sharpened. "Why? Has your sister had a change of heart?"

"Well, sort of. She's just nervous about me going out with you."

"Paranoid is more like it," Julian said, forking a lightly sautéed bit of flaky white fish into his mouth. "Are you still interested in shopping? I thought we'd look at rings."

Her heart plummeted to her feet. "Rings?" she squeaked.

"Just as a lark. On Rodeo Drive. It's a great way to get the rumor mill in gear. And then we can call your sister and meet up at my place. Hank's there while his condo is being renovated, so we can start there and then move on to dinner."

"Hank has a condo?"

He nodded. "Santa Monica. Just off the beach."

Just off the beach... She had a sudden vision of him in his silk shirt patterned in surfboards, khaki shorts and barefoot on the beach. She swallowed her last bit of salad with an effort.

"That's sounds fine," Dixie said. "I'd love to see your house."

"Good."

At that moment Julian was spotted by a small mob of fans who shrieked and squealed and worked up the courage to join them.

"Show time," Julian said dryly to Dixie, then he waved to the group of girls, who nearly collapsed in a heap when their hero called them over. For what felt like hours—but was actually less than fifteen minutes—Julian smiled and hugged and stood for pictures. Several times he drew Dixie near, making it clear that she was with him. For that honor, she received sideways glares and rude sniffs. Incredible.

Thirty minutes later, she and Julian were pulling

into Julian's driveway. Dixie left her car at the restaurant. She climbed out of the Mercedes and walked beside Julian to the front door, which was unlocked. Moments later she was ushered inside a very masculine room done in cream, black and gray.

And Hank was sprawled on a black leather sofa, channel surfing on one of the biggest big-screen TVs Dixie had ever seen. He glanced up, saw her and suddenly stiffened as if he'd been brought before a drill sergeant. "Oh. Hi," he said.

Again, she was swamped by dashed expectations. What did she want, anyway? Some avowal of friendship, or...what? Dixie's mind skittered away from some rather dangerous thoughts regarding Julian's brother. Better to keep her mind on the main goal: her career, and how Julian planned to help her—a plan she needed to formalize with him at the earliest opportunity.

"Hello, again," she responded.

"How was lunch?" Hank asked.

Julian suddenly draped his arm over Dixie's shoulder. "Fabulous," he told his brother. "This girl's one in a million."

Dixie's smile felt as if it might break. She gazed at Hank, but apart from a tightening of his jaw, which she attributed to the fact that he wouldn't appreciate Julian falling for any girl, he seemed rather unmoved by the news. "Is she?" was all he asked, which definitely raised the bar on Dixie's anxiety level.

"Her sister's game for dinner later, after all. Let's go to Dr. Woo's."

Dr. Woo's was a Chinese restaurant so difficult to get into that reservations had to be made weeks in advance, maybe months. Dixie looked askance at Julian, then decided he must know what he was doing.

"What made her change her mind?" Hank asked, flicking off the TV and dropping the remote on the couch as he climbed to his feet. He threw them a dry look. "Did she want to toast your engagement?"

Julian glanced at Dixie, waiting for her to say something. Blushing, she stammered, "She—she's kind of having a hard time with the whole idea."

"I wonder why," Hank muttered. He walked the few steps toward them. Though he was farther away from her than Julian was, Dixie felt his nearness as if it were palpable. "It is kind of sudden, wouldn't you say?"

"It's just going to take her some time to get used to the idea." She swallowed, wondering why her throat was so dry. "In fact, the less we talk about it, the better, for the time being."

"You're engaged, and you don't want to talk about it?" Hank questioned.

Realizing she'd inadvertently raised his antenna on their scam, Dixie blithely waved one hand. "No, no. It's just that Chloe has issues."

"I can't wait to meet her," Hank muttered dryly.

Julian chuckled. "She's one of a kind."

Dixie perked up. She was encouraged that Julian seemed to take Chloe's reluctance to accept him in stride. She smiled back at him.

Hank gazed from one to the other of them, irritated beyond bearing at the romantic picture they made. "I'll keep the engagement talk to a minimum," he promised. "But it's my duty to give you both a toast tonight. I mean, I'm assuming I'll be the best man at the wedding."

"Of course." Julian met Hank's hawklike gaze blandly.

Dixie inwardly gulped. She was not looking forward to this evening any longer. Not at all! She shuddered to think of Chloe's reaction. Good grief. Mount Etna couldn't erupt more than Chloe was bound to! Oh, why hadn't she thought this through? How had she let this happen?

Eye on the prize, she told herself. *Eye on the prize.*

"All right, let's go to Dr. Woo's," Hank said, more as a means to get Julian to remove his arm from Dixie than any serious desire to be in their company one more second than he had to.

"Good, we'll be back later," Julian said. "We've got some window-shopping to do."

Rings, Dixie remembered with a jolt. Window-shopping for rings. She felt Hank's gaze on her and had to look away. Things were really getting out of control, and she didn't have any idea what to do about it!

"DR. WOO'S?" Chloe demanded into the receiver. "Are you out of your mind? You'll never get a reservation!"

"Apparently we don't need one," Dixie advised her sister. "We were going to meet at Julian's, but it's getting kind of late. Can you meet us there? Just use valet parking."

"Oh, yeah! And break my budget for a century! Do you know how much that costs?"

Feeling Julian's eyes on her, Dixie cleared her throat. She was using his cell phone. They'd strolled all over Rodeo Drive and caused a minor sensation in the process and now she felt a headache coming on—big time.

"I don't think you need to worry about it," Dixie said.

"Oh, no. No, no, no. I pay my own way. I'm not having Julian take care of you and me!"

"Will you just come?" Dixie pleaded.

"Well, the food is supposed to be great there." Chloe relented.

"We're going to pick up Hank now. We'll be there in an hour. Just tell them you're with Julian."

"Oh...God..."

Dixie's hand clenched around the receiver. "He's anxious to get to know you, too," she said brightly. "He thinks you two have a lot in common." Choking noises sounded at the other end of the line, and in her peripheral vision she could see Julian's brow furrow as he tried to decipher what was transpiring between Dixie and Chloe. "An hour, okay?"

Chloe groaned, closed her eyes, counted to thirteen and said dourly, "I guess I should ask what this Hank is like."

A sudden vision of Chloe with Hank crossed the screen of Dixie's mind. She blinked several times, finding it difficult to answer.

"Dixie?"

"He's perfect," she said, then slammed down the phone before Chloe could bite on that one.

"Everything okay?" Julian asked.

"Hunky-dory," she said.

HANK PACED around the confines of Julian's living room like a caged panther. He was tense and anxious and unhappy. He glanced at his image above the bar and nearly snarled at his own reflection: black jeans, black shirt open at the throat. Who did he think he was, Julian?

"All I need is a wig," he growled in self-directed fury. But he didn't change his clothes.

What's wrong with me? he asked himself, completely aware that he was acting completely out of character and completely helpless to do anything about it. Dixie had gotten under his skin in a way that was new and confusing. *And she was engaged to his brother!*

Hank groaned aloud. What was Julian thinking? Sure, Dixie was great. He, Hank, could attest to strong feelings in her direction. But she had to be just another gold digger. All women were. But, so what? Julian was a big boy, and he was as savvy about women as Hank was. So, if he wanted to be with her, more power to him. Actually, he deserved to be with a woman he actually *chose* to be with. What harm could it do?

Hank closed his eyes and rubbed his face, more nervous than he'd been in years. For reasons he definitely didn't want to explore, he suddenly remembered his first serious crush. Mary Madeline Langford. He could still recall at age thirteen the very embarrassing way he went about chasing her down. Mary had sent all his male fantasies into overdrive, and he'd followed her around like a lovesick puppy, transfixed by her slender calves and massive breasts and the way she popped gum. Of course, Mary, nineteen, had possessed a boyfriend, a lorry driver with arms the size of tree trunks and a temper to rival the Red Queen. But Hank hadn't been able to get her out of his mind. Only when the lorry driver growled that he would dismantle Hank limb by limb and thoroughly enjoy doing it, thank you very much, did Hank force himself to forget about Mary. In many ways, she was his last unconquerable female, for within a year any fantasies he possessed about the opposite sex had become reality, and subsequently he pretty much lost interest in the game. Much like his older brother, Hank found that women were attracted to his looks and physique. It was flattering and he'd been involved with a number of them, but whenever he hoped he'd finally found her, the girl of his dreams, he was disappointed. They all *wanted* something from him, something he couldn't possibly give because all he ever felt was mild attraction.

And then he learned that money, too, was another pheromone. Though he teased Julian mercilessly about his attraction to females, he shared some of the same problems. And whenever he had a chance to think about his last and latest romantic mistake, it made him damn near shudder. In fact he *was* shuddering, he realized. Now that lady was downright frightening! And though the whole world thought she'd been Julian's lover, it didn't help. Britta had been the most screwed-up individual he'd ever met, and she still called him whenever she was in town.

Ugh. No more thinking about her. Uh-uh.

So, what reason was there to get so excited about Julian's date with Dixie? It wasn't his problem, thank God.

"Amen," he muttered. He was still pacing the floor when he heard Julian's car pull up into the drive. Feeling a little like a deer caught in the headlights, he watched as the door opened. There was Julian in his ubiquitous black jeans and a tan suede fringed shirt, baring a lot of that broad chest, and there was Dixie beside him, cool as ice in that watermelon-shade clingy sundress that made his mouth water.

For the first time in his life Hank felt a serious, serious stab of envy where his brother was concerned.

ON THE WAY to pick up Hank, Dixie had been inordinately quiet. But as they'd turned into Julian's driveway, she'd surfaced from her reverie.

"Before we go any further, we've got to get a few things straight," she said. "Palmer Michaels. You said I'm to be there at two tomorrow?"

"After the meeting with Primitive Cologne at ten."

Dixie drew a breath and nodded. "You still want me to come?"

"Well, yes. It's our bargain."

"I just feel—kind of funny."

"Don't," he assured her. "The Primitive people are great. They'll greet you with open arms."

I'll bet, Dixie thought. She knew they weren't going to like Julian dictating who his Jane would be. But that was his problem. She had a very different one to think about. "Is Palmer Michaels very expensive?"

"I'll pay for the classes," Julian told her, and when she tried to protest, he said, "No way. We've got a deal, and I'm keeping to my side of the bargain."

"And all you really want me to do is act like your fiancée?"

"Yes," he stated firmly.

"I think you're getting robbed."

"I think I'm getting a steal of a deal."

And that's when they walked through the door and Dixie saw Hank dressed all in black and looking rather grim and intense. The image seemed to slam against her brain, and she wondered if she were getting ill.

"You ready?" Julian asked Hank. He examined his brother's black shirt and slacks and said in surprise, "Where are the surfer shirts, dude?"

His surprise turned to shock when Hank growled something unintelligible. What was this? Hank was really having an off day, which was unusual. Julian could certainly get annoyed and have his dark moments, but Hank's disposition was generally sunny.

Hank hardly said a word as the three of them piled into the car. Dixie sat stiffly in the passenger seat next to Julian and Hank sat behind her. She could feel his breath on the back of her neck, and her skin broke out in goose bumps.

Twenty minutes later they were handing their car over to the valet as Chloe pulled up in her ten-year-old Volvo wagon. She climbed out of the car, regarded the valet rather suspiciously, then reluctantly handed over her keys, too. Then she glanced over at Dixie, Julian and Hank. Walking up to Hank, she extended her hand. "So, you're the brother," she said.

He grinned, visibly relaxing for the first time. "So, you're the sister."

Chloe grinned back.

Dixie's heart shrank to the size of a pea. Julian couldn't take his eyes off Chloe, whose black halter top and short khaki skirt showed off a lot of leg and hugged her sumptuous curves. Hank looked at Julian and Dixie and arched a devilish brow and said, "So, I guess we're here to toast the lucky couple, huh?"

Chloe cocked her head and frowned. "Toast them for what?"

Hank winced. "Sorry," he said.

"Toast them for what?" Chloe repeated, gazing from Hank to Julian and Chloe. "Dixie?"

Julian slipped an arm around Dixie's waist, which was just as well because she was feeling rather weak and fluttery. She couldn't speak. She just gazed at Chloe through huge eyes.

Slowly the blood drained from Chloe's face. "Oh, my God," she whispered. "Are you saying...are you saying..." She swayed, and Julian jumped forward and grabbed her. Her body went limp. She gazed up into his face. In horror, she asked, "Are you saying you're *engaged?*"

Julian gazed down at her, holding her waist, barely keeping her on her feet. It was a scene from a romance novel cover if ever there was one. A paparazzo popped from the edges of the crowd and *poof!* snapped their picture.

And for Chloe it was lights out.

5

"I'VE NEVER FAINTED in my whole life," Chloe said again, as if repeating it enough times would ensure that it were true. "Never. In my whole life. Fainted."

She was crumpled onto the red velvet banquet seat, one of the prime tables in the restaurant. It was a bit of a mystery to her how she'd found her way to this position. Had Julian carried her? She didn't dare ask! Had they gotten this table and the red carpet treatment because Julian had stepped forward and caught her before she'd swooned? Or had it been available simply because Julian was *the* Julian? Either way, Dr. Woo's minions had scurried around to make certain she was comfortable, and now she felt like a complete idiot. And the way they were all fawning over Julian now, as if he were some kind of hero who'd saved the damsel in distress, was enough to make any self-respecting normal person retch. And she'd come close to doing it, all right, she thought glumly. In fact, she still felt a little bit queasy though she'd rather be boiled in oil than admit such a thing in front of *the* Julian.

Dixie sat beside her, looking concerned. Chloe wanted to assure her that she was all right, but she was still too discombobulated to even think straight.

And the reason she'd fainted in the first place hadn't gone away. "Engaged?" she whispered in Dixie's ear. She really didn't know whether to laugh or cry!

"Engaged," Hank repeated blankly, sounding as shell-shocked as Chloe felt. He sat on her right, with Julian flanking Dixie's other side.

"This is a joke, right? A very stupid joke to play on good, ole gullible Chloe!"

Dixie licked dry lips and gulped ice water. "No joke," she said out of the side of her mouth.

"Are you out of your ever-loving mind?"

"Most probably."

Chloe could scarcely take it all in. "I need a drink. Get me a drink."

"You'd be better off with a glass of water," Julian suggested. "Or, maybe some herb tea. I can get you some."

Chloe deigned to glower at the man responsible for all this fuss. "A drink," she stated in a voice that could cut glass. "Something with a lot of alcohol."

Hank shot her an appreciative glance. "I'll have what she's having," Hank said to Julian.

"Me, too," Dixie said on a sigh.

Julian gazed from one to the other of them, having been somehow appointed personal bartender for the group. He got to his feet.

"Dixie..." Chloe plunked her elbows on the table and held her head in her hands. At that moment a crowd of females swarmed them, begging Julian for autographs before he could take even a step toward the bar.

That did it. Chloe shot them a withering look, a personal favorite of hers that had destroyed far lesser humans than this particular band of bubbleheads. "Do you mind? We're having a bit of a crisis here, and we don't want to be bothered."

Julian's brows jerked skyward. While the womens'

faces fell in shock, he spread his hands sympathetically, silently agreeing with Chloe. After a few sideways glowers nearly as impressive as Chloe's—and definitely meant for her and her alone—the crowd reluctantly dispersed.

"Not good for your image," Hank remarked in a tone that said he really didn't care one way or the other any longer.

"I'll get the drinks." Julian headed for the bar.

"I'll go, too," Dixie said, but Chloe clamped down on her arm with tight fingers.

"You go," Chloe ordered Hank. "We sisters need a moment."

Hank shrugged and followed after Julian. As soon as she had Dixie to herself, Chloe declared, "Okay, that's it. This has got to end. Now. Soon. Before I go completely around the bend and you throw your life away!"

"Throw my life away! Oh, come on!"

"I understand about the actors' studio. That's good. That's great, in fact. It's really nice of him to help you out that way. But Dixie, *you don't even know him!*"

"Chloe, it'll be okay."

The barmaid came with their drinks while Julian and Hank stayed near the bar, a respectful distance from Dixie and Mount Etna. As soon as they had their double whatever-they-weres in hand, serious drinks for a serious subject, Chloe leaned forward and gave Dixie the older sister evil eye. "I've been patient. A saint, really. But I've about had it with you and this whole 'I don't need to tell Chloe everything' attitude. You *know* you have to tell me."

"What do you want to know?"

"What you're really doing! I know you, Dixie. You

might be a little impulsive, but this is beyond the pale." She peered at Dixie a bit anxiously. "Is he pressuring you in some way?"

"Of course not. Why would Julian have to pressure *me*?"

"Why, indeed," she murmured.

Calling on all her acting skills, Dixie inhaled a deep breath, exhaled slowly, then asked, "Couldn't I just be falling head over heels in love with him?"

"No."

"Well, I am. I—love—him," Dixie stated seriously, and if it wasn't exactly Julian's image she conjured up inside her head at that moment, big deal. So, it was Hank's. So what?

Chloe didn't move even the slightest muscle for the space of three heartbeats. Her gray eyes stared into Dixie's as if she were searching out life's mysteries. Finally, she slapped her palm down on the table forcing the clear liquid whatever-they-weres to jump. Scooping her glass up, Chloe tossed back a healthy dose. She swallowed, sucked in air, grimaced and choked in a strained voice, "Straight vodka!"

"Vodka and Cointreau," Hank corrected her as he appeared at the table again. "With a twist of lemon."

"Enough to kill you," Chloe said, still in that voice that sounded as if her esophagus had collapsed on itself.

"You asked for a lot of alcohol," Hank reminded her.

"Are you okay now?" Dixie asked with real concern.

Julian slid in beside her, his eyes on Chloe, also waiting for her answer. Chloe gazed back at the male model. "I am never going to be okay," she stated firmly and lifted her drink to her lips again.

IF THERE WAS such a thing as hell on earth, this was it, Hank decided. He could not stand seeing Dixie with Julian. Simply couldn't stand it. To keep his emotions in check, he concentrated on Chloe, who was attractive and wonderfully candid and didn't do the least little thing for him.

Just seeing Julian's elbow rub against Dixie's drove him crazy. He'd downed a couple of drinks himself in quick succession, noting that his older brother had barely touched his gin martini. Julian rarely drank. He was too much of a believer in all-around good health. And though Hank generally nursed a couple of drinks over the length of an evening, tonight he felt like drowning himself in buckets of alcohol and behaving like a total sot!

Looking up, he found Dixie's expressive eyes on him, but she glanced away as soon as she realized she'd caught his attention. For a long moment he concentrated on the smooth line of her nape and the soft curtain of hair that fell across her cheek.

They'd ordered dinner and Julian and Chloe had chosen as if they were raving vegetarians, he'd noticed. They probably were. Not that Chloe had managed to do justice to her meal. She was still looking a little peaked, actually. Dixie, luckily, knew how to dig into sesame beef with gusto, and Hank had followed suit. What a perfect girl, he'd thought, then had ordered another drink to squelch the very un-brotherly thoughts he was plagued by.

He'd carried on a lively conversation about why humans were meant to be carnivores for quite a while, which hadn't fazed Julian in the least, and no one else seemed to care. Which really ticked him off, now that he thought about it. He'd made some damn good arguments, and he was about to say as much when Chloe, who'd been relatively quiet for a while, pushed aside her plate, dug inside her purse and pulled out a folded-up piece of newspaper. "Carnivores, schmarnivores," she said. "I'm never going to eat meat." Without another word she started working on a crossword puzzle. "I'm stuck, okay?" she added into the silence that ensued. "What's a six-letter word for 'handsome one'?" she said.

"Adonis," Julian responded instantly, tipping back his martini and finally emptying its contents.

Chloe made a strangled sound and filled in the word. Dixie gazed at her in surprise. "You must really be off your game. I'm surprised you didn't get that one. You're always saying crossword puzzles love words with lots of vowels."

"It's been a rough night," she muttered.

"Give us another one," Julian suggested.

Hank groaned. "Don't do it. Julian's a wordmeister. Now, if you want to talk numbers, I'm your guy. Finance." He pointed a finger in Dixie's direction and winked. "That's me."

"This one's for both of you," Chloe said, directing her attention to Julian and Hank. "Three-letter word for 'British head.'"

"That leaves out king or queen," Dixie said. Like Julian, she'd barely touched her drink—Mandarin Stoli's vodka and Cointreau, a marvelous drink by Hank's standards and based on Chloe's consumption, he felt she might agree. Dixie, however, wasn't as convinced.

"I guess prime minister doesn't fit either," Hank said with a smile that felt slightly lopsided.

"Loo," Julian said.

"Lou?" Dixie asked, her brows drawing together.

"Oh. Bathroom," Hank explained. "The loo. The head? You know?"

"British *head.*" Dixie nodded in understanding.

"I should have come up with that one," Chloe muttered, chagrined. She placed her fingers to her temples and grimaced.

"Are you all right?" Julian asked in concern.

"Never better," she chirped.

"Give me another one," Julian urged her, and Hank could see this crossword puzzle thing was turning into a challenge. He groaned, squinted across the table and asked, "Wanna dance?"

Dixie glanced over at him. She jerked in surprise. "Who? Me?"

"Unless you're in on this…" He gestured to Chloe, Julian and the crossword puzzle.

She smiled, and the dimple that peeked out was heavenly. Julian slid across the seat to let her out without being asked. She scrambled to her feet as Hank extended an arm for her, gesturing for her to precede him. Having never been to Dr. Woo's before, she hesitated.

"Through that door marked Emergency Room," Hank said, his breath near her ear.

With a chill sliding down her spine, Dixie hurried forward, stepping through café doors into a discotheque-type room done in red with a circular dance floor in the center of the room and several couples swaying on the floor to soft music. "I didn't know this was here," she murmured.

"It gets crazy later. Emergency time and all that.

But when it's early…" He shrugged and glanced around the near empty dance floor. "It's nice."

"You come here often?"

Hank made a face. "Used to," he said, refusing to go *there*. He'd spent too many hours baby-sitting beautiful models who refused even to eat the olive in their martinis. Britta was the worst.

Dixie stepped closer, but she kept her own arms stiff. No use getting too close. There was danger there. But there was no use denying that it felt good to be in the circle of his arms, and she tried to hide the little sigh of contentment that escaped her as they gently swayed to soft instrumental music.

"So, Dixie…" he whispered.

"Yes?"

"Why are you with Julian? I mean, really. I know you're not engaged," he said, pulling back slightly so that his eyes could probe deeply into hers. "I know it's a fake."

"Wh-what?"

"You're not engaged. Julian would never get engaged like that." He snapped his fingers and wished he'd had more to drink. The buzz he'd worked so hard for was rapidly evaporating.

"Well, he did."

He pulled back and stared hard at her. Sternly. Determined to get to the bottom of this. Because he couldn't help himself, he let one fingertip trail along the downy softness of her cheek. "Just tell me why you're pretending to be engaged to my brother…."

CHLOE DIDN'T LIKE the way he was leaning so close to her. She didn't like his body in her space. He was just so—big.

"Three-letter word for louse," Chloe told Julian frostily.

"Cad," he answered.

"Wrong!"

"Oh, come on." He reached for the puzzle only to have Chloe snatch it close to her breasts and hug it there as if it were dear to her heart. He'd answered five out of six of the questions she'd reluctantly posed, and now she was seething. And he was as amused as hell! He slid yet closer to her and though her hips stayed in place, her torso drew back as far as it could. His fingers clasped the edge of the paper.

She glanced down, alarmed to see the way her chest was heaving. "You're touching my breast," she pointed out.

"Not yet. But if you pull it any closer to you, I just might."

"I'll scream."

That broke him up. He laughed so hard he thought he might actually suffocate from lack of air. People looked over, grinned, whispered and nudged their friends.

Chloe glanced around in horror. They were making a scene, and it was downright humiliating. "Oh, here!" she declared, slapping the paper on the table in front of him. "Now, move over."

"Why? Does it bother you that I'm so close?"

His breath feathered her hair. "Yes," she admitted tightly.

"Doesn't bother me."

"Oh, fine. Play that stupid little game. Go ahead." She looked away from him, across the room, anywhere but at that massive chest that he so conveniently showed through the open front of his shirt. Did he have to do that? Make such a spectacle of himself? No wonder women threw themselves at him. It was false advertising!

"You've really got a problem with me, don't you?"

His voice was soft. Almost silky. Definitely dangerous. Chloe gazed at him through narrowed eyes. It helped to have a smaller window of vision. Kept him from being so impossibly male. "I've got a problem with you and my sister."

"I'm not going to hurt your sister."

Chloe's attention fastened on his lips. Sensually thin. Masculine. Really, it was just so unfair!

"What?" he asked.

"What, what?" she repeated.

"What's unfair?"

She'd spoken aloud. Burying her nose in her drink again, Chloe fretted over what this meant. "I was thinking about your physical attributes," she said with real honesty.

"You have rather nice physical attributes yourself."

Something in his tone. Some quirk of familiarity and appreciation got to Chloe. "You are a very, very dangerous man," she said.

Julian's blue eyes searched hers. "Is that good or bad?"

Chloe opened her mouth, saw his gaze drop to her lips and felt a bit faint all over again. Turning away, she said with an effort, "I think I need another drink."

"I'M NOT PRETENDING. I am engaged," Dixie corrected him, her pulse going wild. What did he know? Had Julian told him? Was this a test?

"Oh, come on." He smiled and she was mesmerized by the curve of those lips. "Engaged in subterfuge, maybe. But to be married? To my brother? Not likely."

"Maybe you should talk to Julian about this."

"I have. For hours! I thought you might be able to be honest with me, that's all."

A fishing expedition. That's what it was. Hank was on a fishing expedition. Though she should be relieved, Dixie found herself wanting to confess so badly she had to bite her lip and lay her head against his broad chest just to fight for time. His own heartbeat seemed rather erratic. She needed to change the subject—and fast!

"Your hair—" he murmured.

Her pulse jumped. "My hair?" she repeated a bit breathlessly. Could he be feeling even the slightest bit of what she was feeling?

"—is in my mouth," he finished.

"Oh. Sorry." She jerked away from him as if burned.

He gazed at her. They were still locked in dance position, but Dixie was now as far from him as his arms would allow. And she was gazing at him with eyes that looked almost hurt. That bugged him. "Julian said you're going with us to the meeting with Primitive tomorrow," he said. "What's that all about?"

"Again—you should ask your brother."

"Just how good of an actress are you? At first I thought you were probably just run-of-the-mill, like everybody else who throws themselves at him. But maybe you're better than that. Maybe you've really convinced him that you're for real. That you don't have—'' here he made his index and middle fingers sketch parentheses signs in midair ''—*designs* on him. But you haven't convinced me.''

Dixie, who'd been suffering real pangs of conscience, *and* had been laboring under the spell of his own brand of sex appeal, *and* had looked forward to being alone on the dance floor with him far more than she should, *and* had almost made herself believe she really liked him…*really, really* liked him, suddenly decided she'd been wrong, wrong, wrong.

''What are you saying?''

''Oh, come on. What are you really looking for? You can tell me.''

''I don't know what you mean.''

''Somehow—I don't know how—but somehow you've got Julian wrapped around your little finger. He's taking you with us to Primitive Cologne tomorrow. Dropping a gift in your lap that other *actresses* would kill for. What kind of spell have you put him under? What's so special about you?''

What's so special about you?

The words hung in the air. Nasty. Insinuating. Hurtful. And really, really maddening. For a moment Dixie was speechless. Filled with utter disbelief that he could be such a thick-skulled neanderthal!

''You're just looking out for Number One, aren't you? Using Julian to get exactly what you want, and it doesn't matter that he might be falling in love with you.''

''You're wrong!''

''Am I? You're not the first, you know,'' he stated coldly. ''Though you might be the first to actually turn his head. But that's what he's got me for—to make sure certain people like you don't take advantage of him.''

Dixie could scarcely believe the words that were coming out of his mouth—a mouth that she'd found so attractive just scant minutes before! "So, how are you planning to get rid of me?" she challenged.

"Just as fast as I can."

Oh, he was smug! She struggled for a comeback. Some witty *bon mot* that would zing him right where it hurt. But no. Her brain simply shut down.

So she hauled back her foot and kicked him straight in the shin.

At his shocked intake of breath and bit-off cry of pain, she stalked out of the room and back to the table where Chloe and Julian were staring at each other much like a mongoose and a snake might.

Snatching up her purse, she said, "Crossword time over? Then let's get out of here," and sailed out of the restaurant before either of them could protest.

6

VACUUMING. She was vacuuming. And was that *yelling?*

Chloe stepped into the living room and folded her arms over her chest, frowning at her younger sister as Dixie muscled the vacuum cleaner from one side of the carpet to the other. Not a word had been spoken between them since their double date the evening before. A dark cloud seemed to hang low over Dixie's head, so the ride home had been ultra-quiet. And Chloe had her own problems to deal with, namely, her aversion to *the* Julian.

Just thinking about him rose goose bumps on her arms. Briskly she rubbed her elbows and tried hard to forget his silky, challenging voice. The man was sheer trouble, and she was bound and determined to get her sister out of the mess she'd gotten herself into.

It *was* yelling. Or a form of loud muttering as Dixie seemed to be spitting out words between her teeth. Chloe made out "egotist" and "self-serving jerk" and there seemed to be more than a few aspersions made about someone's legitimacy, if she were hearing correctly. Maybe she was worrying unduly. This thing with *the* Julian could be wrapping itself up before it even began.

"Dixie!" Chloe called over the roar of the machine. She'd really tried hard to keep from breaking down first. If Dixie wanted to have a little "me time," so be it. But this was really past the limit of human endurance, as far as Chloe was concerned, and besides she had a lot of things she wanted to say about *the* Julian before Dixie went off to meet him at Primitive Cologne's offices this morning.

Dixie jerked at the sound of Chloe's voice. She stared at her sister. "What?" she yelled.

Exasperated, Chloe stomped over to the cord and yanked it from the wall. The vacuum slowly whined down as if gasping out its last dying breath. "There!" she declared. "So, what gives? You've been acting like—no, cancel that—you've *been* an absolute grouch since last night. What did Mr. Julian do?"

Dixie shook her head. "What are you doing in your bathrobe? Aren't you going to work today?"

"I'm sick," Chloe answered shortly.

"You've never been home sick from work!"

"Well, I'm sick today," Chloe declared in a voice that invited no further arguments. "And what are you doing? You've got a meeting in less than two hours."

"I'm about to get ready." She picked up the cord and prepared to slip the prongs in the outlet, but Chloe grabbed her elbow to stop her.

"By vacuuming?"

"Do you mind? As soon as I'm done, I'll jump in the shower." She took the plug from Chloe's hand and thrust it in the outlet with such determination that Chloe half-expected electricity to jump out of the wall and run around the room in an effort to escape.

"Sheesh…" Chloe lifted her hands in mock surrender and backed away. So much for a good old heart-to-heart with little sis.

But Dixie, having apparently rethought her actions,

unplugged the vacuum, heaved a huge sigh, then flopped down on the couch. She was still in her pajamas and now she propped her elbows on the blue-and-white flannel loose pants, leaned her chin on her hand and gazed forlornly at Chloe.

"What did he do?" Chloe asked again.

"*He* didn't do anything, if by *he* you mean Julian. It was his misogynistic brother."

"Oh," Chloe said in surprise. "Hank? Well, what did *he* do, then?"

"*He* implied that I was only marrying Julian for his money and what he could do for my career. *He* thinks all women are grasping, cheating, lying opportunists!"

"He said that?"

"Well, not in so many words, but that's what he meant. So, I—kicked him," she admitted a bit sheepishly.

"Kicked him?"

"In the shin."

Chloe blinked rapidly in sudden remembrance. Hank had been limping a bit when he came back to the table, but Dixie had been in such a rush to leave that Chloe had been hurried out of the restaurant before she could even really notice. And she'd been dealing with some other issues, as well, for Julian's words and tone and proximity had played havoc with her equilibrium in a way that made her cringe inside this morning.

Dixie's eyes were filled with hurt and injustice and a certain amount of anxiety. "I shouldn't have done it, but he deserved it!"

"Oh, he'll recover. Maybe it'll make him think before he spouts off next time."

"You think so?"

Chloe threw up her hands in exasperation. "Who knows! Men are strange creatures, and Hank, like his brother, is just too good-looking. That's all there is to it. Stop worrying about it. You've got bigger issues to wrap your brain around."

"Mm..." Dixie said, sounding unconvinced. She moved her bare toe around in little circles on the carpet, lost in thought.

"Dixie, honey, you can't marry him. You know you can't."

"Chloe, would you just lay off?" Dixie sighed.

"Just please tell me you're not serious. Please..."

When Dixie slumped further into herself and refused to meet Chloe's eyes, Chloe heaved a sigh. "Then tell me this. Does the man have a last name? I mean, really. You're not going to be Mrs. Julian or anything, are you?"

"I'm sure he has a last name."

"You're sure. But you don't what it is?"

"I forgot to ask."

Chloe stated slowly, "You're marrying him and you forgot to ask his last name."

"It just hasn't come up," Dixie stated shortly, climbing to her feet. "I'll finish this later," she said, sweeping a hand toward the vacuum that still stood at attention in the center of the room.

"Dixie, I just have to say one thing. You won't be happy with him. He's too magnetic. You'll never be able to trust him, and you'll get sick to the back teeth of all the female attention he gets. Believe me, I don't know what's going on in that head of yours, but this charade has got to stop!"

Dixie had made it to the hallway. Now, she turned around and regarded her sister. "Charade?"

"You can't be in love with him!" she blurted out.

"Maybe I'm exactly what Hank said," Dixie said in a blithe tone that belied her inner feelings. "Maybe I'm just out for what I can get."

Now Chloe gazed at her as if she'd sprouted a second head. "Oh, yeah. Like *that's* really you!"

"Well, what if it is? What if I am that gold digger? What if I'm just with Julian for what he can do for me? I'm going to that meeting this morning," she reminded her. "I'm hoping to be in a commercial with him."

"Julian invited you to that meeting," Chloe reminded her right back. "Just because Hank got under your skin doesn't mean you're any of those things. You know yourself. You would never use anyone. You're too straightforward. Now, get back to the real issue. You can't be engaged to Julian."

Dixie opened her mouth, tried to say something, snapped it shut, then shook her head. With that, she just walked down the hall to the bathroom. Moments later Chloe heard the shower pipes groan into action and the rush of pouring water.

"Now what was that all about?" she murmured aloud.

"YOU LOOK LIKE HELL," Julian told Hank as they sped toward the offices of Primitive Cologne on Wilshire Boulevard. Hank was driving, and he'd been running his hand through his hair so much during the drive that strands stood out on end.

"My appearance doesn't matter. You're the one they're interested in what he looks like and you look fine."

Julian lifted a brow at his brother's short tone. "How's the leg?"

Hank's answer was a deeper glower at the road and traffic in front of him. As a small blue Japanese car darted in front of him he laid on the horn.

"What was it again that set Dixie off?" Julian asked in feigned innocence. Hank might be grouching around, but this morning Julian felt on top of the world. He actually pursed his lips and began to whistle a bit. Hank growled beneath his breath, which only improved Julian's mood further. It was so rare to catch his brother out of sorts. Hank was always the eternal optimist.

"She kicked me," Hank pointed out through a jaw that didn't even move.

"I know. You were pretty clear about that last night. What you didn't say was why."

"I just was pointing out that it was kind of fishy that you and she got engaged so quickly. You just met last week and now wedded bliss is on the way! Tell me, has she got something over on you? Is there some deep scandal she's sitting on? No, let me guess, by day you're the romance icon, but by night you're a cross-dresser in a sleazy club on Hollywood Boulevard. She knows the truth, and she's got you by the kahoonies."

"You know what you are, Hank? You're colorful."

"I'm glad you think so."

"I'm glad you're glad."

Hank exhaled heavily. "Okay, so you're not going to tell me. Fine. Don't. But I just don't get why you had to invite Dixie to this meeting. This is your gig, and it doesn't look good to bring in your own Jane."

"Since when do you care about what looks good?"

Julian shot back. "They're not going to care if I ask them to use Dixie in the commercial. She's great-looking. She's got a quality you just can't help but notice. You've seen it!"

"*I've* seen it?"

"Oh, come on, Hank. You practically undress her with your eyes!"

"No, I don't!"

Julian made a sound of exasperation. "Fine. Whatever. All I'm saying is Dixie's perfect for the part. And if Primitive doesn't want her, they'll just say so. Besides, I think they'll like the engagement part of it. Adds an interesting angle to their whole advertising campaign."

"I don't look at Dixie that way," Hank denied again. "She's your—your—*fiancée!* I'm just worried about you, that's all."

"Well, you can stop worrying."

"It hasn't occurred to you that you might be creating professional suicide?" Hank asked.

"What is with you?" Julian swiveled in his seat to gain a clear view of his brother's profile.

"When this hits the fan, it's going to be all over the news. You know that. And yet you act like you don't care!"

Julian struggled with himself for a moment, wondering if keeping Hank in the dark was such a great idea after all. He didn't like Hank's resentment toward Dixie. Maybe if he told him the truth, he wouldn't be so hard on her. "Dixie's as good as it gets," he began, picking through his words to find just the right ones.

Hank snorted loudly.

"Why don't you like her?" Julian asked, truly perplexed. Dixie *was* as good as it gets. And her sister was pretty damn attractive, too, if you liked opinion-ated feminists, which Julian normally steered clear of. But Chloe... For all her bold talk, he'd seen the fear in her gray eyes when he'd moved closer. She was like a deer caught in headlights. Frozen. Maybe a little fascinated. Aware she might be meeting her doom but helpless to do anything about it.

Or maybe that's what *he'd* felt....

He visibly shook his head. He wasn't going there now. No way.

"I like her fine," Hank was saying. "She's not for you."

Now that really got under Julian's skin. "So, who is right for me? One of those women who throw them-selves at me?"

"No, you need someone with more sense," he ad-mitted.

Once again thoughts of Chloe Kingston crowded his mind. She was older than Dixie, although she scarcely looked it. And she acted like a spoiled child half the time, Julian reminded himself. But the translucent quality of her skin and the spark of challenge in her gray eyes seemed indelibly etched on his brain.

"What? No comment?" Hank threw him a look as he pulled into the underground parking lot.

"I want you to be nice to Dixie today. Forgive her for kicking you. I'm sure you deserved it."

"Untrue!" Hank denied, bumping down the ramp as if he were driving in the Indy 500. Julian held tight to his door handle and fervently wished Hank would stop punishing the car. "She kicked me in the shin on purpose with no provocation at all. I was just dancing with her."

"No provocation at all," Julian repeated, amused.

Hank gritted his teeth as he slammed on the brakes in one of the narrow parking spaces. What had he said that was so wrong? Didn't he have a right to his own opinions? "She just got all huffy and flounced out of there."

Shooting his brother an ironic glance, Julian unbuckled his seat belt. "I'll remember to tell her that just as soon as we're in conference with Primitive. Should make for an interesting meeting."

The retort his brother ground out was unprintable.

"AND DO YOU HAVE any other experience besides 'Harrington High'?" the woman in the power suit asked Dixie, pen poised above her clipboard. Her name was Sandra Fowler, and she was not exactly pleased to have Dixie in on the deal.

They were seated around a long oval marble table, backdropped by floor-to-ceiling windows that looked out on rows and rows of buildings. Not exactly a beautiful view, but then Los Angeles was a huge, sprawling city and today it lay under a hot, brown sky.

"Um..." She cleared her throat. Julian sat on her left and Hank was sprawled in a chair across the table and down a few chairs on her right. Julian's denim sleeves were rolled up his forearms, and Dixie caught a glimpse of sinewy muscles that brought to mind his other Tarzan-ish commercial. Sandra Fowler was the woman in charge of that particular advertising campaign for Primitive, and she was currently regarding Dixie as if she were entirely unworthy. Dixie licked her lips. "I've done several commercials," she admitted. "A series, actually."

Sandra's brows lifted expectantly.

"For Kitty-Diggins." At the strange look crossing Sandra's face, she elaborated reluctantly, "Cat litter."

"I figured as much," she said frostily.

Hank coughed into his hand and looked entirely too amused. Dixie shot him a murderous glance.

"It's a national commercial," Julian said.

Hank leaned forward. He was back to surfer shirts and khakis today and he looked as if he'd slept in them. "Is that the one where the cat chases the dog? You're the girl who saves the dog? All the while holding the pink bag of cat litter?"

She shrank inside. It hadn't been the apex of her acting career, but it had paid a few months rent, and that counted for something, didn't it? "Good memory."

"That was on a few seasons ago?" Sandra asked, scribbling rapidly.

Dixie nodded glumly. She shot another sideways glance in Hank's direction, but he'd opened his laptop and was also taking notes. Feeling undeniably depressed, she glanced at Julian, and he winked at her encouragingly. At least he was always nice to her, she thought. Why did it matter so much what Hank thought?

In appreciation she sent Julian a brilliant smile.

"I've seen 'Harrington High,'" Sandra said. "I'm afraid I don't remember you."

Dixie drew a breath. "I was one of the cheerleaders until I got caught cheating on the health test and was sent away to another school."

Hank coughed twice this time, hard. Dixie's glare was hot enough to cut through steel. She could have pointed out that running around half-naked through the jungle wasn't going to be exactly Oscar-nominated material, but since she was with the producers of that particular commercial, she wisely kept her tongue.

"That was also several seasons ago," Sandra added, scribbling madly once again.

Dixie nodded rather fatalistically. This wasn't going the way she'd hoped it would. Bad vibes all around. And therefore it did not bode well for her first appearance at Palmer Michaels' Acting Studio this afternoon. Maybe she really had bitten off more than she could chew.

Tapping the end of a pencil against her teeth, Sandra gazed at Dixie reflectively. "I'd like to see you on film. You don't look exactly like I expected."

Julian's brows drew together quizzically. "What did you expect?"

"Well..." She reached around herself to pick up a part of one of the trade papers scattered on the boardroom table. Unfolding it, she slid it on the table in front of Dixie and Julian's noses.

A grainy black-and-white photo showed Chloe hanging like a limp rag within the clasp of Julian's capable hands while he gazed down at her with concern. The caption read, Fiancée Falls For Her Mane Man.

Dixie swept in a breath. Julian gazed at the photo in fascination, and Hank tried to crane his neck to get a look across the table.

"We'll set up a test later this week," Sandra told Julian and Dixie. "Could you both be here Friday?"

Julian tore his gaze away to silently check with Dixie. She nodded, her thoughts in a whirl.

"Good. We'll be in touch."

In a daze, Dixie shook hands with the Primitive Cologne ad agent, turned and walked into the hallway, Julian and Hank at her heels.

"Well, the word's out, at least," Hank said shortly. "That's what you wanted, wasn't it?"

Julian nodded thoughtfully. Hank's eyes turned to Dixie, and she found her earlier antagonism had all but evaporated. He just looked so marvelous. With a jolt she realized she'd give about anything to lean forward and kiss his lips. Nothing had ever looked so inviting.

"What will Chloe think of this?" Julian asked into the silence that enveloped them.

Oh, God! Dixie thought.

OKAY, so she wasn't sick. Not in the strictest sense of the word anyway. True...she certainly felt discombobulated, but hey, after dealing with *the* Julian all night, who wouldn't?

Chloe toweled her hair dry, then hit it with a touch of the blow dryer. Not too much, or she'd be a frizzed-out wild woman better suited for a stay in an institution than an L.A. law firm. Frowning at her reflection, she heaved a groan of pure guilt. Okay. She had to go in. She'd taken the morning off and that's all her conscience could really stand.

Routine made her feel better. She dressed quickly, grabbed up the paper—Monday's *New York Times* crossword, a cinch—and headed for work. The drive was fairly easy at this time of day and she was stepping off the elevator and through the glass double doors that led to her law firm with a more relaxed frame of mind. This thing Dixie had going with Julian had to be a joke. She would never get engaged after just a couple of dates. That was ludicrous! She was just—exploring her options, Chloe decided, for lack of a better way of putting it. Nothing to worry about.

"Hey, Toni," she said, heading down the hallway to her office.

"Hey." Toni gulped, eyes huge as she watched Chloe's progress.

What's with her? Chloe wondered, pulling her newspaper out of her oversize purse and tossing it onto her desk. But someone had already left her a paper. One of the trades. Not *Variety,* but a decent enough rag, Chloe thought, picking it up. Yawning, she considered heading straight for the coffeemaker.

"Chloe!"

She nearly jumped out of her skin. "Good grief, Ed," she scolded one of the senior partners. "Are you trying to give me a heart attack?"

"They got your name mixed up with your sister's, I see. So, which one of you is really engaged?" He grinned like a jack-o'-lantern. "Keeping something from us, hmm?"

Chloe regarded him with a frown. Ed wasn't normally so, well, giddy in his conversation. He was staid, respectable and downright boring. "I'm afraid to ask what you mean by that."

"Look in the paper!"

She reached toward the one she'd flung on the desk, but he waved impatiently. "No, no, no, no! The one in your hand!"

"This?" She unfolded the paper and the picture of herself and Julian leaped off the page. On legs suddenly wobbly, she sank into her chair. She closed her eyes, waited three seconds, then dared to open them again. The picture was still there.

"Oh, no!"

7

"I CAN'T TALK NOW, Chloe," Dixie said in a hushed voice, cupping the mouthpiece of the receiver to keep others from overhearing. "I'm just outside Palmer Michaels' Acting Studio. I'm about to go to my first class."

"I'm glad you're there. Truly," Chloe said in a taut voice. "But this has got to stop. The whole firm is convinced *I'm* dating Julian! And they're laughing their heads off." A pause. Lowering her voice, she added, "I hate them all."

"Shh! Don't make me laugh."

"*Et tu, Brutus!* It's *not* funny, Dix!"

"We'll talk about it later. I've gotta go. Bye." She hung up before Chloe could rave and rant any more.

Chloe actually sat with the receiver to her ear for ten seconds longer before she hung up the phone. Toni sashayed into her office, dropped some papers on her desk, winked and left.

That did it. In a froth of fury, Chloe snatched her purse by the handle, catching it on the back of the chair, yanking her back so hard that she tripped, banged her knee against the chair and nearly fell to the ground. Counting slowly to thirteen—her own lucky number—she carefully unhooked the strap of her purse, rubbed the knot on her knee and headed for the elevators.

"You leaving?" Toni asked innocently, smiling like Benedict Arnold.

"I've got some things to do."

"Say hi to Julian for me!" she singsonged as Chloe pushed open the glass door to the hallway.

Okay. The gloves were off. Chloe lavished her most brilliant smile on the hapless receptionist. "Oh, I will. Julian and I have a hot tub date this afternoon. We plan to make mad passionate love all evening and through the night. You know." She winked back at her. A "just between us girls" kind of wink. "Then I'm going to rub flavored hot oil all over his body and lick it off drop—by—drop. And then..." Chloe shrugged. "Just don't expect me to be on time to work tomorrow!"

Toni's eyes glazed over, and her jaw hung limp.

My work is done here, Chloe decided as she stepped into the elevator, but she planned on ambushing Dixie when she got home. Yessirree. It was time for the truth, the whole truth, and nothing but the truth.

"VERY ENTERTAINING, Stefan." Palmer Michaels sneered at the guy who'd just finished his interpretation of a shipwreck survivor who'd encountered a civilization of extraterrestrials living on a deserted island.

"Thanks," Stefan muttered.

Dixie felt for him. She *had* found his rendition entertaining, especially when he offered Reeses Pieces from his pocket to the aliens whose parts he'd also played.

But Palmer Michaels was one tough cookie. Clearly, he felt Stefan had cheated by bringing along a prop.

"Now, Miss...Kingston," Palmer said in his precise way, looking at his registration chart. "You are an eagle. And Matt, darling, you're a jaguar. Bring this to life. Make me believe."

For a heartbeat Dixie froze. Her brain just melted. Her first moment in front of this tough crowd and she had to pretend to be a bird? And with Matt darling? Teacher's pet? She'd hoped to have a little grace period before she was thrown to the wolves, so to speak, but apparently that was not to be the case.

What have I gotten myself into?

You're an actress, she reminded herself. *You can do this.*

Never mind that this was the part of acting she hated the most, this belief that one could actually *be* an animal. In Dixie's way-too-balanced mind she believed there wasn't a lot of character motivation to be found in animals. Instinct was instinct. And as an eagle she would be scouring the ground with an eagle eye in search of food. Period.

Well, it's better than flapping my wings all the time, she decided, holding her arms out and allowing herself to soar.

Matt darling slunk on hands and knees into the center of the room and growled low in his throat. He pulled his lips back and snarled. Dixie tried to envision him as a jaguar, but all his snarl brought to mind was the image of Billy Idol in a 1980s video.

Feeling better, Dixie darted quick looks around, examining the top of Matt darling's head and back as she circled around him. Matt darling swiped at her legs several times.

Palmer regarded them both with elevated brows, his nostrils flared in disapproval. Time seemed to stand still as Dixie began to panic. How long was she supposed to do this? What excruciating torture!

Matt darling grabbed at her leg. Dixie jumped away and glanced at Palmer, who sat back and waited in a truly passive-aggressive way. Then her jaguar friend wrapped his paws around her ankle and growled with satisfaction at his catch.

To hell with them all, Dixie decided, yanking her leg free. "I'm in the sky, you idiot!" she yelled at Matt darling. "Like half a mile above you! You can't touch me!"

"Well, excuse me for living," Matt darling muttered, climbing to his feet, folding his arms and regarding Dixie down the length of his nose as if she were some kind of loathsome plague.

"Children, children," Palmer chided, clapping his hands. "Remember, we are *interpreting.* The essence of interpretation is to feel your character. Miss..." He consulted the roster one more time. "Kingston. You can only interpret your own character. Not anyone else's."

Oh, yeah? Dixie thought, schooling her expression to appear to be thoughtfully turning over his advice.

"And name calling is just not allowed." Everyone in the class regarded Dixie disapprovingly as she sat down. It was a harrowing experience, to say the least, and Dixie was suffering serious second thoughts about this class she'd so desperately thought she'd wanted to be a part of.

"Now, Matt, darling..." Palmer's expression grew indulgent. "I saw the jungle beast. Strong, sinewy, skulking through the underbrush. Thank you."

As if on cue everyone in the class clapped politely.

"Skulking through the underbrush," Dixie repeated through a frozen smile later that night as she led another couple to their seats on the patio. Diamond's was only half full. A typical Monday night.

Back at the hostess stand, she reviewed the afternoon again. It depressed her. How she'd longed to be a part of Palmer Michaels's class! How she'd dreamed of being part of the inner circle. Now, she realized it wasn't going to do her one whit of good. What she really needed was a one-on-one acting coach and a big break.

On her own fifteen-minute break she called her agency and left a message for Brandon at L.A. Artists, asking him to call her the next day at home. Everything had happened so fast she hadn't even thought to clue him in. She could just imagine what he must be thinking. And she hadn't even mentioned the potential job with Primitive Cologne. Next, she phoned Chloe, but there was no answer at home, and that was the fourth time she'd called. Where was she?

Back at the hostess stand, she drummed her fingers on the reservation book and tried not to check her watch again. The front doors to the restaurant were open, and down the flagstone entryway and beneath the long, striped awning she saw a Mercedes pull up to the valets. To her mixed horror and delight, Hank stepped from behind the wheel. She waited, expecting Julian to open the passenger door, but Hank apparently was alone, and as he walked toward her, Dixie examined the way he moved; strong, sinewy, skulking through the underbrush....

"I've come in peace," he said, holding up his hands to her expression. "We need to talk about a few things."

"Where's Julian?"

"At the club. Or at his house. I don't know. And he doesn't know I'm here, or he'd probably kill me. But I need some answers, and I see I'm not going to get them from him. I'm hoping you're the reasonable one."

Rehearsed, she realized with an actor's sense. He'd rehearsed these lines. "It's slow tonight. I could be off within the hour."

"I'll wait in the bar."

He strode away with ground-devouring strides that made Matt darling look like a Chia Pet in comparison.

REGRET HAD WOUND its way around Chloe's chest in a constricting vise that would not budge an inch. Why had she said all those things to Toni? Groaning aloud, she reviewed the afternoon and asked herself for the umpteenth time what she hoped to accomplish now, now that she was halfway to Julian's house.

It had all started so innocently. Well, at least it had after she'd shot off her mouth at the firm. But she wouldn't think about that now. There was more than enough time later to shred her conscience over her rash tongue.

But it was the call on the answering machine that had really gotten her going. Brandon, Dixie's agent, had been in a state of shock over her engagement to Julian. His sentences ran together like single words. "Dixieyou'vegottocallmerightaway! Areyoutrulyengaged? Babe! Kitty-Digginscalled. Theywantyoubackformorecommercials! MyGodwhathaveyoudonetoyourhair?"

Chloe snorted. "That's my hair in the picture," she said to the environs of the empty Volvo wagon.

Couldn't Brandon even tell that wasn't Dixie's picture? Sheesh. They didn't look that much alike.

And so she'd waited around for Dixie to phone again, but little sis had been under the radar as far as the phone went. Probably still in that acting class. Chloe had toyed with the idea of going to see her at work, but then a better, scarier idea had planted itself inside her fertile brain. Julian was behind this. And if Dixie wasn't about to tell her the truth, maybe Mr. Wonderful would. If she handled herself right, that is. Asked the right questions, in just the right tone. Not too aggressive. Concerned. The older sister looking out for the younger one.

So, she'd jumped in her car and taken off and now, half an hour into the drive, she was suffering serious second, third and fourth thoughts. She started driving slower and slower and slower, until she actually got waved on by a white-haired lady looking through her steering wheel. Well, if that wasn't the ultimate in humiliation.

Chloe stepped on the gas and with new resolve turned the Volvo into the hills of Beverly Hills. She drove unerringly to Julian's address, noticed several cars in the driveway, all of which she was pretty sure were his, and parked on the street. Gathering her courage, she crossed the flagstone driveway to his front door, hesitated only briefly, then rang the bell.

I'll count to ten, she decided, *then I'm outta here.*

She was at seven when she heard the car pull into the drive. She whipped around and waited like someone at the wrong end of a firing squad. A Bentley, she realized. A British car.

"Hello, there," Julian greeted her with a smile as

he unfolded himself from the driver's seat. "You've come to see me?"

She could hardly blame him for asking the obvious. She'd shown no eagerness for his company to date. Clearing her throat, she opted for plain honesty. "I— yes. Yes, I wanted to see you. I felt we should—see each other. Dixie mentioned your address."

He nodded, as if her words weren't quite as moronic as they sounded. He wore a gray tank top and black gym shorts and sneakers. He'd just come from the gym, she realized, and her gaze fastened on the line of perspiration around his neck. "I've got to take a shower," he said, gesturing to his clothes. "Do you mind waiting?"

"Um…no. Not at all."

He led the way inside, showed her the living room, then left for the shower. She heard the spray turn on as she gingerly lowered herself onto the black leather couch. A bachelor pad, she thought with another undignified snort. Wouldn't you know.

Still, she'd noticed his biceps in a way that was damn near X-rated, she realized with painful honesty. But then, hey. Who wouldn't? The man was a physical specimen. No matter what else he was, he was a physical specimen. Yessirree. Couldn't take that away from him. A physical…specimen.

God. Was it hot in the room? She felt a bit dizzy.

The water shut off.

Chloe, who'd been thinking of walking outside to get some air, froze where she sat. She was still immobilized when Julian stuck his head outside of the room, his hair wet and combed away from his face, and said, "I'll be right there."

"Take your time," she encouraged in a strained voice.

Ten minutes later he emerged in black jeans and a denim shirt, open to the navel, his hair still damp. He was rolling up the sleeves of the shirt as he strolled into the room and Chloe watched this movement as if she were expecting a test on it later. "So, what did you want to talk about?"

She cleared her throat. Bad venue. She should have thought this through. It would have been better to meet at a restaurant, although, based on the evening before, that hadn't served its purpose so well, either. "I think we got off on the wrong foot. I'd like to change that, if I can, and hopefully get into a serious discussion. I mean, get to the truth. No, don't say anything yet. I don't want you to lie to me. Dixie isn't telling me the whole truth, and it's got to be because you won't let her. So, I'm hoping to get you to listen to reason. I know you're not engaged. There's no way it would happen that fast. So, what's really going on?"

Julian regarded Chloe soberly for several moments. Her expression was so mobile, so full of emotion that he could scarcely look away. She was no actress. Every feeling was exposed. No hiding. And she certainly seemed to have no control over her tongue, but then, she'd very eloquently expressed her very real concern about Dixie, all the while desperately trying to keep herself in check. It touched him in a way he hadn't been touched in years. It was so *real*.

"I'm not going to hurt her," he said.

"What's your game, then? Why do you want her?"

"You need to stop worrying so much."

Chloe inched her chin up a few notches. "It's just sex then, right?"

"What?" This was such a left turn that Julian was surprised. He sat down on the ottoman directly in front of Chloe. She leaned back into the leather cushions and crossed her arms, trying to look tough.

"You only want her for sex. You nearly made a pass at me last night. It's just how you are."

Julian started laughing. He couldn't help himself. "I'd hardly ask her to marry me if it were just about sex. And that wasn't a pass, by the way."

"Oh?" She challenged him with lifted brows, wrapping her arms even tighter around herself as if she were guarding her breasts from even the slightest chance he might make good on his threat the night before and actually touch one.

"If I were going to make a pass, you'd know it," he said, irked.

"Well, don't."

"I won't." He jumped to his feet. She was beyond irritating.

"So, are you going to tell me what this charade is all about, or am I going to have to keep guessing?" Now Chloe was on her feet as well.

"Guess away!" Julian declared, flinging his arms wide.

"I think...I think...it's a publicity stunt, to feed your ego. And...I think...Dixie knows it. And she's just putting up with it because you're helping her career!"

"Feed my ego?"

Chloe disregarded the warning note in his tone. Her brain was kicking into gear, and she had a lot more to say on the subject. "Well, here's a news flash. She doesn't need your help. She just got a call from a company who wants her for their commercials. She doesn't need you at all!''

''What company?''

''I don't think that's—''

''What company?'' Julian demanded, advancing a bit so that he glared down at her from his superior height.

''Kitty-Diggins!'' Chloe threw the answer back at him.

And Julian bent over, his anger spent, his humor returning in a burst of hilarity that threatened to actually break a rib if he kept trying to keep it inside.

Chloe gazed down at his shaking shoulders and wondered if it were possible to have a worse day than this one.

HANK SAT at a table around the corner of the bar, a cozy nook guarded by the edge of a rather massive stone fireplace and therefore hidden from the stares of most of this see-and-be-seen crowd. A faint hissing from the gas logs could be heard, though the sound was mostly drowned out by the clink of glassware and muted roar of the bar patrons. A series of booths lined the street side wall, each booth bumped out in a scalloped line of bay windows. Beyond lay Sunset Boulevard and the sparkling lights of a snaking line of endless traffic.

''Could I get you anything else?'' a cute brunette waitress asked with a huge smile.

''I'm fine for the moment, thanks,'' Hank told her, lifting his beer in a salute.

Where was Dixie?

Drumming his fingers on the table, he found himself fighting the itch for his laptop. He always carried it with him. It was everything to the business of being Julian's manager—day planner, account balances, telephone directory, link to the Internet... You name it, the laptop was an all-purpose extra employee, as far as Hank was concerned, and yes, he felt naked without it.

At that moment Dixie wound a path toward his table. The flash of tanned leg beneath her skirt was enough to mesmerize Hank. He sat in silence, watching her approach, and sure as hell hoped there wasn't drool forming in the corner of his mouth.

"Okay," she said, grabbing a chair. "I'm off duty."

"Good." For lack of anything better to say, he offered, "At least Julian isn't here, so the piranhas won't be attacking."

"You mean his fans?"

Hank shrugged. "Sorry. Julian's under attack by women all the time. It's what they do."

Dixie eyed him closely. He didn't *appear* sorry, she decided. In fact, she might go as far as to say he seemed remarkably content with his assessment of women, and the comment needled her. Maybe Chloe's belief that all handsome men were selfish, egocentric Neanderthals wasn't so far off the mark.

Still, he was so blasted attractive. And it was more than just good looks and a killer smile.

The same brunette waitress cruised by and lifted her brows at Dixie, who ordered a plate of sushi and a glass of sparkling water.

"And last night you were eating red meat," Hank said, dolefully shaking his head as if she'd personally let him down.

"I love sushi. And it's the going thing at Diamond's."

"Maybe you and Julian are a match, after all," he said lightly.

The waitress brought Dixie a bottle of Perrier and a glass with a wedge of lime. She poured herself a drink and fought the desire to keep her eyes on Hank. He was wearing one of his ubiquitous surfer shirts. This one with Gauguin-style palm trees and water. For reasons that defied description, she was becoming very fond of those shirts—even if the man who wore them really needled her.

Her order of sushi was delivered on a wooden tray. Hank's gaze regarded the rolled seaweed, rice and crab suspiciously.

"California rolls...dude," Dixie said with a sideways smile.

His blue eyes looked directly into hers. Dixie unwrapped her chopsticks and wished she wasn't so undone by his simplest gesture. What was she going to do about him?

Hank, too, was having a bit of difficulty keeping his mind on track. "So, before we get into everything, give me a little background."

"A little background?"

"On you and your sister. How did you come to be where you are?"

Dixie chewed thoughtfully on her California roll while Hank nursed his beer.

She didn't want to tell him all about herself. It was too personal. Too meaningful. And yet...

"My father left before I was born. My mother died of breast cancer when I was twelve. Chloe raised me from there. She took night classes and worked at a law firm during the day, doing odd jobs, and she's still there. The place would fold without her. So, I'm just trying to do my part now, you know. Pay her back a little.''

This was not what Hank wanted to hear. Well, yes, it was. But no! He didn't want to like her any more than he already did! She was dangerous with a capital D, and he couldn't afford to care about her.

Dixie didn't know what to think of the frown that deepened his face. Was that disapproval? What kind of a jerk was he? "I didn't mean to make it sound like a sob story."

"Oh, no, you didn't," he was quick to assure her.

"And that's not why I'm with Julian," she added just as quickly, realizing he might jump to his own conclusions. "I'm with your brother because I want to be. I want to be—with him," she rephrased. "Just to set the record straight."

"Of course," he said coolly.

"I know you don't believe me, but there it is. And frankly, I don't think there's anything more to say about it."

"So, why did you agree to sit down with me?"

Good question. And the reasons didn't bear examining. "You said you came in peace."

Hank shifted in his seat and decided it was time to take a different approach. "I think you're bad for Julian's image."

"Oh?"

"Not you personally. Any woman who tries to be his fiancée would look the same."

"Tries to be?"

"Don't be offended. Look, Julian's supposed to be

the ideal man. It's what this whole campaign's been about, and it's worked.''

"You mean *your* campaign," Dixie said.

"Whatever. Frankly, I don't think you should be mucking it up. And I don't care how in love Julian is. This is his career. You don't want to be responsible for ending it, do you?''

Dixie's mouth dropped open. "I hardly think I could be responsible for that! Lots of sex symbols are married.''

"But they're not Julian. I'm not making this up.''

"It sounds like you're more worried about *your* career than his!''

"Now, that's just plain mean," Hank said, making Dixie feel like a complete cad, and then he had the nerve to finish with, "If it's money, name me a price, and I'll try to meet it.''

She nearly choked on her sushi. Literally. She coughed into her hand, reached for her glass of water, knocked back a couple of healthy gulps to bring her temper in line, then set down her glass with studied placement. "How melodramatic. As I've said before, take this up with Julian. You and I are done talking.''

"Now who's being melodramatic?" Seeing the line of fury those beautiful lips had turned into, Hank scooted back his chair. One hefty shin bruise was enough.

"I find it hard to believe that someone with as much class as Julian has *you* for a brother! You're the most insulting person on this planet. I was going to apologize for kicking you, but now it doesn't seem like such a good idea!''

"Okay, look, I didn't mean—''

"Hank!" a female voice called above the soft din of the restaurant.

Dixie, half-risen from her chair, decided this was a perfect time to exit. She turned to face a nearly six-foot woman with legs that seemed to go on and on from beneath the hem of an extremely tiny black skirt. A tight lacy black scooped-neck top showed off acres of cleavage, but the woman's face was all angles and eyes and blond bangs. Britta. Supermodel. One of Julian's old flames.

And she was gazing with pure venom at Dixie.

8

ON FRIDAY Dixie was handed a two-page script, given ten minutes to learn it, then thrown into a screen test with Julian. Given that her line was exactly one word, she needed to merely project the image of a ''sexy, but willful, hip and sassy, independent urban woman seeking to escape the asphalt jungle for the real one...''

Like, oh, sure.

Julian, of course, was her urban Tarzan. The scene wasn't hard to learn, but she could feel her heart beating erratically as her whole career hinged on this moment. And Julian's wink of encouragement did nothing to contain the butterflies taking flight in her stomach.

The casting director nodded to her. Sweeping in a breath, Dixie picked up her foot and glanced down at the sole of her pump. Groaning at the imaginary gum, she sighed, said, ''Great,'' then proceeded to lose her briefcase in the process and watch with dismay as imaginary papers skittered across the imaginary pavement. The casting director spoke a few lines, an overlaid narration, and then Dixie looked up in awe as Julian swept into view, grabbed her and swept her away to the steamy jungle.

''Cut. Let's do it again.''

That certainly did not seem like a good sign. They

ran through it again. And then a third time. And then
nobody said anything.

Sandra—numero uno on this project—was missing
in action. That also did not seem like a good sign.

But Julian felt none of Dixie's fears as he gave her
a brief hug and whispered, "You were wonderful."

Was I? she wanted to ask. *Really? You really think
so?*

But she kept her insecurities to herself, not wanting
to sound like every other wannabe actor on the planet.
Instead she gave him a halfhearted smile and asked
herself what she thought she was doing.

It was all Britta's fault the other night, she decided,
sinking onto a hard orange plastic chair on the side of
the set. Her appearance had shaken Dixie's already
shaky confidence in her and Julian's plan. And it
wasn't because she'd known Britta was Julian's ex.
Oh, no. That wouldn't have bothered her. It was learn-
ing the shocking truth that Britta was *not* Julian's ex,
but that she was *Hank's!* That's when Dixie sized up
the long-legged blond beauty and wanted to die.

Hank had inadvertently spilled the beans when he
introduced Dixie to Britta. "I suppose you've gathered
by now that Dixie is Julian's, um, fiancée. Dixie, this
is Britta."

"Hank's fiancée," Britta said with a thin smile.

"Britta…" Hank was long-suffering.

"Okay, darling. *Ex*-fiancée. He broke my heart, you
know," she said in a girlish whine to Dixie.

Her voice had an accent Dixie couldn't quite place,
but the sharpness cut like a razor. Dazed by this turn
of events, Dixie couldn't help repeating, "Hank's?"

"Oh, I know it's such a big secret and all," Britta
declared, flouncing into the chair next to Hank's.

"They always get it messed up. The stupid press. And Hank never wanted to set them straight. Didn't want to shake up Julian's image and all that."

Since Hank didn't want to shake up Julian's image by having Dixie be his fiancée, she didn't think this was the true reason he'd hidden the fact that Britta was with him. Maybe he'd just wanted the privacy, which was understandable, she thought with a sinking heart. Maybe the relationship mattered more than he let on.

"Darling," Britta had entreated, laying a hand on his sleeve. Beautiful fingers with an even more beautiful French manicure curled possessively around his forearm. "I haven't seen you in a while. What are you doing?" She glanced at Dixie. "Damage control?"

I'll show you damage control, Dixie thought, thinking Hank wasn't the only one she'd like to kick in the shin.

"Britta, we're in the middle of a discussion."

"About Julian?"

"Among other things," Dixie answered.

Britta slid her a sideways look, then turned back to Hank. "When will you be done?"

Dixie didn't care what Hank had to say after that. And she certainly didn't care what Britta might have to offer further. In a flash she was murmuring a goodbye to Hank, and one in the general direction of Britta, and then she fled in search of her belongings stowed in the locker in the employee room. But when she tried to get outside to her car unnoticed, she found Hank blocking her way.

"We didn't get anything settled," he said.

"I don't know what you want, anyway. There's nothing to settle." Dixie moved around him.

"Dixie…"

She hesitated, angry with herself for waiting for something more. "What?"

For a moment he seemed at a loss, then he said, "Friday. After the test with Primitive. Let's meet somewhere and talk again."

"No." She'd had enough meetings with him. "I work on Fridays."

"What about the afternoon?"

"No, Hank."

"Then, that's it? You're engaged to Julian."

She nodded. "That's my story, and I'm sticking to it."

"Fine."

With that he strode out of the restaurant and Dixie followed far more slowly, her feet feeling weighted down by lead.

The rest of the week Chloe hadn't been interested in anything Dixie had to say. At first Dixie thought the reason was her sister was siding with Hank. Affronted, she'd attempted to change her mind, but eventually she realized Chloe just wasn't listening to anything Dixie had to say. Worse, she practically wasn't there. For days she'd wandered around like an automaton, causing Dixie to ask if anything had happened. Chloe just shook her head and kept her thoughts to herself. Whatever was cluttering up her mind wasn't open to public view, apparently, either, since when Dixie pointedly asked, "What is on your mind?" Chloe responded sharply, "My mind is utterly empty of thought. There are no thoughts to occupy it. I have forgotten how to think."

And that was all she'd gotten from her sister for the better part of the week, apart from the information that her agent Brandon from L.A. Artists had called. Dixie phoned him back to learn that Kitty-Diggins was rerunning her old commercials and desperate to have her in a series of new ones. When Dixie asked sardonically, "This doesn't have anything to do with Julian, does it?" Brandon responded with unbridled enthusiasm, "Wellofcourseitdoes! Whoarewekiddinghere? It'sallaboutJulian! You'remarryingMr.Romance!"

She almost shouted that she wasn't marrying anyone, but bit down hard on her lip to keep the words inside. "Brandon, I don't know...."

"Thinkmoney," he told her. "Greenbacks. Oh! Guesswhat?"

When Dixie refused to guess, he went right on and told her that "Harrington High" was planning to put Heather Amherst, the girl who had replaced her, in a contract role. Well, that was just peachy. Brandon had no idea how much Dixie hated the idea that Heather Amherst was on a path to success. Heather had flaunted her role in front of Dixie's face, completely oblivious to the fact that the only reason it had become hers in the first place was that Dixie vacated the position. And now she'd been stepped up from recurring player into a contract role!

"Life's hell," she told Brandon, then hung up before she had to explain.

Soooo...

So here she was, hoping against hope that Primitive Cologne would bend to Julian's request so that she wouldn't have to make any more cat litter commercials. She'd actually turned on the television the night before and caught about ten minutes of "Harrington High." One look at Heather had been enough, though.

And there was no one to blame but herself.

Julian, who'd wandered out of the room, returned with a paper cup full of water. He handed it to her, and Dixie accepted it gratefully. "Do you think we're doing the right thing?" she blurted out.

"You mean the engagement?" He gazed at her in concern. "What's the matter?"

"Just the usual."

There had been stories about their engagement in the papers all week long. One famous actress known more for her exploits with her leading men than her ability in front of the camera had made a disparaging comment about the picture taken in front of Dr. Woo's, commenting, "Julian should be a little more careful with starlets who faint at his feet." This, in turn, had begun the rumor that Dixie—though it was really Chloe's picture—was probably anorexic or under the influence of some kind of unnamed substance. Chloe's week-long silence probably had a lot to do with that picture and the actress's comments. There was such an ugly underside to the whole thing.

And the news certainly had affected her co-workers at Diamond's. They stared and shook their heads and made jokes and some even reacted with jealousy. If things kept up this way, Dixie was going to have to take another job whether she got the Primitive Cologne commercial or not.

"How's Chloe?" Julian asked nonchalantly.

"Awfully quiet."

"What do you mean?"

Dixie shrugged and explained about the picture in the paper. "I haven't gotten much out of her all week."

"She hates the idea that we're engaged. When she

stopped by, I tried to put her mind at rest, but I did not succeed."

"When she stopped by?" Dixie asked.

"She didn't tell you? Monday night. She didn't believe the engagement was for real, but I think I did convince her of that, at least. I don't know. Maybe when we go to Hawaii that'll clinch it."

"Hawaii?" Dixie repeated.

"Next Monday. To film the commercial."

"But I haven't got the commercial yet! Monday! For how long?"

"You've got the commercial," he assured her. "We'll be there about a week."

"I can't just up and leave my job at Diamond's!" Dixie protested.

"Dixie!" Julian grinned at her. "*This* is your job. Isn't this what you want?"

"But…"

"Okay." Sandra's voice interrupted as she stepped through a door from the hallway. "We're all set."

"You mean, I'm in the commercial?" Dixie asked in disbelief.

Sandra gazed at her as if she were dense. "That's why we're here."

"She just needed confirmation." Julian rescued her. "Okay, Monday morning, right?"

"I'll have the tickets ready, and I'll notify you. Dixie, I need to know your agency."

"L.A. Artists," she said vaguely, feeling like things were moving way too fast.

"Okay." She walked away without another word.

"Want to have lunch?" Julian invited.

"I've got another class today."

Her tone caught his attention. "The acting studio. How's that going?"

Dixie wrinkled her nose. "Not as well as I'd hoped. I know Palmer Michaels is a friend of yours, but he's a tough guy to please."

Julian laughed. "Palmer Michaels is a pompous ass! Hank's words, not mine, but they're accurate."

"Really? Hank said that?"

"And a lot more. When we first moved to L.A. Hank heard that Palmer's class was a must so he signed me up. He went with me the first day and Palmer thought he was an actor and made him act out a bowl of cereal. Have him tell you about it sometime."

"A bowl of cereal? And I thought I had it bad!" Dixie declared in relief.

"Palmer's class isn't everyone's cup of tea. Drop out, if you want. I did."

"And here I thought you were friends, and I was looking a gift horse in the mouth."

"Not a chance."

"Thanks, Julian." She smiled. "I think I'll take you up on that lunch date after all."

"Good. We meet Hank at the Bistro in forty minutes...."

CHLOE RUSHED into the Bistro fifteen minutes late, scouring the tables with a somewhat frantic eye. Past a pane-glass wall that divided the front room from a covered patio she saw Hank's familiar form. Hurriedly, she scooted around the diners to meet him. "Sorry I'm late. It got crazy at work right before lunch. Always, always happens on Fridays."

"No problem. Julian won't be here for another half hour or so."

Chloe perched on a chair, leaned her elbows on the table and gazed severely at Hank. "We've got to break this up before things get worse. Did you read what that witch said about me in the paper?"

"She meant it about Dixie," Hank reminded her, amused in spite of himself. Chloe felt even more passionate about Dixie and Julian's relationship than he did.

"Which is even worse!" Chloe fumed. "They can't get one thing right. It's all speculation and innuendo, and it really ticks me off."

"So, how do we initiate this breakup?" Hank asked.

"I don't know. I need time to think." Chewing on her lower lip, she pulled out that morning's *New York Times* crossword, which she'd stuffed in her purse. It was a real bear, which had also really ticked her off. "I hate crossword puzzles," she declared a moment later, stuffing it back inside.

"Are you starting to believe in this engagement?" Hank asked her.

Chloe ground her teeth. "No," she said, without any real conviction. "But it just can't be! She can't have fallen for *him*. I know he's your brother, but come on. Women are all over him, and he does nothing to discourage it!"

"Well, Chloe, it's partly his job."

"Nice work, if you can get it," she declared. "He doesn't want Dixie. I don't know what's going on between them, but something doesn't add up."

"I think he does want Dixie," Hank made himself say. He hated saying it. Hated admitting it. But all signs pointed to a true romance afoot.

"No." Chloe was positive. "He's too interested in himself."

Hiding his own feelings over the issue, Hank said, "It sounds like you've fallen for him, as well."

"*What?*" Chloe was on her feet in the blink of an eye.

"Don't worry about it." Hank waved her back to her seat. "Happens all the time."

Words failed her. Truly failed her. It had started with this morning's crossword, and now they wouldn't even form on her tongue. Chloe, who'd really taken a liking to Hank, found that she was fast losing interest in either brother! She stabbed a finger in front of Hank's nose and declared with passion, "I have not fallen for your brother! He's too self-absorbed, and he's too pretty. And so are you!"

"How do you really feel?" Hank asked with false innocence.

"This was a bad idea. You're no help." Chloe shook her head and crumpled back in the chair. "Do you think I should have a drink before I go back to work?"

Hank snorted. "I like the way you think."

"Better make it a virgin," Chloe said on a sigh as Hank signaled the waiter.

"It's cocktail time somewhere in the British Empire," Hank responded, but he ordered two virgin cosmopolitans, and when they came, lemonade-pink liquid shimmered in mega-martini glasses. He picked his up and Chloe grasped hers and they smiled at each other and toasted.

And that was the picture that met Dixie and Julian's eyes as they walked into the Bistro together. It was a toast of shared commiseration, but it looked like a celebration.

Jealousy ran through Dixie's veins like hot acid.

But it was nothing compared to the primitive fury that consumed Julian upon finding Chloe making eye contact and sipping drinks with his brother.

JULIAN'S SMILE HURT. The muscles of his jaw were locked in a kind of permanent grin that felt as false as it probably looked. He gazed from his brother to Chloe and back again and struggled to keep some kind of composure.

They looked like two naughty children, caught with their fingers deep inside the cookie jar. As soon as Julian and Dixie appeared they put down their drinks in unison, as if the scene were scripted.

"Martini lunch?" Julian heard himself say.

Hank was surprised at his brother's tone, and it showed. "Well," he said, hesitating.

Chloe rescued him. If you could call it a rescue. "We thought we needed some liquid refreshment. Would you like one?"

She'd asked Julian, but it was Dixie who answered. "You're not at work."

"Not at the moment. I, um, wanted to talk to Hank." Chloe frowned a bit. "I've got to get back soon."

"We're doing the Primitive commercial," Dixie said, taking the seat that Julian pulled out for her. "Leaving Monday for Hawaii."

Chloe blanched. "Really?"

Hank couldn't seem to take his eyes off Dixie. "Congratulations," he said a trifle tightly. "You got what you wanted."

That stung. But it was the truth. Dixie glanced away, smarting. Hank sat at her right elbow, and his own forearm lay negligently across the tabletop. All she had to do was move her arm, and they would make contact.

And why that seemed so important was a frightening thought. One she refused to consider.

"Crossword puzzle?" Julian asked, spying the folded newspaper sticking from Chloe's purse.

"Touch it and die," she said as his hand automatically reached for the corner of the page.

"I already know they won't let me off work," Dixie said to no one in particular. "If I take the Primitive job, I'll have to quit."

"If?" Hank questioned, lifting his brows.

"Afraid I might be able to answer some you can't?" Julian asked Chloe, his voice teasing. His bad mood was rapidly evaporating as it appeared nothing seriously romantic was afoot. Yet one never knew with Hank, Julian realized. Sometimes women fell for him with the least bit of provocation. Women who, for whatever reason, had no interest in him, but who adored his brother. Could that be what was happening to Chloe?

"You look—grim," Hank said to him. It was all he could do to keep from staring at Dixie now that she was seated next to him. Her perfume was light and citrusy and he wanted to inhale until the scent filled his head.

"Grim?" Julian schooled his expression.

Chloe shot him a sideways glance. "If you think you can really do something here, be my guest." She pulled the puzzle out of her purse and slapped it in front of his eyes.

"No, I'm going to take the job," Dixie said. "It's just—things are moving kind of fast."

"Oh, you noticed?" Chloe said.

"I think ten down is seraglio," Julian said, frowning at the puzzle.

"What's the clue?" Chloe asked.

"Harem."

She grabbed the puzzle and scoured it with her eyes. He was right! How dare he be right again! It just wasn't fair. "Well, you should know that one," she muttered to herself.

Julian cupped his ear toward her. "What was that?"

Downing the rest of her martini, she signaled the waiter. "Another. Make it a double."

The waiter gave her a strange look, shrugged, picked up her empty glass and disappeared. Soon he returned with two of the pink virgin martinis and set them both down in front of Chloe. Chloe glanced at Hank, and they both laughed.

This was definitely a bad sign, Dixie thought, wondering if her expression was as grim as Hank had accused Julian's of being.

"You plan on driving after this?" Dixie asked.

"One of these is for Hank," Chloe offered generously, scooting one of the pink confections Hank's way.

"I don't know," Hank sighed. "That might be more than I can handle."

"What's going on here?" Julian asked suspiciously.

"Nothing." Hank slid his brother a menu and another one toward Dixie.

Chloe downed her drink, winked conspiratorially at Hank, then glanced at her watch. "I've got to get back to work."

"Don't you think you should eat something?" Dixie suggested.

"No time." She leaned down and whispered in Dixie's ear. "I haven't lost my mind. They were virgins. See ya later."

As she left, Julian said to his brother, "Why don't you tell Dixie about your experience in Palmer Michaels' Acting Studio."

"The bowl of cereal?" Hank asked. "Pretty bland." He smiled. "How do you like the classes?"

"Class," Dixie admitted. "I'm a dropout."

"Good for you."

Dixie smiled back at him. He was pretty likeable after all, she decided. But then their moment of conviviality disappeared as he regarded the two of them together, lifted his virgin martini, knocked it back, scooted out his chair and said, "Have a blast in Hawaii, you two."

THAT EVENING Dixie stood at her hostess stand and gazed around rather forlornly. She'd explained the situation to her manager who'd clucked her tongue, shook her head and said, "We're going to miss you."

So much for being understanding. Well, she'd known that was the way it was when she'd taken the job. She'd *hoped* she would one day be in this position because it would mean she'd been hired as an actress. But she certainly hadn't planned for things to work out the way they had. Now she hardly knew how to feel.

Eye on the prize...

A couple of hours before closing, when Diamond's had reached fever's pitch for music, laughter and loud conversation, she was rethinking her nostalgia over her job. She would be glad to leave this craziness for a while, she decided as a disgruntled customer screamed above the din, "I want to talk to the manager!"

There was one in every crowd.

"She'll be right down," Dixie yelled back, which was nothing short of a lie since she had no idea where anyone was at the moment. All the employees were just trying to keep some semblance of order. A typical Friday at Diamond's.

And that's when Hank walked in. He came up to Dixie's hostess stand and waited for long moments before he could gain her attention. Spying him, Dixie did a double take. Then she leaned close so that she could speak in an almost normal voice. "What's up?"

"I just came down for a drink. And maybe some conversation."

"If you mean with me, it'll be a while. We've got— issues here," she said, nodding toward the angered customer who was now yelling at the top of his lungs about how lousy the service was at Diamond's.

"Bad sushi?" Hank asked, bringing a smile to Dixie's lips.

"More a case of not liking the size of the bill, I think."

"I think I'll go to the second floor bar. When you're finished, maybe we could continue that talk?"

The last thing she wanted to do was talk some more about her and Julian's relationship. But she did want to see Hank. Fighting her conflicting feelings, she nodded, then asked, "Where's Julian?"

"Home. He was kind of in a weird mood."

"Why?"

Hank shrugged. "I don't know."

Dixie shook her head. Julian had been rather quiet after Chloe and Hank's departure at lunchtime.

"Hank!" a feminine voice shrilled above the noise.

Dixie glanced around. Her heart sank when she recognized the lovely Britta again.

Hank's groan was inaudible at this decibel level, but Dixie thought she saw a look of annoyance cross his face. That hope died when Britta linked her arm through his and started chatting merrily. She clung to him as they headed upstairs.

Maybe they'd planned it, Dixie thought morosely.

Her first free moment, she phoned Chloe. "Hank's here," she said. "And he's with Britta."

"Where's Julian?" Chloe asked. "Isn't he the ex?"

"Oh…no…" Dixie hadn't really had the opportunity to bring Chloe up to speed. Now she did so in rapid fashion, finishing with, "So she's all over him. It's enough to create serious nausea."

Hearing this, Chloe actually pulled the receiver away from her ear to stare at it. A moment later, she said, "You sound like you like Hank more than you should."

"What? No! Britta's just so much like—Velcro!— it's hard to watch." She mumbled something about getting back to work and hung up.

Chloe set down the receiver thoughtfully, reviewing the conversation. Fifteen minutes later she was in her car, smiling and humming to herself, and on the way to Diamond's. Maybe, just maybe, Dixie was falling for Hank instead of Julian! And if that was the case, Chloe wanted a front row seat while the dreaded Britta was around, just to make sure.

9

THE PLACE WAS humming as Chloe entered Diamond's. Jostled, she had to press herself against the wall to squeeze by the chattering crowds waiting for tables. She finally made her way to the reception stand where a harried-looking girl was being reamed out by a huge bodybuilder type with a shaved head. Dixie was nowhere to be seen.

"Where's Dixie?" Chloe asked a waitress who walked by.

"Upstairs. I'll go get her!"

And that was when the actress who'd maligned Chloe in the newspapers stepped into the restaurant. One moment the crowd was loud and milling about, the next they were separating as if the Red Sea were parting again. Spying Chloe, the actress steamed forward, chin high, as if she were queen of the cinema, which was in reality a far cry from the truth.

"Well, well, well...so, you do work here." She examined Chloe's hair, face and body. Chloe immediately self-assessed—and found she really could have used a couple of extra bust sizes if she were going to take on this woman. For the life of her she couldn't recall her real name.

"Patrice!" Chloe finally declared, as the penny dropped.

"Hmm..." was the actress's answer to Chloe's revelation. "And you're Julian's latest lady friend. I came to see what all the fuss was about. Not much, I see," she added with a mean smile, glancing back toward the crowd, which hung on her every word. Titillated laughter sounded like a ripple. Chloe's blood began to boil as Patrice leaned forward, offering a rather commanding view of some rather impressive cleavage. "You're dreaming, little lady, if you think you can hold a man like Julian."

Chloe tried to hang on to her temper, she really did. It hadn't been that many days since she'd blabbed all those lies to the people at the office, and she'd rued her quick tongue the rest of the week. But Patrice was just *begging* to be brought down a notch or two!

"Not only can I hold a man like Julian, I can get him to marry me," Chloe said.

"It's a publicity stunt!" she sneered. "A woman like you wouldn't know the first thing about pleasing a man." She gave her a once-over, found her wanting and with an elegant little shrug of her shoulders, turned to the crowd for their reaction.

"You should be talking to Julian about that," Chloe retorted, knowing she was heading into dangerous territory, unable to veer off the course to destruction. "He says he's enjoying the best sex of his life. Last time we were together, well, he said some awful nice things about me.... He told me he was glad I was a real person, in every way." Chloe gazed pointedly at Patrice's blatant cleavage. "No miracle bra for me."

Patrice blinked in surprise, and her face turned red. The crowd gasped collectively. The hairs on the back of Chloe's neck lifted. Danger. Warning. She glanced behind her and saw Dixie's manager heading her way.

"What are you doing?" the woman demanded icily.

"Taking care of business," Chloe said with a smile, filled with sudden, utter remorse. What had she done to Dixie? Her urge to see her sister vanished in one instant, but she couldn't just desert her now, not after the stir she'd caused.

"Get out," the manager told her, to which Patrice brightened considerably.

"I, um, there's someone I need to see...."

For an answer, the manager pointed an imperative finger toward the open door. Beaten, Chloe left with her tail between her legs.

"Big mouth," she said aloud to herself. Overhearing, one of the valets responded, "Nice legs, though."

By the time her car was brought around Chloe was torn between hysterical laughter and hysterical tears.

HANK WAS DRINKING himself into oblivion, Dixie decided, watching him surreptitiously as she swiped at a table hidden from his view by crowds of people. And it was really ticking Britta off, by the look of things. Good.

A tug on her sleeve. She glanced around, and the new girl said, "There was someone looking for you but she got thrown out!"

"What? She?" Dixie tore her gaze from Hank and Britta and turned her attention to the girl.

"She got in a fight with that actress, Patrice Reynolds."

Dixie's brain kicked into gear. "Chloe got thrown out of Diamond's?"

The girl related the incident at the hostess stand as she and Dixie hurried back downstairs. Their manager stood with one toe tapping, her expression dark as a thundercloud. She was already furious with Dixie over the Primitive Cologne commercial. Now she looked ready to explode.

"Who was that woman?" she demanded imperiously.

"She helped me." The timid girl chimed in.

"It won't happen again," Dixie assured her. Chloe must have zinged Patrice but good to create this kind of flap! It was actually pretty funny, when she thought about it, though she kept that opinion to herself.

"Maybe it's just as well that this is your last night," the manager said in a huff as she moved off.

Dixie silently agreed. Whether she was ready for this new phase of her life or not, she was moving forward, and Diamond's was a part of her past. Taking over the hostess stand, she concentrated on moving people to empty tables and bringing the waiting line under control. Eventually she could breathe freely again, and as soon as she was able, she headed upstairs for another look at Hank.

Britta caught her halfway down the stairs. "He's drunk!" she spat, as if it were Dixie's fault.

"It happens," Dixie responded, adding as if Britta might not understand otherwise, "too much alcohol consumption."

The glacial look Britta shot her way could have frozen lava. She stomped downstairs and out of the restaurant. Dixie smiled to herself. There was something absolutely freeing about knowing this was her last day of work.

Hank did appear to be under the influence, Dixie realized, as she approached his table. "Hey, dude," she said with a smile. "How's it going?"

"We never got to talk," he said, setting down his beer. "I really wanted to."

"I think you're going to need a ride home."

"Nah...I can catch a cab."

"Want me to drive you?"

He squinted at her, first through one eye, then the other. "Okay," he said.

"Twenty minutes," she told him, then ordered some ice water from the bartender as she returned to her duties.

When she was finished she found him exactly where she'd left him. As soon as she appeared, he got to his feet, swaying just a teeny bit. He followed her out to her car, and she watched as he climbed inside the passenger seat. Definitely inebriated, but still functioning pretty well.

"I'm staying with Julian while my condo's being redone," he said.

"I know."

"Oh, that's right. I told you." He nodded. "Okay."

Dixie hid a smile and drove toward Julian's. It was late, almost two o'clock in the morning, and no lights were on. Hank climbed out of Dixie's car and made his way to the front door, producing a key and managing to thread it into the lock. He flipped on the lights as he crossed the threshold—and then slipped and stumbled across the marble entryway.

"Whoa!" he declared, examining the floor to see what had tripped him up. Not a thing in sight.

"Is Julian here?" Dixie whispered, not wanting to wake him.

"Nah... He's out with the Primitive people. Make sure everybody's happy, happy."

"About me?" Dixie couldn't help asking, wincing as she expected the answer.

"Oh, about everything." He squinted at her and

turned in the direction of the hallway, nearly overbalancing himself.

"Here." Dixie offered an arm around him. "Let me help you."

"I can do it."

"I'm sure you can. But you'll do it better with me."

He squinted at her again as they headed off to his bedroom. "Promise?"

Don't get any bright ideas, she thought, then realized her heart was pounding a little harder, her breath coming a little faster.

Hank's room was at one end of the hall, and they pushed open the door together, the momentum carrying them to the bed where he collapsed on his back and started laughing. "Julian thinks I'm a complete drunk. He thought we were drinking martinis today at lunch!"

"I told him the truth."

"Wha'd he say?"

"Not much." Dixie gazed down at his sprawled form. "Need help taking your shoes off?"

"Nah." He attempted to lean up, twice, then flopped back down and laughed some more. "Well, maybe."

"Here…" Dixie sat on the bed and untied his shoes, pulling them off his feet and dropping them to the floor with two small thuds. When she glanced at him again it was to find him regarding her through half-closed lids.

"Things're happening pretty fast, aren't they?" he said.

"I guess so."

"C'mere…" He gestured with one hand for her to move closer.

More danger, but Dixie couldn't seem to help herself from sliding forward. She inhaled sharply when his hand clasped her upper arm and pulled her slowly, inexorably toward him. "What are you doing?" she whispered.

"I—don't know," he admitted, but the pressure on her arm increased until she was half lying across his chest, her face mere inches from his.

"Yes, you do."

"Okay, I do. I'm trying to kiss you."

Dixie froze. "You're trying to prove I'm not right for Julian."

"Nope." His other hand slid around her nape, and soon her lips were a hairbreadth away from his. "I already know that. I'm doing this for me. I just want—to kiss you."

And he did.

One moment she was stiff with resistance, the next her mouth was pressed against his lips. She told herself to jump up, run out, scream at him for making a pass at her, but she simply sat in wonder, arms propped on either side of his chest, her mouth clinging to his. As soon as he realized she wasn't going to back away, the kiss deepened. Her eyes closed in spite of herself and a soft moan escaped her. It would have been embarrassing except Hank dragged her close until she was sliding onto the bed beside him, one hand feeling the hard muscles of his chest beneath his shirt. His arms encircled her and he sighed softly. "I want you," he whispered.

Dixie swallowed. She wanted him right back. Way, way too much. Her head swirled with thoughts of what she was doing. The betrayal. The absolute wrongness of it! But she couldn't make herself leave. She kissed him and kissed him, and when his hands explored the curve of her body she felt herself melt like butter. Completely. Utterly. Thoughts of lovemaking swirled inside her brain and heated her blood.

"Hank," she whispered, when his lips left hers to nuzzle her throat and neck.

"Hmm..."

I want you, too....

She pressed her face against his cheek, squeezed her eyes closed, prayed for some kind of help to keep her from making such a terrible mistake. *I'm falling in love with him,* she thought helplessly. *I'm falling in love with the wrong brother!*

JULIAN FOUND his front door unlocked and reminded himself to give Hank a piece of his mind for leaving the place open to every burglar around. Might as well take out a Rob Me First sign, he thought darkly. There was a car parked across the street he didn't recognize. Probably casing the place at this very moment.

He locked the door behind him, stretched and walked into the kitchen. He was dead tired. The people from Primitive hammered out detail after detail for their trip to Hawaii, and he just plain didn't care. Of course, they'd demanded to know all about Dixie, which was fine, and the good news was that they'd been impressed with her bright professionalism—and the way she'd looked on camera. So that, at least, was working, though he was starting to have serious second thoughts about this charade. Sure, it kept the women at bay, but there were other complications he didn't want to think about.

Like Dixie's sister, Chloe. What a piece of work. Sometimes he didn't get her at all. He reached into the refrigerator and pulled out a carton of orange juice. Yawning, he grabbed a glass, then nearly dropped it when a feminine voice said, "Hey, there," from behind him.

Julian whipped around. "Dixie! My God! For a minute I thought someone had walked into my house uninvited. Hank left the door open—again."

She glanced around nervously. "I was just helping him get home. He was at Diamond's, and I didn't think he should drive. He wasn't completely bombed, or anything, but it just didn't seem like a good idea, so I drove him here."

"That's your car across the street?"

Her head bobbed. "I didn't want to park in your driveway, in case you weren't home, which you weren't, so I guess that was a good idea." She laughed a bit tightly. "Anyway, that's what was going on. I wanted to make sure he got home safely. That's all. You know." She gave a pretty little shrug, then asked in a rush, "So, how was the meeting with Primitive?"

"Uh…" He was having a tough time keeping up with her fast-paced chatter. "Fine. They love you. We're all set."

"Really? Good. Good. That's just terrific. Couldn't be better." She looked around herself, heaved a theatrical sigh and said, "Well, I'd better be going. It's late. See you later, I guess. Bye."

She was gone in a flash and Julian stared after her, orange juice carton in one hand, glass in the other. He poured himself a drink and walked back into the living room. Sinking onto the couch, he stared across the room.

His mind tripped back to lunch and Chloe's prickly annoyance at his stepping into her crossword puzzle world. He'd filled them out for years. Airplane trips had started the compulsion, and it had just kind of escalated. Hank had no interest in crosswords, so it was kind of nice to find someone who might actually appreciate the same things he did. Except Chloe didn't appreciate him at all. She damn near hated him.

What had first amused him was fast starting to really bother him. Why did she dislike him so much? What was it about him that was so wrong, when obviously she didn't find Hank's company a problem? In fact, she'd been smiling and upbeat with Hank when they'd arrived—and had only started glowering when he'd appeared.

"Chloe," he muttered to himself, setting down the glass of orange juice on the coffee table.

Running his hands through his hair, he shook his head slowly.

What the devil is wrong with me?

THE SCREECH that met Dixie's ears made her leap from her bed in real terror. She ran down the hall to her sister's bedroom, then realized Chloe was already up and awake and somewhere in the living room. Hazarding a glance at the clock, she saw that it was barely 6:00 a.m.

No wonder she felt like death warmed over.

"What's wrong?" Dixie demanded, rubbing her face as she headed down the hall. Her eyes felt like sandpaper. She couldn't open them past a squint.

Chloe stood in the center of the room, clutching the newspaper to her chest. "Nothing."

"Something in the paper?"

"Dixie…" She gazed at her sister, her eyes full of anguish. "I did it again."

"You did what again?"

"She thought I was you and I just let her go on."

"Who?" Dixie reached for the paper, but Chloe shook her head and clutched it tighter. "Oh…Patrice Reynolds?"

"Yes! You know about her?"

"Something happened at Diamond's last night that got you kicked out." Dixie yawned.

"No kidding." Her voice was full of misery. "She was making such nasty remarks about me. Or about you, depending on how you look at it."

There was no color in Chloe's face. She was stark white and looked about to faint. At least that's what Dixie's limited vision led her to believe. Grabbing her sister's arm, Dixie led Chloe to the couch and forced her to sit down. But Chloe was stiff as a board and all she could do was perch on the edge of the cushion.

"So, what terrible thing did you say in return?" Dixie asked.

Chloe groaned and dropped her head into her hands, reluctantly sliding the paper in Dixie's direction as if giving up the map to the treasure. Dixie scanned the article, which described Patrice's skirmish with Dixie and detailed how Dixie was then fired.

"I wasn't fired! I quit," Dixie declared, miffed.

"They think I was fired!" Chloe moaned. "And that's because they think I'm you. I should have never done it. I'm sorry, Dixie. I'm so sorry. I don't know what's wrong with me. I'm just letting my mouth run away with me, and you know I'm bad, but I'm usually not *this* bad!"

Dixie nodded, since it was the absolute truth. Chloe wasn't shy about her opinions, but neither was she generally so out of control. Glancing down at the ar-

ticle, she asked, "Was she really wearing a miracle
bra? I've always wondered about those."

Chloe made some choking sounds but wouldn't
look up. After a moment of consideration, she said
instead, "I think it was pure silicon."

"Well, at least you didn't make a crack about her
standing too close to a heater and melting."

Chloe finally lifted her head. "I would've if I'd
thought of it."

"Probably just as well you didn't."

Sighing, she climbed to her feet. "It's really going
to hit the fan over this one. Your fiancé is not going
to be happy."

Dixie nodded. She supposed she should care more,
but this morning her thoughts were tortured more over
Hank than Julian and her career. She was in love with
Hank. Period. And she couldn't imagine what she was
going to do about it.

"I'd like to go to bed for a week," Chloe said.
"Thank God it's Saturday, and I don't have to go to
work."

"I probably should warn Julian about the write-
up," Dixie said. She wondered if Hank were awake
yet. No, it was too early. But what would he think
about last night when he did wake up? Would it even
prick his conscience? It had decimated any chance she
had for sleep. Would he even remember?

"Where are you going?" Dixie asked Chloe as her
sister wandered back down the hall.

"I'm putting a cold washcloth over my eyes and
lying on my bed, and then I'm going to get up the
courage to call Julian. This isn't your fault, Dixie. It's
mine. I've got a couple of hours to think of what I'm
going to say, and then I'm going to tell him what I

did. I'll have to take my punishment. It will not be a pretty sight.''

"Think I'll go back to bed, too," Dixie murmured, heading down the hall even as she spoke. But her reasons were different than her sister's. She just wanted to climb under the covers and dream about Hank.

BRRRINNNG! BRRRINNNG!

Hank surfaced to the insistent ringing of the telephone. There wasn't an extension in his room, so he stumbled to his feet and was halfway down the hall to pick it up before he fully realized where he was. At Julian's. And it was Julian's phone ringing. The answering machine picked up, and he listened to Chloe's voice, sounding rather subdued, asking Julian to call her.

And that's when he remembered kissing Dixie.

It woke him better than a bucket of cold water poured over his head. For several moments he stood frozen, reliving the events of the night before, wondering if he'd dreamed part of it. He could recall the taste of her lips as if the kiss had just taken place.

He was yawning as he walked into the living room, and that's when he saw Julian sprawled on the couch, looking mighty uncomfortable yet sound asleep.

Guilt gnawed at Hank. His brother was engaged to Dixie, and whatever had been the impetus for that engagement, it was nonetheless a fact. And he'd been lusting after her since the moment they met. And last night he'd kissed her. And he knew he would kiss her again if he could—and a hell of a lot more.

"Hey," he called to Julian who slept like the dead. "Hey!" He grabbed his leg and shook it.

Julian growled at him, tried to turn over, nearly fell

off the couch and reluctantly opened one eye. "I'm on the couch," he said, as if discovering it for the first time.

"Don't tell me you were drinking, too," Hank said, feeling some effects from his beer drinking in the twanging headache at his temples.

"Uh-uh. I just couldn't sleep." He sat up and asked, "What time is it?"

"About ten."

"I didn't fall asleep until five."

Hank gave him a searching look. "Something wrong?"

Julian drew a breath, shot his brother an unreadable glance, then shrugged. He seemed to be struggling with something, but Hank didn't wait to hear what it was. "You didn't hear the phone. Chloe called. She wants you to call her."

"Chloe wants *me* to call *her?*"

"That's what she said."

Julian listened to the message and remarked, "She sounds serious."

"Give her a call," Hank suggested. "I'm heading for a shower."

Julian rubbed at his growing beard and made a face. Yes, he wanted to call her back. Yes, he wanted to talk to her. And yes, he was making too much of the fact that she'd actually phoned him.

After a moment of self-flagellation where he struggled to put his feelings in some kind of order, he dialed Chloe and Dixie's number from memory. It was Dixie who answered. "Oh, hi," she said. "Chloe ran down to pick up some coffee and a latté. She should be right back."

"Do you know why she called me?"

A hesitation. "Julian, she said some things last night that are in the paper. The paper quoted them as if I said them, but it was a mix-up at Diamond's. Chloe let Patrice Reynolds believe she was me, and things kind of..."

"Which paper?" Julian demanded, then hung up and strode to the porch to get his own copies. He scanned the gossipy column he hated the most and there it was, plain as day. Thinking what the Primitive Cologne people might make of this, he phoned back, and this time Chloe took the call. "I want to see you," he told her tersely. "Right now."

"I'm not—feeling well," she said in a small voice.

"Well, that makes two of us," he said grimly. "The Bistro. In an hour."

10

Chloe gazed at Dixie through sorrowful gray eyes. "Just want you to know, you're my beneficiary. In case I don't return."

"He's not going to murder you," Dixie said calmly.

Chloe felt absolutely wretched. In all her years of being Dixie's big sister and pseudo-parent, she'd never failed her so completely. "What's wrong with me?" she asked, truly flummoxed. "It's like I've caught some dreadful disease that has destroyed my brain and left my tongue to fend for itself."

"Just apologize. Patrice probably deserved everything you gave her. I wish I'd been as quick-witted with Britta!"

"Britta insulted you?"

Dixie stopped herself. No. Britta had just clung to Hank in a way that had infuriated and nauseated her, and she'd wanted to get her away from Hank any way she could. "Come on," she said in lieu of answering. Picking up her purse, she headed for the door.

Chloe's brow furrowed. "Where are you going?"

"You didn't think I'd let you face the lions alone, did you?" Dixie held the door. "We're in this together."

"If I wanted your interference, I would have asked for it," Julian said testily.

"You're laboring under the misconception that I care what you want," Hank answered cheerily. "I only care what I want, and I want to be there when you take on Chloe Kingston."

Julian sighed. "I don't deserve this," he muttered as they walked into the Bistro together. A table of women looked up, brightened and started chatting animatedly with one another.

"Your fans are coming your way," Hank observed as he and Julian sat at their usual table.

The women stood in a group, giggling nervously. They asked for Julian's autograph, which he gave with a smile that Hank could tell was more forced than usual. Chloe had really gotten to him.

"Personally, I think what she said is kind of funny," Hank declared.

"You're laboring under the misconception that I care what you think," Julian retorted.

"Ouch. Someone got up from the wrong side of the couch."

"I need to talk to Chloe one-on-one. This vendetta she's got against me has got to stop if we're ever going to get the public to believe in my engagement and start ignoring my love life."

Hank regarded him thoughtfully. "Is that what this is really about?"

Julian, who'd picked up his menu though he knew it by heart, threw it down in disgust and met his brother's watchful eyes. "Hank, stop testing me about this. I'm engaged to Dixie. Accept it. There's nothing more to say!"

"Okay, okay." He lifted his hands in surrender. "Easy, boy."

"What is it that you cannot accept?" he demanded.

Hank's gnawing guilt turned to out-and-out self-loathing. He opened his mouth to answer, but nothing came. He wanted to tell Julian the truth, but the truth was too unpalatable to reveal.

I'm in love with your fiancée.

"What?" Julian demanded again, impatience stamped on his features.

"Julian…"

Hank's hesitation cut through Julian's frustration like a knife through butter. He realized his brother had something weighing on his mind. Suddenly Julian wondered if Hank could be falling for Dixie. He'd suffered such an aversion to their engagement that it stood to reason there was something else driving him. Something more! But did Julian dare believe—hope, in fact—that this could be true? If it were, then the greatest obstacle in the way to his winning Chloe's love would be miraculously removed!

Julian came back down to earth with a bang. What the hell was he thinking? Julian demanded of himself, shocked to his core. That wasn't what he wanted! He was furious with Chloe. Flat-out enraged that she could so carelessly cut a swath through his life like some kind of evil destroyer. He didn't want her love. He wanted her surrender!

Hank, meanwhile, was hunched over his espresso. Confession was good for the soul, so they said, and though he really didn't want to have to do this, it was way past time. "Have you ever wondered—" he began, then cut himself off in mid-sentence and stared past his brother.

Julian turned to see what had captured his attention. Chloe had just entered the restaurant—with Dixie.

Watching their approach with a jaundiced eye, he said tautly to Chloe, "I see you brought reinforcements."

Chloe, though full of contrition, was hardly down and out. "So did you," she said, nodding toward Hank.

"I insisted she let me come." Dixie spoke up. "I know you're probably furious with her—with both of us," she added hurriedly. "And we deserve it. There's no excuse, really, but this celebrity stuff is new to us and it's hard to turn the other cheek and ignore it when someone's so terribly rude!"

"What exactly did Patrice say?" Hank asked. He could hardly look at Dixie. All he could think about was her long legs and smooth skin and soft, giving lips. It was enough to make him break out in a sweat.

"She was rather clear on her assessment of my chances on hanging on to a man like Julian," Chloe said crisply. She couldn't make herself meet Julian's eyes, though he sat directly across the table from her. Instead she concentrated on his hands, but her mind seemed to be stuck on the thought of what those strong fingers were capable of when it came to running them down her body. Her mouth was dry as a desiccated wasteland. She hadn't believed she could feel worse than she already had, but now she knew she could.

"She thought Chloe was me," Dixie said unnecessarily, clearing her throat. Julian was staring at Chloe in a way that made Dixie nervous. He was really, really angry, she realized. Really.

Though she dreaded meeting Hank's eyes because images of his naked body ran through her brain like evil imps, playing and replaying and replaying last night's events, she still needed some support here.

Drawing a breath, she met his gaze with trepidation, pleading silently for his help.

Hank cleared his throat. "What's done is done. You and Dixie are heading for Hawaii on Monday. Let's focus on that."

"I want to talk to Chloe alone," Julian said in a tone that dared her to object.

Chloe visibly swallowed. "Okay," she said in a small voice.

"Um..." Dixie gazed anxiously from one to the other of them. "I guess I'll go...with Hank?"

This was a bonus Hank hadn't anticipated. A chance to be with Dixie alone! How, he wondered, could he turn it into a whole Saturday afternoon? The answer came from Dixie's own lips. "Should I drive?" she asked. "I've got my car."

"Great idea." He scraped back his chair and clasped Dixie's hand, pulling her from her seat before anyone could come up with another idea. "Julian can take Chloe home."

"Oh. Wait." Chloe shook her head.

"His bite is worse than his bark," Hank informed her with a pat on the shoulder. Then he practically yanked Dixie away from the two of them and headed for the door.

"Are you sure she'll be all right? I mean, he's really mad."

"Yep."

"You're not instilling confidence in me."

Hank grinned as Dixie, nearly stumbling from his bum's rush out the door, fell into the circle of his arms. "Let's get outta here and get to know each other," he said, feeling as if he'd been given an unexpected gift.

Dixie, caught in the spell of his laughing eyes and

strong arms and the memory of his lean, muscular body, simply breathed, "Yes," and to hell with recriminations. *Eye on the prize,* a little voice nagged inside her head.

The prize is Hank, she snapped back silently, quelling that little voice into submission, at least for the time being.

CHLOE STARED at the menu but the words were simply black squiggles as the image of Julian's stern, handsome face seemed imprinted upon her retinas for all time. Still, it was better than facing his disgust. Sheesh, he could make her feel wretched! Not that she didn't deserve it, but holy, moly, the man seemed to be carved in ice.

Clearing her throat, she refused to look up. But out of her peripheral vision she saw the slight movement of his head as he looked up from his own menu to give her another hard stare.

"So, the method of punishment today is silence," she said at length when she could bear it no longer. "I thought you wanted to talk to me alone."

"I do. I'm just not sure where to begin," he told her, which caused her to lower her menu a bit.

Chloe's conscience twinged her. "I'm sorry," she said, so softly as to be a mere whisper of air.

"What?" He cupped his ear.

"I said, I'm sorry. I'm sorry I caused so much trouble." She lifted her chin. "But I'm not sorry I told off that abomination to the female sex. She was nasty!"

Julian slowly shook his head at her in amazement. "You said we'd had the best sex ever."

Color flooded Chloe's face and beat there, humiliation a red flush that stained her face and neck. "I was—using literary license."

"You were lying."

"Of course I was lying!" She dropped the menu and leaned her elbows on the table. "But she was beyond rude! She told me—well, she thought she was telling Dixie—that I couldn't hold on to a man like you. I just made a remark about her not being...real."

"Chloe, you can't say things like that in public. It goes on record."

Chloe...

She was reeling from the sound of her name on his lips, that very British accent wrapping around the syllables in a way she found utterly entrancing. Gazing at him, she felt total despair. She was attracted to him. No way to lie to herself any longer. Very, very attracted to him. But he was much too handsome! An egotist without even trying, in Chloe's eyes. And he had to be selfish and vain and controlling.

"You're a celebrity!" she blurted out in despair.

Julian searched her earnest face, itching to reach over and smooth out the lines that furrowed her brow and brought such anxiety to those deep gray eyes. "I'm aware of that. And yes, it has its drawbacks, but it's too late to worry about that now." He hesitated. "Why do you care?"

"I don't care. Not in the way you mean. Why would I care? Maybe Dixie should care, but then she wants to be an actress, so it's all the same thing anyway. It doesn't matter to me. I'm just her sister. No one should even listen to me."

"The gossip columnists are listening," he replied.

"I said I'm sorry!"

At that moment a new wave of customers noticed

Julian. Out of the corner of his eye he saw them heading his way, and his impatience returned. *Not now,* he thought.

Chloe saw his expression change and then heard the footsteps of the group as they surged around their table. For a moment she caught Julian's eye. He was pretty darn sick and tired of this song and dance himself.

"Could we have an autograph?" one asked breathlessly.

"Sure."

She dug frantically through her purse.

"And a picture," another one said, leaning into him as if he were some personal friend instead of a complete stranger. But that's how the public felt about celebrities, Chloe observed silently, as they went through several pictures while Julian mustered up a dutiful smile and remained ever pleasant. Finally, when they'd exhausted their requests, they merely stood around in dumb adoration, refusing to retake their seats.

Chloe bit her lip. It was impossible for Julian to tell them to get lost without coming off as a jerk. But she was already in hot water for shooting off her mouth, so she couldn't really step up to the plate and tell them to scram, either. But Julian was gazing at her, waiting, and she suddenly realized he *wanted* her to take charge.

Clearing her throat, she smiled at the group of women who shot her sideways glances. They didn't want to look at her too closely. In fact their body language showed that she was clearly not invited within the circle of their fan club. To hell with that, Chloe thought and said in a deceptively nice voice, "Julian's

going to be in another commercial for Primitive Cologne, which I think is coming out this fall?'' She
raised her brows in a question and Julian nodded,
watching her closely. ''Be sure to look for it,'' Chloe
finished in a voice that told the group clearly, ''This
interview is over.''

Lips frowned and chins lifted as the women, after
several gushing goodbyes, slowly drifted away. Julian's gaze was surprisingly warm as he said, ''You're
pretty good at this.''

''Not mad at me anymore?'' Chloe questioned.

''I'm trying to figure out a way to harness your
natural gift for taking charge.''

''Really...'' This was a side to Julian she found
terribly intriguing, and one she desperately needed to
avoid if she were to hang on to her sanity.

The waiter came by their table and Julian asked
Chloe, ''You want lunch?''

''Sure.''

When she ordered a chicken Caesar salad, he said,
''A woman after my own heart,'' which also intrigued
her beyond reason.

When the waiter left, he smiled in a thoroughly
charming way that she knew had to be an act and
asked, ''What are we going to do after lunch?''

HANK LOOKED UP from his perusal of Dixie's thigh,
where her skirt had risen about three inches above her
knee, and saw the white BMW convertible whiz by
them. Sucking in air, he slouched in his seat and said,
''Britta!''

Dixie shot him a look. ''Britta?''

''She must be going to Julian's,'' he said, as they

were winding their way into Beverly Hills. "Turn around. We can't go there. She'll eat us alive!"

"What do you want to do?"

"Let's go to the beach. Good God, I can't wait until she leaves town again!"

His words were music to Dixie's ears. She obeyed his command as soon as she was able and soon they were heading west to the beach. "Where do you want to go?"

"Well…would you like to see my condo? It's under renovation, but it's on the beach. I mean, unless you have something you have to do?"

"Nothing I can think of," she said, trying to remember all the reasons she should avoid this man. She was, after all, ostensibly engaged to his brother, and though that was fast losing any meaning in her world, it was an undeniable fact.

"Good," he said, sounding way too satisfied.

"So, what's the deal with you and Britta?" Dixie asked. "I mean, you looked pretty cozy last night."

"Ha! She's a piranha in high heels. Don't even think she's anything else!"

"But you were engaged to her once."

"Engaged!" His face registered such horror that Dixie had to smile. "Not on your life! That was all her doing. She just told everyone she was engaged, and when the press questioned Julian he denied it, but it didn't matter. Speculation ran rampant, and I was just glad they thought she was involved with my brother instead of me." He grimaced. "Unfortunately, Britta still believes there's something between us, and since you and Julian got engaged, she's been calling and finding me and pretty much being a stalker. Think I could get a restraining order?"

"Hmm...more publicity."

"You're right," he said, deflated. "Maybe I just need to get involved with someone else," he added lightly. "Maybe then she'd get the message."

"Maybe." Dixie's pulse speeded up despite her stern warnings to herself not to read too much into his words. "But you don't want to get involved with a woman, anyway, do you?"

He frowned. "What do you mean?"

"You said they're all after something, usually money, as I recall. So why, then, would you ever want one?"

Hoisted on his own petard, Hank bent his head in conciliation. "Maybe not all of them."

"Oh, really?"

"There are one or two worth knowing."

"Such a ringing endorsement for my entire sex," Dixie said dryly. "Oh, don't stop now. Keep the compliments flowing, by all means!"

"All right, all right. I may have been a little hasty in my assessment of all women, but in my defense, all the women I've known have been after something. Julian, too. Well, until you, that is."

Dixie lifted her brows. "Oh, I'm off the gold digger list? How did that happen?"

"I got to know you," he said simply.

That pretty much ended their conversation until Hank said, "Turn here," and soon she was winding through neighborhoods in Santa Monica, a few miles north of Venice and Manhattan Beach. She realized Hank lived along one of the nicer streets, and that his condo was really one of a four-unit building beachside with Hank's condo on the upper level overlooking a commanding view of sun and sand and surf.

"Wow," she said softly as she pulled into the drive.

As they got out of the car, Hank explained, "Julian's an industry unto himself. I've helped him make money, and that's made me money, too. It's a symbiotic relationship—works both ways. He wanted to live in Beverly Hills, but I like the beach."

"I like the beach, too," Dixie said without thinking, shielding her eyes from a bright April sun and gazing along the glimmering, rippled sand to the eye-hurting sparkle of the Pacific Ocean. She turned to him. "Can we go for a walk?"

"Your wish is my command."

They took off their shoes, and Hank reached for her hand. Dixie placed her palm in the strong warmth of his and felt a frisson of something like fear slide down her spine. She was playing with fire. This wasn't right.

"We should have picnicked," Hank said suddenly, "since we ran out on lunch."

"You think Chloe's all right?"

"Oh. Yeah. Julian gets upset, but it doesn't last long, and you know, I don't think he was all that mad at Chloe. It was something else."

"He sure acted like it was Chloe. Maybe he was mad at me," she said, on a sudden thought.

"How could he be mad at you?" Hank stopped and gazed down at her. She felt herself melting beneath the heat of those blue eyes. He actually reached out and grazed her cheek with his knuckles, sending Dixie's heartbeat into overdrive. But then, coming to himself, he said a trifle huskily, "Let's go get that picnic and come back."

"Okay…"

CHLOE PERCHED herself on Julian's black leather couch and sniffed again at the decor. Now that he'd gotten over being infuriated with her, she could stop feeling like she was about to face a firing squad and settle back into her usual good humor. Well, usual state of mind, maybe, since Dixie had accused her of being too acerbic more than once.

It was late afternoon and getting later. She'd agreed to go back to his place with him because she'd believed Dixie and Hank would be there. Julian had practically said they would be, and so she'd shrugged her shoulders and followed him to his car. Once inside the Bentley, however, she'd nearly fainted when he'd suddenly leaned over and kissed her full on the lips!

"Thanks," he said on a smile, pulling away. "Friends, now?"

"Um..." She'd struggled for some kind of reply.

"I was upset earlier," he admitted when she couldn't respond right away. "Sorry."

"No reason to be. I shot off my mouth and I shouldn't have."

"I think the damage will be small," he assured her. "But thanks for easing the fans away. Sometimes they don't take hints well."

"They don't take hints at all. I swear, you need a full-time force field around you just to keep them at a safe distance. How do you stand it?"

"I signed up for this. It's a little too late to complain about it now."

"I'd never be able to stand it."

He smiled. "You're pretty good about being my force field, though. Like I said before, thank you."

"No problem." Chloe squinched down in the seat, feeling the need to pull her shoulders in close and keep up her own little force field. The man was just too damned attractive. That was it. And though normally that aspect was a complete drawback, she was having serious trouble remembering her own feelings on the subject.

And her lips still throbbed from that single kiss. Well, throbbed was probably too extreme a term. Tingled. Felt electrified. Couldn't forget. Hungered for more.

"What?" Julian asked.

"Did I say something?"

"I think you did, but it sounded kind of strangled."

After that she concentrated on making her mind a blank, and when they entered the house to find Hank and Dixie missing in action, she'd nearly turned around and walked out again. But the phone was ringing. The people from Primitive, and Julian had spent the greater part of the next hour explaining the true source of those comments—herself—and soothing the corporate crazies' worries. He'd apologized to her twice for being so preoccupied, but since it was Chloe's doing that had started this, she could hardly complain.

"Where is Hank?" Julian demanded to the room at large at one point, frustrated. His brother normally handled these kinds of situations.

"I guess he's with Dixie," Chloe responded, but when she tried to call their house, no one answered.

Finally, as the sun began to set, he hung up on his last call and declared, "The answering machine can take the next one. I'm done!"

"I'm sorry," Chloe said again, more heartfelt.

"Oh…" He waved it away. "I really couldn't care less anymore. Would you like something to drink? A glass of wine?"

"Sure."

She could use a little liquid courage. And when he came and sat down across from her, their knees nearly touching, she knocked her drink back as if it were some life-giving elixir. Julian regarded her with amusement.

"You know, those were virgin cosmos we were drinking yesterday," she said. "I'm not a raging alcoholic."

"I know. So…you can have another glass of wine, then?" He lifted the bottle in a question.

"Sure…"

He refilled her glass with Chardonnay and Chloe clutched the stem tightly in one hand. When she realized he'd barely sipped at his first drink, she stopped in mid-motion to her lips and demanded, "Are you trying to get me drunk?"

"Yes," he said without hesitation.

Chloe met his gaze and wondered if she were completely losing her mind. "Well, it's working," she grumbled to which he laughed aloud. She sipped a bit more slowly at the wine and wished she had a handle on her own good sense. She was fast losing control of the situation. He was so blasted good-looking and nice. That was it. He was *nice!* "What is your last name?" she demanded.

"Ashby."

"Oh, so you do have one!" She took a gulp, instantly forgetting her own warning to herself, then watched as he refilled her glass yet again. "You really are trying to get me drunk," she concluded, to which he just smiled and topped off his own glass. "You haven't even finished one."

"I'm working on it."

Chloe was losing track of the situation in a big, big hurry. He was sitting way too close to her. ''I tried the puzzle today and failed miserably. Do you have a copy?''

Anything, anything to get him to get up and move away from her!

Julian found the paper and turned the page, settling himself next to her once again as if it were the most natural thing in the world. But it wasn't natural. It was wrong, and the flush on her skin wasn't just from the wine.

''Five-letter word for sexual attraction,'' he said.

Chloe nearly spilled her wine. To make certain that didn't happen, she took a huge swallow to lower the liquid. ''Ardor?'' she suggested.

''Good guess, but wrong.'' He folded the paper and gazed at her in a way that sent warning signals feathering down her arms. ''Chloe.''

For a moment her brain didn't make the connection. The synapse was long and she didn't want to hear it anyway. But then his meaning rushed at her with the strength of a freight train! *He was interested in her!*

''I don't think that's a word for sexual attraction,'' she told him, embarrassed by the breathless quality of her voice.

''I think it is.''

''I'm in deep, deep trouble....''

''We both are,'' he agreed in a husky voice that sent Chloe's blood rushing hotly through her veins.

And then he leaned forward to kiss her again, and Chloe just sat there and let it happen, eyes wide-open, heart thundering, brain begging for more wine so that she could lie to herself later and blame it all on the alcohol....

11

THE PICNIC ENDED with a spectacular fluorescent orange sunset and a stiff April breeze. Dixie and Hank hurriedly packed the leftover sandwiches and cookies and plastic wine cups and their half-drunk bottle of champagne and headed back to his place. "I don't think you should drive yet," he said, as he produced a key and led the way into the shadowy interior of his condo.

Dust sheets covered the furniture, and the smell of freshly done Sheetrock and paint clung faintly to the room. When Dixie walked into the kitchen she admired the caramel-colored granite counters and terracotta tiled floor.

"An interior decorator," he said with a shrug when she complimented his taste. "I just want it to be done soon."

She walked down the hall and peeked into the hall bathroom, which was still under renovation, and then into the bedroom. Here the walls were smoothed and painted a faint yellow. Dust sheets also covered the bed, nightstands and chest of drawers. A desk sat in an alcove, the only piece of furniture currently not under wraps, and Dixie saw that someone had been working there.

"You've been hard at work," she guessed.

"I came here yesterday afternoon for a while. Britta

was calling and I needed some time to think.'' Hank had deposited the picnic basket in the kitchen but he still carried the bottle of champagne. He poured Dixie a glass.

"I thought I was supposed to be getting ready to drive," she said.

"You don't have to leave yet," was his enigmatic answer.

"Aren't you having any more?" She lifted her glass at him.

"I had my quota of alcohol last night," he said, yawning. With that he pulled the dust sheet off to expose a king-size bed with a deep blue comforter. He flopped down on the bed and spread his arms wide, sighing contentedly. "I can't wait to be back here. Not that Julian hasn't been great. But this is mine."

"One of these days I'll know what that's like," she said, sipping her drink thoughtfully. "I was living with Chloe, then I ran up to San Jose and lived with the guy I was supposed to marry, and now I'm back with Chloe."

"You want to be independent?"

"Of course I do." Seeing that her glass was empty, Hank poured the rest of the champagne into the plastic chalice then resituated himself on the bed. Dixie wandered around the room, not wanting to leave, but sensing she should very soon. For reasons she wondered about later, she found herself telling him all about her ill-fated love affair, her decision to move to San Jose and her reasons for returning to L.A. "And that's about all there is to that," she finally finished. "I was working at Diamond's and trying to figure out what to do when Julian showed up and presto, here I am." She tried to snap her fingers and failed.

"Except that you're not with Julian," Hank said.

Dixie, who had been gazing out the window and the now-black ocean waters, didn't like the sound of that. She shook her head and wagged a finger at him. "I shouldn't be here," she said, then added boldly, "but I want to be."

"You're engaged to my brother."

"But I'm not in love with him."

Hank stared at her lips. These were the words he'd so longed to hear. They floated in the air, almost as if they had substance. But what about Julian? "Does Julian know how you feel?" he asked cautiously.

"I think so."

That wasn't good enough. "You *think* so?"

Setting her now empty glass on the desk, Dixie tumbled onto the bed beside him, her blond hair fanning out around her head, her amber eyes smoky and seductive and sending messages to all parts of Hank's body that he was afraid to respond to. "I want to kiss you," she told him, and the words were heartfelt, full of unspoken wanting.

"Okay…"

He didn't move. He let her decide. But to his everloving astonishment she leaned in for the kiss without further trepidation, pressing her warm lips to his with complete abandon. Carefully he let his arms surround her, and just as uncarefully she cuddled up against him and let her smiling lips nuzzle his face.

"Mmm…" she said, gentle laughter lurking somewhere inside. "This is nice. I've wanted to do this for sooo long!"

What about Julian? his brain yelled again, but Hank was fast losing interest in anything that particular organ had to say. His heart was thumping, speeding up, charging toward Dixie like a thoroughbred to the finish line. *Get a grip,* he told himself, but then her hands slid down his back and it was all over.

He tried one last-ditch effort to save himself, and her. "Dixie," he moaned on a half-protest. "I can't."

In her slightly inebriated state, Dixie felt wounded by his rejection. She completely disregarded that he might be thinking of his brother because to Dixie, Julian was not a factor. She and he both knew the situation for what it was: a farce. And it seemed like Hank should know that, too. "Because of Britta?" she asked unhappily.

"Good Lord, no!"

"Then?" Her amber eyes gazed questioningly, longingly into his.

The last vestige of his control broke. To hell with it, he thought, wrapping his arms around Dixie and dragging her close, molding her soft angles to his harder ones. It wasn't champagne that made him drunk; it was kissing her. He pulled her atop him and their fingers willingly undid buttons and swept clothes away to a mingled heap on the floor.

Dixie let her hands slide over the muscles of his chest. It was so...wonderful! And that nagging voice inside her head was dulled by gallons of champagne, and she leaned down and tasted his throat with the tip of her tongue.

Hank made a strangled sound and proceeded to drag her mouth to his, thrusting his tongue deep inside her mouth. There was no room for waiting. Neither of them wanted time to think.

With hurried movements and soft sighs, they explored each other with ravenous hunger. His hands molded the soft contours of her body, and when one palm massaged her breast, she arched upward. But when his knee nudged her thighs apart, Dixie had one last cold rush of reality. "Should we?" she whispered.

"Shouldn't we?" he responded in a voice thick with desire.

I love you, she thought, but couldn't say it.

I love you, he thought, but kept the declaration firmly under wraps.

Then Hank moved against her and Dixie simply melted with desire, loving him, loving the moment, wanting him like she'd never wanted anyone in her life. She let his tongue and mouth and hands ready her, and when it was time she helped guide him inside her. It was glorious! Unbelievable. She met the urgent tempo of his thrusts inside her with increasing ardor. She loved him. She'd fallen in love with him, and it felt so right to make love to him. When the world exploded, she rode the tide and relaxed, falling, falling, falling from a great height, stunned by the joy and pleasure of loving someone so completely.

Later, wrapped in his arms and with the weight of one of his legs thrown possessively over hers, she kissed his smooth chest and cuddled close, refusing to let even a moment of reality break this wonderful dream.

It was Hank who brought her back down to earth. "We have to tell Julian," he said softly. "As soon as possible."

"But not yet..." she whispered, and began kissing him all over again.

CHLOE SQUINTED at Julian's face. She'd been talking a mile a minute, trying to keep both their attentions on the crossword puzzle, failing completely. But Julian had grudgingly gone to make coffee when she'd begged for some and now he held a cup out to her, which she reached for and promptly tipped onto the cream-colored area rug.

"Oh, my God! I'm sorry!" She leaped to her feet. "Quick! I need a cold, damp rag." She swayed slightly, and Julian's strong hands steadied her.

"It's okay."

"It's not okay!" She stumbled toward the kitchen, realized her reaction time had definitely slipped with her consumption of wine and stood blankly at the edge of the kitchen, surveying her surroundings.

Julian moved past her, dampened a dish towel and returned to the living room to sop up some of the coffee. Chloe was right on his heels. "Here, let me," she said.

"Sit down." He smiled at her as he dabbed at the stain.

"No, I need to—"

"Sit down," he ordered more firmly. "Don't worry. I'll get it cleaned. I need to anyway."

She back sat with a thump. Moments later Julian sat beside her. "I'm a trial to you," Chloe said, embarrassed. *And now I'm half-drunk!* She remembered then, vaguely, that Dixie had said he didn't really drink much. Not part of the diet regimen. She suddenly felt sick.

"You okay?" he asked.

His breath was warm against her cheek. The whole place was warm. She realized she wasn't going to be sick, but she definitely needed to cool things off. "I need some fresh air."

Stumbling to her feet, she used his forearm for support. Then she walked to the French doors across the back of the living room, but Julian beat her to them. He threw them open, and they both stepped onto a slate patio. A stiff little breeze whipped Chloe's untamed locks around her face. Stars glittered in the heavens, the smog blown clear by the brisk wind, the sky dark and thick as velvet.

Chloe inhaled deeply and closed her eyes. "What am I doing?" she said, her eyes flying open as she realized she'd spoken aloud. She was further shocked when he came up behind her, wrapping his arms around her waist. And when he leaned down and kissed the side of her neck, she shivered as if with malaria! "Better yet, what are *you* doing?"

"Kissing you." His hands tightened on her waist and he slowly rotated her until she was facing him, wide-eyed. She felt shaky all over. Her fingers dug into her forearms for support.

"I don't think you should. I don't think I want you to."

"I think you do want me to."

"You're so certain."

Those amazing blue eyes gazed calmly into her gray ones. "Yes."

And then his mouth captured hers, and Chloe muttered a squeak of resistance. She should protest. Really, really protest, but holy, moly, his tongue was doing incredible things inside her mouth, and she could only stand in absolute wonder as tiny thrills of pleasure shot through her body right down to her toes!

"I can't do this to my sister!" she choked as soon as he allowed her up for air.

"I'm not in love with Dixie."

"Oh, no...don't tell me that...she...might be...in love with you!"

He shook his head, dragging her close, so that her body felt the hard, sculpted muscles of his chest and the strength of his thighs. Now, she really was going to be sick. She was reeling. But it was guilt and fear and something else that made her head spin, not alcohol.

"She knows how I feel."

"I don't think she does!"

"You don't have the whole story," he said, his voice deeper than normal, his attention riveted on her lips so that Chloe felt compelled to wet them with her tongue. He groaned and closed his eyes, and the next kiss propelled her up against the French doors.

"Julian..." she whispered, too undone to think clearly. Her body was sending her messages she'd never gotten before. This was too much.

"Let me make love to you," he said thickly, and that was all it took.

She shut her brain down completely. When his hand moved beneath her blouse, her breasts seemed to meet his touch with a will of their own. A little moan of pure pleasure escaped her lips as his hands undid the buttons and swept aside the two halves of her blouse and his mouth followed their tender exploration. When his lips closed hotly over one nipple, Chloe's legs simply gave out. He caught her in his arms, a chuckle escaping his lips that was a half groan of answering desire.

How they got to the bedroom Chloe didn't fully remember later. But strong arms lifted her, and she recalled faintly the feeling that a man from another century was dragging her away, intent on branding her as his own. And she was all for it, kissing him with abandon, touching him with fingers grown bold with desire, pressing her bared breasts against his chest until they were writhing on the bed together and there was no line between his passion and her own.

I'm in love, she thought in wonder. Eagerly she helped him off with his clothes, just as eagerly he helped divest her of hers. And when they were lying naked, both lost in throes of passion, Chloe found a rather primitive side of herself she hadn't known existed. She wrapped her hands in his hair and dragged his mouth back to her breasts, arching her back and making sounds that later would suffuse her with embarrassment. But in the heat of the moment she had one hot, shining thought: she wanted his possession.

Julian felt every signal as if it were pounding in his brain. He kissed and caressed and when her own urgency threatened to outmatch his, he drove into her in a way that left them both gasping and reaching and thrusting toward ultimate pleasure.

Chloe reached that pleasure a heartbeat before him and they both cried out. She clung to his broad shoulders like a life raft, her body shuddering in tandem with his. It felt like centuries, eons before she came back to herself enough to know where she was and with whom.

Gazing at his sinewy shoulders and mane of black hair, the sprawling length of him covering her body, she could scarcely believe the events that had passed had actually happened to her.

I made love to Julian, she thought in that strange, faraway state.

As if hearing her thoughts he lifted his head and gazed into her eyes, his own satiated and slumberous. Softly, he kissed her lips, gently tugging at the bottom one with his teeth.

Chloe pulled her lip away from his possession, shocked to feel renewed ripples of passion. "I think we may have made a really big mistake," she whispered.

He frowned and shook his head. "No."

"Julian. I don't do this kind of thing."

"Neither do I." She laughed without humor, but he kissed her hard on the lips to stop her. "I don't," he stated flatly. "But…"

Her heart caught in her throat. "But?"

"But I want to do it again."

And with that he showed her exactly what he meant.

THEY DROVE in relative silence back toward Julian's, neither of them able to think of what to say. Dixie did not want to tell Julian. Not now. Not yet. Not when everything was so fresh and new and wonderful.

"Let me talk to him," Hank said. "It'll be okay. He just needs to hear it from me."

"Hank, it's not quite the way you think it is. He's not in love with me. We're not in love with each other."

"But you are engaged."

"Well…yes…sorta…" She winced. Should she tell him the truth? Or would that just add insult to injury when they faced Julian with this news? She had no idea how he would really react. They were engaged, for all intents and purposes, and there was a high probability he would really object to her having slept with his brother.

"It doesn't matter anyway," Hank said, steeling himself. "He thinks he's with you, and it's not going to be pretty when he finds out the truth."

"Have you ever—had something like this happen before? With another girl?"

"Never. It was just an understood thing."

Dixie felt like a complete heel. "Do we have to tell him tonight?" she asked in a small voice.

"I think so."

As they approached the house, Dixie slowed the car until they were barely creeping the last few feet to Julian's driveway. "I'll go in with you," she said.

"I think this is better if I do it alone."

"Not on your life," she declared, slamming her door and scurrying after him to the front door. To her shock Chloe threw open the door just as she reached for the handle.

"Dixie!"

"Chloe!"

"Chloe," Hank repeated, examining her closely. She looked wild-eyed and scared.

"Are you all right?" Dixie demanded, grabbing her by the arm. "Did he hurt you?" she asked, her voice rising.

"What?" Chloe held her head in confusion.

Dixie turned on Hank. "Just how angry does your brother get about things? It wasn't Chloe's fault that Patrice said all those awful things! Julian should know that!"

"No, no, no." Chloe lifted both hands and waved Dixie's words away.

"Where is Julian?" Hank asked.

"In bed." She cleared her throat. "I think. I was just—waiting for you to arrive and take me home."

"You were?" Dixie asked.

"Oh, well, I mean, I could have caught a cab. I, um, fell asleep."

"The couch isn't the most comfortable piece of furniture," Hank said, his mind already tripping past Chloe to what he was going to say to his brother.

"What?" Chloe glanced back at the couch. "Oh. No, it isn't. I guess." She swallowed. "Can we go home now?" she asked Dixie in a voice that was so unlike herself that Dixie grew more concerned.

"Are you sure you're all right?"

"Fabulous. A-one. Couldn't be better. But I need to get home and go to bed. Right now. Okay?"

"Go on," Hank told Dixie. It was all he could do to keep from leaning over and giving her a goodbye kiss. But that would have to wait.

"You're not going to do anything tonight," Dixie told him, warned him actually.

"If Julian's in bed, looks like there's nothing to do but go to bed, too."

"He's in bed." Chloe nodded several times. "Yep. Nothing to talk about tonight."

"You sure you're all right?" Dixie asked, when she finally tore her eyes from Hank's retreating form and started to the car with her sister.

"One hundred and ten percent," Chloe said.

"He didn't do anything that was—"

"No. He didn't do anything. Okay?" Surfacing

from her abstraction, she brushed back a tangle of hair and asked, "So, where were you and Hank?"

Dixie smiled a bit sickly. "We weren't doing anything much, either."

"Good. Nobody was doing anything, then."

"Nope. Nothing."

"Well...good..."

And they completed the rest of the journey in silence, each locked in her own personal hell of secrets left untold.

12

WHEN CHLOE didn't want to talk about things, she could be as closed up as an oyster. Not that Dixie was in a particularly chatty mood on Sunday, so the conversation between the two sisters consisted only of a few long yawns, a couple of comments like, "Late night last night, huh?" and a great deal of giving each other lots and lots of space. The same scene was being played out at Julian's, though Hank made a few half-hearted attempts to engage his brother in a meaningful conversation, attempts that were ignored by a very preoccupied Julian.

Feeling like a thief, Hank snuck into Julian's den and placed a call to Dixie, only to have Chloe pick up the receiver on an anxious, "Hello?" He hung up rather than ask for Dixie. It just all seemed so... wrong! *If I smoked, I'd be lighting my last cigarette before the firing squad....*

Chloe fingered the phone for long moments after Hank's call. She should be flogged. Put on the rack. Forced to never solve a crossword puzzle again. Made to watch a line of handsome men parade in front of her who shake their fingers and tsk-tsk her, laughing at her silly prejudices now that she'd slept with the handsomest of the bunch, Julian Ashby. She'd done something she'd never done before: succumbed to her most secret desires, and she'd awakened in Julian's arms after a brief comalike state of pure satiation to flay herself alive with recriminations! *My brains fell out somewhere and I can't find them.*

Dixie stayed in bed till noon, staring at the patterns the shadows from the leaves outside her window made on the ceiling. *It must have been a dream,* she thought, reviewing the events of the night before. Then she punched her pillow into a hard ball and squeezed her eyes shut and hoped she would somehow get over this feeling of helplessness. And that the dream would return.

Julian worked out at his gym, signed autographs and, when asked if he was engaged by worried fans, nodded grimly. *I'm going quietly out of my mind,* he decided when he returned to the house late in the evening. All he wanted to do was phone Chloe and find out what in God's name had happened that had sent her flying away from him in a panic.

By eleven that night Dixie and Chloe were pretending to watch the news while both their sets of eyes strayed to the telephone. Hank and Julian were trying to figure out how to place calls that would neither be eavesdropped on by the other, nor picked up by the wrong party. And so the night wore on, and by the time Monday morning broke hazily across the eastern horizon, all hell broke loose.

"The afternoon flight's been canceled." Sandra sounded panicked to Julian's ears. He eyed the clock blearily. Barely 6:00 a.m. "I've rebooked you and Dixie on the 10:00 a.m. flight, so I hope you're packed."

Julian threw off the covers. "Hell, no, I'm not packed!" he declared. "Have you called Dixie?"

"Not yet, I—"

"I'll do it." He hung up and punched out Dixie and Chloe's number. The phone was snatched up on the second ring with Dixie's voice saying anxiously, "Hello?"

Disappointment fell like a curtain. "Dixie it's Julian. They've moved up our flight. We're leaving at ten o'clock this morning." Strangled noises of panic sounded from her throat. Before she could ring off, he asked, "Is Chloe there?"

"She's in the shower."

So early? But then his brain kicked into gear and he realized she would be getting ready for work. He debated asking Dixie for her work number, but Dixie was already slamming down the receiver in her haste to make their new time.

It appeared to Dixie that Hank had not had a chance to bare his soul to Julian, since he'd said nothing about it, so what did that mean? With a sound of frustration, she sped off to pack her bags. She just didn't have time to think about it now.

Hank appeared at the jamb of Julian's bedroom door about thirty minutes later. "What's up?" he asked, running a hand through his hair and yawning.

Julian explained about the flights and then asked, "Why aren't you coming on this trip with me again?"

"I just didn't think you needed me." This was patently untrue since Hank always traveled with his number-one client, but with Dixie in the picture, Hank had gotten his nose a bit out of joint. And now, with everything else, he didn't know if he could stand watching them work together.

Julian nodded, distracted. "Then I'll see you later."

He took a cab to the airport and was relieved to find Dixie there already, waiting for him. She seemed to be half-expecting him to say something to her, but for the life of him he didn't know what that was. Eventually, she shrugged her shoulders and asked, "Have you seen the papers?"

He groaned all over again. "I never want to see the papers again!"

She nodded in agreement. "The tabloids are saying you're off the dating market for good, because of me. Of course, it's still Chloe's picture, but oh, well..."

"When the commercial comes out, that'll get cleared up."

"Oh, I don't care," Dixie assured him hurriedly. "At least you got what you wanted, right? What we were aiming for?"

Julian glanced away, struck by her comments. "Let's get the flight," he said a bit gruffly, and they headed for the jetway together.

CHLOE COULDN'T HELP herself from calling home from work and checking her messages. A part of her was beginning to feel very hurt and bruised. Good grief, how could Julian make love to her so thoroughly, so wonderfully, so fabulously and then simply not call? One quick ringy-dingy to Dixie this morning to change their flights and that was it. Didn't the man have any feelings? Any sense of fair play?

"You stupid idiot," she berated herself, swiping the papers from her desk in one swift, frustrated move of her arm. Of course, that meant she would just have to gather them up again, but tough. She listened to her home phone ring its obligatory four rings before the answering machine picked up with mounting anxiety.

Please, please, please let him have called!

"You have two new messages," the computer voice intoned.

Two messages! She sat up straighter, glancing at the clock. They were just catching their flight. He could have phoned.

"AlohaDixie. It'sBrandon. Kitty-Digginswantsyou bad! HavefuninHawaii. Callwhenyougetback. We'll-setupameeting."

Chloe drummed her fingers impatiently. "Come on, come on!"

The second message clicked on. "Alohaagain!" Brandon's voice rang out, sinking Chloe's heart. "Youwon'tbelieveit! 'HarringtonHigh'wantsyouback! Heather'sout! Out! Callmeandwe'lltalk."

Chloe dropped her head in her hands and reminded herself that she was a complete and utter idiot. He'd said he didn't sleep around with other women, but what good was a Hollywood icon's word, really? She'd just been a number. One in a long line.

And he was engaged to her sister!

"Chloe?" Toni ducked her head inside the office. "Just who is Julian dating? You, or your sister? It's your picture, but they keep calling you Dixie."

"Dixie's engaged to Julian," Chloe stated in an unhappy voice.

"But all those things you said…about you and Julian…."

"I was making it up. It's called lying. I'm a great liar."

Toni gave her an uncertain look and scooted out of the office. Chloe debated on buying up all the tabloids and reading every last iota of gossip, but the thought just gave her a headache. She was suffering a love hangover and it was pure hell.

"What are you looking for?" Toni asked her ten minutes later when she discovered Chloe rummaging in the cupboard beneath the sink in the coffee room.

"Arsenic," Chloe declared.

"Arsenic?"

"I'm looking for aspirin," Chloe explained in a long-suffering tone. Honestly, didn't anyone have a sense of humor anymore? "I'm not well."

"You look a little tired," Toni agreed solicitously. "Maybe you should go home."

Well, great. Now she even looked bad. Chloe wanted to fling herself onto the floor and have an out-and-out fit, but instead she considered Toni's advice. "You know what, I just might."

And for the second time in the last week she did what she never, ever had done before: jettison work because she was almost sick.

IT WAS EARLY afternoon when the plane landed in Honolulu since Hawaii was three hours behind Los Angeles. Dixie stepped off the plane and was greeted with a lei. Julian stepped off the plane and was greeted by adoring fans, his arrival having been trumpeted by the people at Primitive Cologne.

All in the name of business, Dixie realized tiredly, then was taken aback when she was also hounded by a group of reporters and paparazzi wanting every detail of her and Julian's upcoming nuptials.

Julian grabbed her by the arm and steered her away, smiling and waving to the horde of people, ducking her into the safety of a limo standing nearby.

"My bags," Dixie protested.

"They'll bring them."

Their hotel was right on the beach, extravagant to

the extreme, the lobby opening straight onto the sands of Waikiki Beach. A bouquet of white plumeria and bloodred anthurium and spiky birds of paradise awaited her in her room. Dixie gazed around the spacious apartment, noticed the connecting door, debated on knocking but decided to step onto her lanai instead and examine her oceanfront view. It was beautiful enough to bring tears to her eyes, but when she recognized she was crying, she also recognized the true source of her tears.

She was in love with the right brother, engaged to the wrong one.

And Hank hadn't called after their night together.

You didn't call him, either, she reminded herself, but that was because of Julian. Couldn't he have found a way to reach her? Or were all his words of love just talk, since he didn't seem to have had his heart-to-heart talk with Julian.

Several hours later it was Julian who knocked on the connecting door first. "Ready to go to dinner?" he asked. He wore a dark blue shirt, open to the navel, and a pair of black slacks. He looked, she admitted, devastatingly attractive, but she found herself yearning for one of those surfer shirts so popular here in Hawaii.

Dixie, in a lemon yellow sundress, which made her realize how desperately she could use a tan, slipped her arm through his and inhaled and exhaled heavily. She was his fiancée, at least for the duration of this trip, and she'd better start acting like it.

SUNGLASSES were the ultimate piece of apparel, Hank decided. They hid his identity. Had he been suffering from the effects of too much imbibing, they would also be hiding a pair of bloodshot eyes. But today, they simply hid the fact that he was Hank Ashby, Julian's brother. No one generally recognized him anyway, but with a pair of sunglasses on his face, his anonymity was assured. Oh, sure, Julian couldn't get away with such tricks. Not with all that hair and his penchant for baring his chest, but he, Hank, was traveling incognito, and on this flight to Honolulu, that's just how he wanted to be.

He didn't really know what to do. He certainly did not know why he was flying to the scene of the crime just so he could be tortured by his brother making goo-goo eyes at the woman he loved. Okay, Julian didn't make goo-goo eyes. Neither did Dixie, for that matter, but hell, it was going to be torture if they were even on the same island together, which, he supposed, was inevitable.

I'm a glutton for punishment, he thought miserably, sinking down in the seat. And with that he dozed off in search of some of the sleep he'd missed the night before, and the time passed.

He awakened as the wheels touched down in Honolulu. By that time he'd pretty much decided he should turn around and take the next flight out. Deplaning from first class, he stood for a moment in the airport, wishing for some sign to tell him what to do next.

"Excuse me," a feminine voice said, as one of the passengers tried to brush past him.

Hank lifted his sunglasses and stared at the offender. "Chloe?"

She nearly fell over at the mention of her name. She gasped and literally clutched her chest, as if her heart were about to leap from her rib cage. Leaning in for a better look, she asked, "Hank?"

''What are you doing here?''

''What are you doing here?''

They laughed at their in-unison queries, then Hank asked, ''Were you on this flight? I was on this flight.''

''I was in coach,'' she said.

''I was in first. So, are you going to find Dixie?''

''I guess. Are you going to find Julian?''

''I guess.''

They stared at each other for a long moment. ''Does Dixie know you decided to join her a day later?''

''Uh-uh,'' Chloe admitted. ''And Julian?''

''Nope.''

''I've booked myself into a nearby hotel,'' Chloe said, wrinkling her nose a bit at the admission. ''I didn't want to be in the exact same one.''

''Why not?''

''I just didn't.''

Hank was feeling better by the moment, though he couldn't exactly say why. ''Let's get a cab. I haven't got a reservation, but wherever you're staying sounds fine to me.''

''You don't want Julian to know you're here?''

''I don't know what the hell I want!'' he expelled on a frustrated sigh.

''Me, neither!''

They climbed into the cab with huge smiles on their faces. Absurdly Hank felt like shaking her hand, as if they were allies in crime. And Chloe, feeling the same way, reached out and did just that, giving his hand one hard shake in unspoken, unexpected partnership.

THE DAY'S SHOOT was on a remote part of the island that looked enough like a jungle to suit the powers that be at Primitive Cologne. At first Dixie had looked forward to the task, but fifteen hours into the shoot with no end in sight and a throbbing black eye from where Julian accidentally whacked her with a vine, she was feeling less enthusiastic. And Julian himself was an absolute bear! He growled and scowled and generally looked dark, gloomy and, yes, still handsome, but who the hell cared? She was beginning to believe Chloe's theory about good-looking men completely. As the day wore on, she determined she didn't like either Ashby brother and wished to high heaven neither one of them had ever crossed her path!

"We might need more makeup," one of the production assistants said, grabbing her chin and turning her face to and fro. "Nasty shiner."

"Well, we know who to blame," Dixie said with a tight smile.

"Now, now. It was an accident."

Yeah, right, Dixie thought, feeling completely uncharitable on everyone's behalf. Chloe had left her a message on her phone to call Brandon, and on one of her breaks she'd managed to find a phone. Brandon's euphoria over Kitty-Diggins and her return to "Harrington High" should have buoyed Dixie's spirits, but it didn't. And when he'd gone on to tell her that her nemesis, Heather Amherst, had been booted from the show, falling victim to some mysterious cheerleader demise, she'd said rather waspishly, "What? Did she fall off the top of the human pyramid or something?"

Brandon had rushed right on with oohs and ahs over her fabulous association with Julian, and then had bemoaned the fact that Julian did not appear to be gay, after all. Brandon, apparently, had been hoping. He finished the conversation with, "Whatacryingshame! Ifiguredhewasstraight!"

They finally stopped for the day around seven o'clock, but by the time they got back to the hotel and Dixie made it through the shower, it was close to nine. Making a face at the connecting door, Dixie took her juvenile self downstairs to the bar, thought about one of the tropical drinks, decided she was too unhappy to stand a depressant like alcohol and wandered onto the beach.

Gazing across the sand at the creaming surf, feeling the warm breeze against her cheek, smelling the scents of ocean and the coconut aloe she'd spread on her own hot skin, she sighed and searched for inner peace. She was just going to have to get out of this faux engagement. Primitive Cologne or no. Julian or no. Kitty-Diggins and "Harrington High" or no. It was time to put things back on track.

As soon as the decision was made Dixie felt much better. Lifting her chin and closing her eyes, she let herself drink in the moment, a smile spreading across her features. If she couldn't get out of her blue funk and enjoy the beauty of Oahu there was something wrong with her.

Up the beach, twinkling lights and the ripple of conversation caught her attention. A thatched-roof circular cabana with stools all around was open for business, and the business was tropical drinks with umbrellas and getting to know the other vacationers. Touching her bruised cheek and eye, Dixie knew she probably looked like she'd been in a fight. No amount of makeup could disguise the vine beating she'd taken when she was up close and personal.

But what did she care? At this point, it was a conversation piece, and she was in the mood to talk to people who knew nothing about her, anyway.

She'd wrapped herself in a sarong done in tropical scenes in varying shades of blue. Now she took off her sandals and let them dangle from her fingers as she slogged through the sand toward the cabana. Coming from the shadows into the light, she was momentarily dazzled by the refraction off the rows of bottles stacked in a pyramid in the center of the cabana and nearly touching the ceiling. The bartender, who looked native Hawaiian, greeted her with a huge smile. "Aloha, pretty lady. What would you like?"

Dixie gave him an ironic look. Pretty lady? With her shiner? "I think I'll—" She broke off in surprise. From her point of view, on one side of the bottles, she could see the forearm of the customer directly opposite her. It was male and it lay on the bar, but the short-sleeved shirt with all the surfboards was one she'd seen before—and not in Hawaii!

Sliding over a space, she was stunned to see that, yes! It truly was Hank. And then her surprise turned to out-and-out shock, because his companion for the evening was her own sister!

"Chloe!" she declared, stepping into full view.

Other customers glanced around with interest. Chloe, however, surfaced slowly, then waved a sheepish hand at Dixie. "Hi, there! I was wondering if we'd see you tonight."

"Are you drunk?" Dixie demanded, all her frustrations rising up at once.

"*Moi?*" She threw a hand to her chest and looked affronted. "Not enough time yet. And you know I wasn't really drinking those pink martinis at the Bistro. That was just for Mr. Wonderful's benefit."

This speech might have been more believable if Chloe hadn't slurred the last part, making it sound like Misser Wunnerfall. Dixie turned her attention to Hank, who was regarding her silently. Not a good sign, given their last communication was of the carnal kind. "And you?"

"I'm here—for Julian. I'm his manager." For some reason both he and Chloe found this very entertaining, and they looked at each other and broke into laughter.

"Let me buy you a drink," Hank offered, lifting his own glass up for her inspection. Like Chloe's, Hank's hurricane glass was filled with a frozen white concoction and fingers of some red-colored substance ran down the inside glass in dripping crimson lines. "A lava flow," he told her.

"I swore I'd never drink again after last night," Chloe said. "But Hank's pretty persuasive."

"Oh, how I know!" Dixie murmured.

"But I like these better than Chardonnay," she said, lifting her glass and turning it around for serious examination. "What's in 'em again?"

"Rum," Hank decreed. "And some...other stuff."

"We deserve this, don't we?" Chloe asked.

He nodded. "Yes, we do!"

Chloe nodded sagely, and Dixie wondered if she were about to nod off on the bar entirely. She and Hank shared a happy look and clinked glasses while the bartender caught Hank's order and went to make one for Dixie.

But Dixie felt angry and hurt, and the more Chloe and Hank acted like buddies the more she wanted to scream. "I'm really not interested in a drink," she said primly.

Hank leaned forward and grabbed her forearm.

Dixie pulled back, but not before he demanded, "Who gave you that black eye?"

"It was an accident." She tried to twist her arm from his grasp, but Hank held on tight.

"What kind of an accident?"

"Let go of me!" She jerked her arm back and nearly de-stooled him. Hank scrambled around for support, and it was Chloe who put her arm around him and reseated him. That did it. Dixie couldn't help the fount of fury that rose up inside her and met her willing tongue. "Don't ever touch me again! Go find Britta, or maybe Chloe! I don't care. But next time you plan on drinking champagne and picnicking and pulling off the dust sheets, look somewhere else!"

"Dust sheets?" Chloe questioned, struggling to focus.

"Dixie!" Hank protested. "I'm not—with Chloe!"

"Good God, no," Chloe answered, rearing back to look at Hank as if he'd lost his mind.

"You could have fooled me," Dixie choked, and then, because it was just too humiliating, she turned sharply away and ran straight into Julian's broad bare chest and steadying grip.

IT HAD BEEN a bad day from beginning to end, and Julian knew it was all his fault. He'd tried hard to put the energy required for his jungle-man persona into the shoot, but all he'd done was scowl and growl. And he'd felt terrible when Dixie got hit by the vine, but even his apology had sounded curt and unfeeling.

And it was all because of Chloe. He loved her. Had probably loved her from the first moment she'd examined him with those cool gray eyes and spoken her first acid words. She was so incredibly feisty, yet it was a cover-up for a tender heart. It amazed him that he found the woman he loved by getting engaged to her sister, but there it was.

After a shower, a glass of some kind of pineapple juice and a talk with himself in the mirror, Julian had knocked on Dixie's door, intending to apologize for his behavior. But she hadn't been around, so he'd wandered downstairs and outside and eventually to the bar and the scene that met his eyes. Chloe! With Hank!

And Dixie had been standing there with tears in her eyes, and now he was clasping her forearms to keep her from bolting. "What's going on here?"

"Are you somehow responsible for her black eye?" Hank demanded, sounding as cross as a bear himself.

Julian nodded. "I let go of the vine too soon. I'm sorry. I wanted to come apologize again," he said to Dixie's blond crown. She wouldn't lift her eyes to meet his. "And for being so out of sorts."

"Never mind," she whispered urgently. "Please let me go. I've got to get out of here!"

"Wait." Julian drew a deep breath, deciding it was time to take the plunge. "I wanted to explain why I was in such a bad mood, too. Something's been bothering me for a while now. I can't—go on with this engagement. I know I'm the one that wanted it," Julian rushed on when Dixie finally lifted her head to stare at him in disbelief, "and I appreciate everything you've done for me, but it's not fair to you. I'm not being fair to anyone because…because…" He tore his eyes from hers to look toward Chloe. "I'm in love with your sister."

13

HANK AND CHLOE'S mouths dropped open simultaneously. Julian dragged his eyes from Chloe to gaze into Dixie's strained face.

"Do you mean it?" Dixie asked in a voice that seemed to have forgotten how to work.

"Yes, I mean it." Julian gazed at Chloe with a tenderness that was impossible to miss. The fact that Chloe's jaw lay nearly on the sand kind of spoiled the effect, although, as Dixie thought about it, maybe it was just about perfect. Her sister looked poleaxed, and with Chloe, that was hard to accomplish!

"I'm sorry," Julian apologized to Dixie. "You're just about perfect, and you've been more than terrific over this whole thing. Anything I can do to help you in the future, just let me know. I'd be happy to open any doors for you, but I think your career is on its way. You've got more than enough natural talent to get ahead, and I suspect I'll be saying, 'I knew her when' along with—''

"Who the hell do you think you are?" Hank demanded harshly.

"—the rest of the world."

Dixie swung a look at Hank. She was still too poleaxed herself to do more than stare. Hank's fists were clenched, and he'd climbed off his stool and was standing on the balls of his feet, legs apart. He looked ready to do serious physical battle.

Julian's brows were a straight line of consternation. "What's this?" he asked Hank.

"Damn you," Hank growled. He'd never wanted to hit his brother before. He'd never wanted to hit anyone before. But he sure as hell wanted to bury his fist in Julian's handsome face right now. Dixie did not deserve this. And though a part of him was filled with relief that Julian wasn't in love with her, another part wanted to defend her honor with every breath he possessed!

"Hank," Dixie protested in a strangled voice.

In the tense moment that followed, Chloe awoke from her stunned stupor. The last few moments had telescoped into one thought: Julian was dumping her sister.

"I knew it!" she bit out tensely. "I just knew it!" She gazed at Hank in disgust. "If you're going to hit him, get on with it. Oh, forget it," she added in the next breath. Elbowing Hank out of the way, she planted herself directly in front of Julian. "Of all the egotistical things to say! You're an overbearing jerk, do you know that? Who do you think you are? Using women like pawns. Picking them up just to throw them away! Dixie's ten times the human being you are. A billion times! But it doesn't surprise me. I've never trusted a pretty boy. They're all the same, and yes, I almost believed you were an exception, but I was wrong!" She paused for a breath, tamping down the little happy voice that nagged in her brain, reminding her that *the* Julian had stated *he* loved *her!* That, of course, was completely beside the point!

"Chloe..." Dixie clapped a hand to her forehead,

afraid her head might explode from too much information. Chloe had unfortunately recovered from her momentary fuzziness, and every syllable was being bit out with force.

"And furthermore, women do not deserve to be treated with such contempt. Just because you're good-looking does not mean we need you. In fact, I'd venture to say that all good-looking men are a liability we women can't afford. Too much emphasis on physical appearance and not enough on what's inside. Unformed, that's what you are. And you, too," she said in growing annoyance as Hank stood in readiness. "For Pete's sake, make up your mind! Take a swing at him! Unless that pretty face is too profitable for you to ruin!" she declared, pointing a finger at Julian's nose.

Hank's fury at Julian couldn't be sustained in the face of Chloe's high dudgeon. "Do you mind?" he asked her. "I'm having a pivotal moment with my brother."

"Oh, please." She lifted her hands and backed away.

"You didn't feel this way after we made love," Julian said to Chloe.

Hank's head swiveled sharply from Julian to Chloe, but the movement yanked at the alcohol-shrouded parts of his brain. The lava flow had kicked in mercilessly and he suddenly felt like it would be a better idea to focus with one eye closed at a time, just to keep things from spinning. Hitting Julian was getting to sound like a better and better idea, but he was having trouble hanging on to to exactly why this should be. Still...

Hank lurched at his brother, making a halfhearted stab at connecting his fist to Julian's jaw.

"Hank!" Dixie's voice sounded from a long way away, as if it were coming from a watery hole.

"Cut it out, Hank," Julian snapped, pushing him away with such ease that even through his haze, Hank was infuriated.

Well, to hell with him! Hank thought, and without further consideration, he launched himself at Julian, full body. *Thunk!* Hard flesh met hard flesh. The momentum crashed them to the ground. Julian made an oof sound as he connected with the beach, and Hank's breath whooshed out. Above him, Hank heard Dixie and Chloe yelling at him. Or at least that's what he thought it was until he heard Dixie's voice saying in utter disbelief, "You slept with Julian?"

"Get off me!" Julian demanded, but his voice was weak. The kick to his solar plexus had rendered him damn near helpless. Hank's body was a bullet and Julian felt darn near annihilated.

"I—didn't plan on it," Chloe's voice answered.

"You." Dixie was flat-out stunned. "You—slept—with—*Julian?*"

"At least he's not gay," Chloe answered on a weak laugh.

Hank rolled away from Julian and stared up at the stars. Things were definitely blurry, but Chloe's last comment got through his addled brain and he started to laugh. Glancing toward Dixie, he realized she was bent over. When she lifted her head he saw her face was lit with mirth. She looked at him, clapped a hand to her mouth to stop the laughter and managed to gasp out, "Are you all right?"

"Who said I'm gay?" Julian demanded.

"It was just a rumor." Chloe swept the thought away with one uncaring hand.

"Is that why you slept with me?"

"Are you crazy?" Chloe demanded, glaring at him.

"I just want to know why you slept with me. That's all." Julian's face was carved in stone. He wished to high heaven that he could collect his breath enough to climb to his feet, but Hank had taken care of that in a really big way.

In the silence that followed, while Chloe struggled to come up with some kind of answer that made sense rather than the bald truth that she loved Julian right back, Dixie said, "The reason I made love to Hank was because I love him."

That caught their attention! Julian and Chloe and Hank all looked as if they wanted to clean out their ears and recheck what they'd heard. Then Julian and Chloe turned from Dixie to Hank. Julian finally clambered to his feet, extending a hand to his brother as one brow arched. "You and Dixie made love, yet you wanted to kill me for making love with Chloe?"

"It's not the same thing." Hank was still reeling from the soft warmth of her words. *Because I love him.* She meant *him.* Hank Ashby! It was incredible. Dusting himself off, he accepted Julian's lift to his feet. The two brothers gave each other a long look, both of them unable to fight the smile that slid over their lips.

"You dog," Hank said to Julian, grinning.

"Double dog," he responded, punching his finger against Hank's chest.

Dixie's mouth had gone dry. She'd laid her feelings on the line and still she didn't know what Hank truly felt for her.

Chloe stood a bit apart, certain the earth was going to open up and swallow her whole. This night wasn't real. There was nothing about this whole scenario that rang true. Nothing.

Julian's arm reached out for her, dragging her close. "Don't leave me in suspense," he said against her hair.

She swallowed. "I don't quite know what to say."

He tilted up her chin with one finger, staring at her through the soft, warm night. "You love me, too," he said.

"Arrogant male," she whispered. "I do not."

"Oh, yes, you do."

Dixie kept her attention fixed solely on Chloe and Julian. She wasn't even really surprised. She should have known about their feelings for each other. It was so obvious in hindsight. What she didn't know was how Hank felt, and with each passing second, the worry and fret was excruciating!

"Dixie," he said softly, coming up beside her.

"Did you know about them?" She cut him off, suddenly unable to hear anything he had to say. "I should have known. Chloe's been acting so strange. Worse than usual."

"I heard that!" Chloe declared, trying to peek over Julian's broad shoulder, but he refused to let her, his arms sliding around her waist, pulling her close. It was pure heaven, as far as Chloe was concerned, and she just wanted to let her eyes drift shut and have him carry her off to some distant Nirvana.

"All that crossword stuff," Dixie babbled on. "And Chloe's continued put-downs about how handsome Julian was. All that complaining and fretting and making a hubbub."

"I heard that, too!" Chloe cried, a moment before Julian swooped in for a kiss.

Dixie gazed at them, their silhouettes dark against the night sky, long tresses blowing in the gentle breeze, Julian's muscular arms enclosing and shielding and protecting her. Poignancy clogged her throat and absurdly, she felt like crying.

And then Hank's arms slid around Dixie's waist from behind, pulling her against his broad chest. Her heart raced lightly and she could feel the ka-thunk of his against her back. "We couldn't have made love unless we were in love," he breathed in her ear, "but it's nice to hear you say so."

"Oh, Hank!" All her tension rushed away.

And with that his mouth found hers and the kiss they shared seared them together.

In the long moment that followed, Julian asked soberly, "Who said I was gay?"

Everyone broke into peals of laughter.

FOUR MONTHS LATER Chloe, Dixie, Julian and Hank sat at Java Beach when Chloe, chewing on her lower lip in consternation, declared she was stumped by that Saturday's *New York Times* crossword puzzle.

"No, don't help me," she declared, slapping at Julian's hand as he was about to drag it away from her.

Hank ignored them by leaning over and nuzzling Dixie's neck. "I think this is my favorite part of you," he said.

"People are staring." But Dixie made no attempt to push him away.

"I said don't help me!" Chloe declared, glaring at Julian.

"What? I didn't move," Julian protested.

"Yes, you did."

Smiling indulgently, he consoled himself by playing footsie with Chloe beneath the table, unmindful of the other patrons who couldn't stop themselves from staring at the now famous foursome. The media had been having a field day with their twin romances. Two sisters and two brothers, and *the* Julian, to boot! The summer had sped by in a dither of hot copy, but Dixie, Hank, Chloe and Julian had managed to ignore the worst of it.

At least until the new Primitive Cologne commercial hit television sets across the country. And with her new contract on "Harrington High" and a few Kitty-Diggins commercials added to her résumé, Dixie's celebrity star had risen right along with Julian's. It was definitely a time for celebration, and the four of them were engaged in a friendly argument over where to eat lunch. Hank was opting for Mel's Diner, but Julian had put his foot down. Three chicken Caesar salads had won over Hank's desire for a juicy hamburger.

Dixie craned her neck to look at Chloe's handiwork. "Looks like 'marry me' in the center of the puzzle," she said.

"It is 'marry me,'" Chloe stated in a long-suffering voice. Honestly! These neophytes. "It's a song. Like 'Marry Me, Bill,'" she said. "That old song by that Fifth Dimension singer. But it doesn't fit."

"Marilyn McCoo," Hank supplied. "And the name of the song is 'Wedding Bell Blues,' not 'Marry Me, Bill.' Those were just some of the lyrics."

"Oh." Chloe frowned. "Well, okay. Then what's another song that starts with 'marry me'?"

"Why does it have to be a song?" Julian asked.

"Because it's marry me *something*. There are five letters there. What else could it be?"

"What else could it be, indeed?" Julian asked softly.

Nothing on his face gave him away, but Dixie sharpened her gaze on him. He regarded her blandly, then turned his attention back to Chloe's bent head. Dixie glanced at Hank, whose lips twitched. A dead giveaway. "Maybe it's a request," she suggested a bit breathlessly.

"A request?" Chloe shook her untamed curls and looked as if she wanted to yank them out of her scalp. "Marry me...today," she ruminated. "No. I think the second letter's an *H*."

Julian's smile flashed, but Chloe wasn't looking up to see it. "I think you're right," he said.

Chloe shot him a sharp glance. "You're not even looking at it!" she declared, then glancing around she realized Dixie, Hank and Julian were all staring at her with varying degrees of amusement and indulgence. "What? Have I got something caught in my teeth?"

"Nope." Dixie grinned like a goblin.

"Have you all lost your minds at once?" Chloe demanded. A moment later, her heart lurched in disbelief. "Oh...my...God." With a shaking hand, she slowly filled in her own name, realizing all the letters fell in place like dominoes. "How...?" she asked the man she loved.

It was Hank who answered. "He's *the* Julian."

"I don't believe it!" Chloe's face flooded with color. She bent over the puzzle, so thrilled she was afraid she'd burst.

"So, what's your answer?" Dixie prodded gently.

"I..." Her pen worked like mad, her brain on another plane. Gasping, she started laughing so hard she nearly choked.

"Chloe?" Dixie asked, glancing worriedly at Hank and Julian. They seemed remarkably unconcerned. "Chloe! Are you okay?"

For an answer she shoved the puzzle beneath Dixie's nose.

The line beneath *Marry me, Chloe* read *Ditto, Dixie.*

Dixie's answer was a slow smile and a pair of shining eyes.

THE DAY HAD BEEN fraught with problems from beginning to end, mostly because it was nearly impossible to plan a double wedding that included a celebrity and expect the media to leave it alone. A serious amount of planning had been put into the event, and now it was almost a reality.

"Did you see the headlines?" Hank asked, nervously pacing the narrow confines of his condo's living room and tugging on the bow tie of his sleek black tux. "Every paparazzo in the greater Los Angeles area is trying to figure out where our wedding will be. They know it's today!"

"They don't know it's here," Chloe said, pacing just as nervously. Her short white dress was a carbon copy of her sister's, white lace and simple lines.

"They don't know it's all of us," Julian added, tugging on his tie, as well. For once in his life, he hadn't unbuttoned his shirt to his navel—but he was thinking about it.

"Wanna bet?" Dixie asked on a sigh as she drew back the curtain and looked at the growing assembly on the beach.

Hank groaned. "It'll be a dead giveaway when the minister arrives."

"Uh-uh." Chloe shook her head. "He's incognito."

Ten minutes later a man on a beach rider bicycle rode past the group on the beach and turned a block away. Carefully, he parked his bike against one of the apartments at the end of the row. Even more carefully and casually, he strolled around the back of Hank's condominium and let himself through the lock at the back gate.

With that, their minister sneaked through the rear entrance and into the living room.

"Very California," Hank greeted him with a grin.

The minister glanced down at his surfer shirt and flip-flops, grinned, then let Dixie lead him to the bedroom and the garment bag already smuggled into the place earlier.

And then the men in black tuxes, the women in white lace dresses and crowns of plumeria, Dixie Kingston became Hank Ashby's bride, and Chloe Kingston became Julian Ashby's.

And they lived happily ever after...dude.

The Cupid Caper

Darlene Gardner

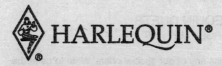

HARLEQUIN®

TORONTO • NEW YORK • LONDON
AMSTERDAM • PARIS • SYDNEY • HAMBURG
STOCKHOLM • ATHENS • TOKYO • MILAN • MADRID
PRAGUE • WARSAW • BUDAPEST • AUCKLAND

Dear Reader,

It was inevitable that I'd write a book with a private eye as a main character. Not because I loved those old movies with Humphrey Bogart playing Sam Spade, which I do. But because, like the hero in *The Cupid Caper,* I have a detective in my family.

That's where the resemblance between the detective agency in my book and my sister Lynette's business ends. She doesn't have an octogenarian secretary or a hunky partner, although years ago she did a brief stint as one of three female detectives for a wealthy rancher who was trying to copy the television series *Charlie's Angels.*

Gee, I wonder if my sister has the meddling gene that makes my heroine such a good detective. Come to think of it, maybe that's why she's always telling me to stay out of dark alleys and to trust no one.

Enjoy!

Darlene Gardner

Books by Darlene Gardner

HARLEQUIN DUETS
39—FORGET ME? *NOT*

Don't miss any of our special offers. Write to us at the following address for information on our newest releases.

Harlequin Reader Service
U.S.: 3010 Walden Ave., P.O. Box 1325, Buffalo, NY 14269
Canadian: P.O. Box 609, Fort Erie, Ont. L2A 5X3

To my son Brian,
because he *really* wants me to dedicate a book
to him. But, most of all, because he gave me
his Wartortle card for good luck.

1

SAM CREIGHTON BRUSHED the snow from the shoulders of his black leather jacket, stomped the stuff off his fair-weather shoes and cursed his brother.

Why would Jake track him down, leave an urgent message for Sam to come to Philadelphia and then post a note on his office door saying he'd gone out of town?

Especially because mere hours before, Sam had been in sunny Florida on a quest for the perfect sailboat, dreaming of the open seas and an itinerary he'd make up as he sailed along.

He'd wanted to stay in Florida minding his own business, but Sam found he couldn't ignore Jake's message. So he'd hopped a plane to Philadelphia and traveled straight from the airport to Jake's town house only to find it shut up tighter than a gagged mime. Next, he'd come here to his brother's downtown office.

He looked up and down the hallway and made a face. The dim lighting was probably meant to camouflage the dreadful condition of the carpet and the paint peeling from the walls. It was so dark, he could barely read the sign on the door.

Jake Creighton Investigations.

The stairs he'd just climbed were rickety, the air musty, the atmosphere creepy. It was like something out of an old Humphrey Bogart movie. Except Bogey would be inside his office, sitting behind his desk smoking a cigarette, not leaving a note asking his brother to hold down the fort until he got back.

How, exactly, did Jake expect him to do that?

Leaving sun-soaked Florida for the frozen tundra of the northeast had been bad enough. But this transcended lousy. Surely his brother realized that investigating violated Sam's cardinal rule: Thou shalt not butt your nose into the business of others.

Besides, Sam knew zip about being a private detective. He'd spent the last eight years on the floor of the New York Stock Exchange as the owner of an investment firm that handled orders for small brokerages around the country.

Then, a month ago on his thirtieth birthday, he decided he'd had enough of the frenzied life. He'd sold the business and hightailed it to Florida to shop for a boat to sail wherever the mood took him. It certainly wouldn't have brought him to Philadelphia. In the middle of February yet.

Sam surveyed the dingy hall once again. The first thing Jake should do was find another location for his office. In business, presentation was half the battle.

Making a mental note to check into alternative locations while he was in town, Sam tried the door. Locked.

He rubbed the back of his neck. Jake must have been in an all-fired hurry to get out of town to forget about the details he usually held supreme, such as leaving Sam keys to his town house and office.

Apprehension dripped down Sam's body in a cold trickle, washing away the annoyance. Was it possible that Jake hadn't left town of his own volition?

Sam shut his eyes tight, trying to think like a detective. If Jake were in danger, he was pretty sure it hadn't caught up to him. Otherwise, he wouldn't have time to leave a note.

Most likely, the note meant that his brother was just fine, which annoyed Sam all over again. But not as much as the locked door. How, exactly, was he supposed to get inside?

Sam bent down and lifted the worn mat, searching for a key that wasn't there. He reached up and ran his fingertips alongside the top of the door ledge. Nothing.

Finally, he pulled his wallet out of the back pocket of his black jeans and took out a credit card. One swipe and he should be in.

Ten minutes later, with sweat beading his brow, Sam flicked the credit card up and down through the narrow opening between the door and the wall for the umpteenth time. Nothing.

Up and down. Up and down. Up and freaking down.

He was just about to swish the card again when a smooth, long-fingered hand took it from him. The barrel of a gun pressed against his backbone. Hell. A lady cop. It had to be a lady cop. How was he going to explain this one to the long, smooth arm of the law?

"You have about ten seconds," a throaty voice hissed near his ear, "to explain what you're doing breaking into this office."

"*Trying* to break in," Sam corrected dryly. "As you can see, I haven't managed it yet."

"Don't get smart with me, buster. Start talking." She punctuated the command by jabbing the gun deeper into his back. But something about the gun didn't feel right. Either it had an ultrathin barrel or...

Sam whirled and took a look for himself.

Or it was a tube of lipstick.

"Hey, that's not a gun," he exclaimed.

"Don't get self-righteous with me, especially because you're not Jake Creighton."

His eyes lifted from the lipstick-masquerading-as-a-gun to the heart-shaped face of a woman in her mid-twenties, who was definitely not a cop. Unless, of course, she was a cop under deep cover as...

He squinted and stared at her, not quite sure what she was supposed to be. A wig of bouncy red curls covered her hair. Fake freckles, which looked like they had been applied with that lipstick, dotted her face. Her voluminous trench coat fell nearly to the floor, but wasn't quite long enough to cover white bobby socks worn with a pair of Mary Janes.

She looked like Susie Q meets the *X-Files*.

"Who are you and what are you doing here?" she asked in a tough-girl voice at odds with her appearance.

She had moxie, he had to give her that. She was alone in a seedy office building with a stranger, but she seemed completely unintimidated. It was probably because she knew karate. She shifted and her trench coat parted, giving him a glimpse of long, luscious legs. Kickboxing, he corrected. With those gams, she was probably an expert kickboxer.

"I'm embarking on a life of crime—"

"Exactly what I thought," she interrupted, thrusting the lipstick at the air like it was a sword and she was giving him a warning. He stifled a smile.

"—fighting," he finished. "Crime fighting. Not crime."

"And why should I believe that? How do I know you haven't offed Jake and stashed him somewhere?"

"Because I'm his brother," he said and held out a hand. "Sam Creighton's the name."

"Jake's brother?" She gaped at him, her mouth a perfect O as she ran a calculating gaze over him. Considering how much he liked her eyes on him, he was eager to feel her hand in his, but she pointedly ignored it. Finally, he dropped his hand.

"Jake's brother wouldn't need to break into his office," she said. "Let's see some ID."

She might not be a cop, but she had the lingo down. He handed over his credit card, but she looked so dubious that he pulled his wallet out of his back pocket and flipped it open, removing his driver's license.

"Eeeouwww," she exclaimed as she examined the license. "If this is you, it's a *really* bad photo."

He leaned over and took a look. "I do look like Rocky Raccoon, don't I? Wonder how they get that black eye effect?"

"Hey, back up, buster." The tough-girl voice was back, which wasn't so much intimidating him as it was turning him on. So, after all these years, he understood why some men stayed home to watch *Xena, Warrior Princess.*

She looked back and forth between Sam and the driver's license, as though deciding whether or not to believe him. Her eyes were the color of grass in the summertime, rimmed by a deeper green and dotted with gold. They couldn't have been more bewitching.

"If you're Jake's brother," she asked, giving him back the license, "how come you're breaking into his office?"

"You've heard of kleptomania, right?" he asked, deciding to have a little fun. "I have breaktomania."

"Breaktomania?"

"The obsessive need to break into locked places."

She narrowed her pretty eyes. "Then how come you haven't managed it?"

She had him there, especially if she'd spent any time at all watching him fumble with the credit card. He shrugged. Time to swallow some pride. "Because Jake forgot to leave me a key."

Evidently, that answer convinced her he was telling the truth. "Mallory Jamison," she said, holding out her hand. Finally, at long last, he got to touch her.

The connection was electrifying, like a bolt of lightning in a clear blue sky. A sizzle went up his arm and through his body, traveling to all kinds of interesting places. He breathed in her essence. She smelled like sunshine and orange blossoms, scents that somehow suited her.

He smiled at her long and slow, noting she was tall enough that he didn't have to bend too far to look into her eyes. Hers widened, as though she felt the sizzle, too.

She pulled her warm hand out of his grasp much too soon. His instinct was to grab it back but he squelched it. He didn't want her to point that lethal lipstick at him again.

"Jake probably didn't think you would need a key," she said, snatching the credit card out of his hand. She stepped in front of him and inserted the card once again in the skinny space beside the unyielding door. "All you do is give the card a little jiggle. Like this."

The latch immediately popped, and the door swung open. A satisfied smile graced her painted red lips when she turned and held the credit card out to him.

"I thought all good private eyes knew how to do that."

"I'm in the early stages of breaktomania." Sam repocketed the card. "I have the urge to break in, but I haven't figured out how to do it yet."

"You are a private eye, aren't you?"

"Oh, sure," Sam said. Granted, he was angry at his brother for getting him into this situation but he didn't want to scare away a potential client. Jake was bound to come home soon. From the looks of things, he desperately needed some business. "Just call me Sherlock Creighton."

She walked deeper into the office, putting distance between them as she pulled off her coat. "So, Sherlock, where's Jake?"

"He left a note saying…"

Her coat was completely off now, making him completely forget what he'd been about to say. Her curvaceous figure was squeezed into a cherry-red dress a couple sizes too small and more than a couple inches too short. Her legs, bare but for the bobby socks, seemed to go on forever.

But it wasn't the kind of dress meant for seduction. Instead, it was a child's dress, with a white collar and matching belt. Come to think of it, nothing about her computed. From the curly red wig to the faux freckles to the patent leather shoes.

"Go on," she said, waving a hand in a circular motion. He tried, but he still couldn't speak. A "wow" was lodged in his throat. "You were telling me about that note that you have in your hand—the one Jake left. What does it say?"

His voicebox finally managed a rusty-sounding question. "What did who say?"

"Not who. What. The note." She put her hands on her hips. The motion emphasized how nicely that too-tight dress outlined her generous curves. "What did the note say?"

"Wow," he said, the word finally making its escape.

"Wow?" Her brows shot up. "Jake wrote you a note that said wow?"

"No. Of course not," Sam said, valiantly recovering some of his equilibrium. How best to explain his verbal slip? "It said 'How.' As in, 'How the hell you doin', Sam?'"

"Very friendly," she commented, leaning against a wall and crossing one long leg over the other. She was killing him here. "But did it say anything informative? Like where he is?"

With a concerted effort, Sam switched his focal point from her legs to her face. What had that note said? "He didn't say where he was going," Sam finally answered triumphantly, because he'd managed to answer at all. "He only said that he'd gone and wants me to run the business until he comes back."

"Oh, no," she exclaimed.

Unaccountably, her comment stung. "Look. I'm no whiz at breaking and entering, but I'm sure I'd get the hang of it if I practiced."

He wasn't prepared for the way she rushed across the room and laid a hand on his arm. Or for the way he felt heat even through the leather.

"You've got to help me find him. You've just got to."

He tried not to get lost in the green depths of her eyes and made his lips form words. "First, I think you'd better tell me who you are."

"I already told you. I'm Mallory Jamison," she said, as though that explained everything.

"Forgive me for saying so..." He cleared his throat, and commanded his body to stop reacting to her touch. It didn't work. "But that's an awfully... unusual...getup you're wearing, Mallory."

Her hand flew to her red wig. Then she gave an honest-to-goodness giggle. "I can't believe it. I was in such a hurry to get here I forgot I was wearing this."

"*Why* are you wearing that?"

She did a curtsy, tilted her head and smiled. "I'm Little Orphan Annie."

"You don't look like any Orphan Annie I've ever seen," he said. If Daddy Warbucks got a load of her, he'd faint dead away.

"Funny you should say that," Mallory exclaimed, shaking her head. "That's exactly what my client said."

"Your client?" All sorts of thoughts ran through his mind, making him reluctant to voice his next question. "What kind of business are you in?"

"It's a party-gram business," Mallory said. "Clients hire us to dress up as characters and deliver upbeat messages for birthdays, anniversaries, bar mitzvahs, you name it."

"This is your business?"

"Oh, no. This isn't my kind of thing. It's my sister Lenora's business. I've just been helping her out since I got out of college."

"And when was that?"

She frowned as she mentally added up the years. The total seemed to surprise her. "Three years ago."

"If it isn't your thing, why don't you quit and do something else?"

"Oh, but I couldn't. Not until the business starts doing better. My sister needs me. Take today. Lenora's taking some time off, so I went to a little girl's birthday party as Little Orphan Annie and sang 'On the Good Ship Lollipop.'"

She looked so proud of herself, he hated to disappoint her. But somebody had to tell her. "It was before my time, but that's Shirley Temple's song. I'm pretty sure Annie sings 'Tomorrow.'"

"Oh, no," Mallory exclaimed, bringing her hands to her cheeks. She even had pretty hands. Slim and long-fingered. "No wonder the mother was so displeased." She tapped one of those long fingers against the side of her mouth. "Although the father seemed to like me. He watched my performance so closely, he didn't seem to notice the curious way his wife kept elbowing him in the ribs."

"I'll bet," Sam said.

"I've never been Annie before. The last time somebody requested her, my sister played the part."

"Let me guess." He considered her intently. "Your sister's a lot, uh, smaller than you are."

"She's a pixie," Mallory said. "You should see the trouble I had fitting into her dress. I could barely zipper it. The whole time I was tap-dancing, I thought it was going to rip."

"You tap-danced?"

"Of course I did. Everyone knows Annie tap-dances."

"Sorry to tell you this, but that's Shirley, too."

"Oh, no."

"Oh, yes."

"Oh, great." Mallory rolled her eyes. "That does it. I've got to find Jake."

"I already told you. He didn't say where he was going," Sam said as renewed impatience at his brother flared up in him. He'd put a downpayment on the perfect boat, but that wouldn't hold it for long. "He didn't say when he'd be back, either."

She grimaced and clutched at her wig. Something that resembled panic flashed in her eyes.

"I have to find him right away. I can't afford to wait," she moaned, then snapped her fingers. The panic had turned to speculation. "You said you were a private detective, right?"

"I believe *you* said that."

"But aren't you going to run the business while Jake's gone?"

"Well, yeah," Sam said, nodding slowly.

"Then I can hire you to find him for me," she finished.

"Hire me? You want to hire me to find my own brother?"

"Why not? Neither of us knows where he is, and I need to find him. It makes perfect sense that I should hire you."

"It doesn't make sense to me," Sam said, shaking his head. Especially to his rampaging hormones. Nothing had made much sense since he'd turned around and seen her lipstick being pointed in his direction.

"Don't tell me you can't use the business, because I won't believe it." Mallory made a sweeping motion with her hand. "Look at this place. A lot of potential clients wouldn't even venture into this part of town."

She had him there. It was no use denying that his

brother's fledgling agency was having trouble attracting clients.

"That's true, but—"

"I have money. Not lots. But some."

"I don't doubt that you do, but it just seems strange. Not only is he my brother, but he owns this agency."

Mallory opened her mouth to speak, but apparently thought better of it because no sound came out. She clamped her lips shut and regarded him with an intensity that made his pulse beat faster. She looked as though she was trying to figure out a puzzle, and he was one of the pieces.

"Exactly how much do you know about what your brother's been doing lately?" she asked.

He frowned. Somehow, that wasn't the question he'd expected. He cast his mind back to the last time he'd seen his brother and came up with a Christmas weekend at his parents' winter home in Florida. But not this past Christmas. It had been the Christmas before that.

"I don't keep tabs on him. Jake's a grown man. He doesn't keep me posted on what he's doing." Something occurred to Sam. Something he'd rather not consider. "Why? Should I know about you?"

"Uh-huh." Mallory stood up taller, and the dress inched up higher on her luscious legs. "I'm Jake's fiancée. That's why I want to find him."

2

"HIS FIANCÉE?" SAM STARED in shock at Mallory. He hadn't known that Jake had a fiancée.

Finding out that his brother was going to marry this woman, who sent his blood rushing to all kinds of unwise places, was almost too much to process. "Since when does Jake have a fiancée?"

"Since six months ago." As if sensing he was staring at her bare ring finger, she rubbed the empty space. "We haven't gotten around to getting the ring yet, but that doesn't mean we're not perfect for each other. We knew it the first night we met. It only took him a week to ask me to marry him."

"Oh, really." Sam rubbed his forehead. The long engagement sounded like his brother. The quick popping of the question didn't. Sam didn't remember Jake as being so rash. He liked to take his time and think things through.

"Aren't you going to ask why I want to find him?"

That was the logical follow-up question, but Sam had such an aversion into others prying into his affairs that he tried his darnedest not to stick his nose into theirs. He wondered if private eyes could operate on a need-to-know basis. He opened his mouth to speak.

"It doesn't matter why you want to find him. We're the outfit for the job." The voice making the declaration was slightly breathless, scratchy with age and definitely not Sam's. He turned to see an elderly woman with hair whiter than the snow falling on Philadelphia standing in the open doorway. She was so small he doubted she topped five feet.

"Who are you?" he asked.

"The young whippersnapper wants to know who I am," she muttered, moving to an empty desk across the office with a spryness that defied her age. She dug into an oversize black purse and pulled out a photo of two impish-looking boys, a stack of novels and a paperweight in the shape of a spy glass. "I'm Ida Lee Scoggins, the secretary for Jake Creighton Investigations, that's who I am."

"Since when?" Sam asked as Ida Lee arranged her possessions on the desk and flopped into the seat. She was so tiny she had to raise her elbows to rest them on the desk.

"Today's my first day, and I'm rarin' to get going." She rubbed her hands together. "No need to fill me in. I heard it all. A missing person. A mysterious dame. A crackerjack case. Woo-wee. Let's get to work, Jake."

"Pssst," Mallory said, drawing the old lady's attention. "Jake's the one who's missing. That's his brother Sam. Sam's running the agency until Jake gets back."

"Fine with me. I get along well with all my bosses. Says so on my résumé." She dug in the immense black purse again. "Wanna see it?"

"No, I don't want to see your résumé," Sam said. Judging by the state of Jake's office, he was pretty sure his brother couldn't afford a secretary. "I want to know why, if Jake hired you, you don't know what he looks like."

Ida Lee screwed up her wrinkled face and scratched her nose. "My eyesight's not so good," she said finally.

Sam suspected there was nothing wrong with Ida Lee's eyesight, but darned if he could prove it.

He looked back at Mallory in time to see her fiddling with her wig. She pulled it off and glorious dark curls tumbled free. Immediately, his fingers itched to touch her hair. His brother's fiancée's hair. Hell. Ida Lee, he could deal with later. For now, he had to find some way to control his physical reaction to his brother's girl. Either that, or he was going to take her into his arms and kiss her.

"What you waiting for?" Ida Lee asked in her gravely voice.

"Excuse me?" he said, wondering why Ida Lee was advocating that he kiss Mallory. With a gnarled finger she tapped the tape recorder that had magically appeared on her desk.

"I got the tape running. You gonna ask the dame when was the last time she saw your brother alive or what?"

"Jake's not dead, Ida Lee," Mallory said. "He's running scared."

"The mob's after him, isn't it?" Ida Lee sounded excited. "He's afraid if they catch him, they're gonna put some concrete overshoes on him and toss him in the Schuylkill River, right?"

"He's not running from the mob." Mallory's face crumbled dramatically. "He's running from me."

Sam had been so fixated on the delectable way Mallory looked without the wig that he couldn't speak. Now he again took in the voluptuous body stuffed into a dress several sizes too small and the beautiful face alive with misery and he couldn't keep from speaking.

"Why would he run away from you?" he blurted out, forgetting about his need-to-know policy.

"He says he needs time to rethink the engagement, but I'm afraid the thought of getting married is scaring him. Anyone who's seen th... I mean us, together knows we're perfect for each other. I need to make him see how wrong he is to be frightened of true love before it's too late."

Jeez, Sam thought. This was getting worse by the minute. Not only was he developing a rapidly heating case of the hots for his brother's fiancée, but she was desperately in love with his brother. Not good. He forced himself to think rationally about what she'd just said.

"If your love is as true as you say it is, it'll survive. Maybe you should let him have that time to think."

"No," Mallory protested. "Thinking could ruin everything. When it comes to love, you don't think. You feel."

She tossed her head, shaking out her long, dark curls. Her breasts strained against the bodice of her tight red dress. A ball of heat formed in his belly and uncurled, whipping its tendrils out to what felt like every part of his body.

Once again, he was speechless, but the ringing of the telephone saved him from having to make a reply. He crossed the office and pounced on the receiver before Ida Lee could pick it up.

"Hey, that's my job," she growled.

"Jake Creighton Investigations," he said, suffering her glare. Maybe he should have let her pick up the phone, but with a voice like hers, she'd scare clients away.

"Sam, it's me." It was Jake, his missing brother. "Boy, am I glad you're there."

Relief that Jake was safe flooded Sam, but it was quickly replaced by anger. "You should be glad. If I was where you are, you wouldn't be standing right now. How could you do this to me?"

"I know, I know. I should have left a key, but sounds like you got into the office just fine. The one to my town house is in the top desk drawer."

"That's not what I meant, and you know it."

"Aw, Sam, don't be angry. I wouldn't have called you if I had anyone else to turn to. But I couldn't just shut down the business."

"Then why leave at all?"

"It's...complicated. I just can't be there right now."

"Sam?" Mallory crossed the office to stand within a few feet of him. "Who's that on the phone?"

"Nobody important," Sam told Mallory, covering the receiver. Blood ties ran thick. Even though his brother was acting like a rat, he wasn't ready to rat on the rat. Not yet, anyway.

"Is somebody there with you?" Jake asked.

"Yeah." Sam turned his back and whispered into the receiver, low enough that Mallory couldn't hear. "Your fiancée."

"My fiancée?" Panic flared in his brother's voice. "Whatever you do, don't tell her where I am."

"I don't know where you are," Sam said, exasperated.

"Believe me, it's better that way. Then I won't have

to worry about you slipping and telling her. Listen, I've gotta go.''

''Go? You can't go. I need to get back to Florida and finalize the deal on my boat. Besides, I've got problems here, not to mention a case.''

''A case? We got a case? Take it.''

''But I haven't told you what the case is yet.''

''Doesn't matter. I need the money,'' Jake said. ''I know you haven't done a case before, but I have faith in you.''

''Flattery's not going to work. You get your butt back here. I'm not—''

''The phone line's breaking up, bud,'' Jake interrupted before Sam heard what sounded like brother-generated static. ''Listen, I gotta go. I'll call in a couple of days.''

The phone line went dead, leaving Sam staring at the receiver.

''He hung up on me,'' he said, not quite believing it. Granted, with their four-year age difference, he and Jake had never been close. But his brother had been the kind of kid who laid out his underwear the night before he put them on. This newfound irresponsibility came as a shock.

''Who hung up?'' Ida Lee asked.

''Jake.''

''The boss?'' She sounded relieved, calling to mind one more thing Sam hadn't discussed with his brother. Namely, if he'd hired an octogenarian secretary. ''So the mob let him call?''

The mob? Sam hadn't thought of that. Maybe Jake had been forced to make the call, except…except that made no sense. ''The mob's not like the cops,'' he told Ida Lee. ''They don't give you one phone call.''

"That was Jake?" Mallory's voice rose an octave, and she thumped him on the arm. "Why didn't you tell me that was Jake? Did he say where he was?"

Sam shook his head. "He didn't say much of anything. Except that I should take the case."

"My case?"

"Yeah, but he didn't know you were the client."

"Doesn't matter," Ida Lee cut in. "The boss says you should take the case, you have to take it."

"Jake's not here, so I'm the boss," Sam said. "And the boss does what the boss wants to do."

"Please say that doesn't mean you won't take my case," Mallory pleaded. The desperation that surrounded her words was as tangible as smoke.

Hell. He didn't want to be in the middle of his brother's relationship, but Jake had put him there. And darn if he didn't understand Mallory's side of it. Jake was her fiancé, after all. Either he wanted to marry her or he didn't. His brother should be man enough to discuss either decision with her face to face.

"I'll take the case," he said. The moment the words were out, he knew he was going to regret them. That is until she threw her arms around his neck and she pressed her soft body against his. Oh, brother. His pulse beat heavily in his throat, and he amended his thought. Sorry, brother.

Mallory drew herself from him way too soon, and Sam reminded himself she'd only embraced him because he'd agreed to find Jake. The man she loved.

"I'll need a retainer," he said. He didn't know much about being a detective, but he did know business.

Mallory rummaged through her purse, then raised those green, green eyes to his. "I'm a little short right now. It sure would help if you charged me by the hour.''

"Don't do it," Ida Lee warned.

"Why not?"

"Don't you read detective novels?" she asked, tapping the stack of books on her desk. "She'll stiff you for sure."

Considering the state of his body, Sam almost grimaced at Ida Lee's unfortunate choice of words. "I'll charge you by the hour," he told Mallory.

"You'll be sorry," Ida Lee said. "Beautiful dames who show up out of the blue can't be trusted."

"Neither can secretaries who can't identify their boss."

That shut her up, but Sam doubted it'd be for long. "Don't worry," he told Mallory. "I'll find my brother."

"Well?" She stared at him with her eyebrows raised, obviously waiting for him to do something.

"Well what?"

"Aren't you going to do a star-sixty-nine?"

"Of course I am," Sam said, unwilling to admit he hadn't thought of it himself.

He punched in star-sixty-nine, found the number from where the last call was made and dialed it. After a few rings, someone picked up the receiver. Music and loud conversation blared in the background as a gruff voice came over the line.

"House of the Seven Veils."

The voice definitely didn't belong to Jake, but that didn't mean his brother wasn't nearby. "Hello. Can you tell me if there's a Jake Creighton there?"

"Could be," the voice said. "We got a lot of men here."

"Can you ask around?"

"You want to know, come down here yourself."

"Where's here?"

The voice rattled off an address that Jake scribbled down, then the dial tone sounded in his ear.

"Well," Mallory said expectantly. "Where's Jake?"

"House of the Seven Veils."

Ida Lee let out a loud whoop. "Oh my, oh my. Can I pick me out a wild boss or what? I just knew this job was going to be exciting. The Seven Veils! Can you imagine that?"

"Exactly what kind of a place is the Seven Veils?" Sam asked Ida Lee, but his attention was on Mallory. Her lungs filled, almost bursting the seams of her dress, as she drew in a deep breath. She seemed to be bracing herself for the answer.

Ida Lee grinned, hardly able to contain her excitement. "It's one of those nekkid-lady places. You know, a strip joint."

LENORA WAS GOING TO kill her.

No, scratch that. Lenora would think death was too good for her. Her big sister would probably chase Mallory around the room with one of her high-heeled pumps, intent on tattooing her. It would be a new brand of torture. Call it pure heel hell.

Not only had Lenora commanded Mallory to stay out of her business, but she'd specifically forbidden her from playing Cupid by trying to talk Jake out of rethinking their engagement.

Yet here Mallory was, driving to a strip club with Jake's hunky brother, the man she was paying to hunt

Jake down. What's more, she was masquerading as the fiancée of the man her sister loved.

Granted, it sounded bad. But it made perfect sense.

If Mallory had told Sam the truth about who she was, one of two things would have happened.

Either he would have refused to take the case outright, seeing as she was the sister of the fiancée rather than the fiancée herself. Or he would have gone straight to Lenora to find out where his brother might have gone.

Lenora wasn't packing up her broken heart and leaving for her refuge at their parents' house in Harrisburg until tomorrow. If Jake spoke to her before then, she'd know that Mallory had once again meddled into her affairs. Not only would her sister get angry, but she'd call off the search.

Mallory couldn't let that happen. Making sure Jake recognized that he and Lenora were in the throes of true love was of the utmost importance. But there was the ripple effect to think about, too.

If they didn't get back together, Lenora would be so heartbroken she might leave Lenora's Party-Grams in Mallory's hands indefinitely.

Considering how Mallory had botched her first solo performance, that would be bad. Very, very bad. Especially because Lenora loved the wretched business almost as much as she loved her fiancé. And Mallory didn't love it at all.

No. Mallory's only choice had been to utter the little white lie about being engaged to Jake. She just needed to make sure Lenora didn't find out about it.

"When we get to the club, wait for me in the car." Sam drummed his fingers on the dashboard and sent her a worried look. She knew he wouldn't have agreed to her coming along at all if she hadn't been the one with the transportation. "Mallory, I want you to promise."

She took her left hand from the wheel, slipped it under her left hip and crossed her fingers. It was the same thing she'd done before telling Sam she was his brother's fiancée.

"Sure thing," she mumbled.

He seemed to relax after that, and she had to fight the urge to sneak a peek at him. Not that she wasn't sure what she'd see. Her mind had already taken a snapshot and processed the film.

He was quite a head turner, this brother of Jake's. And he was Jake's brother. If the resemblance hadn't been quite so strong, she wouldn't have let him in Jake's office. Jake was a looker, but Sam was what the laboratory came up with when it went back to the drawing board.

The new, improved version.

He was taller and leaner than Jake, his hair a few shades darker so that it was nearly the color of his inky-black jacket. Jake appeared smoothly shaven even at midnight, but Sam had a five o'clock shadow that gave him a rakishly sexy air. Jake's blue eyes were nice, but Sam's were a richer, darker shade—like the water in the deepest part of the ocean.

If desperation hadn't driven her, she'd never have told a hunk like him that she was engaged. To his brother, no less. Darn.

She refocused her attention on the road, which was covered with a fine mist of snow. Considering that they were heading into a shadier part of town than where Jake's office was located, Mallory didn't mind the frosty stuff. It whitewashed the grime.

A low-slung building that had obviously once been a warehouse was situated back from the road. A neon sign above the door cast a garish red shadow on the snow. Bare-Naked Nudes, it proclaimed.

The House of the Seven Veils.

Mallory maneuvered the car into a parking lot and listened to the tires crunch gravel and snow. The front door of the club flung open while she was parking the car. Two men staggered out, their arms encircling each other as they sang an off-key tune and wove their way to an SUV with the rear end bashed in.

"I shouldn't have let you talk me into bringing you here," Sam muttered under his breath when she shut off the ignition.

"You didn't bring me here," she pointed out. "I brought you here."

"That doesn't mean you should be here." The overhead lights in the parking lot were so dim, his hair blended into the darkness, leaving only his face visible. It was a good face. Strong and vulnerable at the same time. His brows creased as a muscle worked in his square jaw. "Lock the doors, and just *stay in the car* until I get back. I'll be as quick as I can."

She smiled at him as the cold night seemed somehow warmer. She wasn't a helpless female who fainted at the first sign of trouble, but his concern touched her. She reached out, her fingers coming to rest just above his jaw. His skin was bristly and warm. Very warm.

"Has anybody ever told you that you're sweet when you're worried?" she whispered and watched his lips part. He had a sexy mouth, the lips wide and curving. The air in the car had cooled when she shut off the ignition, and she could see his breath. Her hand rotated, wanting to feel his breath on her fingers, wanting to touch his lips. Before she reached his mouth, he jerked backward. Her hand fell away.

"Just stay here," he repeated, his voice less steady than it had been a minute ago. Then he was out of the car, striding toward the entrance of the strip club.

Mallory shook her head from side to side. "Stupid, stupid, stupid," she said aloud. "You must not caress the brother of your fake fiancé."

She thought for a moment, and her hands dropped from the wheel. She tapped the side of her face with a forefinger and bit her lip.

"Of course," she continued slowly, "I'm not *really* Jake's fiancée, so touching his brother isn't *really* wrong."

Except Sam thought it was. The stricken expression that had descended over his face when she'd touched him came back to her. It didn't take a genius to recognize it as guilt.

"Darn," she said, and repeated her new mantra. "You must not caress the brother of your fake fiancé."

She filled her lungs with air, vowing to stick to her resolve at least until they found Jake and got this whole mess straightened out. Then she got out of the car.

Just because she wasn't going to caress Sam didn't mean she was going to listen to him.

What guarantee did she have that Jake wouldn't disappear out the back door once Sam found him? He was a man on the run from commitment, and it was her duty to show him the error of his ways. Besides, it was freezing outside.

She gingerly made her way across the parking lot, slipping and sliding on patent-leather shoes that weren't made for traipsing in the snow. She was almost to the entrance when a figure materialized at her side, the white of her hair blending with the snow so her small, pointed face appeared magnified.

"I'll case the joint for you and cover the back exit," Ida Lee said conversationally as she fell into step with her, as though her appearing out of the blue in the parking lot of a strip joint wasn't really, really odd. "If I see Jake, I'll pounce."

"But you don't know what he looks like," Mallory reminded her.

"Details, details. He looks like his brother, right? I'm good at family resemblances. Not to mention well versed in the art of private investigation."

Mallory narrowed her eyes. "How'd you get here anyway?"

Ida Lee snapped her fingers. "Darn. If only I'd thought of coming with you, I wouldn't have had to take a cab."

"Did Sam say you could come?"

"He didn't say I couldn't," Ida Lee shot back. She reached into her black bag and thrust an object at Mallory. "Here. You'll need this radio communication device."

"It looks like a child's walkie-talkie." Mallory turned it over in her hands. "Hey, isn't this a picture of Barney the Dinosaur?" A suspicion formed in Mallory's mind. "Did you get this out of your grandchild's toy chest?"

"Can't hear you." Ida Lee cupped her hand to her ear, as though her hearing was as bad as she claimed her eyesight was. Mallory was about to argue the fact, but they'd reached the front door. It swung open and loud music blasted them, as did warm air and a blue-gray haze of cigarette smoke.

Mallory walked inside, followed by Ida Lee. Holding the door open was an unsmiling behemoth she assumed was the bouncer. He was at least six feet five, with a granite jaw and itty-bitty eyes that darted to and fro. Looking for trouble, she assumed.

Ida Lee tugged at his sleeve, and his tiny eyes traveled downward from their great height to focus on her. "You got to tell these people to stop smoking so much," she growled. "It's like the inside of a pipe in here."

He brought his left hand to his mouth. In it was a cigarette. He inhaled the smoke deeply into his lungs and then blew a blue stream into her face.

Ida Lee glowered at him. Then she lifted her foot, which was encased in a heavy boot, and brought it down full force on his instep.

"Ow," he yelled, tears filling his beady eyes.

"That'll teach you to respect your elders," Ida Lee said. She stood on tiptoe and shouted into Mallory's ear. "I'm going to go blend in."

In only a few moments, she'd disappeared into the crowd, leaving Mallory alone with the whimpering behemoth. She walked away from him. Fast. Ten steps later, she stopped, her eyes riveted on the woman performing on stage.

The lower half of her was artfully covered by a blue veil, but that wasn't the part of her body commanding Mallory's attention. Dangling yellow tassels jiggled as the dancer gyrated and whirled, but her incredible chest didn't move.

Mallory took a look at her own, teensy-by-comparison, attributes, then brought her gaze back to the stage. Still, the tassels jiggled. Still, nothing else did.

"No way are *those* real," she said. From the avid looks on the men's faces surrounding the stage, a comment like that might have incited a riot. But Mallory didn't have to worry. Nobody was paying attention to her.

"What do you mean, you needed to get out? Aren't I woman enough for you?"

The voice was so shrill, it rose above the pulsating music, like a car alarm sounding on a busy street. A few feet from Mallory, a slight woman with frizzy blond hair pointed an accusing finger at a big, tall man. His lower lip trembled, and his Adam's apple bobbed. Her attention snagged, Mallory moved closer to the couple so she could better tell what was going on.

"Aw, honey. I'm sorry," the large man said so softly that Mallory had to strain to hear. "You know it's you that I love."

"Then what you doin' here?" The woman raised a huge, black purse over her head. Like Ida Lee's, the purse looked like it weighed a good twenty pounds. Mallory wondered if the handbag section at Macy's department store was having a big-bag sale.

"Not the purse, honey," the man pleaded, his beefy hands held out in front of him. "Please, not the purse."

His plea didn't make a dent. With her face contorted in rage, the blonde swung. The purse crashed through the man's hands and landed a solid blow on his chest.

"Ow, that hurt," he cried.

"It'd hurt more if I left you, Shea Cooper." She punctuated her comment by hauling her purse once again over her shoulder, preparing to whack him again.

That did it for Mallory. Didn't the blonde see that

her man was hurting, physically and emotionally? That he loved her despite her masochistic tendencies with the purse? She moved quickly, putting herself between the couple.

"The basis of any good relationship is forgiveness." Mallory shouted to be heard above the music. "You heard Shea. He apologized. You should forgive him."

"Who in tarnation are you?" The woman took a step forward. Her eyes glittered dangerously. "Are you here with my man? Is that how you know his name?"

"Why, no. I heard you call him Shea. I—"

"How dare you come between us, with your fancy makeup and your big hair..."

Mallory patted down her hair, insulted to the core. It had always been curly, yes, but she wouldn't call it big. Long, yes. Unruly, maybe. But not big.

"...and try to tell me how to run my life."

The blonde made a sharp backward movement with the arm that held the purse, which to Mallory took on the proportions of one of those big, black wrecking balls that destroyed concrete and mortar.

Uh-oh. The blonde was too far gone to realize Mallory was only trying to help. And everyone knew that hell hath no fury like a woman who thought another female was out to snatch her man.

The blonde was no longer intent on beating up poor Shea. Instead, she was going to pummel Mallory.

3

THE HOUSE OF THE Seven Veils was so smokey that Sam wished a strong wind would blow through the place so he could better see the patrons. Considering the dim lighting, even a typhoon might not do the trick. Only the stage was illuminated, with lights streaming down on the strippers who brought droves of customers into these kinds of clubs.

Sam had never been one of those customers. He thought a woman with a little mystery was sexier than one who let it all hang out. Besides, the strippers didn't have anything he hadn't seen before.

He glanced toward the stage to confirm his thought, then did a double take. This stripper had *more* than he'd ever seen before. Her proportions were more out of whack than a Barbie doll's. He wouldn't be surprised if she toppled over under the tremendous weight of her chest.

Even as he gaped at her, beholding the rare sight, he found himself thinking that he preferred women who were more realistically endowed. Like Mallory. Inside that tight red dress of hers, he'd bet her rounded breasts were soft but firm.

He looked away from the stripper and her stupendous chest and refocused his search for his brother. He needed to get control of this crazy pull Mallory had on him. And fast.

When Mallory had touched his face and gazed into his eyes in the car, his body had started to overheat. A few more seconds shut away in that dark intimacy with her, and he would have hauled her into his arms and kissed her senseless. He'd mustered the will to move away, but now he was fantasizing about her breasts. His brother's fiancée's breasts.

Granted, he was angry at Jake for getting him into this situation, but he was still his brother. And a loyal brother didn't have hot sexual fantasies about his brother's fiancée.

The sooner he found Jake and got the heck out of Dodge, the better. Then he could sail into the sunset on that sleek catamaran he had waiting for him in Florida, and his brother and Mallory could get back together. Unless, of course, Sam found a way to sabotage the getting-back-together part and talked Mallory into taking a sail with him.

Oh, great. Now he was fantasizing about being the instrument of destruction in what Mallory called true love. He was slime. No, worse than slime. He was muck. The real honest-to-goodness kind that lined the bottom of trash heaps.

The vibrating, atonal music that had passed for a song ended, which allowed him to clearly hear one woman accuse another of playing around with her man. Sam immediately sympathized with the transgressor. He wasn't playing around with Mallory, but he sure wanted to.

He turned toward the voices, curious to get a look at the players. A feisty blonde with wild hair and even wilder eyes was shooting murderous looks at a taller, dark-haired woman with long, curly hair. A dark-haired woman in a trench coat.

Hell. The woman was Mallory.

The crazed blonde had her purse raised overhead. Sam shot into action, shouldering his way through the crowd. He reached the fracas in just enough time to throw himself between Mallory and the avenging blonde.

"The purse!" yelled the chunky guy standing behind Mallory. "Watch out for the purse!"

Thwack!

Said purse hit Sam a heavy blow on the shoulder, sending him reeling. That was no ordinary purse she was brandishing. It had to be weighed down by bricks, either that, or slabs of cement. For a second, he saw stars. Then soft hands steadied him, and the wonderful scent of sunshine and orange blossoms enveloped him. Mallory's scent.

"Are you all right, Sam?" she asked, her voice tinged with anxiety. He saw two of her, blinked until she morphed into one, nodded, then straightened. No purse was going to be the undoing of Sam Creighton. Even if it did contain bricks.

"Get outta my way and lemme at that hussy," the woman with the weapon yelled as a battle cry. All she was missing was war paint. "No one messes with my man and gets away with it."

Sam rubbed his shoulder and kept his body between the woman and Mallory. No way was he moving. Mallory weighed a good fifty pounds less than he did. She might not survive a blow from The Purse.

"She's not with your man." Judging by the sneer on the blonde's face, she didn't believe him. Sam had promised himself mere minutes ago to keep his hands off Mallory, but now he had no choice but to touch her. He slung an arm over her shoulder, pulling her soft body against his. "She's with me."

"You expect me to believe—"

"Believe this," Sam said, turning Mallory's chin with two fingers. He could tell the instant she figured out what he was going to do. Her eyes filled with wonder and her lips parted in surprise. It was a double dose of temptation he would have been powerless to resist even if the avenging blonde had not been watching.

He brought his mouth down on the soft sweetness of hers, claiming her lips in a swift, hard kiss that packed even more punch than the crazed blonde's purse. Especially so because Mallory was kissing him back. Music was playing again, and his heart mimicked the sound of the drums, thumping way too quickly in his chest. His stomach knotted, his body hardened, his soul soared. Then his conscience kicked in, and he drew back.

He stared into Mallory's confused eyes, not even sparing a glance to find out if the blonde believed their act. If it had been an act at all. It sure didn't feel like one.

"Honey, it's true," he heard the guy with the beer belly and the soft voice say. "I don't want nobody but you."

The double negatives notwithstanding, Sam could have said the same thing about Mallory. His brother's fiancée. Hell.

He tore his guilty gaze from Mallory. He needed another whack to knock some sense into him. He should pay the blonde to thump him one more time with her purse, is what he should do.

"Hey, you." The behemoth who'd been standing

guard by the door tramped up to Sam, his torso so thick that his arms stuck out from his sides at forty-five degree angles. He jerked a thumb the size of most people's wrists at the nutty blonde, who was preparing to drag her man out of the club by his shirttail. "You botherin' that woman?"

"Bothering her?" Mallory stepped between Sam and the bouncer before Sam had a chance to answer. "She smacked him with her purse. Where were you when that was happening?"

"Watchin'," the behemoth said unapologetically. "I thought she was gonna smack you."

"Then why didn't you stop her? You're a bouncer. Why didn't you bounce her?"

"Me, I only bounce men," the man said. "Everybody likes to see a coupla females in a catfight."

"What kind of bouncer are you?" Mallory erupted, advancing on the bouncer and poking him in the chest with her forefinger. "I bet the owner of this place would like to hear how you fell down on the job. Where is he? I demand to talk to him."

A red flush started on the bouncer's thick neck and climbed slowly northward. Sam grabbed Mallory's index finger, removing it from the man's massive chest. "She's just kidding."

"I am not kidding." Mallory shot Sam an indignant glare. "I—"

"She's a practical jokester. Can't believe a word she says," Sam interrupted, turning Mallory forcefully by the shoulders.

Sam quickly ushered Mallory away from the bouncer before she could reply. "I can't believe you did that," she sputtered.

"Did you want to get us thrown out of here?"

"He wouldn't have done that to us. He didn't do it to Ida Lee," she said. Sam was about to ask what Ida Lee had to do with anything when she continued, "Besides, his boss would want to know he thinks it's fun to watch the customers beat up on each other."

"We're talking about a man who owns a strip club. He probably thinks combat is good for business. I can almost hear him." He imitated the style of a vendor selling concessions at a ball park. "Catfight here. Catfight here. See your catfight here."

"I still think the owner should be told," Mallory said stubbornly.

"Yeah, well, I think you should have stayed in the car. And I definitely think you shouldn't have gotten between that blonde and the guy she's with. What were you thinking?"

"I was thinking the two of them shouldn't risk everything they have together because of a silly misunderstanding."

"So you knew them?" Sam asked as her actions began to make a little more sense.

"Never saw them before in my life."

"Then why…" Words failed him.

She put her hands on her hips and shook her head. "Do you honestly think I should have stood by and done nothing when I thought I could help?"

"Well, yeah," Sam said.

"Well, I couldn't. Why do you think I followed you in here instead of staying in the car?"

"Because you're contrary," Sam answered, scowling.

"I am not!"

"I rest my case."

"Oh, okay. Maybe I am contrary," she said, un-

expectedly surrendering the point. She did so with a
gracious smile that revealed an adorable dimple in her
left cheek. At least, he thought it was a dimple and
not one of the dots of red lipstick she hadn't washed
off yet. He had to stop himself from bending down
and exploring the spot with his mouth. What was it
about her that he couldn't resist?

"Ida Lee to the dame. Ida Lee to the dame."

The scratchy voice of Jake's octogenarian secretary
seemed to be coming out of Mallory's stomach, and
Sam saw why when she unclipped a walkie-talkie
from the pocket of her trench coat.

"Oh, I forgot to tell you. Ida Lee's here casing the
joint," Mallory said, and Sam wondered if things
could get any worse. She pressed in the transmitter
button on the walkie-talkie. "Mallory here."

"Who?" Ida Lee asked.

Mallory gave Sam a sidelong look and shrugged.
He caught a glimpse of a purple dinosaur on the
walkie-talkie. "I don't think Ida Lee knows my
name," she said, then pressed the transmitter button
again. "It's the dame. Over."

"Why didn't you say so in the first place?" Ida Lee
shot back. "Just checking in to say that the bird's still
out of the coop and nowhere in sight. Got one more
quadrant left to check, though. Over and out."

Mallory fastened the device back onto her trench
coat. "Ida Lee hasn't seen Jake. Have you?"

"No," Sam said. But since he'd spotted Mallory
scuffling with the blonde and her purse, he hadn't
looked anywhere but at her. "But I haven't finished
looking yet."

"I'll help you," she said, then fanned herself.

"Gee, it's as hot as Hades in here. No wonder those strippers shed their clothes so fast."

Before Sam could stop her, she'd shrugged out of her coat. His eyes popped. His heart stopped. His breathing quickened. Then his brain sounded a red alert. Mallory had taken her coat off at the worst possible time.

The strippers were between acts, which meant all eyes weren't on the stage. Most of them in the immediate vicinity focused on Mallory. An owner of one pair stared so hard Sam thought his eyes might pop out of their sockets.

"Mallory, put your coat back on." Sam tried to shield her with his body from the bug-eyed man. The ploy didn't work. It exposed her to a man on the opposite side of them. His gaping mouth was open so wide he could have caught flies—big ones.

"Why would I do a fool thing like that? It's got to be eighty degrees in here."

She shook out her hair as she talked, and it fell in glorious, dark spirals around her shoulders. With her tight red dress and curvy body, Sam thought she looked like a sex goddess, who had risen up from under the cover of her big, bulky coat. A wolf whistle came from somewhere nearby. Unfortunately, Sam wasn't the only one who looked at Mallory and thought about sex.

"Come on, Mallory. Put the coat back on," Sam urged. "Men are staring at you. That one over there is salivating."

She laughed. "Oh, come off it, Sam. They're only staring because I'm still dressed in costume. They've probably never seen a Little Orphan Annie as old as I am."

"I don't think that's—"

"Hey, shweetbuns." A man with a long-necked beer in one hand sidled up to them, interrupting what Sam had been about to say. He gave Mallory a lopsided leer and waved the beer. Some of it sloshed onto the floor. "When you gonna shtrut your shtuff?"

"Strut my stuff?" Mallory looked at him in confusion. "What stuff? I don't have any stuff."

Sam rolled his eyes. If Mallory had any more stuff, the police would make her get multiple concealed-weapon permits. The man pointed at the stage with his bottle. More beer spilled onto the floor.

"Sure you have shtuff," the man said. "When you gonna get up on shtage and show it?"

"On stage?" Mallory's eyes got so wide, Sam could see a ring of white all around the grassy green. It would have been comical if she weren't the focus of so much male attention. She turned those shocked eyes to Sam. "He thinks I'm a stripper," she squeaked, then turned back to the drunk. "I am *not* a stripper."

"Then why you dreshed like that?"

"I'm Little Orphan Annie, that's why."

The man threw back his head and whooped. "An orphan like you can come live with me anytime, shweetheart."

"That's going too far." Sam took a threatening step toward the man, and Mallory could only stare at him in wonder. His jaw hardened and his eyes turned steely. Sam was all set to defend her, for the second time since she'd stepped into the House of the Seven Veils. "The lady's no stripper. You owe her an apology."

"Hey, I didn't mean nothin' by it," the man

drawled, backing up. He raised both palms in a hands-off gesture, and his beer bottle crashed to the floor. ''I didn't know the shweetheart was your lady. Sorry, shweetheart. But it's not my fault you look like a shtripper.''

''I thought I told you—''

''Sam, let it go.'' Mallory put a restraining hand on his arm. His muscles were tense, telling her he'd been ready to slug the man. For her. ''I'll put my coat back on.''

Sam hesitated, and the man disappeared back into the crowd. Mallory shrugged back into her coat. The music started again and a veil-clad dancer pranced onto the stage. Just like that, the attention shifted from Mallory to the stage. Mallory's attention, however, was riveted on Sam.

Without giving a second thought as to what she was about to do, she closed the distance between them and kissed him on the cheek. It wasn't as heavenly as kissing him on the lips, but it was better than nothing.

''Thank you,'' she said. ''The way you defended me was really sweet.''

''Someone had to do it,'' Sam muttered, looking everywhere but at her eyes. ''I might even have to do it again if we don't get you out of here.''

''But we haven't finished searching yet,'' Mallory exclaimed. ''We can't leave until we find Jake.''

''Jake's not here.''

''But Jake has to be here. He made the call from here, didn't he? I have to find Jake.''

A cocktail waitress who'd been serving a nearby table turned and regarded them. She had blond hair teased into a virtual bees' nest, a cloud of heavy perfume and a skirt even shorter than the one Mallory wore under her coat. "You looking for a Jake? I maybe could help you out with that."

Sam gave the waitress a dubious look. "You're telling us you know Jake Creighton?"

The waitress cracked her gum and balanced a tray of drinks on her ample hips. "I dunno. Not many people 'round here use last names. But maybe I got some information."

She looked at them expectantly, then raised her palm. Sam sighed, then reached into his back pocket for his wallet.

"Not so fast," Mallory said, then addressed the blonde. "Suppose you tell us what Jake looks like first."

"I got 'im," Ida Lee called, dragging a man by the collar of his shirt. A man Mallory had never seen before. He had a mustache, curly blond hair and the fear of diminutive, elderly women in his eyes. "He's not too smart, though. Answers to the name of Jake. If I was in hiding, I wouldn't use my own name."

"I'm not in hiding." The man's voice trembled. He looked so unlike Sam that Mallory wondered if Ida Lee had been telling the truth about her failing eyesight. "And my name *is* Jake."

"That's not the Jake I'm talking 'bout," the cocktail waitress said. "The other one has dark hair. About six feet tall. Blue eyes, I think." She nodded at Sam. "Kinda looks like him."

"Pay her," Mallory told Sam. He opened his wallet and took out a twenty, which the waitress grabbed and tucked into the side pocket of her short skirt.

"This Jake," the waitress said, "he left ten or fifteen minutes ago with Patty Peaks. You just missed him."

"Jake left the club with another woman?" Mallory couldn't keep the shocked disappointment out of her voice. If Lenora found out, she'd be devastated.

"See. I'm not the Jake you want," the man with Ida Lee cried. "Please tell Grandma Moses to let me go."

"Grandma Moses?" Ida Lee tightened her grip on the man's shirt collar. "It's Grandma Gumshoe to you, buddy. I've a mind to stomp you with my boot again."

"Let him go, Ida Lee," Sam said. "You heard the lady. Our Jake went off with Patty Peaks."

"Who's Patty Peaks?" Mallory asked, only slightly aware of Ida Lee's captive struggling to get free. Finally, the old lady's grip relaxed and he gained his independence and ran like the dickens.

"Friend of mine," the waitress answered.

"You got an address for this Patty Peaks's crib?" Ida Lee insinuated herself between Mallory and Sam.

"Maybe I do. But it'll cost you extra." This time, the waitress looked straight at Sam. She was no dummy. She knew who the moneyman was. He sighed heavily, got out his wallet again and drew out another twenty.

"Nah," she said when the bill was tucked safely away. "Patty don't got a permanent address. She usually crashes with friends."

"No address?" Sam shook his head in disgust. "If you didn't have an address, why'd you say you did?"

"I didn't say I had an address." The bottled blonde cracked her gum. "I said *maybe* I had an address."

"Do you know where Patty Peaks and Jake went?" Mallory asked.

The waitress eyed Sam again. "Maybe."

"That's not going to work this time, sister," Ida

Lee told her, lifting her boot. "You better sing like a canary or I'll stomp the information out of you."

The waitress backed up a step. "Okay, okay. I don't know where they went. Patty didn't say. I didn't ask. Wasn't any of my business."

Mallory tried to stem the despair she felt rushing through her. There was nothing they could do. Her future brother-in-law was about to make the biggest mistake of his lifetime by indulging in a one-night stand. An awful thought occurred to her. If it was a *one*-night stand.

"You haven't seen them together before tonight, have you?" she asked the waitress. Even Mallory could hear the undercurrent of panic in her voice. "I mean, do they arrive together? Sit at the same table? Leave together?"

"I never seen this Jake before, but Patty don't spend her time at tables, honey. She ain't no customer. She's one of the dancers." The waitress paused as Mallory digested the terrible revelation. "You might've caught her act. She just finished up a little while ago."

Mallory's eyes got wide with horror. "You don't mean she's the one with the..." and she made a curving motion in front of her chest.

"Yeah," the cocktail waitress said dryly. "Why'd you think she uses the name Peaks? Patty's the one with the Alps on her chest."

4

MALLORY TOOK IN HER sister's teary baby blues and droopy mouth and was very glad Lenora didn't know that Jake had run off the night before with Patty and her peaks.

No use heaping anguish upon misery.

Besides, Mallory didn't want to believe that her future brother-in-law had spent the night with a breast man's greatest fantasy. Maybe, just maybe, he was that one single man in a thousand who had mounds of resistance.

If not, she'd personally see to it that Jake's lapse with Patty was his only one.

"Really, I'll be fine," Lenora said in a voice that broke and shook. "I just need a little time."

Yeah, right, Mallory thought.

The rented brownstone she shared with Lenora in northwest Philadelphia doubled as their office and was always open for business. No matter that the only walk-in client they'd ever had requested The Invisible Man.

Today, Mallory had returned from breakfast at a coffee shop around the corner to blinds shut so tight it seemed more like midnight than midmorning.

Lenora was still in her pajamas and, more alarmingly, she wasn't wearing makeup. Her sister played tennis in full face paint, for heaven's sake. Mallory had once witnessed her approach a synchronized swimmer to ask what brand of foundation wouldn't wash off in the pool.

Despite what she claimed, Lenora wasn't fine at all.

"You don't have to put on an act for me. I know you're heartbroken." Mallory put an arm around her sister's shoulders and squeezed gently. Lenora was two years older, but never failed to make Mallory feel protective. She was china-doll pretty, a petite blonde who made Mallory wonder how they'd sprung from the same gene pool. "Why, when I get my hands on Jake, I oughta—"

"What do you mean when you get your hands on him?" Lenora's chin came up. "You won't meddle again, will you, Mallory?"

"Me? Meddle? Why would you ask that?" Mallory tried to look innocent, but her sister wasn't buying it.

"I meant what I said. This is none of your business. I don't want you anywhere near him."

"But—"

"No buts, Mallory." Lenora dabbed at her nose with a tissue. "If Jake needs time to be sure he wants to go through with the marriage, I'm going to give it to him."

"How can he not be sure?" Mallory erupted, no more able to hold her tongue than she could a flake of snow. "You two are perfect for each other. Everyone can see that."

"Stop it, Mallory." Lenora sniffled. She went through a series of rapid eye blinks. "This isn't like the time you threatened to tell everyone the head cheerleader stuffed her bra with socks if she didn't give me a fair tryout for the squad. You can't make Jake love me."

"But Jake does love you! You're perfect for each other. Like Heathcliff and Cathy. Only human."

"If you paid as much attention to what's happening in your life as you do mine, you'd have your own...Heathcliff, for example," Lenora said before getting up and walking into the kitchen.

"What's that supposed to mean?" Mallory trailed after her, opening blinds along the way.

"I bet you can't remember the last time you had a date."

"I never meet anyone I want to date."

"Never?"

"Well, almost never." If circumstances had been different, Mallory would want to date Sam. Heck, she'd want to do a whole lot more than date him. Last night, at the club, his lips had moved over hers, and she'd learned that she could crave a man more than a double hot-fudge sundae. "But that doesn't have anything to do with what we're talking about."

"It has everything to do with it." Lenora got a wineglass from the cupboard and took a half-full bottle of chardonnay from the refrigerator. "You should stop worrying so much about everyone else and start going after what you want."

Before Lenora could pop the cork, Mallory had the bottle of chardonnay back in the refrigerator. Lenora watched, her hands on her hips, as Mallory filled her wineglass with milk.

"I want for you not to drink wine in the morning." She handed the milk to her sister. "And I want you to talk to me. You're obviously miserable."

"And milk's going to make me feel better?"

"Strong bones and teeth can't hurt." Mallory was relieved when her sister sipped at the white stuff, her pinky extended. When she set down the glass, there was a white line above her lip, but Lenora looked pretty even with a milk mustache. "C'mon, Lenora, talk to me."

"Okay." Lenora dabbed at her eyes. "You're right. I am miserable. I'm also angry."

"Good, good. This is good."

"I'm so angry that I've started to reevaluate my feelings for Jake."

Bad, bad. That was bad.

"I'm thinking I should test the waters, see what's out there."

"No! You don't want to do that," Mallory said while the horrors of Lenora's past love life flashed before her eyes in slow motion. She'd spent years making sure her sister didn't marry any of the assortment of losers she'd dated. She hadn't relaxed until Jake came along. "Jake's the man you're going to marry."

Lenora blinked, drying her tears. "Since that's debatable at the moment, I was thinking about calling Vince to see if he wanted to make another go of it."

"Vince DelGreco!" The thought of Lenora getting back together with Vince sent Mallory's heart into palpitations. Despite his jet-black pompadour greasier than motor oil and his insistence that neither disco nor Elvis were dead, the guy was a pasty-faced lounge lizard.

Vince hung out in bars dispensing pickup lines. Once, before he knew she was Lenora's sister, he'd asked her to help find his lost puppy in the cheap motel across the street. Shudder.

He wasn't worthy of the title lizard. He was more like a gecko. A lounge gecko.

Be calm, Mallory told herself. She never got anywhere with her sister when she gave her emotions free rein. "Come on, Lenora. Get serious. Did you know Vince thinks he can get a handle on what women really want by reading *Cosmo?*"

"Is that why he was always trying to get me to take those weird sex quizzes? I always wondered about that."

"Tell me you're not going to call him," Mallory pleaded. "Give Jake more time. I'm sure he'll come to his senses."

"Maybe I will give him a *little* more time," Lenora said, sniffling. "As soon as I pack, I'm leaving for mom and dad's anyway. That is, if you can still handle the business."

"I can handle the business," Mallory said, hoping she sounded more confident than she felt. Just that morning, she'd placed a classified advertisement in the newspaper on Sam's advice. Considering that the ad might generate more business, she wasn't so sure it had been a good idea after all. "Just promise me you won't call Vince."

"I'm not making any promises. It would serve Jake right if I got back together with Vince. At least Vince appreciates me."

Mallory worried her bottom lip, more sure than ever that she'd done the right thing in hiring Sam to find Jake.

Sure, she longed to tell Sam who she really was. But she couldn't risk losing his support. Not with true love on the line and DelGreco the Gecko lurking in the wings.

Finding Jake was no longer important. It was crucial.

SAM YANKED OPEN THE door of Jake's refrigerator, searching for liquid salvation after a frustrating day trying to locate a brother who didn't want to be found.

Since Sam was still simmering over Jake's treatment of Mallory, maybe it was a good thing he'd come up empty.

He'd be worried about his brother if they hadn't trailed him to the House of the Seven Veils. But, in view of the circumstances, Jake warranted something other than worry. What kind of a man ran out on a fiancée as wonderful as Mallory and took up with a stripper? Jake didn't care how big Patty's chest was, it couldn't compare with Mallory's heart.

Not that Sam was a saint. Patty's peaks might not do it for him, but he'd sure like to get a peek at what Mallory had under her blouse.

Fat chance of that happening. He didn't agree with the way Mallory let her emotions rule her actions, but he admired her passion. Unfortunately, she ached as deeply as she loved. Last night, Mallory's despair had been so complete that she seemed inconsolable. It would be a long time before she took up with another man. Let alone the brother of the one who had broken her heart.

It was a good thing he was getting on a sailboat and leaving for parts unknown just as soon as he found his brother. Otherwise, he couldn't be held accountable for what might happen to Jake's nose.

Cool air blasted him. He was still holding the refrigerator door open, surveying the contents of the fridge.

Bean curd and alfalfa sprouts. Wheat germ and bran muffins. Vegetable juice and soybean milk. Yech! It was enough to turn a burger-loving, beer-guzzling man's stomach, which he would have pegged Jake for.

But the truth was he didn't know enough about Jake to hazard a guess as to what kind of food he ate. Sam had made his laissez-faire policy clear when he'd left home after high school. *Live and let live.* So, even though New York City was just a skip away from Philadelphia, neither brother had made the trip more than once or twice.

He was about to close the refrigerator in horror when a glimpse of redemption stopped him. Beer. Hallelujah. Sam popped open the tab on the can and took a healthy swig. His eyes watered. His taste buds rebelled.

A glance at the label confirmed his fear. It wasn't beer at all, but a nonalcoholic substitute. Ew.

"Jake, I don't know you anymore," he said aloud. He bent down and swilled water straight from the kitchen tap, swirling it around in his mouth before swallowing.

A few seconds later, the doorbell rang. He picked his way through the clutter he'd strewn about to make Jake's pristine suburban town house seem less creepy, fully expecting to open the door to a stranger looking for Jake.

Instead of a stranger, Mallory stood on the doorstep, her glorious hair shoved under a bald cap, her eyebrows thick and coal black. A jagged scar crisscrossed her left cheek.

"Hey there." She smiled up at him from beneath a pencil-thin mustache, looking glowingly beautiful instead of like a woman suffering the depths of despair. "I have to deliver a party-gram later tonight and thought I'd stop by on the way to see what kind of progress you've made on the case.''

"The case?" Sam's eyebrows rose as she came into the town house. He'd spent the day searching for that rat Jake, but he'd no longer thought he was working for Mallory. "After what we found out last night, I thought you'd given up on Jake."

She didn't answer right away. Instead, one by one, she undid the buttons on her voluminous trench coat. Remembering the last time she did that, Sam crossed to her side to speed up the process. His knuckles brushed the nape of her neck as he slid the coat off her shoulders and he heard her soft gasp. By the time she flashed him, his brow had broken out in a light sweat.

Only there was no sexy little dress under her coat this time. She was wearing an artfully ripped black singlet that clung to her curves like plastic wrap. The sleeves had been torn off. Another of the rips bared most of a curvaceous leg. A large, red *M* was emblazoned across her chest.

Sam had enough friends back in New York who were professional wrestling fans to have recognized the costume. It had been made popular by The Maniac, a Goliath of a wrestler with bulging biceps and the pecs and abs of a superhero.

His signature move was the Maniac Mash, during which he took a flying vertical leap and landed outstretched on his prone opponent. Mallory wasn't moving, but Sam still felt as though he'd been hit in the gut by an air-bound wrestler.

"Of course I haven't given up on Jake," she said. He tried not to stare at her, but it was no use. Walking to the hall closet would've cost him too much eye time, so he tossed the coat over the back of a chair.

"I don't understand," he said, a statement that was all encompassing. First, why was she dressed like The Maniac in drag? Second, why was she wasting her time on a two-timer like Jake? He decided he wanted an answer to the second question more than the first. "Aren't you angry with Jake?"

"You bet I'm angry," Mallory said, and he thought her pretty mouth belonged not under the mustache but beneath his mouth. The way it had been beneath his mouth last night. "But we don't actually know what Jake and Patty did after they left the club."

Sam had a pretty good guess, but he tried to sound noncommittal. Just in case, by some miracle, he was wrong. "That's true. We don't."

"Besides, even if they did," she paused, "*indulge* themselves, I can't throw away everything I have with Jake because he made one little mistake."

Sam still couldn't take his eyes off her mouth, but he no longer liked the words coming out of it. Noncommittal be danged. Loyalty was an admirable trait, but there was such a thing as going too far. "I wouldn't call it a little mistake," he said.

"Believe me, I'm going to make Jake pay for this. But he'll come around to my way of thinking when we find him."

"You're sure about that?" he asked, loathe that his brother should hurt her. A protective instinct kicked in, and he moved closer to her, as though his presence would shield her from harm.

"Of course I am." She tilted her head back and met his eyes. She had such great bone structure that she might be one of the few women alive who could inspire desire while wearing a bald cap. When she spoke again, it was in a whisper. "Don't you know how rare it is for two people to be completely right for each other?"

He took in the lovely line of her scarred jaw and the tempting curve of her mustachioed mouth. He breathed in her now-familiar scent of orange blossoms and sunshine, and for one crazy moment, he thought she was referring to them. How would it feel to be loved by a woman with a heart as big as Mallory's?

He inched forward, intending to kiss her the way he'd kissed her in the club before guilt had coursed through him. Guilt because she was his brother's fiancée and not his. His brother. To whom she'd just declared her devotion. He stopped no more than six inches from her lips.

"You really love him, don't you?" he whispered back.

For a moment, she didn't answer, but just stared at him through half-closed lids. She looked as though she were in a trance.

"Mallory?"

She blinked at him. "Huh?"

"My brother. You must really love him."

"Your brother?" She seemed to emerge from the trance. "Oh, my gosh. Yes. Your brother. He's a great guy. That's why I want to find him. That's why I stopped by. To see what progress you've made on the case."

Sam straightened. He then rubbed his jaw, casting his mind back on what he'd done that day. She was still staring at him, so he took a few steps backward and found it easier to think.

"I didn't make much progress," Sam said. "I went

back to the House of the Seven Veils this morning, thinking I might track down Patty, but the place was closed. Then I spent hours driving around Philadelphia trying to figure out where my brother might have gone.''

"You're joking, right?" she asked.

"Why would I joke about something like that?"

"Because driving around…" Mallory's words died, and he noticed she was looking at the treasure trove of private-eye novels sprinkled over the coffee table. Sam Spade. Phillip Marlowe. Spenser. Fletch. The fictional detectives were all represented. "Where did you get those?"

"Ida Lee. She thinks I should study. Oh. And get a fedora."

"Not a bad idea," Mallory said. "The studying, not the fedora. Those detectives really knew how to solve a case."

"Yeah," Sam said, "but they were make-believe cases. And they got clues."

"That's it," Mallory said, pointing at him. "That's what we're missing. We're in Jake's home, right? He must have left a clue behind as to where he was going."

"What kind of a clue?"

"I'm not sure." Mallory tapped her lush bottom lip with a forefinger. "Maybe a travel brochure. Or a piece of paper he'd written something down on. I say we do a search."

"We can't do that." Sam's mind rebelled at the word *search*. "It'd be an invasion of his privacy."

"That's why they call it private investigation and not public investigation." Mallory was already walking through the town house, picking up books and magazines searching for he didn't know what. "Besides, the way I see it, it's for his own good."

"How's that?"

"It's in Jake's best interests to be found, because then he can get on with the rest of his life."

With her. She didn't say it aloud, but she didn't need to. Once they found his brother, Jake and Mallory would patch up their differences and get on with the rest of *their* lives. And Sam would get on his boat and get on with his, which is what he wanted, after all. He frowned.

"Please, Sam. It's really important that I find him." Her gaze locked with his. They were separated by fifteen feet, but he could feel the connection across the room.

He didn't say anything for a full ten seconds, then gave a curt nod. "I'll look upstairs."

Fifteen fruitless minutes later, Sam came downstairs to find Mallory sitting at the kitchen table going through a short stack of bills. He noticed that Jake had attached Post-it notes to the envelopes to remind himself when they should be paid.

"Any luck?" she asked, looking up from the bills.

"I still don't have a clue where he went." There wasn't so much as a crumb out of place in his brother's town house. He was so alarmingly neat that ants probably boycotted his place.

Mallory shrugged. "There's nothing left to do, then, except search the garbage."

"You've got to be kidding."

"Your brother's a neatnik, pal. He didn't leave clues strewn about the house like a normal person, so we need to see if he threw any away."

As she talked, Mallory took newspapers out of a

bag marked To Be Recycled and spread them over the kitchen tile. Before he could stop her, she picked up the garbage can and dumped it. Sam took an instinctive step backward, but Mallory got down on her hands and knees for an up-close-and-personal view.

"Oh, my gosh," she exclaimed as she examined the contents on the floor. "This could be Mr. Clean's garbage."

Sam came closer and watched as Mallory picked up a resealable bag into which Jake had stuffed an apple core. Her next find was one of those plastic microwavable containers that had held a frozen-food dinner. It was spotlessly clean. She held it up.

"He even washes his garbage."

"This doesn't seem right, Mallory," Sam said while she continued to rummage. "How would you like it if someone went through your garbage?"

"Are you kidding? I'd be flattered someone loved me enough to care about what was in my garbage." Mallory lowered her eyes as if she'd said too much. Again, Sam found himself inwardly cursing his brother.

"If Jake doesn't want to go through your garbage," he said, "he's a fool."

"Thanks," she said, blinking up at him. Again, he felt that connection, but then she looked down and it was gone.

"Eureka," she said a moment later, picking up a piece of paper that had a name, address and telephone number on it. "This might be the clue we're looking for. Does the name Father Andy O'Brien mean anything to you?"

"Never heard of him."

"Hmm. This is interesting. Jake dated this the day before he went missing."

"Jake dates his scrap paper?"

"I'd rather him do that than date Patty Peaks," she said. "But dating scrap paper is too weird, even for Jake. I think he wrote down the date and time he was supposed to meet with this Father O'Brien."

"Why would Jake go to a priest?"

"That's what I was going to ask you. Do you think he went to this Father O'Brien to confess his sins?"

"We're not Catholic."

"Oh, my gosh." She clutched her heart, right above the *M.* "Is it possible he's thinking about a career change? Of maybe becoming a priest? Of becoming *celibate?*"

She paced the room as though the thought was too much to bear. She was so upset that Sam felt guilty for wishing she was on the mark. A celibate brother couldn't touch her luscious skin the way he wanted to.

"I think you're jumping to conclusions," he said to assuage the guilt.

"There's one way to find out," Mallory said decisively. "We visit Father O'Brien to see if he has any idea where Jake is."

She started walking toward the door.

"Are you sure you want to go dressed like that?"

"Like what?" She looked down at herself. "Oh, darn. I forgot. I have that gig tonight."

"You mean The Maniac in drag thing?"

"In drag?" Her face fell. How someone could look so beautiful in a bald cap like that, Sam didn't know. "I'm not in drag. You don't think I look like The Maniac?"

Sam rubbed the back of his neck. The Maniac probably ran six feet six, two hundred seventy-five pounds. He had wild eyes, bulging muscles and body hair. He didn't have sweetly curving hips and breasts that called attention to the *M*.

"Nope. I can definitely tell you're not him."

She put her hands to her face, and they were trembling. Something deep inside him trembled in sympathy. It went against his grain to offer unsolicited advice, but this was different. If he didn't do something fast, she was headed for another fiasco à la Little Orphan Annie.

"Look. We'll go see Father O'Brien tomorrow. Right now, you can practice your act on me and I'll help you work out the kinks."

"You'd do that for me?"

That and anything else she asked. Especially if it involved skin-to-skin contact. Sam nodded.

She gave him a grateful smile and took a deep breath. "Okay, when I get there, I'm going to pound my chest and do the Tarzan yell. Then I'll say something catchy like, 'I've been searching the jungle looking for a birthday girl.'"

Catchy? Sam grimaced. The only thing that would catch her was a catcall. "You're confusing The Maniac with Jungle Jim. He's the wrestler who does the Tarzan yell."

"You're kidding."

"I'm not kidding," he said and had to grin. Letting his friend George drag him to Wrestlemania VIII last year hadn't been a waste of time after all.

"Scratch that, then. Lucky thing that wasn't going to be my main event. After I swing my ball and chain—"

"Sorry to interrupt, The Maniac doesn't have a ball

and chain. That's The Jailbird. He's the one who wears the black-and-white striped singlet.''

"Scratch the ball and chain, too, then." She squared her shoulders. "I'm just getting to the best part. When they take out the cake, I'll step in and light the candles from my lightning rod."

"Uh, Mallory. I hate to tell you this, but—"

"The Maniac doesn't have a lightning rod?"

"Storm Warning's the one with the lightning rod."

She put her hands on her hips and sighed. "Then what does The Maniac have?"

Sam tried not to roll his eyes. He didn't expect her to know the ins and outs of professional wrestling, but The Maniac was such a phenom he'd crossed the line into popular culture. He'd become even bigger than Hulk Hogan.

"He has it all," Sam said. "Super strength, super size, super moves. Even a super slogan. 'The Maniac isn't crazy. Whoever gets in the ring with him is.' He's like the superhero of the wrestling set."

"So you're saying the candle bit won't work?"

"Not unless you figure out how to light them with super vision, but even The Maniac doesn't have that." She was making a supreme effort to keep her lower lip from trembling and failing badly. "Speaking of which, you could use a little supervision."

"I could use more than that." She paced across the room. "This is a disaster. Why did I tell Lenora I could handle the business by myself? She's not even going to have a business to come back to."

He crossed the room and put his hands on her shoulders, wanting only to comfort her. Until she looked up at him with her dewy eyes and her quivering lips. Then he wanted to do much more than comfort her. Hell.

"I've got an idea." He gave her a rueful grin when he realized he was only going to tell her his G-rated idea. The other idea he'd have to squelch. "Didn't you say this was for a little girl's party?"

She nodded. "Usually it's the boys who go for the wrestlers, but this girl is crazy about them."

"Perfect," Sam said, "then my plan will work."

"You have a plan?"

"You bet I do. Watch this."

He reached out for the *M* that was on the front of her costume, and his fingertips brushed her breasts. Her breath caught, her mouth parted and she lifted her eyes to his. The moment stretched, and he saw his reflection in her pupils. His own eyes were dark with desire, his face tight with it.

Summoning willpower he didn't know he had, he pulled the *M* off its velcro backing, turned it upside down and refastened it. Quickly. So his fingers wouldn't linger on her lush softness. So his mouth wouldn't come down and taste it.

Then, as gently as he could, he peeled off her mustache. His fingers brushed her lips in the process, and his gut clenched. She didn't move, but stood perfectly still, her eyes still on his, as his hand moved to her bald cap. He removed it, watching as her hair tumbled around her shoulders in thick, dark waves.

His hands wanted to keep on touching her, so he thrust them behind his back. He cleared his throat as he surveyed the transformation.

"Goodbye, Maniac," he said. "Hello, Womaniac."

She stared down at the *W* that was now gracing her chest. He watched her smile grow wide an instant before she flung herself into his arms, peppering his face with kisses.

He laughed, feeling even more powerful than The Maniac. That is until she got too close to his mouth, and he thought about what his brother would do if he saw them like this.

Gently, he put Mallory from him. Forget about the candles. If Jake had super vision, he'd incinerate Sam.

5

"DID I THANK YOU FOR suggesting I go to that party as Womaniac?" Mallory asked the next morning. She and Sam were walking up a snow-shoveled sidewalk to the address they had for Father Andy O'Brien.

"I believe you did. Oh, let's see, about five times on the drive over here." Sam rubbed his jaw, making her wonder what it would feel like to rub her face against his skin. Her mouth went dry at the thought. "Like I told you, it was nothing. Just a simple matter of matching the client's need with the solution that best fit."

They were fifteen miles west of the city center in a neighborhood of grand, old houses set close to roads that grew heavier with traffic each year. Father Andy's house was as impressive as the others, a massive two-story structure with a stone facade and an entranceway featuring a stained-glass door. No church adjoined the property, bringing up the possibility that the priest was retired.

But Mallory was barely thinking about the good Father and the questions they needed to ask him. She was thinking about Sam and the amazing fact that her praise was embarrassing him. The only thing more amazing was that the slight flush on his face was turning her on. She bet his skin was flushed like that after he made love, too. She cleared her throat and made her mind get out of his bed.

"It wasn't nothing. It was a great idea," she said. "It let those little girls know that a woman can do anything she puts her mind to. It was wonderful for their self-esteem."

"Except for that tiny one who kept practicing The Maniac Mash by leaping on me."

"She probably only did that so you'd keep catching her," Mallory said. Their arms brushed, and her breath caught. It hardly mattered that she was wearing her trench coat and he had on black leather. She still felt the sizzle. "I was tempted myself."

"Really?" By the surprised look on his face, at which she couldn't stop stealing glances, that wasn't something she should have said to her fiancé's brother. Darn.

"Not that I would have done it," she added quickly, forgetting that they had reached Father Andy's front door.

"Of course not," he said, but kept on gazing at her. He had a wonderful face, with lean cheeks, a strong jaw and that sexy stubble she'd rubbed against just yesterday when he'd kissed her. The air around them seemed to heat, and Mallory wouldn't have been surprised had the snow on the nearby trees melted and dripped.

She could certainly use some of that melting snow around her face, especially because Sam Creighton was strictly off-limits.

She was pretty sure why that was presenting such a problem. She'd had a glimpse into his heart when he'd rescued her at the club, and it had attracted her even more than his handsome face. But her motivation to keep her hands off him couldn't be stronger.

Sam was willing to help Jake's fiancée, but she doubted he'd offer assistance to the floozy two-timing his brother. If she surrendered to temptation and threw herself into his arms, that's exactly what he'd believe her to be.

"Um, Mallory?" Even his voice was sexy, a low-throated purr that seemed to vibrate inside her.

"Yeah?"

He inched closer to her, and she could smell a heady mixture of soap, shampoo and heat. "One of us should ring the doorbell."

"Yeah," she agreed as her eyes dropped to his mouth. His lips parted, and she drew in a breath as she swayed toward him.

The door sprung open as if by divine intervention. Guiltily, they sprang apart.

The man who stood in the doorway was tall and slender with an angular face set off by long, flowing gray hair. Tiny wire-rimmed glasses were perched atop his long nose, but it was difficult to look anywhere but at his colorful tie-dye shirt and loose-fitting purple pants.

"Sorry." Sam recovered his wits first. "We must be in the wrong place. We're looking for Father Andy O'Brien."

"That's me," the man said. From somewhere in the house, rock music blared. "Welcome, my children."

When Mallory realized her jaw had dropped open, she snapped it shut. Something about him was vaguely familiar, but he didn't look like any priest Mallory had ever seen. She started to say so when Sam stuck out a hand.

"Nice to meet you, Father," Sam said. "We're—"

"I know who you are." He took their hands in turn and clasped them warmly. "I can't tell you how glad I am that you decided to come. I was saddened when you canceled your appointment."

"But—"

"Come. Let's get you in out of the cold." He ushered them inside a house that could have been featured in a decorating magazine. It was a virtual showpiece, with gleaming wood floors, oriental rugs and a majestic grandfather clock that chimed the hour.

"Forgive me, Father," Mallory said as she took in the opulence, "but aren't priests supposed to take a vow of poverty?"

He threw back his head and laughed so hard she counted five silver fillings in his back teeth. "I'm an advice consultant, not a priest. Whatever gave you the idea I was a priest?"

"The 'Father' in front of your name," Mallory said.

"Oh, that." He waved a hand. "People have been calling me that for twenty-five years, which is about as long as they've been coming to me for advice. What I want to know is why don't they go to their own fathers for advice?"

"Probably because Dad only knows best when he isn't yours," Sam quipped, and Mallory wondered at the edge to his voice. Was he talking about his own father?

"No matter," the man said before she could puzzle on it any longer. "I wouldn't be where I am today if people didn't come to me for advice. Though my editors at the newspaper know not to call me Father in print."

Suddenly, Mallory knew why the man had seemed

familiar when he opened the door. "Oh, my gosh. You're Andy! From the 'Dear Andy' column in the newspaper."

"Why, yes, I am. I'm not often recognized."

"I can see why." Mallory tilted her head as she regarded him. "You don't look anything like that photo they have with your column."

"You don't like the one they're using?"

"Oh, I do, but it puts fifty pounds on you. Did you know some people call you Adipose Andy? Which is a shame, since you're really quite thin."

"I have lost weight recently. Do you think I should have a new photo taken?"

"Oh, most definitely. I—"

"Mallory," Sam interrupted. "We didn't come here to talk about Andy's weight."

The advice columnist put his hands on his hips. "Andy sounds so informal. I prefer to be called Father Andy."

"Okay," Sam said, sighing. "We didn't come here to talk about *Father* Andy's weight."

He was right, of course. They were on an all-important mission to find Jake and save Lenora from heartache and Vince DelGreco. But Mallory didn't see any harm in helping someone in need along the way.

If Sam had seen Father Andy's mug shot, he'd feel the same way.

"Of course you didn't," the advice columnist cut in, then muttered under his breath, "although I don't see how it hurts for me to be on the receiving end of the advice for a change." He pasted on a smile. "Come right this way to my office."

The office was as impressive as the rest of the house, with bookcases built into the walls and stretching to the ceiling. The desk was mahogany and gleaming, the chair behind it made of the finest leather, the carpet a rich burgundy. Father Andy sat down and indicated they should do the same.

"First of all, let me assure you my advice is most valid. I've been doing consulting work on the side for years."

"What kind of consulting work?" Mallory asked, thinking it was a novel concept to charge people for advice. She did it for free.

"Anything and everything. One of my specialties is premarital counseling. That's why you're here, is it not?"

"Actually, we—" Mallory said.

"The moment I opened the door, I knew you were sweethearts. I could tell from the way you were looking at one another."

Mallory exchanged a quick glance with Sam, which was so heated that she couldn't deny what Father Andy had said.

"Don't look so shocked," Father Andy continued. "It's perfectly natural for the lust to accompany the love. Now, why did you make the appointment?"

Sam shifted in his chair. "We don't have an appointment."

With a puzzled frown, Father Andy reached across his desk for a leather-bound book and flipped it open. He ruffled through the pages until he found the one he was looking for. He scrutinized it, then looked up at them. "You're not Franny Delaney and Danny Franconi?"

"Try Sam Creighton and Mallory Jamison," Sam said.

"Hmm." Father Andy tapped his chin. "Well,

that's very odd. I can always spot the lustbirds, and I pegged you two right off. If I hadn't opened the door when I did, you would have been all over each other.''

''We would not have been,'' Mallory said forcefully. Too forcefully.

''Methinks the lady protests too much,'' Father Andy said.

''Mallory's engaged to my brother,'' Sam said, wiping the knowing look off Father Andy's face, where concern now replaced it.

''Oh, my,'' he said. ''You two really do need advice.''

''We're not here for advice,'' Mallory said before he jumped to any more conclusions. ''We're here because we're looking for Jake Creighton, Sam's brother. My fiancé. We hoped you could help us.''

''You want me to help you complete your love triangle?''

''It's not a love triangle,'' Sam said. ''It's a love line. Mallory and Jake. It doesn't have anything to do with me.''

''Hmm,'' Father Andy said. ''Methinks the gentleman protests too much.''

''Look,'' Sam said, and Mallory could tell he was losing his patience, ''was my brother here to see you or not?''

''If he was,'' Father Andy said, ''why do you think I would tell you?''

''For the last time,'' Sam said, ''we are not trying to complete some sort of kinky love triangle.''

Father Andy laughed. ''If you think that's why I won't tell you if he was here to see me, you're seriously underestimating me. I like kinky.''

Mallory thought she'd better change the subject.

Quick. "We'd really appreciate anything you can tell us."

"You're missing the point." He seemed offended. "What kind of an advice consultant would I be if I blabbed my client's secrets all over the place?"

"We don't want to know Jake's secrets," Mallory said. "We want to know where he is."

"Forget it." Father Andy flipped his gray hair back over his shoulder and turned his long nose in the air. "They don't call me Father for nothing. My office is like a confessional. Nothing said here is repeated."

"JAKE WAS THERE," Mallory said five minutes later as she opened the passenger-side door of Jake's rental car. "I can feel it."

Sam could feel it, too, but he wasn't sure it was a good feeling. He was starting to think the sailboat in Florida could wait. The longer they went without finding Jake, the longer Sam could spend with Mallory. Never, in all his life, had he enjoyed a woman's company more.

Of course, spending time with her had a flip side that could only lead to disaster. The longer he stayed in Mallory's company, the closer he came to kissing her again. If Father Andy hadn't opened the door when he had, it would have happened already.

"But why did Jake go to see Father Andy?" Mallory mused as she settled into the passenger seat. "What kind of advice would he need, unless..."

"Unless what?"

"Unless he went to Father Andy for advice on whether or not to get married. Oh, my goodness. Do you think this means he's considering ending the relationship altogether?"

Her grass-green eyes were alive with panic, drilling into Sam once again how very much she loved his brother. Hell. No matter that his libido was thrumming and his arms wanted to clasp her to him, his heart wanted to wipe the panic out of her eyes.

"You don't know that." He tried to sound soothing instead of jealous, which was what he was. "Even if that's why Jake went to Father Andy, he could have left more sure rather than less sure of wanting to be married."

"Do you really think so?" Mallory looked so hopeful his spirits sank lower than the floor of the Grand Canyon.

"Yeah." Sam tore his eyes from her and put the keys in the ignition. "No man in his right mind would break up with somebody like you."

"You think so?" He heard the smile in her voice.

"I know so," he said and turned the key in the ignition.

"Don't start the car!" Mallory's hand shot out and covered his. His reaction was instantaneous. Daggers of desire shot through his body, stunning him with their power. He turned, and his eyes locked with hers. The air between them grew heavy, but he couldn't allow himself to act on what he thought he saw in her eyes. Not when she'd just been obsessing over whether his brother still loved her enough to marry her.

"You gonna tell me why I shouldn't start the car?" he rasped, and only then did she seem to realize she was touching him. She took her hand away, and he felt bereft.

"Father Andy," she said, which was the last thing he expected her to say. She gestured out the car window. "He's leaving."

The advice columnist was striding toward a sleek sports car parked in the driveway, his shoulders hunched against the wind. Sam had parked on the street, slightly uphill from Father Andy's luxurious house, so it was a good bet the advice columnist didn't know they were still in the vicinity.

"So?" Sam asked.

"So I have a hunch he knows something." She grew animated as she talked. "Think about it. We know Jake was here, even though Father Andy wouldn't confirm it. Maybe he's going to warn Jake that we're on his tail. We need to follow him."

Sam let out a heavy sigh. He wasn't cut out for this private eye business. He was willing to go some lengths to help Mallory find his brother, but he thought he should draw the line at following a private citizen. Still, he'd promised to help her.

"Even if I wanted to follow him, I'm not sure I can," he said, looking for a loophole. "See that car he's driving? That's a Maserati sports car. He's going to take off out of here like mad."

"But you'll try." She looked at him with such trust his resolve melted. Hell.

"I'll try," he said and started the car. The sports car was already descending the hill. Sam was about to press down hard on the gas pedal so he could catch up, when he realized that something was out of whack.

The sports car was moving like a slug through mud.

"I thought you said that was a fast car," Mallory said.

"It is, but the good Father must have slow reflexes," Sam said, inching his rental car forward.

"Don't get too close," Mallory warned. "You're supposed to keep about ten car lengths behind."

"You've followed people before?"

She flashed him a smile. "No, but I do watch TV. Ideally, you keep at least another car between you and the one you're following."

"Unless a grandpa shows up driving a Ford Model T roadster, that ain't gonna happen," Sam said.

There was a traffic light at the bottom of the hill, and Father Andy reached the intersection with the light green. He executed a slow left turn, inching the Maserati sports car through the rotation.

"Oh, no," Mallory exclaimed. "The light's going to turn red. Step on the gas, Sam. If you don't, we're going to lose him."

Sam sped to the bottom of the hill just in time for the light to turn yellow. He touched the brake once, preparing to stop.

"What are you doing?" Mallory yelled. "Go!"

"But the light's red."

"Go," she yelled again, and he checked both ways to make sure no cars would broadside him in the intersection. Knowing he was going to regret it, he pressed down on the gas pedal and screeched through the turn.

"There. Was that so hard?" Mallory asked an instant before he spotted flashing red and blue lights in his rearview mirror.

"It's a cop," he said.

"Can you lose him?" she asked breathlessly, but the madness of the moment was gone. He'd run a red light, but he wasn't about to try to shake a cop.

"I haven't lost my mind," he said as he pulled the car to the shoulder of the road, but he wondered if that were true. If he'd ignored the note on Jake's office door asking him to run the business while he was gone, he'd be basking under the sunny skies by now, the sail of his boat flapping in the wind. Instead, he was in Philadelphia getting a traffic ticket with a woman he desired but couldn't touch.

The cop sauntered up to the car with his hat pulled low and black shades covering his eyes. He was a solid six feet two and two hundred-plus pounds—one of those tough-guy cops who inspired either glee or fear, depending upon whether he was for you or against you.

Sam was pretty sure the cop was against him.

"Driver's license and registration," the cop ordered in a voice edged with flint.

Yep. The cop was definitely against him.

Mallory stuck her head around Sam and gave the cop a sunny smile. "You really should work on your curbside manner."

"What did you say?" the cop and Sam spit out at the same time. Mallory ignored Sam and addressed the cop.

"Your curbside manner is atrocious. Didn't your mother ever tell you to turn your frown upside down? Especially when you're in town."

The cop's face contorted into a ferocious scowl. Sam closed his eyes and grimaced.

"Driver's license and registration," the cop repeated.

"Gee, you don't have to be so surly," Mallory muttered, earning her an elbow from Sam. He prayed she'd gotten his message to keep quiet while he retrieved the documents and handed them to the cop.

"Didn't you see the red light back there?" The cop's shades were so dark Sam couldn't tell whether he was looking at the documents or at Sam. He tried to look innocent while he thought about how he was going to answer.

"Of course he saw it," Mallory piped up before Sam could speak. "He said to me just before he ran it, 'Mallory, the light's red.'"

"Mallory," Sam whispered between clenched teeth. "You're not helping."

The cop's mouth thinned. "Then you're saying you ran the red light deliberately?"

"Only because we didn't want to lose Father Andy."

"Mallory!"

"You were following a priest!" The big cop scowled. "I might be able to give you a ticket just for that."

"He's not really a priest. He just—" Sam started to explain, but the cop didn't want to hear it.

"Get out of the car and spread 'em," he barked, and Sam's head started to throb. Apparently, the cop wasn't taking any chances with someone low enough to tail a man of the cloth.

Ten minutes later, they were back on the road, traveling in the direction Father Andy had taken before Sam's expensive left turn. "Thanks a lot," he told Mallory.

"I thought he'd be more sympathetic."

"Oh, yeah. And why not? We had the perfect excuse. Following a priest because he wouldn't divulge something told to him in confidence."

"Father Andy's not a priest."

"Yeah, well, I doubt it would've made much difference to Dirty Harry. He didn't seem to think tailing somebody was a good enough excuse to run a red light.''

Mallory tapped the side of her mouth. "People who are that surly generally have something eating them up on the inside. I know a good therapist I could recommend. Do you remember that policeman's name? I could call him at the precinct."

"That's not a good idea," Sam said. What was it with her? Didn't she see that meddling caused nothing but trouble?

"Sure, it's a good idea. Think how much happier he'd be if he talked to somebody."

Sam didn't much care about the happiness of a cop who'd just slapped him with a ticket, but he doubted Mallory would feel the same. He tried another tactic. "But think how much surlier he'll be when you talk to him."

He was tipped off to the fact that she wasn't listening to him by the way she was leaning over the dashboard, peering through the windshield.

"Oh, my gosh." She pointed to a sleek red sports car in the distance. "I see Father Andy's car. I can't believe we caught up to him."

Considering the Maserati was only traveling about twenty miles per hour, Sam believed it.

"He must not have taken any turns." Sam slowed the rental car to a good following crawl.

"What a stroke of luck!" She clapped her hands and bounced in her seat. "Now we can find out if he was going somewhere that will lead us to Jake."

Jake, Sam thought. It always came back to Jake.

He tried to focus on driving very slowly, but his attention kept wandering to Mallory's profile, which was intent on the road. How many more clues did he need that she was fixated on his brother?

A long mile later, Father Andy took a right turn and the Maserati sports car slowly, very slowly, climbed another hill. Near the summit was a brick structure too large to contain a single family. Unless it was the crowd of kids from *Cheaper by the Dozen.*

Colorful play equipment, including a snow-covered swing set, filled a fenced yard. Somebody had built a lopsided snowman complete with a top hat and carrot nose, and Mallory could make out the beginnings of a snow fort.

Mallory frowned. She'd been so sure that Father Andy would lead them to Jake that she hadn't considered the possibility of failure. Now she wondered if she'd been wrong. The big house on the hill didn't look like the kind of place Jake would hang out.

Father Andy was pulling into the driveway of the house when Sam's cell phone rang. Her heart sped up as he flipped it open. Maybe all this was unnecessary. Maybe it was Jake.

"Now's not a good time to talk, Ida Lee," Sam said, crushing her hopes. He pulled the car to a curb across the street from the house while Mallory watched Father Andy disappear inside the structure. Sam listened for a couple of moments, then rattled off the address of the place and hung up.

"Ida Lee said she needed the address for her records," Sam said. "She also said she needed to be where the action was, but I told her I needed her in the office."

"I doubt there's going to be much action around here for a while anyway," Mallory said and settled more comfortably in her seat.

"Why do I get the feeling you're going to suggest we wait?"

"Private eyes don't call it waiting." She smiled at him, liking the way his shoulders moved inside his jacket as he stretched. "They call it surveillance."

"I don't remember Dick Tracy doing this." Sam shook his head, rustling his dark hair. "But then, if I were Tracy, Ida Lee would have called me on my two-way radio wristwatch, not on my cell phone. And either Prunetop or Flattop Jones would be inside that house."

"Dick Tracy's in the comics, right?"

He slanted her a look. "He's only the most famous comic-book detective there is."

"I thought so, but I wasn't sure. I didn't read comic books growing up."

"I can sympathize." Sam leaned back against the headrest. "My mom's an English teacher who's a literature snob. I had to sneak comics into the house. Oh, man. She was so against me reading them that I had to hide them in the attic."

"So she never found out?"

"Oh, she found out all right. She opened the overhead door to the attic one day, and they came crashing down on her head." The soft sound of his chuckle reverberated through Mallory, making her tingle. "Holy avalanche, Batman. The way she carried on, you would've thought I was stashing nude pictures of Cat Woman."

Mallory smiled at him. She liked sharing confidences with him while they sat in the car, the cozy atmosphere at odds with the shivery winter cold. It made her feel as though she could tell him anything.

"That's not the way it was in my house," she said.

"My dad was hooked on the Sunday comics, and my mom couldn't get enough of *Mad Magazine*."

"And you're telling me you didn't realize you were living in paradise?"

"To me, paradise was the literature section at the county library." She smiled. "It drove my parents crazy that I wasn't interested in reading what they read."

"So did you major in literature in college?"

"Philosophy," she answered. "Unfortunately, I didn't take into consideration that there aren't a whole lot of jobs out there for philosophy majors."

"Is that why you took a job at your sister's business? Because you needed a job?"

Mallory frowned, because it hadn't happened quite that way. Lenora had come to her, tears streaking her beautiful face, and talked about how her business would fail unless she took on a partner. Of course Mallory had offered. "I took the job to help Lenora out."

"Lenora's not your responsibility."

"Of course she is. She's my sister."

He laughed shortly, without humor. "You don't think she should be responsible for herself?"

"Well, yes. But that doesn't mean I can't help her get what she wants."

"What about what *you* want?"

"I want to help Lenora." She frowned at him. Why couldn't he understand? "Just like you want to help Jake."

"It's not the same thing."

"Why not?"

"Because you're doing the party-gram thing because it's what your sister wants to do. I'm not going to become a private detective to please my brother.''

''I thought you already were a private detective.''

''Are you kidding? I've never even seen *Columbo*.''

''Then why did you say you were a private eye?''

''*You* said that. I went along with it, because I didn't want to lose Jake a client.''

''Aha,'' she accused. ''So you *were* helping him.''

''Only because I thought he'd be back by now, and I'd be off sailing in my twenty-eight-foot catamaran.''

''So you're a sailor?''

He laughed. ''Not hardly. Up until a couple weeks ago, I was a floor broker on the New York Stock Exchange. I owned a firm that handled orders for small brokerages that don't have access to the floor.''

''Wow. Sounds exciting.''

''I wouldn't put it quite that way. Hectic, yeah. Pressured, sure. Competitive, most definitely.''

''So what happened?''

''One day, I was shouldering my way through the crowd, trying to get to the trading post, and it hit me that I hadn't seen the sun in three days. My whole life was taking place there on the floor.''

''So you sold the business just like that?''

''Just like that.'' He snapped his fingers. ''I'm going to spend the next few years experiencing all I've been missing. That's why I'm buying the sailboat.''

''I thought it was already yours.''

''It's on the way to becoming mine. I put a downpayment on it, but before I could finalize the deal Jake called asking me to help him out.''

Jake. She'd been enjoying Sam's company so much that she'd almost forgotten she was pretending to be Jake's fiancée. Suddenly, the reason for her pretense seemed silly. She and Sam had made a connection. He'd understand why she was going to extremes to get their siblings back together. It wouldn't matter that she was the sister of Jake's fiancée and not Jake's fiancée herself.

"I was surprised when he called," Sam said before she could broach the subject of who she really was. "Me and Jake, we make it a point not to stick our noses in each other's business."

"But that's what good brothers and sisters do," Mallory protested, amazed he didn't realize that. "If you didn't think so, you wouldn't be sitting here with me."

"Oh, no." Sam gave his dark head a vehement shake. "I was hoodwinked into doing this, remember? Don't get me wrong, I want to find Jake, too. My boat's waiting. But I wouldn't be doing this if you weren't his fiancée."

Mallory felt as though a thousand bees had just descended on her with their stingers extended. "Why does it matter who I am?"

"Are you kidding? A fiancée has the right to know if there's a husband in her future. Not that I would have told Jake that if he hadn't dropped me in the middle of this."

Mallory didn't need to ask what rights the sister of Jake's fiancée had. Sam had already given her the answer: a big, fat zilch.

She clamped her mouth shut and stared back at the house. She needed Sam to find Jake. He had access to his brother's office, his town house and his records. As much as she wanted to tell Sam the truth, she couldn't. Not when true love was at stake.

6

SAM WONDERED IF every stakeout was as arousing as this one. He doubted it.

He and Mallory had stopped talking ten minutes ago, and he was doing his best to pretend he was staking out the house on the hill. But the woman at his side was much more intriguing.

It hardly seemed to matter that she was dressed in jeans, boots and a sweater instead of the body-hugging costumes he'd seen her in previously. He could easily picture what her body looked like under those clothes.

Oh, jeez. This was bad. He should think about something other than his brother's fiancée, such as the catamaran waiting for him in Florida. But when he did, he pictured Mallory inside the cabin, her luscious figure barely covered by a bikini, her finger beckoning him to come join her on the bed where they would…

A series of sharp raps on the driver's-side window interrupted his erotic fantasy. He turned to see Ida Lee peering at him, her face magnified by the glass, and the fantasy died a mournful death. He rolled the window down halfway, and cool wind blasted through the car.

"What are you doing here?" Sam asked.

"I told you I was bored. What did you think I was going to do? Stay in the office by my lonesome while you and the dame have all the fun?"

"That *is* what a secretary usually does," Sam pointed out.

"Yeah, well, I ain't no usual secretary. I've been thinking on it, and I've decided my position should be upgraded to executive assistant. Sort of a do-anything kind of job."

"You go, girl," Mallory piped in. "A woman doesn't get anything in this life unless she goes for it."

"We don't even know if Jake is going to go for her being a secretary," Sam protested, but it was as if he hadn't spoken.

Ida Lee let herself into the back seat of the car and shut the door on the winter cold. She scooted forward so that her white head was positioned between Mallory and Sam.

"Fill me in on what's happening," she demanded.

"Nothing's happening," Mallory answered, which put Sam in his place. He'd been so aware of her that he'd barely kept his hands off her, but obviously she hadn't felt the same way. Probably, he thought darkly, because she had this love thing going on with his brother. "We're just sitting here, watching the house, waiting for Father Andy to leave."

"You're spying on a priest?" Ida Lee covered her mouth with small, wrinkled hands.

"He's not a priest," Sam explained. "He's an advice columnist. He writes the 'Dear Andy' column for the *Times*."

"Get out of town!" Ida Lee's small eyes turned bright. "I love Andy. I wrote him a letter once back when me and Edgar were having problems. I couldn't sleep on account of Edgar's snoring, and it was making me mean as a june bug in February."

"What did he advise?" Mallory asked.

"All kinds of things. Separate beds, separate rooms, earplugs, surgery."

"Did any of them work?"

Ida Lee shrugged. "I never found out. It was easier just to get rid of Edgar."

Sam wished he could get rid of Ida Lee, but there were a lot of things he wished for and couldn't have. Like Mallory.

"There's Father Andy now," Mallory said, and Sam was grateful to have something else to think about.

The advice columnist was standing on the threshold of the open door, pausing there as though saying his goodbyes. After a moment, he pulled the door closed and moved across the porch and down the steps. The wind had picked up, and Father Andy swayed as he made his way to his Maserati sports car.

Sam was so intent on the scene that he was surprised to hear the back door of the car open. He swung around in time to see Ida Lee sliding across the seat.

"Wait," Sam said. "Where are you going?"

"To get his autograph."

"You can't do that," Mallory cried. "We're staking him out."

"Fiddlesticks," she said. "A chance like this comes around only once in a lifetime."

Sam grabbed for her as she slid the rest of the way across the car seat, but all he came up with was her scratchy plaid scarf. Ida Lee hurried across the street straight for the advice columnist. She caught up to him before he opened the door of his car.

"Somebody has to talk to her about keeping a low profile on a stakeout," Mallory muttered as Ida Lee dug into her gigantic purse and produced what looked to be an autograph book and a pen.

She talked animatedly to Father Andy for a few minutes, probably about the clamorous Edgar, before he got in the sports car and drove away. Moments later, Ida Lee gave a coast-is-clear sign. Sam and Mallory got out of the car and crossed the street.

"I don't know much about detective work," Sam said when they reached her, "but I do know you don't ask subjects under surveillance for their autographs."

"Nonsense," Ida Lee said. "It was a diversionary tactic. While I was talking to him, there was no chance of him noticing you two in the car."

"Not even when you got out of it and ran across the street?" Mallory asked.

"Come on," Ida Lee said, ignoring them and dashing up the porch steps. For eighty-plus, she was unusually spry. She'd already rung the doorbell. "We're trying to find out if Jake was here, right?"

"Let's not tell her," Mallory told Sam out of the side of her mouth. "We could try a diversionary tactic."

"Too late," Sam said. Somebody had opened the door, and Ida Lee was already striding through it. Sam put a hand at the small of Mallory's back, telling himself he wanted to guide her through the door, but knowing it was just an excuse to touch her.

"What's that noise?" Mallory asked a second before she realized the answer to her question.

It was the sound of children. They were everywhere. Little ones sat on a mat drawing in coloring books. Older ones were clustered around a television set watching a nature documentary. Toddlers played pat-a-cake with teachers.

"Oh, my gosh," Ida Lee exclaimed. "We're in the land of the Lilliputians. I haven't felt so tall since I read *Gulliver's Travels*."

A woman with salt-and-pepper hair and a sturdy build left a group of children in the corner and approached them. Her smile mimicked the happy face on her yellow T-shirt.

"G'Day," she said with an accent that Sam pegged as Australian. "Welcome to G'Day Care Center. If you're here to pick up one of the little ones, I hope you remembered your permission form."

"Oh, darn." Ida Lee snapped her fingers. "I done forgot. But I didn't come to pick Buddy up. I came to visit. I'm his granny."

Oh, no, Sam thought. Here she goes again.

"Buddy?" The woman looked confused. "There's no Buddy here."

"That's 'cause he only lets his granny call him that." Ida Lee searched the room and pointed out a dark-haired boy about five years old. "He's that one over there."

"Jerry? Just a minute, I'll bring him over."

"What do you think you're doing?" Sam whispered the moment the director of the day-care center was out of hearing range.

"I'm gaining her trust so she'll be more likely to confide in us," Ida Lee said. "Private eyes do it all the time. If she thinks we're related to little Jerry there, she'll open up like a faucet."

"But we're not related to little Jerry," Sam said.

"She doesn't know that."

The director of the center came across the room, holding little Jerry by the hand. "Your granny's come to visit, Jerry," she said when they were almost upon them. "Right there."

Jerry stopped in his tracks, opened his mouth wide and let out an ear-splitting yell before he went sprinting in the opposite direction.

"That's what I get for making him eat his brussels sprouts and lima beans at dinnertime," Ida Lee said. "No respect."

The woman's eyes narrowed. "Please leave," she told Ida Lee, pointing toward the door. "Now. Before I call the police."

Sam thought of the oversize cop with the attitude problem and took the octogenarian secretary by the arm. "Come on, Ida Lee. You've got to do as she says."

"But it's cold out there!" she protested as he ushered her toward the door.

"Then get in my car, turn on the heater and wait," he ordered.

She stuck out her tongue at him but did as he said. He closed the door behind her, turned and walked back to where Mallory stood by the director.

"I want you two out of here, too," the director told them. Her face no longer mimicked the happy smile on her shirt.

"Oh, but we're not with that lady." Mallory flashed her a look that was all innocence, but the director wasn't buying it.

She jerked a thumb at Sam. "Yeah, right. Then why'd he call her by name?"

"She's very friendly," Mallory said. "She introduced herself on the way in. Isn't that right, Sam?"

"Um, sure," Sam said, but the director appeared

unconvinced. "I mean, yes. Definitely. Never saw her before in our lives."

She narrowed her eyes. "Then what *do* you want here?"

"We're looking for someone," Mallory said, then hastened to add. "Not a miniature someone. An adult someone."

"Who might that someone be?"

"My brother," Sam answered. "Jake Creighton."

"Oh." The woman drew out the syllable. "Father Andy said the two of you might come by, but I thought it'd take you longer than this to find me. It sure took your brother longer."

"Are you saying Jake's been here?"

"Yes, he's been here." She pursed her lips and regarded them solemnly, as though considering how much to say. "You better come into my office."

The office, tucked into a corner of the day-care center, was a photographer's showplace. The walls were plastered with photos of children, a montage of innocence. The color images had obviously been taken recently, but the walls also contained a large number of black-and-white photos with yellowed edges. Sam examined them, discovering most of those photos pictured infants.

"These babies in the photos are so cute, but I don't remember seeing any when we came in," Mallory said. "Are they in a different part of the center?"

The director shook her head. "G'Day doesn't take infants anymore. These shots were taken years ago when this building was a home for unwed mothers."

Sam frowned. She'd sounded matter-of-fact about the building's history, but he had a feeling there was a clue to Jake's whereabouts in there somewhere. Only he didn't have the skill to figure out where.

"Did you work here then?" Sam asked.

"I started working here thirty years ago, right after I emigrated from Australia. Things have changed, but I've always enjoyed working with the little ones." She paused. "Now suppose you tell me why you're tracking your brother."

"We want to find him, is all." More accurately, Sam thought, he *needed* to find him. A half hour alone in the car with Mallory had taught him that he'd best get away from the temptation she presented before he did something he regretted. "He disappeared and didn't tell us where he was going."

"I can't help you there. He didn't tell me where I was going, either."

Sam heard Mallory sigh, a heartfelt noise that affected him to the core. He couldn't let this be a dead end, not when she had so much invested in finding his brother.

"Please don't tell us you're bound by professional ethics not to reveal what you and Jake talked about."

To his surprise, the director laughed. "I'm not Father Andy, and Jake isn't one of my charges. Professional ethics don't apply here."

"Then what did you talk about?" Mallory asked.

"Children," the director answered. "He asked all kinds of questions about the children."

"Was there anything specific he wanted to know?" Sam asked.

After a moment of thought, the director nodded. "He wanted to know about the babies. He seemed very interested in what happened to the babies."

THE FIRST THING SAM noticed when he pulled his rental car to a stop in front of Lenora's Party-Grams was that the sign advertising the business didn't contain Mallory's name. The second was that it wasn't big enough.

The size of the sign probably didn't matter anyway. In its own way, this out-of-the-way location in northwest Philadelphia was just as faulty as the one his brother had chosen for Jake Creighton Investigations.

The way to generate clients for a business was to place its headquarters in a high-traffic area. Either that, or advertise in a high-traffic area.

Neither Jake nor Mallory and her sister had adhered to that basic principle.

But Sam didn't think it was the right time to mention that to Mallory. She'd been unusually silent during the drive from the G'Day Care Center. After years immersed in the commotion of Wall Street, Sam usually enjoyed silence. But he missed her incessant chatter.

He walked her to the door, unable to keep himself from touching her, even if it were only a hand on her arm.

She turned, and against the backdrop of the fallen snow, Jake noted her eyes seemed greener. Even though she was looking at him, her mind, as usual, was on Jake.

"My head hurts from thinking so much," she said, and he could see her breath in the cold afternoon air. "But I still can't make sense of why Jake went to that day-care center."

Sam had been thinking about his brother's motives in visiting the center, too. He had a theory, but he wasn't eager to share it. But when her eyes turned sad and her mouth drooped, he knew he was going to.

"Has Jake ever told you how he feels about having children?"

Mallory shook her head, surprising him. He would have figured the children issue to be a major topic of discussion among engaged couples. If Mallory were his fiancée, she'd know he wanted children. Lots of them.

"Seems to me that Jake's doing some soul-searching about marriage and what it means." Sam licked his lips, finding the next part hard to admit. "I think him going to Father Andy and then that day-care center are good signs."

"You do? How?"

"Father Andy does premarital counseling, right? Maybe he sent Jake over to that day-care center to show him how rewarding being a father could be."

"You really think so?"

It was just a theory, one he wanted to be wrong, but there was such hope in her eyes that he couldn't disappoint her.

"Sure. I wouldn't be surprised if Jake showed up in the next few days on his knees asking you to forgive him."

"Really?"

He swallowed, not wanting to picture the scene. "Really."

Mallory beamed at Sam, filled with new hope. If Jake came knocking at the door to beg Lenora's forgiveness, she'd be free to tell Sam she wasn't and never had been engaged.

"Thank you," she whispered, standing on tiptoe to kiss his winter-cooled cheek. She felt his body tense, the way hers did whenever he came near her, and knew that the sexual attraction flowing between them was close to spiraling out of control.

Spurred by the knowledge, she drew back and met his passion-dark eyes. Her shiver had nothing to do with the chill. She silently repeated her mantra: You must not caress the brother of your fake fiancé. Then quickly, before she did some caressing she'd regret, she turned and let herself into the apartment.

She closed the door and leaned against it, hoping he'd forgive her when she confessed her deception.

But she couldn't think about that now, not when her mission to get her sister and Jake back together was so close to being a success.

The message light on the business answering machine was blinking, but she ignored it and took the steps two at a time. She was much more interested in the messages on the machine in Lenora's bedroom.

The red light winked at her, giving her hope that Jake had called Lenora about reconciling. Mallory pressed down the message indicator without a second thought. Privacy be danged. True love was at stake here. She held her breath as she waited for Jake's voice to come over the recording.

"Hey, doll. Sheldon Burns here."

Sheldon the Sloth! Mallory covered her mouth in horror. Lenora had gone out with the Sloth before she'd dated the Gecko. As far as Mallory knew, he'd never held down a regular job. The last she heard, he was sponging off his parents.

"Give me a call, why don't cha? The number's…"

Mallory hit the delete button before Sheldon could recite his telephone number. She thought of it as an act of kindness. Her sister was in such a vulnerable state that she might do something crazy, such as date the Sloth again.

Mallory would make sure that didn't happen. Jake was the perfect man for her sister, especially now that he was coming to his senses. The dalliance with Patty Peaks seemed to be over, and he was thinking marriage and family. Sam had said so.

She tapped a finger on the side of her mouth. Just because Jake hadn't contacted her sister at the apartment didn't mean he hadn't spoken to her. Whenever Lenora was upset, she ran home to their parents. Maybe Jake had figured that out.

A minute later, Mallory had her mother on the line.

"Hello, dear. No, no. You're not interrupting anything. Your father and I were just watching *I Love Lucy.*"

"Can I talk to Lenora?"

Her mother laughed so uproariously Mallory had to hold the receiver at arm's length to protect her eardrums. "That Lucy is such a card," she said, still chuckling. "Did you say something, dear?"

"Lenora," Mallory repeated. "Can I talk to Lenora?"

"You could if she was here, but she's not."

"Not there? But she said she was going to visit."

"She *was* here," her mother said. "But you know how your sister is when the weather's dreary. She was already in such a state that I suggested she go down to the vacation house in Hilton Head."

"Did she go with Jake?" Mallory held her breath, willing the answer to be yes.

"Jake? Why, no. He's the reason she's in a state. I thought you already knew that."

"So you're saying she went to Hilton Head alone?"

"Alone?" Her mother seemed distracted, and Mallory could hear the television laugh track in the background. Her mother chuckled along with it. "Oh, no, no. She didn't go alone. She said something about taking a friend along."

A friend? The wheels in Mallory's mind turned as frantically as if a hamster were exercising on them. If Lenora hadn't taken Jake, who had she taken? "Which friend?"

"She didn't say." Her mother laughed again. "Listen, dear, I've got to go. This is the episode where Lucy and Ethel are scarfing down those chocolates. No matter how many times I watch these reruns, I still hope they save the day."

Mallory hung up. Without her mother guffawing in her ear, it was easier to think about which friend Lenora might have taken to Hilton Head. Unfortunately, the possibilities that popped to mind were Sheldon Burns and DelGreco the Gecko.

Regretting that she'd deleted Sheldon's phone number, she reached under her sister's nightstand for the telephone book. Minutes later, she was talking to him.

"Lenora? Did you say this was Lenora? Man, doll, I didn't think you'd call back. Nobody else has."

"You mean you haven't talked to Lenora?" Mallory asked.

"I'm talking to you now, doll."

"This isn't Lenora. This is Mallory."

"Mallory?" There was a pause. "I was going to try you next."

"You were? Why?"

"I know you and me didn't see eye to eye when I was dating your sister, but I was thinking you might want to lend me a hundred bucks."

"I'll do something better, Sheldon," Mallory said as sweetly as she could. "I'll send you the classified employment section of the newspaper."

"Ah, Mallory, you don't—"

She depressed the dial tone before the Sloth could get in another plea. Where did her sister dredge up these losers? At least Lenora hadn't gone off to Hilton Head with Sheldon. Unfortunately, that left Vince.

Squaring her shoulders for courage, she looked in the white pages under DelGreco and quickly dialed his number. She got an answering machine instructing her to dial his cell phone number.

"Oh, please don't let him be en route to Hilton Head," she muttered as she dialed.

Vince picked up on the first ring, obviously in a car. Disco music and traffic noise warred in the background. "Disco DelGreco tuning in."

"Vince, this is Mallory Jamison. Can I speak to Lenora?"

There was a slight pause. "Lenora? Why would you think Lenora was with me?"

"Because she said something about calling…" The import of what he'd just said hit her, flooding Mallory with relief. "You mean my sister isn't with you?"

"Nope."

So far, so good. "Have you talked to her lately?"

"Not in the past year."

"Well, that's a relief," Mallory couldn't help saying aloud. "Sorry to have bothered you."

"Hey, babe, wait," Vince said before she could ring off. "So Lenora mentioned me?"

Oh, no. "Just in passing. She didn't mean anything by it."

"So she's been thinking about me?"

"I didn't say that."

"Didn't have to. Wouldn't mention me if she wasn't thinking about me. Hey. What happened to her engagement? She dump that Creighton guy?"

"No, no." Mallory was afraid the panic she felt would seep into her voice. She tried to steady herself. "She's still engaged. Very engaged. Extremely engaged."

"Don't believe you, babe. You and me, we got off on the wrong foot. Once me and Lenora start up again, I'll take you disco dancing. It'll be fun. You'll see."

Ugh. "Lenora doesn't want to date you again."

"Won't know that unless I call her, right?"

"No, no." The panic had Mallory in a stranglehold. She barely managed to choke out her next words. "Don't call her."

"Oh, oh, I love this song," Vince said as one disco song blended into another virtually indistinguishable from the first. He sang along with the lyrics.

"So you won't call her, right?" Mallory asked over the music.

"Why not?"

"She's not home," Mallory said desperately.

"She'll be home sooner or later, babe. Thanks for the heads up. Knew she still wanted me."

"Vince, wait—"

"Gotta go, babe. The music's calling. Disco DelGreco tuning out."

Minutes later, Mallory walked downstairs dejected and not only because her eardrums would never be the same again.

Despite what her mother had said about Lenora taking a friend to Hilton Head, her sister had most likely gone off alone. Now, thanks to Mallory, she had Sheldon the Sloth hunting her for a loan and DelGreco the Gecko looking for love.

She needed to find Jake. And fast.

She was about to leave the apartment when she spotted the nagging message light on the business answering machine. She couldn't ignore it, not when Lenora viewed incoming calls as a cause for celebration.

She depressed the button and listened to one prospective client put in a request for Zippy the Pinhead and another ask for Peppermint Patty. Both parties said they'd gotten the name of the business from the classified ad Sam had advised her to put in the newspaper.

Lenora would have viewed getting two calls in one day a coup. Mallory called it a headache. She had only the vaguest idea who Zippy and Peppermint Patty were, but at least she now knew who to ask for help. Coincidentally, it was the same person who could put her new plan into motion—the one she'd just hatched to find Jake.

As soon as she called the prospective clients back and tracked down some costumes, she'd pay Sam a visit.

A little voice in the back of her head told her it would be safer all around if she stayed away from Sam until Jake turned up.

''Shut up,'' she told the little voice and picked up the phone to make the first of her calls.

The sooner she got her work done, the sooner she could go to Sam.

7

"YOU'RE SURE THIS is going to work?" Sam asked, eyeing Mallory warily.

They were standing in a back room of Jake's town house beside a file cabinet so organized it had taken Mallory only seconds to locate his brother's credit card statements. Sam was holding one of them in his left hand, looking down at the account number conveniently printed across the top of the statement.

"Sure, I'm sure. All you have to do is call and pretend to be Jake."

Sam shook his head, troubled at the thought of impersonating his brother. He wasn't cut out for this private eye stuff, that was for sure. But, on the other hand, he'd promised Mallory he'd find his brother.

What's more, Sam was getting worried. Jake had promised to check back in a few days the first time he'd called, but the phone had been silent. Granted, Sam wasn't as close to his brother as he should be, but it wasn't like Jake to renege on a promise.

Jake still deserved a pummeling for what he was putting Mallory through, but Sam wanted to find him healthy and unharmed before he harmed him.

"Okay, I'll do it," he said grudgingly, "but I doubt they'll give that information out to just anybody."

"You're not just anybody. You're the guy who knows his account number and his mother's maiden name.'' Mallory lifted the receiver and handed it to Sam. ''Now dial.''

He did, aware of her eyes on him for the duration of the phone call. She looked so hopeful that he realized he'd do just about anything to avoid disappointing her.

''You were right,'' he told Mallory when he hung up the phone. ''They asked for the last four digits of the account number and our mother's maiden name. After that, I was on Easy Street.''

She closed the gap between them and laid a hand on his arm. Her touch excited him, but he reminded himself that the excitement shining from her eyes wasn't because of him. She was excited because they were getting closer to finding his brother.

''Don't hold back,'' she said, and he almost groaned. If he didn't hold back, she'd be crushed to his chest while he kissed her senseless. ''Tell me about Jake. Has he charged anything in the last few days?''

Sam nodded, aware that his self-control was about to snap if he didn't move away from her.

''He put something on the card last night,'' he said as he moved two paces. He couldn't bring himself to make it three. ''A room for two nights at the Stay-and-Go Inn in Scranton.''

''Scranton?'' She was as surprised as Sam had been. The city was a few hours north of Philadelphia and no vacation destination, especially not in the winter. ''Why would Jake go there?''

''There's one way to find out.'' Sam made his way to the phone again, dialed information and jotted down a name and address on a piece of paper.

''Who are you calling?'' Mallory asked when he

depressed the dial-tone button and let it back out again.

"The Stay-and-Go," he answered. She shot across the room, snatching the receiver from him. Their hands touched, and electricity crackled. Their eyes met and in hers he saw an acknowledgment of the dangerous attraction that was between them. Oh, brother.

"You can't call that inn." Her voice was as shaky as the hand that had put the receiver back on the cradle. "If Jake finds out we're on his trail, he'll vanish again."

"Then what do you suggest we do?"

"We can drive to Scranton in a couple of hours. We have to go up there and confront him."

"Tonight?"

"Yes, tonight. We've got to act fast before things get worse."

For the last fifteen minutes, Sam had been soaking in the way her soft yellow sweater clung to her breasts. Her dark hair looked so sexy swinging around her shoulders that he had to keep fisting his hands so he wouldn't run his fingers through it. It was taking a Herculean effort to keep his distance.

Now she was telling him they were going to spend the next two or three hours locked up in a car together. He doubted things could get much worse.

HE WAS RIGHT. BY THE time the Stay-and-Go came into view more than a hundred miles later, Sam was desperate to get out of the car.

It hardly mattered that the hotel was unremarkable, with a beige facade and four banks of double-tiered rooms shooting out from a small, undistinguished lobby.

To Sam, the Stay-and-Go was salvation, delivering him from the little demon who'd been sitting on his shoulder for the past two hours.

Nothing had deterred the demon, not even a discussion of how Mallory should portray Zippy the Pinhead and Peppermint Patty. It didn't matter that they were two of the least sexy comic-book characters ever created. The demon had refused to budge.

Instead, he'd borrowed a slogan from the telephone company. Only the somebody the demon had urged Sam to reach out and touch happened to be his brother's fiancée. Hell.

Sam had barely brought the car to a stop when he made his escape. He opened the door and leaped out, forgetting about melting snow's propensity to freeze when the temperature dipped below thirty-two degrees.

His legs shot out from under him, and his rear end came into quick, hard contact with the icy ground. He gazed heavenward. "Okay, I get the message," he muttered under his breath as he rubbed his smarting behind. "I need to cool off."

Mallory was out of the car in seconds, slamming the door and rushing to his side. "Are you all right?" Her face was pinched with concern as she extended her arm. "Here, let me help you up."

It was funny how life worked, Sam thought. Here he'd been jumping out of the car to keep from touching her and that very action caused her to touch him. Surrendering to the inevitable, he let her help him. Her hand felt so good in his that, when he was standing, he found he couldn't let it go.

"Got to make sure you don't slip, too," he said to save face. She smiled at him with eyes that sparkled like pretty green jewels. Face saving be damned. He wasn't about to let go of her, not when that smile had been all for him.

Moments later, they walked through the lobby door hand in hand. A mighty gust of wind followed them, scattering the papers on the registration desk and knocking the spindly, dark-haired clerk backward. When the clerk stepped back to the desk, he was missing his hair.

A quick look around revealed that the miniature artificial palm tree behind the desk could have used a barber.

Sam caught the man's eye and raised his brows, trying to direct his attention to the toupee hanging from the tree. The clerk mimicked Sam's eyebrow lift, but his gaze wandered to their joined hands.

"I get it." The clerk waggled his eyebrows, which represented the only pieces of hair on his head. "You two want a room for the night."

Sam dropped Mallory's hand. That's what he got for trying to help out. It reminded him of one of the many reasons he'd adopted a policy of noninvolvement. The clerk's toupee was none of his business.

"Uh, mister, you lost your hair," Mallory pointed out.

"Again!" The man patted his bald head. "This wind is going to be the death of me yet."

Mallory jerked her thumb at the palm tree, and the clerk plunked the toupee off the fronds and settled it on his scalp. Backward. Which is where Sam would have left it.

"Your hair's on backward." Mallory made a circular motion with her index finger. She leaned across the registration desk. "May I?"

The clerk nodded and obligingly lowered his head toward her. Mallory happily rearranged his toupee, murmuring, "The color doesn't quite compliment your eyebrows. If I were you, I'd do something about that."

"Do you really think so?" the clerk asked, patting his fake hair.

"Oh, definitely." Mallory cocked her head to one side and studied him. "You should try a less inky black. Maybe a charcoal. Or an ash. I think you'd be much happier."

Sam cleared his throat. He knew Mallory well enough by now that he wasn't shocked that she was dispensing toupee-care tips to a complete stranger. That didn't mean he thought it was right.

"We were hoping you could help us," he cut in, giving the clerk a look that was all business.

"Certainly," the clerk said, straightening. He looked like a Chia Pet that had stuck a limb in an electric outlet. If Sam had been the one dispensing advice, he'd have advised the clerk to go au naturel. "You wanted a room, right?"

"What we'd really like is a room number," Mallory said. "We're looking for my fiancé."

The clerk's expression disintegrated into confusion. "Your fiancé?" The clerk pointed to Sam. "Then who's this guy?"

Sam was about to tell the clerk that his relationship to Mallory wasn't any of his business when Mallory chirped up. "Sam's my fiancé's brother."

"Whatever." The clerk lifted his brows again, making Sam wonder why Mallory had bothered to explain. "But even if you were Big Brother, I couldn't give out a guest's room number."

"But you can ring his room for us, right?" Mallory

smiled so luminously Sam didn't think any male could refuse her. He certainly couldn't. He'd proved that when he agreed to help her find his missing brother. "My fiancé's name is Jake Creighton."

"Just a minute." The clerk punched some keys on the computer in front of him, then studied the screen. "I'm sorry, but my records indicate Mr. Creighton checked out this morning."

"This morning?" Mallory exclaimed. "But I thought he paid for two nights."

The clerk shrugged. "If he registered for two nights, he changed his mind. Why do you think we call this place the Stay-and-Go? People stay, and then they go."

Mallory swallowed her disappointment. She'd been sure they were on the verge of finding Jake and straightening out the mess he was making of his and Lenora's love life. Not to mention her own.

"Can you tell us if he paid for a single or a double?" Sam asked, and Mallory looked at him in surprise. It hadn't occurred to her that Jake might have someone with him.

"Our singles and doubles are the same price," the clerk said, looking down at his computer, "but it seems to indicate here that he was traveling alone."

"So he didn't have a woman with him?" Sam asked, and Mallory easily followed his train of thought. Sam feared his brother had run off with Patty and her peaks, which was ridiculous. A one-night stand she could believe, but not a long-term affair. Jake loved Lenora. Besides, they'd been trailing Jake for days and there had been no further sign of Patty. Just because Patty hadn't been back to the House of the Seven Veils didn't mean she was with Jake.

"Do you know how many people come through here?" The clerk shook his head. "How am I supposed to remember if he had a woman with him? I don't even remember the guy."

"Thanks." Mallory smiled at the clerk. He'd said his records indicated that Jake was traveling alone. That was enough for Mallory. She had renewed faith in her future brother-in-law, who, after all, was in love with her sister. She turned away from the registration desk, her spirits buoyed.

"You jumped to the wrong conclusion, Sam. Just because Jake left the strip club with a woman who has the Grand Tetons in her blouse doesn't mean he brought her to Scranton."

"Wait a minute." The clerk's voice stopped them from walking out of the lobby. They both turned toward him. "Did you say something about the Grand Tetons?"

Mallory nodded, an ugly sense of trepidation filling her.

"*They* were here," the clerk supplied, then reddened slightly. "I mean *she* was here."

"But you said you couldn't possibly remember all the people who come through the hotel," Mallory protested.

"I don't remember them all," the clerk said dryly, "but every once in a while, something catches my eye."

"Like the twin peaks," Sam said, and the clerk nodded.

Mallory closed her eyes as disappointment came crashing down on her, all the harder because her hopes had just been lifted.

The terrible truth was that Jake hadn't only left a bar with a stripper. He'd run off with one.

MALLORY KEPT HER EYES straight ahead as Sam slowly and deliberately navigated his rental car down the snowy interstate, but she hardly saw the fat flakes that were collecting on the highway. She was too preoccupied trying to fit together the pieces of an increasingly difficult puzzle.

How did Jake's visits to Father Andy and the G'Day Care Center tie into his association with Patty Peaks? Was it possible that he'd been deciding whether to marry and have a family, as Sam had suggested, and come away from his soul-searching convinced he'd rather have a fling with a stripper?

She frowned, trying to rationalize what they'd learned at the Stay-and-Go to what she knew about Jake Creighton.

In her gut, she knew that Jake was a decent sort. The kind of responsible, hard-working man that her sometimes-flighty sister needed to fill in her blanks.

What's more, aside from Romeo and Juliet, she'd never seen two people more in love than Lenora and Jake. They were masters of the long, smoldering look. They held hands. Heck, they even completed each other's sentences. Love emanated from them, like the smells of cinnamon buns and powdery doughnuts from a bakery.

Never would she have dreamed that Jake would do something as irresponsible as follow a stripper around eastern Pennsylvania. The way he looked at Lenora, she wouldn't think he'd notice other women.

She frowned. Okay, scratch that. This was Patty

Peaks she was thinking about. Still, it didn't compute, unless...

"Commitment phobia," she said aloud.

"Pardon me?"

The snow was coming down so heavily that the world in front of them resembled a vast white blanket. Sam had the windshield wipers on double time, but as soon as they flicked the white stuff away, new snowfall took its place.

"I think Jake's suffering from commitment phobia. I was watching a new talk show the other day, and—"

"I thought literature was your thing, not trash TV."

"It's not trash TV. This was more erudite than other talk shows. The show doesn't have transvestites or call girls or male strippers as guests."

A corner of his mouth lifted. "Just the commitment phobic?"

"Exactly." She breathed easier. "And now that I think about it, the symptoms fit like a glove." She shivered. "By the way, can you turn up the heat?"

Sam reached down and adjusted the switch for the heater. "The only thing colder than my brother's heart," he muttered, "is this night."

She ignored him, although she thought it was kind of sweet that he was jumping to her defense. After all, he didn't know Jake was cheating on Lenora. He thought his brother was two-timing *her.*

"Anyway," she went on, "the host of the show advocated treating the problem with cognitive-behavioral therapy."

"I'm sure a talk-show host is very knowledgeable about these things."

"Cognitive-behavioral therapy is more commonly called exposure therapy."

"Too bad Jake's not here right now," Sam said. "We could put him out in the snowstorm and see if it works."

"Not exposure to the elements," Mallory said. "Exposure to whatever frightens him."

"Which would be?"

"Le…" Mallory started to say her sister's name, but remembered her masquerade just in time. "Love," she finished. "All we need to do is find Jake, expose him to his beloved and he'll come around."

Sam let out a long breath, and she sensed that he was mentally counting to ten. "So I guess this means you're not buying the theory that he's just a cad?" he finally asked.

"Certainly not," Mallory refuted, then lowered her voice. "I've never told anyone this before, but I have an irrational fear of squirrels."

"Squirrels?"

"Yes. Have you ever taken a good look at one? Those beady eyes. Those quivering whiskers. The way they infiltrate bird feeders. They're just rats with bushy tails. Now, intellectually I know they're not going to hurt me. I mean, come on, they have tiny little claws. But I freak out when one comes near me."

"Which pertains to Jake how?"

"He reacts the same way to commitment. That's his irrational fear. That's why he's off somewhere with Pilfering Patty."

"Who stole your man."

"She's *trying* to steal him. I'm going to get him back." For Lenora.

That decided, Mallory refocused her attention on the highway. Trouble was, she could barely make out where the road ended and the shoulder began. Traffic had tapered off considerably since she'd last paid their surroundings any mind. She noticed that Sam wasn't traveling more than twenty miles per hour and that he'd switched on the turn signal. The world, as they knew it, had turned white.

"This storm kicked up so fast that it's going to be hours before the plows can get through." He slanted her a meaningful look. "Call me blizzard phobic, but if we don't stop now, I'm afraid we'll get stuck out here."

"But why are we pulling off here? It doesn't look like there's anything off this exit."

"There was a sign a mile or two back advertising a hotel that's supposed to be just up the side of that hill."

Now that they were off the main highway, the night was so dark that the car's headlights provided the only illumination. Through the swirling snow, Mallory could barely make out the narrow, two-lane road that snaked upward.

"Are you sure there's a hotel up there?"

"If there isn't, I say we sue for false advertising," he said, and Mallory waited for the panic to claw at her. After all, they could freeze to death if he were wrong. Surely, the car couldn't make it more than a few miles in the driving snow.

Then, right before heading up the mountain, he winked and gave her such a devastating smile that she would have welcomed the opportunity to stave off freezing by sharing body heat.

Just like that, in the space of that wink, instead of panic, she felt calm.

The panic didn't come until Mallory finally spied

the outline of a multitiered building through the snow and caught the name in lights atop it.

Sweetheart Suites.

Oh, great. Just what she needed when she was trapped in a blizzard with a sexy man she couldn't caress.

A love nest.

8

FIFTEEN MINUTES LATER, Mallory and Sam followed a Sweetheart Suites employee down an extravagant hallway festooned with gold fixtures and striped red-and-gold wallpaper. Above each door was a miniature statue of Cupid, his arrow poised to make a strike for love.

"Am I correct in deducing that you two have no luggage?" the man asked. He was so frightfully thin that Mallory thought the red jacket he wore paired with matching red slacks made him look like an anorexic tomato.

"Yep," Sam said. "No luggage."

He glanced back at them over his bony, red shoulder. "It's just as well. I don't suppose, when it comes right down to it, that our guests need luggage."

Before they could reply, he picked up his pace, walking so briskly that Mallory wondered if he were a marathoner in training. Either that, or a man with such disdain for hotel guests that he thought he could shake them.

After Mallory had convinced Sam that the client was responsible for expenses and checked them into the hotel, the red-jacketed man had appeared as if by magic. Mallory barely had time to adjust to the exorbitant price tag of a suite before he was sprinting off with the order that they follow him.

"What did you say your job title was?" she called after him, her voice raised to make up for the distance he was putting between them.

"I'm Beau, your honeymoon concierge," he said, as though it pained him to utter his occupation.

Mallory sped up, alarmed that he'd reached the conclusion they were newlyweds. She didn't notice that he'd come to a stop and would have plowed into him if Sam hadn't grabbed her by the waist and pulled her against the hard length of his body.

Desire gushed through her in a warm rush, making her voice thick. She dared not turn around and look at him for fear she might try to ravish him. "But we're not on a honeymoon."

The concierge raised a brow as skinny as the rest of him. "It won't be the first time someone got into one of our rooms on false pretenses, and I assure you it won't be the last. But, I can hardly toss you back out into the snow."

He unlocked the door, which was painted a golden hue, and stepped under Cupid's bow. As he entered the room, he made a sweeping gesture with one scrawny arm.

"Monsieur and *mademoiselle*," he said, emphasizing her unmarried status. "Your accommodations."

The room was like nothing Mallory had ever seen. The walls were coated with gold paint. From them hung paintings mounted on black velvet and featuring famous lovers—Romeo and Juliet, Cleopatra and Marc Antony, Lady and the Tramp. The furniture was French provincial, the fireplace log-burning and the red carpet so luxuriously thick the heels of Mallory's winter boots sank into it.

Beau strode through the spacious accommodations,

opening a door that led to the bathroom. It was fit for a sultan, its focal point a red heart-shaped hot tub that percolated with bubbles.

Finally, he stepped onto the raised platform that held the suite's centerpiece. An extra-large bed, covered with a red-velvet spread, dominated the middle of the room. It, too, was heart-shaped. At the foot of the bed was another statue of Cupid, this one three-feet tall. The naked, winged infant was aiming his arrow straight at the pillows.

It was as though somebody had hired Bozo the Clown to design a seduction palace.

"I'm afraid there's been a mistake." A guffaw rose in Mallory's throat, and she tried to stifle it. She heard Sam let out a chuckle and dared not look at him. "This appears to be a honeymoon suite."

"Of course it's a honeymoon suite. Sweetheart Suites caters exclusively to honeymoon couples." Beau gave them a disapproving glance. "Or to those pretending to be honeymoon couples."

"So you're saying all the suites look like this?"

"We have some with a Roman theme, but those are booked months in advance. Hedonism is quite a big seller."

"Never mind. This'll do," she said, getting control of her laughter. "Just show us where the second bed is."

Beau gave her another one of those patented eyebrow lifts. "We've found, in our extensive research, that newlyweds prefer to sleep together."

"Then we'll order a cot."

"A cot? You must be joking, mademoiselle. Honeymoon couples do not sleep on cots."

Sam touched her arm. A funny little shiver went

through her body, but she attributed it to the aftereffects of the cold. Sam was as sexy as men came, but no way could passion flare in so clownish a suite.

"Why don't I book us another room?" he whispered while Beau stared at them. His arms, which resembled two pickup sticks, were crossed over his chest.

"No!" Mallory whispered back. The cost of this room was already taking a huge chunk out of her monthly expenses. "I can't afford to pay for two rooms."

"I can. Let me take care of it."

"I'm the client. I'm the one who pays the expenses." She looked around the suite, with its corny decorations and splashes of red paint. She'd be wary of spending the night with Sam anywhere else, but this place could never put her in the mood for love. "We're both adults. We can handle this."

"Are you two going to whisper sweet nothings to each other all night or are you going to let me know if there is any other way I can be of service?"

"I hadn't realized you were being of service," Sam said, and Mallory recognized irritation in his voice. Beau's surly attitude must have gotten to him. "What exactly is it that you do?"

"I make certain that our honeymoon couples have their every need met," Beau said. "I arrange for special activities and answer any questions they may have."

"I have a question," Mallory said. "Why are you a honeymoon concierge when you so obviously hate the job?"

"The job is very satisfactory, mademoiselle," he

said, but Mallory noticed how he bristled. Bingo. She'd hit on his problem.

"Oh, come on, Beau. Everybody else might love a lover, but you don't. Don't tell me this is what you want to do with the rest of your life."

"Of course it isn't," he snapped, his control breaking. "Do you know how hard it is to smile when you haven't had a date for six months?"

"Then maybe you should work on your personality."

"What did you say?"

"Your personality, Beau. You're very sarcastic. Women don't find that attractive in a man."

"Oh, really? And here I thought sarcasm was an aphrodisiac. Not," he said haughtily, "that I am sarcastic."

"Sure you are. We'll get a second opinion if you don't believe me." She tugged on Sam's arm. "Sam, don't you think Beau is awfully sarcastic?"

Sam did think so, but that was beside the point. He'd been ready to dismiss Beau without a tip and be done with it. But not Mallory. For some reason, she was meddling in Beau's life. Just as she meddled in everyone else's life they came across.

"Mallory, just let Beau go."

"I can't do that. This is for his own good. Isn't that right, Beau?" She didn't wait for him to answer. She didn't let his scowl frighten her off, either. "Our mission is to get you a date. First off, we have to establish whether there's anyone you'd like to date."

"Oh, I can't believe—"

"Beau," Mallory interrupted. "Do you want help with your problem or do you want to spend the rest of your life alone and miserable?"

He scratched his head. "Oh, all right. There is this cocktail waitress who works at the hotel bar, but I doubt she'd go out with me."

"Have you asked her?"

"No, but—"

"No buts." She crossed the room until she was standing directly in front of Beau. "Practice on me. Pretend I'm the cocktail waitress and ask me out."

"Do I have to?" He sounded like a five-year-old boy trying to get out of taking a bath.

"Yes. Now ask me."

He sighed. "Angel—"

"Stop right there. Don't start off by calling her by an endearment. Some women really hate that."

"But Angel's her name."

Mallory made a face, but refrained, just barely, from asking heaven to help her. "In that case, go on."

"Angel, I was wondering, if maybe, well, perhaps you might want to go out with me sometimes."

"No, no, no." Mallory shook her head with each negative she uttered. "That won't do. You need to be forceful. Confident. I'll show you how it's done. Come over here, Sam."

"Oh, for Pete's sake, Mallory, I don't think—"

"You can help Beau." She took him by the hand and made him face her. "Show him how to ask a woman out on a date."

Sam wasn't the least bit interested in improving Beau's love life and got ready to say so. Then he became aware of Mallory's soft hand in his, of her green eyes locked on his, of that heady smell of sunshine and orange blossoms. The passion with which she attacked life seemed to surround them both. He took a step closer, bending slightly so he could breath in her scent. Her green eyes darkened.

"You're the most enchanting woman I've ever known," he whispered. "Would you—"

"Yes," Mallory answered, and he moved to close the gap between himself and bliss.

"Oh, for goodness' sake, how is that supposed to help me? He didn't even finish the question." Beau's voice was an unwelcome reality check. Sam stilled inches from Mallory's lips and reluctantly straightened.

Mallory backed up a step, but she and Sam were unable to look at anything but each other.

"The point is to be straightforward and honest, Beau," Mallory said, staring at Sam. She wet her lips, and he nearly groaned. "Just go ask her out."

"Oh, all right. I'll give it a try," Beau said and Sam heard him turn to leave the room. Get out, get out, he thought as the door opened. But Beau didn't leave. "I almost forgot," he called. "Smile."

A flashbulb went off, effectively breaking their gaze. Sam turned reluctantly to see Beau brandishing a camera. "I'll get your official honeymoon photo to you tomorrow afternoon," he said.

"But we're only staying the night," Sam pointed out.

"Then make it a good one," Beau said haughtily before he shut the door in their faces.

Mallory hurried to the door and opened it. "There's that sarcasm again, Beau," she shouted down the hall. "Gotta work on that sarcasm."

Sam took a deep breath, telling himself it was a good thing Beau had broken the mood of a moment ago. Concentrating on all the things he liked about

Mallory was dangerous, so he focused on something he didn't like. "Anybody ever tell you that you should work on staying out of other people's business?"

"Oh, sure. All the time. Never does any good, though. Who else is going to help the Beaus of the world?"

He was about to argue the point, but didn't think it would do much good. Telling Mallory not to care about people around her would be like trying to blot out the sun.

Instead, he walked around the room, past a table made to look like a pair of pursed lips and a gold banister that held pewter figurines of embracing nudes. The decorator had obviously gone to a lot of trouble to stock the suite with items meant to create a passionate mood. Too bad they were all so corny.

He picked up one of the nudes and his mind immediately conjured up a picture of Mallory's lush body sans clothes. He blinked the image away with great difficulty and put down the figurine.

Corniness aside, maybe he shouldn't take any chances.

"I could still get another suite," he offered.

"Not when I'm footing the bill, you can't. This room is big enough for the both of us." She affected a western drawl à la John Wayne. Good. John Wayne wasn't sexy.

In her pacing, she passed a marble coffee table that had two white T-shirts laid out on it. She picked up the top one and shook it out. It was emblazoned with two interlocking red hearts. A gold-and-orange fire raged behind them. Feel The Heat In A Sweetheart Suite, it read.

The saying couldn't have been sillier, but the look

that passed between them was pure passion. It felt to Sam as though the ridiculous fire pictured on the T-shirt had come alive inside his body.

"At least I have something to wear to bed," Mallory murmured and practically sprinted for the bathroom. "I'm going to take a bath."

Beau had told them the heart-shaped hot tub doubled as a bathtub, and Sam pictured Mallory shedding her clothes and stepping naked into the bubbling water. He closed his eyes, willing his body to stop responding to her, but his erection was so hard it was almost painful. What was happening to him?

A few days ago, he would have laughed at the notion of a hot tub shaped like a heart. Now the idea of a woman stepping into one was turning him on. Not just any woman. Mallory of the big heart and zest for life. He needed something to take his mind off Mallory's glorious naked skin, so he picked up the phone and dialed his brother's town house.

As expected, he got the answering machine. His next call was to the office.

"'lo?" The voice sounded as though it belonged to a very young child.

"This isn't Jake Creighton Investigations, is it?"

"Jake who?"

"No. I'm not Jake. I'm Sam."

"Sam who?"

"Never mind." He was about to hang up when he heard what sounded like the phone being wrenched away from the child.

"Jake Creighton Investigations." Ida Lee's scratchy voice came over the line, which was exactly what he needed. There was nothing like a snarling senior citizen to get his mind off seduction. "You got a case, we got a solution."

"Ida Lee. Sam here. Who was that who answered the phone?"

"Oh, that was my grandson Bubba."

"Your grandson's at the office with you?"

"Of course not. What do you think I am, cracked? The only people who go down there after dark are criminals. I had the calls forwarded to my place."

"Have there been any calls?"

"You're not gonna believe this, but yes. We got a call from a woman who said Little Orphan Annie recommended us and another from a guy who claims he was referred by somebody called Womaniac."

Oh, great, Sam thought. Just what he needed. Two more cases when he could barely handle the one he already had. "Please tell me you didn't set up appointments with them for tomorrow?"

"Appointments? I was supposed to set up appointments?"

"That is what a secretary does."

"I already told you. I've decided I'm more than a secretary," she said. "I'm an executive assistant."

"How about assisting me by calling them back tomorrow to see when they want to meet." It pained Sam to make the request, but prompt attention to clients was good for business. And, despite it all, he wanted his brother's business to succeed.

"All right, all right," Ida Lee groused. "Where are you anyway? I tried your cell phone and didn't get an answer."

"We're probably out of the service area."

"Who's we?"

Sam sighed. He hadn't wanted to get into this, but

Ida Lee *was* the agency's secretary. He told her about getting caught in the snowstorm after trailing Jake and Patty Peaks to Scranton. "I'm stuck at a hotel in the Poconos with Mallory."

"Who's that?"

"Mallory," he repeated, then remembered that wasn't what Ida Lee called her. "The dame."

"You're with your brother's girl?" She lowered her voice. "She's two-timing him, isn't she? I could've told you that would happen. In the books I read, it always does."

"She's not two-timing Jake. I'm with her, but I'm not *with* her," Sam said. Only silence came from the other end of the line. "Oh, never mind. Here's the number."

He hung up, but not before Ida Lee warned him to be careful of beautiful dames packing secrets. Except there was nothing mysterious about Mallory. She was a woman so in love with his brother that she was willing to believe he was commitment phobic instead of what Sam knew him to be.

A nincompoop.

His brother didn't deserve Mallory, but Sam had learned a long time ago that life wasn't fair. Because he was the older of the two brothers, Sam had to fight their domineering father for independence at every turn. Finally, it had seemed his only recourse was to distance himself from the family. Jake had merely sat back and enjoyed the gains Sam's battles had gotten him.

Shaking off the memories, Sam spied an armchair in the corner of the suite. It was conspicuous solely because it looked normal. Releasing a deep breath, he sat down.

And had the chair spring to life.

It took him a moment to realize the thing was moving and more than a few more to locate the power switch and turn it off.

A vibrator would have been bad enough when he was trying to keep his mind off sex. A vibrating chair was worse.

A magazine lay on the glass table next to the chair, and he picked it up and flipped through it. He shut it fast and checked the front of the publication for the title: *Hot Hints for the Honeymooner.*

He pulled his sweater over his head and fanned his face. He didn't think he could get any hotter.

Moments later, the door cracked open and Mallory walked out. She'd washed the curls right out of her hair, which fell long and straight to her back, but that wasn't the part of her commanding attention. She was dressed in the smaller of the two T-shirts, and it barely covered her bottom. The word *Heat* stretched across her full breasts. For a moment, he couldn't breathe.

"I left the extra-large T-shirt for you," she said.

"Mallory?" He voice was so raspy her name was barely recognizable.

"Yes?"

He cleared his throat. "Remember what you said about this suite being big enough for the both of us?"

She nodded.

"It won't be unless you put on the extra-large."

A blush climbed up her cheeks that was so becoming he almost groaned. She disappeared into the bathroom without another word. Moments later, she emerged dressed in a T-shirt that fit her like a sack. But the damage was done. He'd already seen the outline of her body in the smaller of the two shirts, and he couldn't get the picture out of his mind.

His eyes followed her as she crossed the room and sat on the edge of the massive heart-shaped bed, the spot in the room farthest from where he was.

He was unprepared for her giggle.

"It's a water bed," she said, tucking her legs under her and bouncing into the middle. She overbalanced and fell onto her back. Mirrors stretched the length of the ceiling above the bed. He watched the bed undulate and the sack shirt inch up her thighs to reveal a staggering length of bare leg. "Isn't this the corniest room you've ever seen?"

It was undoubtedly corny, just as her T-shirt was unquestionably tacky. Just as he was undeniably aroused.

"I'm going to get ready for bed, too," he said gruffly. Once inside the bathroom, he leaned the back of his head against the closed door. His gaze fell on the valentine-shaped tub. She'd drained it, but he could picture her inside the water, gloriously naked. How was he going to survive the night without touching her?

He shut his eyes while his conscience warred with itself. Why shouldn't he act on the sexual attraction that was sizzling between them? Jake, after all, was off indulging himself with another woman. Nobody would blame Sam. He let out a heavy sigh. Nobody, that is, but himself.

It didn't matter that his brother didn't deserve her. Mallory loved Jake. And because he was Jake's brother, she trusted him. Only a snake would take advantage of a woman in a situation like this. He turned the faucet on cold, hoping he didn't prove to be a reptile.

He ignored the purple "Passion Pellets" on the lip of the tub and stepped into the frigid water. His toes began to turn blue, but he doubted the bath would cool him off.

He could only pray that Mallory would be in bed when he got out of the bathroom, the red-velvet covers pulled up to her chin.

INSTEAD, SHE WAS SITTING on a red shag rug in front of the fireplace sipping champagne. Champagne, for Pete's sake. The nectar of seduction. She'd poured a second glass for him and greeted him with a soft smile. His body hardened. Never mind that the fire was gas and the logs were artificial. What was going on inside him was definitely real.

"Beau came by with a bottle, and I didn't want it to go to waste. He brought food, too," she said, lifting the silver covers off two silver plates. "Fried oysters with caviar on the side and chocolate-covered strawberries for dessert. Get this. Sweetheart Suites keeps a frozen supply of oysters and strawberries on hand because they're supposed to be aphrodisiacs. Did you ever hear of anything so corny?"

"Nope," Sam said, but he didn't think it was safe to talk about aphrodisiacs. Especially because nothing could have made him want her more than he did at that moment. The fire cast a soft glow over her that made her look even more beautiful than usual. Her bare feet were tucked under her, and her long hair cascaded down her back. He might have succumbed to the temptation to take her in his arms if her lower lip hadn't trembled.

He was instantly at her side. Her face was so expressive that he was starting to be able to read the nuances of her emotions and he could tell she was upset. The passion fled, and in its place came concern.

"What's wrong?"

"It's Beau," she said, sniffing and trying to smile.

"Aaah," Sam said, immediately understanding. A few strands of her hair had dried haphazardly, and he smoothed them back from her forehead. "I take it he didn't have any luck with that cocktail waitress?"

The expression on her face crumbled. "He was pretty unhappy. Apparently he told her he'd do anything to please her, and she asked him to please get lost."

"At least she was polite about it," Sam said, trying to latch on to something positive. He didn't care if the honeymoon concierge got a date, but Mallory did.

"Maybe I could find somebody else who'd date him," she mused. "There must be someone out there for him."

Trust Mallory's soft heart to convince her head that a virtual stranger's problem was her problem.

"It's not your job to find Beau a girlfriend." He sensed that she was about to protest and laid two fingers against her lips to silence her. Reason wasn't going to work, so he'd remind her that they had their own problem. "Besides, we've got our hands full trying to find Jake. Remember?"

At the mention of his brother, Mallory drew back just enough that his fingers dropped from her lips. She gave him a shaky smile and lifted her champagne glass. "To finding Jake," she said.

"To finding Jake," he repeated as their glasses clinked.

The glasses were engraved with two cartoon hearts, complete with bug eyes and puckered lips, reaching for each other with chubby red arms. The design transcended silly, but it didn't seem silly with Mallory by his side. Sam choked down some of his champagne. He had it bad if cartoon hearts could turn him on.

They spent the next ten minutes eating in companionable silence. Oysters had never been one of Sam's favorite foods, but they were both hungry after the long drive. They didn't talk again until they were almost finished with the chocolate-covered strawberries.

"Sam, why doesn't Jake ever talk about you?" Mallory asked, licking some chocolate from her bottom lip. "Before you showed up in town, I didn't know he had a brother."

A brother. Maybe if she kept bringing up Jake, Sam would remember why he shouldn't want to kiss the chocolate off himself. "We're not close," he answered shortly.

"Why not?"

He shrugged and popped the last strawberry into his mouth. "I left home at eighteen. Jake was four years younger. We were never close to begin with. After that, we drifted further apart."

"Do you mean you left home to go to college?"

"No. I mean I left home for good. I never went back."

"But why?"

Sam hesitated, because this was a subject he seldom discussed. After a moment, he found, to his surprise, that he wanted to tell Mallory about it. Other women had asked him about his past, but he'd never gotten a sense that they were truly interested in his answers. With Mallory, he didn't doubt that.

"I left home to get away from my father," he said. "He wanted to lead my life for me, and I wouldn't let him."

She tilted her head, the firelight turning her skin golden. Her expression was puzzled. "What do you mean, he wanted to lead your life for you?"

"He pushes. He always has. When I was a kid, he needed to approve my choice of friends, clothes, music, sports, everything. It got worse as I got older. He's a lawyer. He refused to put me through college unless I became one, too."

"So you rebelled?"

"I didn't see it as rebellion. I wanted to major in business, not to drop out of school and join a rock band. But my father couldn't accept my decision. So I dropped out of the family and put myself through school."

She looked troubled. "But that doesn't make sense. Jake's not a lawyer. If your father had so many problems with you majoring in business, why did he let Jake become a private eye?"

"Probably because I paved the way for Jake to do whatever he wanted to do. The old man was easier on him because of the way I reacted to all the pushing he did."

"And now you don't see your parents anymore?"

"I do see them," he said, neglecting to mention that he'd been less than an hour from their Florida home last week and hadn't dropped by. "Just not much. I'm never again putting myself in a position where my father can tell me what to do."

"But people who care about other people have opinions on what they should do."

"Then they should keep those opinions to themselves."

"Oh, really? So when we find Jake, you're not going to tell him you disapprove of how he's been acting?"

He frowned. "You know that I will."

"I rest my case. The reason you'll express your opinion is because you love him."

No, Sam thought. Oh, he did love Jake. Quite a lot actually. But more likely the reason he had such a strong opinion about Jake's infidelity was because he loved Mallory. The knowledge resonated through him, stunning in its intensity.

He loved Mallory. His brother's fiancée. Oh, jeez.

He should have seen it coming, but he hadn't. The more time he spent with her, the more he appreciated the amazing capacity of her heart. Even as he'd tried to stop her from getting involved with everyone around them, he'd wanted her to turn her attention on him. She was a woman who loved deeply, and he wanted all that passion and intensity for himself.

She'd moved closer to him as she made her point, and the firelight flickered over her, highlighting her beauty. With her long mane of hair and shining green eyes, she looked like a goddess. But it wasn't just her looks that attracted him, it was the woman she was underneath her skin. A woman he didn't know nearly enough about.

Because he couldn't help himself, he picked up a strand of her dark hair and slid it back and forth between his fingers. Her eyes darkened, and she let out a breath. He could smell chocolate. Never again would he doubt that it was an aphrodisiac.

"You talk as though the needs of the people you

love are more important than your own needs," he said. "I bet you were one of those girls who worried more that your friends would have dates for the prom than if you would."

He recognized surprise flickering in her eyes. "How did you know that? I set up so many people in high school and college that they called me The Matchmaker."

"Did you date much?" he asked, although he suspected he already knew the answer. She shook her head, and he tucked the strand of hair behind her ear.

"There wasn't time," she said. "There always seemed to be so much to do."

"For others, you mean. There was so much to do for others."

"It's important to me that the people around me are happy." She reached out a hand and touched his cheek. "I want you to be happy, too, Sam. That's why I said the things I did about your family."

"*You* make me happy." The words poured out of him before he could stop them. His fingers moved to her face, and he cupped her cheek, reveling in the soft, satiny feel of her skin. "All I have to do is look at you, and the happiness just wells up inside me."

Her eyes changed, grew darker. He thought he glimpsed desire in them before she lowered her lashes. "I can't believe that. I bet you say that to women all the time."

"I've never said it before, because it's never been true before. I don't know if I can explain how you make me feel. It's like there's a light around you that's always shining, making everything brighter."

"You mean like a floodlight?"

He laughed. "No. Like the light from the sun. I

think it's your warmth. I've never met anyone as caring as you are."

"You're caring."

"Me?"

She nodded. "You don't want anyone to know it, but you are. You came when your brother needed you. You rescued me from that woman and her purse in the bar. You're going way beyond the call of duty to help me."

"Maybe my motives for helping you aren't as pure as you think they are." He could hear her breathing quicken to match his own. He tipped up her chin with a forefinger so he could see into her eyes. He hadn't been wrong. What blazed in them was desire.

He moved toward her as though in slow motion, giving her time to draw back. Instead she came forward. Their lips met in the softest of kisses, and his fingers tangled in her damp hair, holding her loosely, giving her time to reconsider.

He knew it was wrong, but he couldn't stop himself. Especially not when she traced the outline of his lips with her tongue. He groaned, and pulled her toward him, thrusting his tongue inside her mouth in fierce possession.

He felt her full breasts crush against his chest, and pulled her onto his lap to give him better access to all her treasures. His hand stroked her thighs and snaked beneath her T-shirt to capture one of her breasts. His breath caught when he reached bare flesh and felt her nipples tighten.

He buried his face in her neck and trailed kisses up her hairline. He'd been yearning to do this since he first saw her. Denying himself had been eating at his soul. And why? For a brother who didn't deserve her.

A brother who was off with some stripper. A brother he loved.

He shut his eyes tight, trying to forget about Jake, but he couldn't.

"Aw, hell," he said, lifting her off his lap and setting her on the floor beside him. He got up, putting distance between them before he changed his mind.

"Sam, what's wrong?" Mallory looked at him with dewy eyes and swollen lips. It took all his willpower not to rush back to her side.

"I can't do this," he ground out between his teeth. His white T-shirt had come loose from his jeans, his dark hair was tousled and his feet were bare. Mallory had never wanted a man more.

"Why not?" she asked, but the answer immediately occurred to her. Jake. Sam couldn't make love to her, because he thought she was engaged to his brother. "I mean," she amended in a sad voice, "of course you can't."

He covered his face with his hands and shook his head. "That was really low. I shouldn't have taken advantage of you like that."

Mallory's mouth dropped open. He was apologizing for something that was as much her fault as his. More, because she'd tempted fate by inviting him to sit by the fire, knowing full well what she wanted to happen. She should tell him right now that she wasn't engaged to Jake and never had been.

"Sam, I..." The confession caught in her throat as she realized she couldn't tell him the truth. Considering that Patty Peaks and DelGreco the Gecko were on the scene, she needed to find Jake more desperately than before. She couldn't take a chance that Sam would stop helping her search for his brother, not when her sister was in danger of losing her true love. Not when Mallory still had the power to do something about it.

"Don't say anything." Sam crossed the room to the love seat and removed the cushions from it. "We should get some sleep. You can have the bed. I'm going to sleep in the bath."

His head down, he dragged the cushions in the direction of the bathroom. As he moved away from her, every stride seemed like a step on her heart. "You could stay out here, you know," she whispered.

He paused, but didn't look at her. "We both know what would happen if I did, and I'd rather not hate myself in the morning."

As he shut the door to the bathroom, it occurred to Mallory that Sam had no good reason to hate himself. But when he found out she'd been lying to him, he might very well hate her.

9

THE SNOW HAD STOPPED falling and the plows had come through by the time morning came, clearing the roads for their drive back to Philadelphia. They accomplished the trip in silence, with Mallory wondering how she'd gotten them into this mess.

She'd had the best of intentions when she told Sam she was engaged to Jake, never dreaming things would spiral out of control this way.

Sure, she'd thought Sam was a hunk from the get-go. But in the past, she'd been certifiably hunk proof. Able to look but not interested enough to touch. Then again, those other hunks didn't have the facets Sam did. They wouldn't make the sacrifices he had for Jake or for her. They wouldn't have stopped last night because their honor wouldn't let them continue.

She wanted to do a whole lot more with Sam than touch, but with Jake on the lam, it was imperative she adopt a new mantra. Something along the lines of, "You must not make love to the brother of your fake fiancé."

Not only that, but Lenora was losing sight of the fact that Jake was her true love. Mallory's phone call to the Gecko hadn't helped. It had sent him scurrying after her sister, muddling matters even further.

The hard truth was that they were no closer to finding Jake than they'd been at the beginning of their search.

It was a royal mess, is what it was. Especially because Sam was beating himself up because he thought he'd betrayed his brother. A brother who wasn't Mallory's fiancé.

Who would have thought a tiny white lie in the name of true love could lead to this?

"Sam, about last night—" she said when they crossed into the city limits. He immediately silenced her by slicing his hand through the air.

"I don't want to talk about it. I'm taking you home, and we're going to forget any of this happened." His eyes were bloodshot. Mallory's best guess was that he hadn't slept the night before. She'd barely slept herself, and she hadn't been trying to stuff cushions into a heart-shaped hot tub.

"But—"

"Mallory, there's nothing to talk about." He ran a hand over his jaw. "As much as I want to, I'm not the kind of guy who moves in on his brother's fiancée."

Before she could protest further, his cell phone rang. He quickly flipped it open, leaving her no choice but to drop the conversation. She watched his face turn sober as he listened to the caller. After a few moments, he flipped the phone closed.

"Who was that?" she asked.

"Ida Lee." He rubbed his jaw again, but kept his eyes on the highway. "She had the office calls forwarded to her place last night but turned off the phone when she went to bed at ten o'clock. When she checked for messages this morning, there was a call from Jake."

Mallory's heart sped up. "Did he say where he was calling from?"

"He spent last night at the town house. Ida Lee thinks he may still be there."

IDA LEE WAS WAITING on the doorstep when they pulled up to Jake's town house. Her heavy black purse was slung over her shoulder, making it sag so much she looked like Quasimodo.

"Now let me get this straight," she said, addressing Sam. "You got some clout with that brother of yours, right? You can tell him how much help I've been in this investigation."

"You've been helping?" Sam asked.

She bristled. "Course I've been helping. Watch this."

She gave her purse a mighty swing, letting it thwack against the door. "It's too cold to knock," she explained. "Hurts the knuckles."

"Ever heard of doorbells?" Sam stepped in front of her only when he was sure she wasn't going to take another swing. Getting beaned by a purse once in a lifetime was enough. He pulled a key out of his pocket. "These things work even better," he said.

As soon as they were inside the town house, Sam recognized that something was different. The clutter he'd not-so-artfully strewn about the place was gone, replaced with neat stacks of newspapers and magazines. He ran a finger over a table surface. It came away clean. Horror of horrors. Someone had dusted.

"Yep," he said. "Jake's been here."

He walked deeper into the town house, looking for more concrete evidence that his brother was no longer missing. He found it on the kitchen table.

"It's a note!" Ida Lee exclaimed, rushing over to the table and grabbing for it.

Sam reached it first.

"Catch up with you later, bro," the note read. "There's something I gotta do first. A man goes a little crazy when he's in love."

Without speaking, Sam handed the note to Mallory, knowing he wouldn't be able to keep it from her. She read it while Ida Lee, on tiptoe, peered over her shoulder.

"What does he mean by that?" Ida Lee asked. "Is he gonna stand on the steps of City Hall buck nekkid and howl at the moon? Now, that'd be crazy."

Mallory didn't say anything and, after a moment, Ida Lee noticed her silence. "You're thinking he's gonna run off with that stripper lady again, aren't you?"

"Ida Lee," Sam warned, his voice low. Didn't she see the shocked hurt on Mallory's face? "We don't know that."

"He was up in Scranton with her, so it's a pretty darn good guess." Ida Lee studied Sam. "You're worried about the dame here, aren't you? Don't. She might look soft-hearted, but she has a flinty edge. All dames do."

Ida Lee was right. Mallory was tough. She'd get over Jake's betrayal and move on with her life. The beginnings of a plan wormed its way into Sam's mind. He was in perfect rebound position. What's more, after last night, he knew Mallory wasn't immune to him. When she realized his brother was a lost cause, he'd be there to pick up the pieces.

The edges of Mallory's mouth drooped, and Sam tried to ignore what was happening. But then her lower lip trembled, and he could no longer fool himself. She might desire him, but the lip tremble proved it was his brother she loved. The knowledge was like a spear through his heart.

As soon as they found Jake, he was out of there. Even though the sunny seas no longer seemed quite so beckoning.

"Ida Lee's just talking off the top of her head," Sam said as he realized the most astounding fact of all. If Mallory wanted his brother, he wanted her to have him. No matter how much it hurt his heart. "She doesn't know Jake's with Patty."

"She's being sensible." Mallory lifted her chin. "Jake went off with Patty once. We can't rule out the possibility that he's with her again."

Sam blew out a long breath, feeling her pain as acutely as if it were his own. "Tell you what. Consider the decks cleared. I'm not going to charge you for the case."

"Not charge me?" Her green eyes widened. "Why not?"

"I didn't find him, did I?"

"You're not through searching."

"You can't mean you still want me to look for him."

"Of course I want you to keep looking for him. Why do you think I hired you?" She stood up straighter. "In fact, I think you should call the credit card company again. We know he's close, right? Maybe he's made another purchase."

"Right," Sam said, marveling at Mallory's loyalty to his brother. Jake's note had said he was in love, and Sam doubted he meant with Mallory.

"Well, did you find out anything?" Mallory asked

five minutes later after he hung up the phone. He hesitated, not wanting to tell her what he'd discovered.

"Just spit it out," Ida Lee said, and he figured that was as good advice as any. Mallory would know sooner or later anyway.

"The latest charge on his card is for several thousand dollars." Sam hesitated, his gaze on Mallory's pinched face. He remembered what she'd said about Jake not getting around to buying *her* a ring. "It's from McGuffin Jewelers."

The room was quiet for a moment before Ida Lee's voice rang out in the silence. "Oh, my goodness gracious. He bought that nekkid lady an engagement ring."

No sooner had Ida Lee uttered the line than the doorbell rang. "I bet that's the groom-to-be now," Ida Lee predicted.

"Jake wouldn't ring his own doorbell," Sam said, starting toward the door. Ida Lee shouldered him aside, but Mallory was closest to the door.

"I'll get it," she said, figuring she couldn't just stand there in shock all morning.

She swung the door open to reveal a petite blonde with a cupid's-bow mouth and an achingly beautiful face. A blonde who was supposed to be in Hilton Head.

"Mallory?" Lenora asked.

Mallory's first instinct was to go to her sister and gather her into her arms, offering comfort for Jake's betrayal. But her sister was no more aware that her fiancé had betrayed her than Sam was that Lenora was Jake's fiancée. Oh, Lordy.

Mallory's second instinct was much, much stronger

than the first. She followed through on it, slamming the door in Lenora's surprised face.

"Who in the dickens was that?" Ida Lee asked.

They could hear muffled pounding on the door and her sister's voice calling, "Mallory, I know you're in there. Let me in right this minute."

Mallory knew she should obey her sister's command, but she couldn't bring herself to open the door. Not with Sam standing behind her.

"You better not be in there with Jake." Lenora's voice grew louder, shriller. "Not after I told you to stay away from him."

"Who's that?" Sam asked.

"It sounds like a love triangle," Ida Lee said excitedly, bouncing on the balls of her feet. "Who'd of thought Jake had three dames instead of two?"

"Jake doesn't have three dames," Mallory refuted.

"Let me in," Lenora cried. "Darn it, Mallory, open the door!"

"Open the door, Mallory," Sam said, his voice dangerously low. Her sister, she could ignore. Sam, she found she couldn't.

Taking a deep breath, she opened the door and looked into her sister's irate face. Lenora didn't wait for permission to enter, but shouldered her way inside the town house.

"I can't believe you slammed the door in my face. And what are you doing here anyway? I told you to stay away from Jake. But you never listen. You..." Lenora stopped abruptly, looking back and forth between Sam and Ida Lee.

"Who are these people?"

Ida Lee spoke before Mallory could answer. "Who are you? We were here first."

"What does being here first have to do with anything?" Lenora threw up her pretty hands. "This is Jake's place, so I have more right to be here than anyone."

"How so?" Sam stepped forward, towering over her tiny sister. "Who are you anyway?"

"She's my—" Mallory started.

"I'm Jake's fiancée," Lenora said defiantly before Mallory could finish. "That's who I am."

"You can't be Jake's fiancée," Sam said slowly, his gaze sliding back and forth between the sisters. "Mallory's his fiancée."

Ida Lee gasped, covering her mouth with a hand. "Here I thought the dame was the one two-timing Jake. And all this time, it was the other way around. I should have known it. All dames are alike. They reach down your throat and pull out your heart."

Ignoring Ida Lee, Lenora tipped her head to regard Sam. Mallory couldn't bring herself to look at him. "I can't imagine how you got the idea that Mallory and Jake are engaged when he's *my* fiancé," Lenora said.

"Wait just a minute here," Ida Lee said. "This is confusing as all get out. Does Jake have two fiancées or three?"

"Three?" Lenora asked. "Where do you get three?"

"Well, there's you. The dame here," she said, jerking her thumb at Mallory. "And that lady who likes to get nekkid."

Lenora blanched. "What lady who likes to get naked?"

"That stripper down at the House of the Seven Veils. Her name's Patty Peaks on account of her gigantic bosoms. Jake said he was gonna do something crazy. Far as we can tell, it was buying her a rock.''

Lenora's brows drew together, and her pretty mouth parted. She clutched Mallory's arm. "Is that horrible woman telling the truth, Mallory? Did Jake buy another woman an engagement ring?''

"Hey, I'm not a horrible woman," Ida Lee protested. "I'm that three-timer's executive assistant.''

"He's a two-timer, not a three-timer," Mallory refuted. Tears filled her sister's eyes and tore at Mallory's heart. She put an arm around Lenora. "Except we don't know that for sure, honey. We don't know if it was an engagement ring he bought, either.''

"We just think it," Ida Lee cut in. "On account of him spending the night with Patty in Scranton.''

Tears trickled down Lenora's face. "I can't believe I decided not to go to Hilton Head only to subject myself to this.''

Mallory hugged her, giving Ida Lee a furious glance. "Don't cry, Lenora. Like I said, we don't know anything for sure.''

"Lenora?" Sam's eyes cut into Mallory over the top of her sister's blond head. She felt sick. "Isn't Lenora your sister?''

"Yes, she's my sister," Mallory answered, figuring it was past time she introduced them. "Lenora, this is Jake's brother, Sam Creighton.''

"His brother?" Lenora glanced at him with a hurtful look in her eyes. From the confines of Mallory's arms, she declared, "I hate you!''

"Me?" Sam pointed at his chest. "What did I do?''

"You're related to Jake, aren't you?''

"Yeah, but—''

"I bet you spend nights with women you aren't engaged to, too. I bet it runs in the family."

"He just spent the night with the dame here, and they're not engaged," Ida Lee said helpfully. "Hey, maybe it does run in the family. He thought she was engaged to Jake when he was doing it. Didn't you, Sam?"

He didn't answer, but just kept staring at Mallory, his expression inscrutable. Nausea churned inside her stomach. She'd wanted to tell him the truth herself, but he'd found out about her deception in the worst possible way. How would she ever explain it all?

"And you," her sister said, pointing a shaking finger at Mallory as she backed away. "You were meddling again when I told you not to."

"I was just trying to help," Mallory murmured.

"To help? How did you in any way help?"

"I was trying to get you and Jake back together. I didn't want either of you to make a mistake. Him, with Patty Peaks. Or you, with Vince."

"What does Vince have to do with it?" Lenora asked. "You called him, didn't you? That's why I have that message from him on my answering machine."

"I only called him to make sure you hadn't gone to Hilton Head with him."

"That's exactly what I should do. On second thought, maybe I should follow in Jake's footsteps and do something crazy," Lenora said, and Mallory hoped it was something innocuous, like lending Sheldon the Sloth money.

"Do you like to get nekkid and howl at the moon, too?" Ida Lee asked.

"Of course not." Lenora's expression turned defiant. "I'm talking about calling Vince."

"Lenora, you can't," Mallory cried, thinking that the Sloth was looking better all the time. At least he was too lazy to keep in touch.

"Don't tell me what to do. I won't stand for it this time."

"Isn't Vince the Gecko?" Ida Lee asked.

Lenora's tear-streaked face turned puzzled. "Who?"

"The dame here says your ex-boyfriend looks like a gecko. You know, one of those lizardlike things that scurry about eating bugs."

"Vince does not look like a gecko!"

Leaping lizards. Just what Mallory didn't need. Her sister coming to the defense of one of nature's lowest life forms. "I meant it in a good way," Mallory said, trying to repair the damage.

"Just stay out of my business, Mallory Jamison. If I want to take up with Vince, I'll darn well do it," Lenora said before she spun on her high heel and headed for the door.

"Hey, girlie, wait," Ida Lee cried, following Lenora out the door. "I took a cab over here. You think I might catch a ride?"

Mallory reached for her coat, intent on saving her sister from what could be the biggest mistake of her life, but she never made it to the door. Sam stood in front of her, blocking her way.

As always, whenever she got near him, her heartbeat accelerated. This time, the thump-thump-thump had more to do with dread than passion. What must he think of her?

"Where do you think you're going?" he asked, his voice low.

She gulped. "After Lenora. I need to stop her."

"Funny. I would have thought you needed to tell me what's been going on."

He had a point there. Mallory met his eyes, then felt so guilty she dropped her gaze. She sighed, knowing he was right. When he took her coat out of her hands, she let him. He threw it over the back of a chair and crossed his arms over his chest.

"I'm waiting," he said.

She rubbed the side of her nose, shuffled her feet, drew a breath for courage. "I was never engaged to Jake."

"I figured that much." His voice was a monotone, making it impossible for Mallory to figure out what he was thinking. "What I'm wondering is why you said you were."

She still couldn't look at him. "Lenora told me that Jake was talking nonsense, saying he wasn't sure they should get married. I was desperate to find him. I figured you'd be more likely to help me if I told you I was his fiancée."

"You could have told me the truth."

"Yeah, right." She rolled her eyes, not an easy trick considering she was looking at the floor. "Like you would have helped me if you knew I wasn't engaged to him. You're the one who doesn't like to stick your nose in anyone else's business. You wouldn't have helped me stick my nose in Jake's."

He seemed to consider that. "Okay. I'll buy that, but why didn't you tell me you weren't engaged to Jake last night at the hotel?"

His words were so raw it was obvious that she had

hurt him. Her deception had undoubtedly ruined any chance they had of being together, but she needed to make him understand about last night. Finally, she raised her eyes.

"I wanted you. You can't imagine how much," she said softly. "But Jake was off with Patty, and I was afraid Lenora was with Vince. If anything, I needed to find Jake more than I needed to before. I couldn't tell you."

He was silent as he regarded her, and she still couldn't tell what he was thinking. He wet his lips.

"Let me get this straight. You and Jake never had a romantic relationship?"

"Never," she answered. "I only wanted to find Jake for Lenora."

He lifted an eyebrow. "You're not engaged to anyone else, are you?"

She shook her head. "Not at the moment."

He didn't say anything, but kept regarding her with that dark blue gaze. Her knees turned weak and her stomach churned. She heard her mother's voice in her head. *Nothing good ever happens to a liar.*

"I'll understand if you can't forgive me," she said, her voice soft as she once again lowered her eyes.

"I shouldn't forgive you," he said, moving closer to her. He took her by the arm, and she expected him to usher her out the door and tell her not to come back.

"If you never want to see me again, I'll understand that, too."

He leaned closer still. "After what you did, that would be a perfectly reasonable request."

She found the courage to look up at him and was surprised by what she saw in his eyes. It definitely wasn't censure.

"Hey, you don't look angry," she accused, her eyes narrowing. "What's going on here?"

He didn't answer but hauled her the rest of the way into his arms, closing his mouth over hers. It was firm and hot and definitely not angry. She speared her fingers into his hair and felt the warmth of his skin at the nape of his neck. Then she kissed him back, barely believing that she was wrapped in his arms, exactly where she never thought she'd be again.

Her heart swelled with emotion as his lips stayed locked with hers in a succession of long, drugging kisses. They turned her insides to a hot puddle of need and crept into her heart.

"Does this mean you're not angry with me?" she asked when they paused for breath.

"I was angry," he said against the side of her mouth, "but I got over that real fast when it sunk in that you weren't engaged to my brother."

"Where do we go from here?"

He nipped the side of her mouth, sending a delicious shiver down the length of her body. "You know that Little Orphan Annie dress you were wearing the first time we met?"

"Yeah," she said, drawing in a sharp breath when his hand dipped under her sweater and found her bare breast.

"Do you think that maybe you could put it on?"

"I could," she said as her nipples pebbled, "but I'm not thinking clearly enough to find it. Besides, I think I popped the seams."

"All the better," he said, pushing up the sweater and moving his mouth to her breast. He suckled. "I was so turned on the first time I saw you that all I did was pray that those seams would pop."

She giggled, then moaned because of the clever things his mouth was doing. She threw her head back, giving him freer access. He kissed his way up her neck until he was once again even with her mouth. His lips hovered over hers. "What do you think about going downstairs so we can put that futon in Jake's basement to use?"

"You mean the ugly orange-and-green plaid one?" she asked. The futon was by far the tackiest piece of furniture in the town house.

"Yeah," he confirmed, smiling. "Since I saw you on that heart-shaped water bed last night, I seem to have developed a taste for everything tacky."

She giggled again. "Don't tell me you found that sexy?"

"Darlin'," he drawled, "if you were lying on a two-by-four, I'd find it sexy. I was never so frustrated in my life."

She started at the top of his shirt, unbuttoning her way down his chest. "I think we can do something about that," she said, placing a kiss in the hollow of his neck and trailing her lips through the downy softness of his chest hair. She felt him shudder.

Tiny hairs teased her hand as she stroked his chest, and she moved her hand lower until she felt his arousal through his jeans. She kissed him deeply, and he trembled against her when she moved her hand.

Her legs were swept from under her, and she felt herself being lifted, then lowered to the sofa. "What about the futon?" she asked, smiling up at him.

"It's too far away, so we're going to have to christen it later," he promised as he pulled her sweater over her head, leaving her upper body bare. For a moment, he stared at her, his eyes like blue flames. "And forget about the dress. I'd rather take your clothes off than have you put any more on.''

She smiled at him, shimmied out of her leggings and gave herself up to the heady sensation of being loved by this incredible man.

Much later, after the sun had set and they'd dined on Chinese food that had been delivered to the door, she curled up against his big body in the downy softness of his bed.

Her eyelids were heavy, her body sated from their lovemaking. Sleep was just a breath away.

"Mallory?" he said against her hair.

"Hmm?"

"If you ever pretend to be engaged again, I'm gonna hunt down that blonde from the strip club."

"Why would you do that?" Mallory murmured.

"So I can sic her, Ida Lee *and* their purses on you."

10

MALLORY AWOKE THE NEXT morning to the smell of coffee and a sweet, sexy lethargy that seemed to have invaded her bones. She opened one eye and stretched out an arm, instantly disappointed that the side of the bed that Sam had occupied was empty. She brought his pillow to her nose and drew in the lingering scent of him.

Ah, making love with Sam had been sweet bliss. She might have thought she'd imagined how good the first time had been if there hadn't been a second time. And a third. By the end of the evening, the futon hadn't looked quite so tacky.

Their lovemaking had been all the more precious because of the way he held back the night before when he thought she was engaged to his brother.

How could she not love a man as gallant as that?

She smiled to herself, certain that this wild, warm feeling churning inside her was love. It dwarfed anything she'd felt before for the few men she'd dated but hadn't cared enough to keep around.

Subconsciously, she must have been waiting for a man with the right combination of honor, chivalry and caring. She'd been waiting for Sam.

Smiling, she pulled one of Sam's T-shirts over her head, used the bathroom and padded into the kitchen on bare feet just as he answered the phone.

He was standing by the stove with his back to her, bare to the waist. His hair was tousled and he was barefoot, his only clothing a pair of faded jeans. His broad shoulders tapered to a trim waist, a tight bottom and long legs.

Her mouth curved into a smile, because she knew what all that glorious male looked like naked.

He was frying eggs and putting strips of bacon into a sizzling pan while he cradled the phone between his shoulder and ear. Mallory came up behind him and encircled his waist. He felt warm and wonderful and she wanted him all over again. He turned around, smiled at her with crinkling eyes and dropped a quick kiss on her lips.

"Okay, Jake," he said, speaking into the phone. "I guess you know what you're doing."

Mallory instantly became alert as the events of yesterday came back to her. Jake and the engagement ring he'd bought for Patty Peaks. Lenora and her threat to take up with DelGreco the Gecko.

How could she have let so much time pass without doing something about those impending disasters?

Sam reached under her T-shirt to stroke her hip, and she knew how.

"Is that your brother on the phone?" she whispered, batting his hand away so she could think. "Where is he?"

Sam shook his head, a gesture she couldn't interpret. Did he mean he didn't know where Jake was or that he didn't want to tell her?

"You know I'd stand up with you, bro. Uh-huh. Uh-huh. Well, I can't tell you what to do. Yeah? Okay, then. I'm behind you."

Behind him? Behind him for what? Mallory tugged

on Sam's arm. "What?" she implored. "What's he going to do?"

Sam shook his head at her again. "Okay. Okay. See you in a couple of days then," he said, nodding. Then he hung up.

The receiver was barely back on the cradle when Mallory peppered Sam with questions.

"What did you mean you'd see him in a couple of days? Did he tell you where he is? Is Patty Peaks with him? Does he know about Lenora and the Gecko?"

"Easy, darlin'," Sam said, laughing and taking her more fully into his arms. "Don't I get a better good morning greeting than that?"

He lowered his head to claim her lips, making her forget about what they'd been going to discuss. Even though they'd made love repeated times the night before, tiny little thrills still coursed down her body.

"Good morning," he said, nuzzling the side of her neck in the spot he'd discovered the night before. The one that made her purr.

"Good morning," she murmured and gave in to another leisurely kiss. Sam's kisses, she thought dazedly, were more effective than a jolt of caffeine in getting the heart pumping and the blood racing. She might be able to give up coffee altogether.

"Now that's what I call the proper way to start the day," he said when he drew back. He grinned at her, looking so young and carefree that she smiled back.

"Did you sleep well?" he asked, holding her loosely in the circle of his arms.

"When I slept," she answered, which got her another grin from him. A wicked one, this time.

"Sleep's overrated," he said, lowering his hands to cup her bottom and pulling her more fully against him.

Sensations screamed through her body, but something important was nagging at the back of her mind. Something so important that she mustered the will to draw back from him and the security of his arms. She needed to think, and she couldn't do that with him touching her.

When he stopped clouding her senses with his touch, it came to her. Jake. They'd been discussing his telephone conversation with Jake. She put her hands on her hips.

"Were you trying to distract me, Sam Creighton?"

"Seems to me I was trying to kiss you, but I'm glad you found it distracting." He raised his eyebrows. "Want me to distract you again?"

She did, but now wasn't the time. "Later," she said.

"I'll hold you to that." He turned back to the frying pan and flipped the bacon. He seemed to have entirely forgotten about his brother.

Because Mallory didn't want to risk getting near him again, she raised her voice. "That was Jake on the phone just now, wasn't it?"

"Yep." He turned around, and the sight of his chest was almost enough to distract her again. A lock of dark hair fell across his forehead, making him look boyishly handsome. "Is this later enough?"

He grinned and made a grab for her, but she danced out of reach. If she let him touch her again, she'd never get her questions about Jake answered.

"What did you and Jake talk about?"

Sam crossed his arms over his chest and regarded her with amusement. "You're not going to let the subject drop, are you?"

"Nope," she confirmed.

"Okay. You win. We talked about eloping."

For the space of a heartbeat, Mallory's breathing stopped. Did Sam mean that he intended to elope with her? She hadn't projected that far into the future, but now that the thought had occurred to her, she was certain it was what she wanted. To marry Sam. To have his children. To grow old with him.

To love him for the rest of her days as much as she did at this moment.

"He wanted my advice, but I told him only he could make a decision like that," Sam finished. "So he decided to do it."

Mallory had been so stunned by the revelation that she wanted to marry Sam that she'd missed an entire sentence. "Who decided to do what?"

"Jake decided to elope," Sam said patiently. "That is who you wanted to talk about, isn't it?"

It shouldn't have been surprising that Sam hadn't meant he wanted to elope with her. Just because she had fallen in love with him didn't mean the feeling was reciprocal. Of course he'd been talking about his brother. His brother? Horror washed over her like spray from a cold shower.

"Oh, my gosh." Her hands flew to her face. "Did you just say that Jake was going to elope?"

He nodded. "Yep."

The next thought was so horrifying that Mallory had a hard time voicing it. "With Patty Peaks?"

Sam shrugged, as though the identity of the bride was of little consequence. "I *think* that's who he was talking about."

"Didn't you ask?"

He shook his head, his arms still crossed over that magnificent chest. "Didn't think it was any of my business."

"You're his brother. Of course it's your business!"

"That's a matter of opinion, and it's not mine."

Mallory paced from one side of the room to the other, unable to believe what she was hearing. Sam loved Jake. She knew he did. That was one of the things she loved about him. How could Sam not understand that it was his duty to prevent his brother from making a terrible mistake? How could he not know that Jake marrying Patty Peaks would be a disaster of terrific proportions?

"We can't let Jake go through with this."

Sam looked taken aback. "Excuse me?"

"Jake isn't thinking clearly. He hasn't been since he ran out on Lenora. She's the one he loves, not Patty Peaks."

"Jake is a better judge of which woman he loves than you are."

"Not at the moment, he isn't. Look at how erratic his behavior has been since he left town. Consorting with strippers. Asking columnists for advice. Visiting day-care centers. If he gave himself more time, he'd realize who he loved."

"Obviously, he doesn't want to give himself more time."

"But he'll be making a terrible mistake if he doesn't!"

"It's his mistake to make."

He looked so intractable that she could have screamed at him. Her sister's happiness was at stake here. Not to mention his brother's. And, quite possibly, Mallory's own sanity. Who knew how long Lenora would stay away from the party-gram business with her heart shattered. She needed to make Sam see reason for all their sakes.

"We've got to stop the wedding," she declared.

Sam raised both of his hands with his palms facing outward. "Whoa. I don't want any part of this. There's no way I'm stopping Jake's wedding."

"Then I'll do it myself," Mallory proclaimed. "Just tell me where he is."

Sam stared at her silently, his lips closed. Mallory's spirits sank as it dawned on her that Jake must not have told him where he was.

"You don't know where your brother is, do you?"

"Oh, I know where he is."

Hope bloomed in Mallory's chest. Maybe she wouldn't be too late to stop Jake from getting married, after all. Maybe she could still assure a happily-ever-after for him and her sister. "Where?" she asked eagerly.

Sam didn't hesitate. "I'm not going to tell you."

For just a moment, Mallory thought he was joking. But then she noticed that there was no teasing light in his eyes, no playful grin on his lips. The only sounds in the room were the bacon sizzling on the stove and her shocked gasp.

"But you have to tell me," she implored.

"Why? So you can stick your nose where it doesn't belong?"

"How dare you say my nose doesn't belong in Jake's business? He's the man my sister loves. I need to know where he is."

"No, you don't."

"I can't believe what I'm hearing," Mallory cried. "Don't you care if Jake marries the wrong woman?"

"Darlin', I don't care who Jake marries as long as it isn't you."

The sentiment behind the words was the right one,

but Mallory wouldn't let herself soften. Not even when Sam cracked a smile and slung an arm around her shoulder. "Come on," he said, "let's forget about this and have some breakfast."

She shrugged off his arm and sent him a murderous look. "You can't honestly expect me to sit down to a meal with you after this." She turned on her heel, tossing over her shoulder. "I'm going to get dressed."

She heard his heavy sigh and the fall of his footsteps behind her. "Come on, Mallory, be reasonable. What Jake does is his business, not ours."

"That's a matter of opinion, and it's not mine," she repeated his words back at him. "My opinion is that I can't stand to spend another minute with you."

He caught up to her in the hall outside the bedroom, putting a restraining hand on her arm. She didn't look at him, afraid that the love she felt for him would weaken her resolve to leave.

"I can't believe you're upset over something so trivial," he said.

"Trivial?" She whirled, so angry that she could withstand anything, even overpowering sexual attraction and enduring love. "Your brother's about to make a terrible mistake, you won't lift a finger to help him and you say it's trivial!"

"I already told you. It's not my place to interfere in Jake's life."

"Oh, really. So you're saying if he was about to step in front of a car, you wouldn't pull him back to the curb?"

He let out a short breath. "Now you're being silly."

"I am not being silly. Oh, I should have known this would happen as soon as I found out you were estranged from your family."

"I'm not estranged from them."

"You barely talk to them. You hardly ever see them. You don't know what's going on with them."

"I already explained that." Sam's words were clipped. "I care about them. I just don't think I should get involved in their lives."

"Listen to yourself. Don't you hear how callous you sound?" She shook her head. "I can't believe you're as unfeeling as that."

His eyes narrowed and she saw she'd hit a nerve. "Are you saying you won't be with me because I refuse to meddle in my brother's affairs?"

"That's one way of putting it."

"Did it ever occur to you that your being a meddler is a problem for me?"

"I am not a meddler," Mallory cried.

"That's what they call somebody who's always sticking her nose where it doesn't belong," he said. "I'd say you're the prototypical meddler."

"Call me what you want, but I care enough about *my* sister to want what's best for her!"

"Maybe what's best for her is you leaving her alone to make her own mistakes. Did you ever consider that you're enabling her to be dependent on you? Why else would you be working at a job you dislike so much? You spend so much time looking out for what everyone else wants that you don't have a clue what you want."

She wrenched away from him. "I don't have to listen to this. I'm leaving."

He let out a short, harsh laugh. "So you're saying this is goodbye? After what happened between us last night?"

Tears gathered in her eyes, but she wouldn't let

them fall. In mere minutes, she'd gone from the realization that she loved this man to the certainty that she couldn't have him.

"I'd tell you that I smell bacon burning, Sam, but I wouldn't want to risk having you accuse me of being a meddler," she said an instant before the smoke detector let out a long, angry wail.

She felt like imitating the mournful noise as she let herself into the bedroom, changed her clothes and walked out of his life.

11

MALLORY STARED INTO her bathroom mirror later that afternoon, fiddling with her pointed black witch's hat.

She tilted it slightly off center, deciding that the rakish angle gave her a more sinister look. She touched the green makeup she'd caked onto her face and the long, rubber nose that ended with a wart on its tip. It, too, was green.

Yes, she thought. She looked sufficiently scary.

Getting a last-minute assignment to portray Glinda the Witch had been a godsend. She'd been so busy hunting up the witch's costume and turning her face green that she hadn't been able to dwell on her heartache.

She'd nearly used the impending party-gram as an excuse to call Sam for a costume consultation, but even she had seen *The Wizard of Oz*. She vividly remembered the scene in which Dorothy had flung the bucket of water over Glinda, who had emitted the pitiful cries that she was melting.

Now that Sam was no longer helping her find his brother, she had no reason to get in touch with him. Especially now that she'd calculated what she owed him, written a check and stuffed it into a mail slot.

No. She and Sam were finished.

She loved him, of that she was certain, but she

couldn't build a life with a man who kept himself distant from those he loved.

Pain stabbed at her an instant before she got angry all over again at his refusal to reveal his brother's whereabouts.

If he'd told her where Jake was, she might have been able to prevent a disaster-in-the-making. As it was, she was afraid two disasters were in the making.

Lenora not only hadn't come home last night, but she hadn't left a message where she could be reached. Mallory shut her eyes. She didn't want to, but she had to accept the possibility that Lenora was with DelGreco the Gecko.

The wheels in her brain whirred. Just because Lenora was with the Gecko didn't mean she couldn't do something about it. She might not be able to save Jake from disaster, but there was still time to save Lenora.

She tried to open her eyes, but the heavy mascara she'd applied stuck to her lashes, sealing them closed.

She pried them open, shuffled to the phone on her ruby slippers and dialed the Gecko with the fake green fingernails she'd attached to her much shorter natural ones. The phone was picked up after the first ring.

"Grand DelGreco Station. If you're a babe, you can get on my train."

Eeeeeewwwwww. Mallory made a face. Trust the Gecko to answer the phone with the world's cheesiest greeting. What was Lenora thinking to consort with the likes of him?

"It's Mallory," she said shortly, to the point. "I'm looking for Lenora."

"When you find her, ya think you could talk her into a foursome? Me, you, her and bliss."

"You're even creepier than I remember, Vince."

"I'm not Vince, but I'm willing to pretend I am if he rocks your boat."

"Who is this?" A suspicion formed. The Gecko had a teenage brother who, for some scary reason, had adopted Vince as a role model. "This is Virgil, isn't it? Does your mother know what kind of things you're picking up from Vince?"

"This isn't Virgil," he said, but when he spoke again, it was in a deeper, disguised voice. "You're not one of his mother's friends, are you?"

"I don't know your mother."

"In that case," the smooth voice was back, "wanna get on the Virgil train?"

"I'm gonna whack your caboose if you don't stop it. I want to talk to Vince."

"Man, that guy has all the luck. First Lenora, now you."

Mallory's heart dropped. Please, no. Don't let it be so. "Lenora was there?"

"Yeah, she just boogied out of here with Vince."

Her worst fear was confirmed. Lenora was consorting with the Gecko. Still, maybe it wasn't too late. Maybe Mallory could still make her sister realize what a dreadful mistake it would be to continue to see him.

"Did they say where they were going?"

"Yeah. It was unreal, Vince being the cool guy he is. Who would have thought he'd give up the bachelor life for a chick, no matter how babelicious she is?"

"What are you talking about?" Mallory asked as panic rose in her like the ocean at high tide. During a hurricane.

"He said they were going to City Hall to elope."

Mallory had no sooner hung up the phone than she was rushing down the stairs on her ruby slippers, her long black skirt flowing behind her. She yanked open the door and there stood Jake.

For a moment, she couldn't speak. It wasn't just that, with that brown hair and blue eyes, he looked so much like a preppy version of Sam. It was that he was standing there at all.

"Mallory?" Jake cocked his head and gave her a grin almost as charming as Sam's. "That is you under that face paint, isn't it? Who are you this time?"

"Glinda the Witch from *The Wizard of Oz*," she snapped.

"But isn't Glinda the—"

"What are you doing here?" she interrupted.

"I'm here to see Lenora," he said matter-of-factly.

The nerve of the man. She supposed he'd come all this way to break the news personally that he had eloped with Patty Peaks. "She isn't home. If she were, fat chance you'd have of getting in the door."

Never mind that she was going out. She made to slam the door in his face. He stuck a foot in the threshold, blocking her attempt.

"I must be missing something here." He cocked his head again. "Why would you try to stop me from seeing Lenora?"

"As if you didn't know," she sniffed.

"Why don't you tell me anyway?"

"Because of the way you've been consorting with Patty Peaks, that's why. Didn't you consider how that would devastate Lenora?"

"Why would it matter to Lenora?" He looked confused. "She should be used to that kind of thing by now."

Mallory gasped. She'd never have pegged her sister as the kind of woman who would share her man. Jake must have brainwashed her, but even he couldn't think Lenora would continue their relationship now that he was married.

"You are low, Jake." Mallory shook a long green fingernail at him. "I completely misjudged you. Never would I have thought you'd go off and do a thing like this."

Again, she tried to close the door. Again, his foot was in the way. "A thing like what?" he asked, having the nerve to sound exasperated.

"A thing like getting married!"

"I'm not married. Whatever gave you that idea?"

For the first time since he'd appeared at the door, Mallory's resolve faltered. Maybe she'd jumped to the wrong conclusion, but... "You did buy an engagement ring."

"So?"

"And you did tell Sam you wanted to elope with Patty."

He actually laughed aloud, making her wish she knew one of those witch's spells that could turn humans into toads.

"Patty? She's a very nice person, but I don't want to marry her. I want to marry Lenora."

Those words, so longed for just days ago, lit Mallory's ire. He'd already admitted that he was chronically unfaithful. Now he was assuming that her sister would just laugh off his latest affair and skip to the altar with him.

"Tough luck, buster. After the way you've been sleeping with that stripper, I'm going to do everything in my power to make sure Lenora doesn't take you back."

"Wait a minute." He looked angry. "I'm not sleeping with Patty. I was working a case for her. Not that it's any of your business, but I haven't touched another woman since I met Lenora.''

A blast of wind caught some snow on an overhanging branch and blew it into the apartment, depositing white flakes onto Mallory's face. It wasn't egg, but it could well have been. A part of her wanted to accuse him of lying, but a bigger part of her recognized the ring of truth in his words.

''Now,'' Jake said, ''where's Lenora?''

Mallory covered her red lips with her green hands, thinking about the way she'd misconstrued what was going on between Jake and Patty, sending her sister rushing off to City Hall with DelGreco the Gecko.

''You don't need to protect her anymore, Mallory,'' Jake continued. ''I admit I was a fool. When it came time to set a wedding date, I got cold feet and ran. But it only took me a couple days to realize how much I love her.''

Sincerity was pouring out of him like snow in a blizzard, making her feel that much worse. ''Oops,'' she squeaked.

His blue eyes, so like Sam's, narrowed. ''What do you mean 'oops'?''

''Lenora's with the Gecko.''

''What's a gecko?''

''It's a really small lizard.''

''Lenora has a pet?''

She swallowed. ''I wish. This Gecko is a man. Most people know him as Vince DelGreco.''

''Her ex-boyfriend?''

Mallory nodded.

''So you're telling me she went straight from my

arms to his? That she didn't waste any time in lining up a new man?''

"Oh, no," Mallory protested. "I'm the one who lined him up, not that I meant to. You see, I was looking for you so I could talk some sense into you. But I couldn't find you. Then Lenora said something about calling Vince, but I didn't know she didn't mean it. So I called him to make sure she hadn't. Then he called her. And, before you know it, they're headed to City Hall to get married.''

He swore ripely and started for the street.

"Where are you going?" she asked.

"To stop them.''

"Wait." She hitched up her black skirt and followed him down the sidewalk. "I'm coming with you.''

He turned at her declaration and fixed her with a hard stare. "Stay out of this, Mallory. You've done enough damage already. If Lenora's married the Gecko, it'll be on your head.''

As his car screeched away from the curb, she walked back into the apartment and slumped into a chair. Misery overtook her as she puzzled over how doing the right thing had turned out so terribly wrong.

Ten minutes ticked by before she realized she wasn't cut out to stand by and do nothing. The least she could do was try to set things right. She checked the clock on the wall. She had another hour before she was due to deliver the party-gram.

She grabbed on to her witch's hat, lifted her black skirt and flew for the door.

City Hall, she thought, here I come.

"I STILL DON'T UNDERSTAND why you didn't call a cab after that truck bashed into you," Sam said as his car, with his brother in tow, sped east on Market Street toward Philadelphia City Hall.

Sam had been in Jake's office after meeting with one of the clients Mallory had lined up, wondering how the heck a private eye went about investigating insurance fraud, when Jake's SOS had come in.

"Are you kidding? The office was just five minutes away and cabs take forever," Jake said, then added more softly. "Besides, my big brother wouldn't have been driving the cab."

Trouble was, Jake's big brother would rather have been left out of it. If Lenora wanted to become Mrs. Gecko, there was nothing Sam could do about it. This was between Lenora and Jake. Despite Mallory's protestations to the contrary, it had been from the beginning.

At the thought of Mallory, pain gripped him. At first, he'd been shocked that she'd tossed him out of her life for his policy of noninvolvement. But gradually he'd come to realize that a meddler and a mind-your-own-business kind of guy didn't mix.

Still, his eyes stung every time he thought about going through the rest of his life without Mallory. Losing her was almost more hurt than he could bear.

He thought it ironic that he was speeding toward City Hall, possibly to witness Jake also lose the woman he loved.

"Man, what a day I'm having," Jake said, sighing heavily. "Can you believe, on top of everything else, I totaled the car?"

Sam took a quick look at Jake. Despite the nasty accident, he was scratched but otherwise unhurt. That fact had filled Sam with such overwhelming relief that he'd yet to tell Jake what he thought of the little stunt he'd pulled. He should have done it that morning on the phone, but he was so satiated from loving Mallory that he'd been in an amiable mood.

Unluckily for Jake, his mood had changed.

"What a day you're having! What a month *I'm* having. What were you thinking, going off and leaving me with your business like that?"

"I wasn't thinking much of anything." Jake ran a hand over his mouth, exactly the way Sam did when he was troubled. "This whole marriage thing had me tied up in knots."

"That didn't give you the right to tie my life up in knots," Sam said. "It would have served you right if I'd taken the next plane back to Florida."

"Florida? You're talking about that sailboat you had a deposit on, aren't you?" Jake asked. "Aw, hell, Sam. I'm sorry. I sure hope you didn't lose out on the boat because you were up here helping me out."

Incredibly, until Jake had mentioned the sailboat, Sam hadn't thought about it in days. He didn't know if his deposit had been enough to hold it or not. He'd been so wrapped up in Mallory that securing the boat had become of little importance.

All he'd cared about was Mallory and her growing despondence over the fact that his brother was cheating on her. Only Jake hadn't been cheating on Mallory. He'd been cheating on Lenora.

"Never mind the boat," Sam said, thinking aloud. "You have other things to think about."

"You mean Lenora, don't you? Do you think she'll forgive me?"

His brother seemed so intent on his answer that Sam couldn't withhold it, no matter how much he wanted to. "For getting cold feet, probably," he said. "For sleeping with Patty, that's a whole other issue."

"Ah, jeez. How many times do I have to say this? I wasn't sleeping with Patty. I was working a case for her." He shook his head. "How do you know about Patty, anyway?"

Briefly, Sam filled him in on what had been happening in his absence, giving Mallory the credit she deserved for managing to trail Jake all over eastern Pennsylvania.

"Wow," Jake said. "That's pretty impressive detective work, even though you two reached the wrong conclusion. Patty hired me to find her birth mother, that's all."

Despite himself, Sam was curious. "So that's why that waitress saw you leaving the House of the Seven Veils together?"

"I needed to give Patty a status report on the case and I couldn't catch up with her earlier in the day."

"What about Father Andy? How does he fit in?"

"He was the key to solving the case. Patty's been getting a bouquet of roses every year on her birthday. She never knew who they were from until I tracked down the sender. Turned out Father Andy was a friend of Patty's birth mother. She went to him for advice, and he sent her to a home for unwed mothers."

"Which is now the G'Day Care Center."

"Yeah," Jake said. "The director's been there for thirty years. Fortunately, she was fairly chatty. From there, it wasn't too hard to track down Patty's birth mother."

"To Scranton," Sam finished.

"Right again. The reunion was actually pretty

touching. I got to see it, because Patty wanted me there for moral support.''

The pieces of the puzzle finally fit together. Jake hadn't sought Father Andy to figure out whether he wanted to be married. He hadn't visited the day-care center to research what it was like to be a father. And he hadn't been having wild sex with Patty Peaks in Scranton. Most likely, she'd merely been present while he registered for a room.

If Sam had known Jake better, he would have figured out all those things sooner. He ran a hand over his jaw. "Hell, Jake, how did we become such strangers?"

His brother considered him for a moment. Traffic was fairly heavy, creating a cacophony of sounds: whirring tires, blaring horns, humming engines.

He had to strain to hear Jake's softly voiced answer.

"By staying out of each other's business, that's how."

DIRECTLY IN THE HEART of the city, the granite mass of Philadelphia's City Hall tower climbed nearly five hundred and fifty feet into the sky, acting as a beacon for the temple of local politics that surrounded it.

Gathering her witch's skirt in one hand, Mallory dashed into the courtyard. The sun had been shining brightly overhead for hours, melting the snow and uncovering the huge compass painted on the ground. It was meant to orient visitors to the city, but it didn't help Mallory. She stopped in its dead center and watched the maze of pedestrians enter the four portals of the building.

She'd visited City Hall before, but she hadn't the foggiest idea which set of doors to enter.

"Excuse me, do you know which office people go to for the marriage licenses?" she asked the first person to pass by, a grandmotherly type who reminded her of Ida Lee.

The woman turned to her, let out something that sounded like a cross between a terrified gasp and a scream and hurried away.

It was then that Mallory remembered her green face and Glinda the Witch costume.

She glanced around, noticing that people were being careful not to get within fifteen feet of her. Darn. How was she supposed to get directions when she was portraying one of the most despised characters in American movie history?

"Hey," she yelled to a woman in her twenties who was rushing by, "can you tell me where the marriage license place is?"

Ignoring her, the woman rushed by faster. Witches, Mallory thought, got absolutely no respect.

Giving up on relying on her fellow citizens for help, Mallory picked one portal at random and headed for it. Surely there'd be a directory inside the place.

She was gaining on another small, white-haired woman, but she'd learned her lesson. No way was she asking anyone else for directions. She gave the woman a sidelong glance as she passed. It was Ida Lee.

"Ida Lee," she exclaimed. "What are you doing here?"

Ida Lee looked at her, showing none of the alarm evident in the faces of the other passersby. Instead, she seemed awed. "Criminy, if you know my name, there must be something to witchcraft after all."

"I'm not a witch," Mallory refuted. "Well, I am a

witch. But only for today. This is a costume. It's me, Mallory. You know, the dame.''

Ida Lee scrutinized her. ''So it is. Green's not your color, dear. Even with those eyes. It's too much of a good thing.''

''But Glinda has a green face.''

''You're Glinda? From *The Wizard of Oz?*''

''Right,'' Mallory said.

''But Glinda isn't—''

''This is the last place I would have expected to see you,'' Mallory interrupted. They didn't have time for small talk. ''What are you doing here?''

Ida Lee hesitated, then abandoned their previous topic of discussion. ''What did you think? I was going to miss the boss trying to win back the woman he loves? I'm here to watch the fireworks.''

''But how did you know there were going to be fireworks?''

Ida Lee waved a hand. ''Oh, that. I was at the office with Sam when Jake called and asked if he'd drive him here.''

''Sam's here?''

''There he is now.'' Ida Lee indicated the brothers rushing across the courtyard. They made a handsome pair with their height and dark good looks, but Mallory could only focus on Sam. He was wearing the same black leather jacket he'd had on the first time they met, and it set off the inky blackness of his hair and breadth of his shoulders. Mallory's heart lurched.

''But I wonder who that man is with Sam,'' Ida Lee mused.

''That's Jake,'' Mallory said dryly. ''Your boss.''

''Oh.'' Ida Lee cleared her throat. ''Of course it is.''

Only then did Mallory spare Jake a glance. His eyes

were focused forward, and he looked single-minded on the task of stopping the woman he loved from becoming Mrs. Gecko.

"Yoo-hoo," Ida Lee called, rushing after them. Mallory followed in her wake. For an octogenarian, she could really scoot. "Yoo-hoo. Over here."

The brothers turned in unison, and Mallory watched Jake's eyes roll when he spotted her. Sam, conversely, only looked bewildered.

"I told you to stay out of this, Mallory," Jake said.

Sam screwed up his face. "That witch is Mallory?"

"Yeah, that's her." Jake advanced a step, looking upset. "What are you trying to do? Mess up things for me even worse than you already have?"

"Hey, don't talk to her that way!" Sam protested, which Mallory put down as a male's knee-jerk reaction to another male being less than polite to a female. Especially because Sam held the same opinion.

"Yeah," Ida Lee cut in, "the dame's not so bad."

Jake scrunched his eyebrows and peered at Ida Lee. "Who are you?"

"I knew it." Sam pointed a finger at Ida Lee. "I knew Jake didn't hire you to be his secretary."

"Well, he would've if he had the sense of a tick." Ida Lee rested her hands on her hips. "We got two new cases since I've been working there."

"Mallory solicited those cases," Sam said.

"Well, I helped," Ida Lee said, disregarding the fact that she hadn't.

"Wait a minute. I know that voice." Jake's expression turned incredulous. "Mrs. Scoggins?"

"So what if I am?" Ida Lee said.

"But you're the lady who's always calling trying to get me to buy lightbulbs."

"Hey," Ida Lee said, shaking a finger, "if you didn't want me to join up with you, you should have bought some lightbulbs instead of telling me all those detective stories."

"But I..." Jake stopped, then threw up his hands. "I don't have time for this. I need to find Lenora before it's too late."

He took off in the direction of one of the portals, with Ida Lee, Sam and Mallory following in his path. Unlike Mallory, Jake seemed to know exactly where he was going.

"What are you doing here?" Mallory asked Sam when he drew even with her. "I thought you refused to get involved in your brother's business."

"He asked me to get involved," Sam said, stopping short of telling her more. It had struck him in the car that he'd been wrong to be absent from Jake's life. He knew far more about his friends than he did his own brother, which filled him with remorse. But he'd spent so many years trying to distance himself from the people he loved that he hadn't yet figured out how to rectify the damage.

A gust of cold wind blew in from the north, taking off her pointed hat. He caught it deftly and handed it back. Her hair, he saw, had been spray painted black and slathered with gel. The cast of her face was green, the glue holding her nose in place starting to loosen. She should have looked frightful. So why did he still think she was beautiful?

"Hey, isn't that the dame's sister?" Ida Lee suddenly exclaimed, redirecting their attention to the steps of City Hall.

The petite beauty who'd burst her way into Jake's town house was emerging from one of the portals with a man Sam assumed was Vince DelGreco. Lenora looked delicately beautiful in a calf-length red wool coat with a matching hat. Vince had more gel in his dark hair than Mallory. He was also wearing white bell bottoms that were way too tight.

"Is that the Gecko?" Ida Lee asked. "I think he's kinda cute."

"I think we're too late," Mallory moaned as Sam watched Lenora spot Jake. Lenora's eyes turned hard, but he thought he saw pain behind them. Pain. And something much more visceral.

Mallory rushed forward to where her sister stood with the Gecko.

"You!" Lenora spun around, glaring at Mallory. She seemed unfazed that her sister was done up in cartoonish horror. "You ruined my life."

"She didn't do it with a fleet of flying monkeys, did she?" Ida Lee asked.

"Of course not," Sam snapped, then addressed Lenora. "You should watch what you say to her. Mallory wouldn't be here if she didn't care about you so much."

Lenora looked them all over, then turned a puzzled gaze to Jake. "But where's the stripper you ran off with?"

"I never ran off with a stripper," Jake said. "I was working a *case* for a stripper."

"That's not what Mallory said." Lenora looked at Mallory, who shrank back. "She said you were going to marry the stripper."

"Mallory says a lot of things she shouldn't," Jake said.

"Hey, don't talk about her that way!" Sam didn't

know why he kept defending Mallory, but he couldn't seem to stop himself.

Lenora and Jake both ignored him. They had eyes only for each other, but the magic lasted only a moment before Jake's expression turned bitter.

"I don't see what right you have to accuse me of running off with a stripper when you just got married to a relic from the disco age."

"You talkin' about me?" Vince puffed out his chest. "I ain't no relic. I'm a live wire."

"I don't know what all the hullabaloo is about anyway," Ida Lee chimed in. "They're not married."

"How would you know?" Sam asked in exasperation.

"They can't be married. In Pennsylvania, you can't marry until at least three days after you get a license. It's the law."

"You knew that and didn't tell anybody?" Sam asked incredulously.

Ida Lee shrugged. "Nobody asked me."

The hurt expression on Jake's face didn't fade. "So you and Disco Boy got a marriage license?" he asked Lenora.

"That's Disco Man to you, buddy," Vince told Jake before Lenora could reply. "And you can have her. What do I want with a woman who gets up to the front of the line and dumps me? It's like she's blind or something."

"You dumped him?" Jake asked Lenora, who nodded.

"I shoulda known marriage wasn't for a babe magnet like me," Vince said, then brightened. "Hey, Mallory? That green stuff washes off, right? How 'bout you taking a ride on the Vince train?"

"How 'bout me derailing that train?" Sam asked.

Vince gave him an assessing up-and-down look before backing away, palms in the air, "Okay, okay, big guy. Didn't mean nothing by it. Just wanted a date, that's all."

"I got a niece I maybe could set you up with," Ida Lee offered.

"She a babe?"

"Almost as big a one as you are," Ida Lee said, setting off Vince's swagger. They walked off together, conferring merrily.

Jake hadn't taken his eyes off Lenora, who was gazing back at him in kind. "Why didn't you get a marriage license?" he asked her.

"Because it's you I love, you dope," Lenora said, hitting him on the shoulder. Then they were in each other's arms, murmuring words of love which they sealed with kiss after kiss.

The moment was so private that Sam felt uncomfortable witnessing it, but he couldn't stop watching them. For the first time, it dawned on him that Mallory was right. Jake didn't belong with Patty Peaks anymore than Lenora belonged with the Gecko. The two of them were meant for each other.

They obviously reached the same conclusion, because moments later they rushed off hand in hand to the marriage license bureau, intent on getting a start on their future together.

And, quite suddenly, Mallory and Sam were alone. Mallory glanced up at him, glanced down and shuffled her ruby slippers. Silence yawned between them, deep and uncomfortable.

"Your nose is falling off," Sam said after a moment.

"Uh, thanks," Mallory said, fiddling with it until it was more secure. Crooked, but more secure.

More silence followed.

"I guess this means you'll be heading back to Florida soon," Mallory said, finally breaking the silence. "The boat's waiting, right?"

Florida? The boat? He'd forgotten again, but he wasn't about to tell her that. "Yeah," he said and got a whiff of sunshine and citrus. He didn't need oysters or chocolate-covered strawberries. Her smell alone was an aphrodisiac. "What about you? What are you going to do?"

"Me? I guess I'll just do more of the same." She seemed overwhelmingly sad, which was the way he felt. "That reminds me. I need to get going. I have to be Glinda for a party-gram."

"Glinda? But you're not dressed like Glinda."

"Sure I am. Don't you remember the big scene at the end of *The Wizard of Oz?*" She affected a pitiful voice. "'I'm meeelting, I'm meeelting.' I thought they'd get their money's worth if I did that."

"But that was the Wicked Witch of the West's line."

"Exactly," Mallory said. "Glinda really knows her drama."

"Glinda is the Good Witch of the North."

"Oh, no."

"Oh, yes."

She tried to smile. Despite the way she'd blacked out some of her teeth, it was heartbreakingly beautiful. "Then I'd better go get changed."

She turned and headed across the courtyard, a forlorn figure in her green face paint and black witch's cloak. He wanted to call her back and convince her she needed him, and not only because she was frightfully bad at popular culture, but he didn't quite know how.

Not after the things she'd said to him at the town house.

He stood there for a long time, watching her until she'd faded into the distance, feeling as though his heart was dissolving.

He'd bet the Wicked Witch of the West had never felt such pain, not even when she'd melted into that pitiful puddle.

12

MALLORY BLINKED RAPIDLY, trying to dry her eyes
before tears fell down her face.

So what if she hadn't known that Glinda the Good
Witch of the North didn't have a green face like her
wicked counterparts? One incensed client did not a
business break. It was nothing to cry over.

She rubbed her face, which was still raw from the
hour it had taken to remove the green face paint. If
she were honest with herself, she'd admit that she
didn't feel like crying because of the party-gram business.

She wasn't even fighting back tears of happiness
because of Lenora and Jake's upcoming marriage.

She wanted to weep because she was in love with
a man who couldn't love her back. A man who
thought she was a meddler because she'd been trying
to assure that the course of true love ran smooth.

Was it her fault that Lenora had gotten the impres-
sion that Jake had been carrying on a torrid affair with
a stripper?

Was she to blame because Jake had been half out
of his mind with fear that Lenora had gotten herself
hitched to a gecko?

Would she have been liable if the two of them had
broken up over all the misunderstandings?

She thought over the questions and was surprised at

how simple it was to come up with the answers: yes, yes and yes.

No matter how much she'd wanted to help Jake and Lenora get back together, the hard truth was that she'd nearly broken them apart. They'd found their way back to each other not because of her but despite her.

She pressed her lips together, trying to come to terms with the revelation. Sam was right. She was a meddler. And maybe, just maybe, there was such a thing as too much meddling.

Sam was right about another thing, too. She'd spent so many years trying to help everyone else get what they wanted that her needs had become incidental, so much so that she barely recognized what they were. Now, at long last, she knew what it was she needed.

Sam. She needed Sam. Needed him because she loved him.

He might not love her back, but she'd never know if she didn't ask him. He'd repeatedly defended her in the courtyard when others had taken her to task for her meddling, hadn't he?

If there was a chance in a zillion that he wanted her back, she'd be a fool if she didn't fight for him.

She ran to the closet in the hall and pulled out her trench coat. She was about to put it on when the doorbell rang.

Exasperated at the interruption, she yanked the door open. A three-foot-tall statue of Cupid stared back at her, its arrow pointed straight at her heart.

It was easily the corniest thing she'd ever seen: a naked cherub with wings, carrying a bow and quiver of arrows dipped in gold, yet. Its lips were turned up in an impish grin, one eye closed in an exaggerated wink.

It was also wonderfully familiar, as was the man standing off to the side of the statue. Sam.

"Hello, Mallory," he said, gazing at her so intently that her legs almost gave way.

"Sam." She gulped so hard she almost swallowed her tongue. Her heart sped up, and she tried not to leap to conclusions about what it meant that Sam and the statue had showed up at her door. "Would you like to come in?"

He nodded, picking up the statue under its bow arm and carefully carrying it into the brownstone. "Beau would have my head if Cupid came home missing a wing," he explained.

"Beau? You mean the honeymoon concierge from Sweetheart Suites?"

"Yeah. He let me borrow Cupid," Sam said almost sheepishly. He took something out of his pocket and handed it to her. "He also gave me this."

It was the honeymoon photo that Beau had snapped of them while they'd been staying at Sweetheart Suites. Their bodies were angled toward each other, their eyes locked, their hands poised as though itching to grab one another.

They looked, Mallory thought, as though they were in love.

A wealth of questions swirled through her mind, but she didn't ask any of them. "But I thought Beau hated us," she said instead.

"Not anymore. Seems he took your advice about curbing his sarcasm and not taking no for an answer. He has a date with Angel Saturday night."

"That's great, but..." Her words trailed off when her courage faltered.

"But you were wondering what I'm doing here with the statue."

Mallory gulped. "It did cross my mind."

"I thought..." he started, wet his lips and tried again. "Aw, hell, Mallory. It was supposed to be a party-gram, but it seems I belong behind the scenes, not in front of the door."

"What kind of a party-gram?"

He took a piece of paper from his pocket, unfolded it and cleared his throat. "Love looks not with the eyes, but with the mind, and therefore is wing'd Cupid painted blind?"

"What's that supposed to mean?" Mallory asked.

Sam shrugged, but he seemed nervous. "It's Shakespeare. I'm into popular culture. You're the one who likes literature. You're supposed to know."

She smiled. "Suppose you tell me what it means to you."

"It means," he said, coming across the room to take her softly by the shoulders, "that I've been blind. I realized that while I was watching Lenora and Jake at City Hall. They were so obviously meant for each other that I finally understood why you went to such lengths to get them back together."

Mallory's hand came up to stroke his lean cheek. "I'm the one who's been blind. You were right. I am a meddler. And by my meddling, I almost broke them up."

"Don't be so hard on yourself," he said, twining his fingers in her hair. "I've come to realize that meddling isn't always bad."

Her eyebrows rose. "You have?"

"I have. You only meddled because you love your sister, and anything done in the name of love can't be all wrong." He paused. "Which is why I'm hoping you won't object if I kiss you."

"Do you mean—?"

"Yeah," he said, bringing his head closer to hers. "I mean that I love you, Mallory Jamison. Even if you do meddle too much."

Her lips trembled and the tears she'd tried so hard not to cry before he walked in the door streamed down her face. "And I love you back, Sam. Oh, I love you back."

Their kiss was all the more precious because Mallory had thought they'd never kiss again. She dug her fingers into his thick hair, pulling him against her as she kissed him over and over. Sensations poured over her like falling snow, but there was nothing cold about them.

A long time later, Sam lifted his head.

"I thought about what you said about keeping myself apart from my family, and I think you were right," he said against her lips, gladdening her heart. "I told Jake that I'd fly our parents in from Florida for his and Lenora's wedding."

"I'm so glad, Sam."

"I was also hoping I might introduce them to my fiancée." He drew back from her, and she'd never seen him look so humble. "That is, if you'll marry me."

She grinned. "Just you try and stop me."

"Never," he said, grinning back. "What do you think about a spring wedding? I hear that Philadelphia is beautiful in the spring."

"The spring? Does this mean you're not going back to Florida?"

"Yep," he said.

"But what about the sailboat? The one that will take you anywhere your heart desires?"

"My heart's desire," he said simply, "is in my arms."

"But what are you going to do?" she asked, and he stroked her hip. She laughed. "For a job, I mean?"

"You're looking at the new consultant for Lenora's Party-Grams," he said. "I told your sister my ideas for the business—advertising, changing locations, jazzing up the acts, things like that. She invited me to be a partner."

Mallory frowned. Working with Sam would be a pleasure, but Lenora's Party-Grams wasn't exactly raking in the cash. "I don't think the business can support three people."

"Two," he corrected. "There's only me and your sister."

"What about me?"

"Oh, you'll be doing something else. If you want, that is."

Oh, she wanted to get away from the party-gram business and do something else with her life. She always had, but she didn't understand what he was getting at.

"I have a confession to make," he continued somewhat sheepishly. "I meddled."

"You? Mr. Thou-shalt-not-butt-his-nose-into-the-business-of-others?"

"Yeah," he said. "I talked you up to my brother, told him how you tracked him down and how you solicited those cases. He wants you to join him and Ida Lee at Jake Creighton Investigations."

The solution was so perfect that, for a moment, Mallory couldn't speak. What better job could there be for a woman like her than being paid to meddle? She threw her arms around his neck and beamed at him.

"I thought you'd be happy about that."

"Are you kidding? You working with my sister, me working with your brother. It doesn't get any better than that." Her grin grew broader as something occurred to her. "You know what this means, don't you?"

"I'm afraid to ask."

"I don't see how we're going to help being one big, happy meddling family."

INDULGE IN A QUIET MOMENT
WITH HARLEQUIN

Get a FREE
Quiet Moments Bath Spa

with just two proofs of purchase from any of our four special collector's editions in May.

Harlequin® is sure to make your time special this Mother's Day
with four special collector's editions featuring a short story
PLUS a complete novel packaged together in one volume!

Collection #1   Intrigue abounds in a collection featuring *New York Times* bestselling author Barbara Delinsky and Kelsey Roberts.

Collection #2   Relationships? Weddings? Children? = *New York Times* bestselling author Debbie Macomber and Tara Taylor Quinn at their best!

Collection #3   Escape to the past with *New York Times* bestselling author Heather Graham and Gayle Wilson.

Collection #4   Go West! With *New York Times* bestselling author Joan Johnston and Vicki Lewis Thompson!

Plus Special Consumer Campaign!
Each of these four collector's editions will feature a
"FREE QUIET MOMENTS BATH SPA" offer.
See inside book in May for details.

Only from

HARLEQUIN®
Makes any time special ®

Don't miss out! Look for this exciting promotion on sale in May 2001,
at your favorite retail outlet.

*Harlequin truly does
make any time special. . . .
This year we are celebrating
weddings in style!*

A
Walk
Down
the Aisle

WEDDING CELEBRATION

To help us celebrate, we want you to tell us how wearing the Harlequin wedding gown will make your wedding day special. As the grand prize, Harlequin will offer one lucky bride the chance to **"Walk Down the Aisle"** in the Harlequin wedding gown!

There's more...

For her honeymoon, she and her groom will spend five nights at the **Hyatt Regency Maui.** As part of this five-night honeymoon at the hotel renowned for its romantic attractions, the couple will enjoy a candlelit dinner for two in Swan Court, a sunset sail on the hotel's catamaran, and duet spa treatments.

A HYATT RESORT AND SPA ®

Maui • Molokai • Lanai

To enter, please write, in, 250 words or less, how wearing the Harlequin wedding gown will make your wedding day special. The entry will be judged based on its emotionally compelling nature, its originality and creativity, and its sincerity. This contest is open to Canadian and U.S. residents only and to those who are 18 years of age and older. There is no purchase necessary to enter. Void where prohibited. See further contest rules attached. Please send your entry to:

Walk Down the Aisle Contest

In Canada	In U.S.A.
P.O. Box 637	P.O. Box 9076
Fort Erie, Ontario	3010 Walden Ave.
L2A 5X3	Buffalo, NY 14269-9076

You can also enter by visiting www.eHarlequin.com
Win the Harlequin wedding gown and the vacation of a lifetime!
The deadline for entries is October 1, 2001.

HARLEQUIN®
Makes any time special ®

PHWDACONT1

HARLEQUIN WALK DOWN THE AISLE TO MAUI CONTEST 1197
OFFICIAL RULES
NO PURCHASE NECESSARY TO ENTER

To enter, follow directions published in the offer to which you are responding. Contest begins April 2, 2001, and ends on October 1, 2001. Method of entry may vary. Mailed entries must be postmarked by October 1, 2001, and received by October 8, 2001.

Contest entry may be, at times, presented via the Internet, but will be restricted solely to residents of certain geographic areas that are disclosed on the Web site. To enter via the Internet, if permissible, access the Harlequin Web site (www.eHarlequin.com) and follow the directions displayed online. Online entries must be received by 11:59 p.m. E.S.T. on October 1, 2001.

In lieu of submitting an entry online, enter by mail by hand-printing (or typing) on an 8½" x 11" plain piece of paper, your name, address (including zip code), Contest name/number and in 250 words or fewer, why winning a Harlequin wedding dress would make your wedding day special. Mail via first-class mail to: Harlequin Walk Down the Aisle Contest 1197, (in the U.S.) P.O. Box 9076, 3010 Walden Avenue, Buffalo, NY 14269-9076, (in Canada) P.O. Box 637, Fort Erie, Ontario L2A 5X3, Canada.

Limit one entry per person, household address and e-mail address. Online and/or mailed entries received from persons residing in geographic areas in which Internet entry is not permissible will be disqualified.

Contests will be judged by a panel of members of the Harlequin editorial, marketing and public relations staff based on the following criteria:

- Originality and Creativity—50%
- Emotionally Compelling—25%
- Sincerity—25%

In the event of a tie, duplicate prizes will be awarded. Decisions of the judges are final.

All entries become the property of Torstar Corp. and will not be returned. No responsibility is assumed for lost, late, illegible, incomplete, inaccurate, nondelivered or misdirected mail or misdirected e-mail, for technical, hardware or software failures of any kind, lost or unavailable network connections, or failed, incomplete, garbled or delayed computer transmission or any human error which may occur in the receipt or processing of the entries in this Contest.

Contest open only to residents of the U.S. (except Puerto Rico) and Canada, who are 18 years of age or older, and is void wherever prohibited by law; all applicable laws and regulations apply. Any litigation within the Province of Quebec respecting the conduct or organization of a publicity contest may be submitted to the Régie des alcools, des courses et des jeux for a ruling. Any litigation respecting the awarding of a prize may be submitted to the Régie des alcools, des courses et des jeux only for the purpose of helping the parties reach a settlement. Employees and immediate family members of Torstar Corp. and D. L. Blair, Inc., their affiliates, subsidiaries and all other agencies, entities and persons connected with the use, marketing or conduct of this Contest are not eligible to enter. Taxes on prizes are the sole responsibility of winners. Acceptance of any prize offered constitutes permission to use winner's name, photograph or other likeness for the purposes of advertising, trade and promotion on behalf of Torstar Corp., its affiliates and subsidiaries without further compensation to the winner, unless prohibited by law.

Winners will be determined no later than November 15, 2001, and will be notified by mail. Winners will be required to sign and return an Affidavit of Eligibility form within 15 days after winner notification. Noncompliance within that time period may result in disqualification and an alternative winner may be selected. Winners of trip must execute a Release of Liability prior to ticketing and must possess required travel documents (e.g. passport, photo ID) where applicable. Trip must be completed by November 2002. No substitution of prize permitted by winner. Torstar Corp. and D. L. Blair, Inc., their parents, affiliates, and subsidiaries are not responsible for errors in printing or electronic presentation of Contest, entries and/or game pieces. In the event of printing or other errors which may result in unintended prize values or duplication of prizes, all affected game pieces or entries shall be null and void. If for any reason the Internet portion of the Contest is not capable of running as planned, including infection by computer virus, bugs, tampering, unauthorized intervention, fraud, technical failures, or any other causes beyond the control of Torstar Corp. which corrupt or affect the administration, secrecy, fairness, integrity or proper conduct of the Contest, Torstar Corp. reserves the right, at its sole discretion, to disqualify any individual who tampers with the entry process and to cancel, terminate, modify or suspend the Contest or the Internet portion thereof. In the event of a dispute regarding an online entry, the entry will be deemed submitted by the authorized holder of the e-mail account submitted at the time of entry. Authorized account holder is defined as the natural person who is assigned to an e-mail address by an Internet access provider, online service provider or other organization that is responsible for arranging e-mail address for the domain associated with the submitted e-mail address. **Purchase or acceptance of a product offer does not improve your chances of winning.**

Prizes: (1) Grand Prize—A Harlequin wedding dress (approximate retail value: $3,500) and a 5-night/6-day honeymoon trip to Maui, HI, including round-trip air transportation provided by Maui Visitors Bureau from Los Angeles International Airport (winner is responsible for transportation to and from Los Angeles International Airport) and a Harlequin Romance Package, including hotel accomodations (double occupancy) at the Hyatt Regency Maui Resort and Spa, dinner for (2) two at Swan Court, a sunset sail on Kiele V and a spa treatment for the winner (approximate retail value: $4,000); (5) Five runner-up prizes of a $1000 gift certificate to selected retail outlets to be determined by Sponsor (retail value $1000 ea.). Prizes consist of only those items listed as part of the prize. Limit one prize per person. All prizes are valued in U.S. currency.

For a list of winners (available after December 17, 2001) send a self-addressed, stamped envelope to: Harlequin Walk Down the Aisle Contest 1197 Winners, P.O. Box 4200 Blair, NE 68009-4200 or you may access the www.eHarlequin.com Web site through January 15, 2002.

Contest sponsored by Torstar Corp., P.O. Box 9042, Buffalo, NY 14269-9042, U.S.A.

PHWDACONT2